KICKER'S LEGACY

Sandy Loyd

Published by Sandy Loyd
Copyright 2014 Sandy Loyd
Cover design by Kelli Ann Morgan at Inspire Creative Services
Edited by Pam Berehulke at Bulletproof Editing
Cover Photo by Decker Loyd
ISBN: 978-1-941267-04-2

For more information on the author and her works, please see www.SandyLoyd.com

This book is also available in print from some online retailers.

DEDICATION

To my son, Decker Loyd. Thanks for letting me use the airplane photo and thanks for giving me insight to teenage boys.

Chapter 1

Rain pummeled the windshield with such force the wipers couldn't keep up. Lauren Kane peered out at the watery blur. A fun-house distortion of the road ahead came to mind. The trees waved in the wind, changing shapes like stepping from mirror to mirror.

Lightning struck, framing the shapes as they really were for a stark instant. A roar of thunder followed. The sound reverberated through the car like a locomotive on overdrive.

"Oh my God," Lauren cried out when after another loud thunderous crack, the car suddenly swerved. She stomped on the brake pedal, felt the *thump-thump-thump* of a blown tire, and gripped the steering wheel, fighting to gain control of the fishtailing. The Honda CRV shot off the rain-slick road. Ground cover flew at her fast and furious before she managed to stop.

With a shaky hand, she shifted into PARK and inhaled several deep breaths while sending up a silent prayer of thanks.

Still trembling, she turned to her son sitting in the passenger seat. "Are you okay?" She ran unsteady fingers through DJ's hair and her searching gaze roamed up and down his lanky form.

DJ smiled and nodded, completely unfazed in the way that only a sixteen-year-old boy could pull off, as if this had been a ride at Disney World rather than a near-death experience. Craning his neck, he looked out the window. "Wow! We're lucky we didn't hit a tree."

"Yeah, lucky." Following his gaze, she peeked over the dashboard for a better view of where they'd landed. All she could see, in between the wipers' *swish-swish* uselessly tossing water back and forth, was darkness in the headlights' glare.

Lightning tore through the air. Another earsplitting boom stalked the flash seconds later.

"Really lucky," she murmured as a shiver of fear crept up her spine when the jagged streak of light pointed out exactly how close the vehicle rested to what looked like a sharp drop-off. She glanced back at her son and sent up another thanks that DJ wasn't behind the wheel. Luck or kismet or a guardian angel or whatever other magic out there had been on their side tonight. Her son lacked night hours for his learner's permit and his inexperience just might have killed both of them. As it was, she'd barely regained control of the car.

"This is so cool." DJ took out his iPhone and punched a few buttons.

"What're you doing?"

"Figuring out where we are," he said. "Then I'm putting this on Facebook. Wait 'til Joey hears about this."

"You can get service way out here?" When he nodded, she rolled her eyes and said under her breath, "Technology." Like she needed some little handheld phone to tell her something she already knew? They were on a mountain road halfway between DJ's swim camp and home—thirty miles from home. Worse, they were quite a ways off the road. In the mud. With a damn deluge going on outside and a damn flat tire to change.

What she needed was divine intervention with the weather. Or help in figuring out how to get back on the road once she changed the tire. Would a computer or GPS help her with either? Heck no. No amount of information would do the trick. She was on her own, just as she'd been since her husband's death, which meant bucking up and doing what she'd always done when life threw her in the dryer for a heated spin. Take the ride, then once things cooled down, she'd depend on herself and her street smarts to deal with any and all little surprises, wrinkles and shrinkage among them.

Yeah! I am woman, hear me roar.

But sometimes the best she could manage was a loud meow. "Like right now," she whispered, suddenly missing Jimmy, which seemed pretty lame after fifteen years. Besides, even when he was alive, she hadn't had one hundred percent of her husband. Added to that emotional disconnection, she hadn't been married long enough to form a deep attachment, much less a dependence on him. How could she miss what she'd never had? "That's not the point," she muttered. After all, wasn't having part of someone better than having no one at all?

"What?" DJ asked.

"Nothing." She eyed the bullets of water still hitting the windshield and focused on her situation rather than the past. "Can you call AAA?"

"Sorry." He stuck the phone back into his backpack. "Just lost service."

"Figures." She sighed. "We have to change the tire before we can move the car." Unless they wanted to stay in this precarious spot awhile, they didn't have much choice.

"No biggie." He shrugged, totally unconcerned, and threw his backpack onto the backseat. His hand went to the door handle.

"Yeah, but you're gonna get drenched." Correction, they were both going to get drenched, she thought, staring out the window.

DJ snorted. "I won't melt."

She smiled at the stab at humor. Both knew she'd spoken those exact words no less than a thousand times since he was old enough to understand them. Except at those times it wasn't raining quite as hard and they weren't stranded near a mountain drop-off. "Be careful."

DJ clambered out. After shrugging into her raincoat and grabbing an umbrella, Lauren followed. In minutes she had the hatch open and found the jack and tire iron. DJ hefted the spare to the ground. She tried to shield him with the umbrella, but when the whipping wind pulled it backward too many times, she refolded and tossed the useless item on the ground.

Cold moisture drenched her numb fingers, making it ten times harder to work quickly as she took turns with DJ to loosen the lug nuts. When they'd undone the last one, she stepped out of her son's way while he jacked up the car.

Thank God it was the back tire. Though a good ten feet away, that drop-off was still too close for comfort.

A sudden gust of wind almost knocked her off balance. Shivering, she wished he'd hurry so they could get back inside the car. She hugged herself in an effort to ward off the chill and observed DJ's progress as he pulled the tire off the car. He had to be just as miserable.

She looked behind her and up the hill at the exact moment another bolt of lightning struck. Her breath caught in her throat as jagged fingers of light touched the ground. Those long seconds were enough to illuminate the silhouette of a man standing in front of some kind of truck or van. Odder than that, the headlights were out.

Total darkness set in again. She wiped water off her face and squinted, trying to see through the torrential downpour. Out of her peripheral vision, DJ picked up the spare and stuck it in place, yet her focus remained on the man up the hill. In that time he hadn't moved, in fact, seemed only to be staring at her just as she was staring at him. She shivered again, but this time not from the cold. It was eerie, but maybe that was only her imagination. It was hard to discern anything in this mess. Maybe he was waiting for the worst of the storm to pass. If so, then why not wait in the car? She reached into her pocket for the pepper spray she always carried when she drove alone. If the menacing mystery man meant them harm, she wouldn't hesitate to use it.

"See, Mom," DJ shouted. Her attention strayed to her son, who, unaware of any possible danger, added and tightened lug nuts one by one. Then he whipped his wet hair back and water sluiced off his face, but he only grinned, seeming totally oblivious to the raindrops pelting him. "This is a perfect example of how a car is actually more dangerous than an airplane. People die in car crashes all the time. But according to the statistics, airplane accidents and fatalities are rarer."

Lauren's back stiffened when his shouted words registered. Here they were in the middle of a damn deluge, changing a tire near the edge of a cliff with some weirdo watching them, and DJ was trying to twist her arm about flying. She mentally counted to ten. At six, she relaxed her shoulders, pushed sodden hair behind her ears, and took a deep breath.

"Just hurry," she yelled back. "So, we can get out of this mess." And away from the sinister-looking stranger, she added silently, unwilling to get back in the car without her son.

She glanced back up the hill as another flash lit the sky, and said more to the rain than DJ, "And I've already expressed my opinion on the subject." All signs of the person had vanished. She blinked, not sure she'd actually seen anyone to begin with or if it had been a figment of her imagination. Thunder loomed. She stared into the wet black night and a new thought formed.

Was someone stalking her?

Her heartbeat quickened. More unease raced up her spine as images from her past flashed inside her mind's eye. She tugged the edges of her coat closer together to expel a sudden chill surging through her that had nothing to do with being soaked. Was the past coming back to haunt her? It certainly felt that way, mainly because the tension running through her system now was the same threatening tension she'd experienced right after her husband's killer had been convicted of sabotaging Jimmy's plane. At the time she'd been sure someone had been following her.

"No," she whispered as she shook her head, dismissing the unpleasant memories and forcing herself to continue breathing. She had no reason to panic, not when she and DJ had existed off the radar for almost fifteen years. Her past was just that—in the past—where it would stay.

"But, Mom. Statistics don't lie." DJ's voice drew her attention. "Airplanes *are* safer," he bellowed as he exerted force on the last lug nut.

4

"I go by my own statistics," she said, glad for the diversion, even one that was an ongoing argument. "I don't know of anyone who died in a car accident, but both my father and yours died in plane crashes, so my decision isn't likely to change." He wasn't taking flying lessons in the near future, and no amount of badgering in the rain would sway her.

DJ didn't understand her fears. Fears she'd kept to herself all these years so as not to influence him. She grasped her son's yearning better than he did. After all, his grandfather had been a fighter pilot, and DJ was a Kane. The love of flying was embedded in his DNA, inherited from generations on both sides of the gene pool.

Unfortunately, that particular facet of his personality, or rather its dangerous element, was something she might never come to terms with. How could she, when after already enduring the loss of her mom at age ten, her father's jet had gone down eight years later in a training accident? She'd only been married eighteen months before her husband's fatal airplane crash had cut his life short. In essence, their love of flying had resulted in death, which was the sole reason she was alone in the first place, raising her son without a father or grandfather, so she wasn't likely to change her mind on the subject. Not when he was all she had.

"That's not fair." DJ's displeasure was evident in his frown, despite his voice being drowned out by rolling thunder.

"Maybe not, but get used to it," she said, still shouting. "Life's never fair." Damn, why was he continuing this conversation? In the godforsaken rain? How she wished he'd just drop it. Her only child was nothing if not tenacious once he made up his mind. Another Kane trait, she thought, bending to retrieve her useless umbrella and the tire iron he'd thrown on the ground after working the jack to lower the car.

He grabbed the muddy blown tire and shoved it into the trunk. Once in place, he relieved her of the tool. "You're getting soaked. Get back in the car. I'll finish out here. Make sure we're not stuck."

She nodded. Just like DJ to irritate her one minute, and then turn around and do something so thoughtful the next. They depended on each other, she realized, slipping out of her coat.

Suppressing a shiver, she tossed the coat into the backseat along with the worthless umbrella and slid inside the car, trying not to think about the jeans plastered to her legs. She wiped off the water as best she could before starting the engine. All she wanted at this point was to make it home where they could change clothes and get warm.

"Try to back up," DJ said before he slammed the hatch. A tree and the drop-off prevented her from turning around, so she had to back up at least a hundred feet to make it to the pavement. She waited for him to move out of the way, then shifted into REVERSE and pressed the gas pedal. The motor revved and the wheels spun, but the car didn't move.

"Looks like I'll need to push," he yelled. "Just wait for me to get into position." Seconds later, his slap on the hood indicated he was ready and she eased her foot onto the accelerator while eyeing the rearview mirror.

This time the car moved back a few feet before sliding into the same position because the wheels started spinning. They tried again several times with similar results.

Her gaze shifted forward to glimpse DJ as he swiped water off his face, shaking his head in frustration and mouthing *no good*.

Great. They needed a tow truck, which would probably take hours. Of course, that was contingent on getting cell phone service.

Suddenly headlights reflected in the rearview mirror and lit the darkened area. Her body tensed. Had her mystery man returned? She expelled a relieved sigh, noting the lights belonged to a sleek car that looked nothing like the van or truck she thought she'd seen.

Someone emerged from the car and walked out of the shadows, cutting into its headlights' glow. Several giant steps later he stood next to her side window, and through the *rat-a-tat-tat* of rain hitting the car's roof, his "Are you okay?" was barely audible.

Erring on the side of caution, she stabbed the button so that the window dropped only a few inches. "Yes," she said, thankful to have someone to help them, especially someone who didn't appear the least bit sinister. "We're just stuck in the mud."

"Well, let's see about getting you unstuck." His nod indicated first the inside of the car and then the hood. "Give me a minute to get into position. Then give it some gas and we'll push in tandem." Half a minute later, he shouted from next to DJ, "Go ahead, ease on the gas pedal and back up slowly. When you feel a little traction, give it more gas. Just not too much at once."

After four attempts, she managed to back up until the rear tires touched pavement, allowing enough traction and power to go the rest of the distance.

She jerked the gearshift into PARK and glanced up. The guy now stood at her window again, his short dark hair plastered to his scalp. Water hit the top of his head and formed small waterfalls that rushed over sopping clothes to drip from his shirtsleeves and the edges of his baggy shorts.

"Thank you for stopping," she offered, rolling the window all the way down. After all, it seemed kind of silly to be wary of him when he'd helped her. Yet, not wanting to let him know how desperate their situation had been with no phone service, she added, "You saved me from having to call a tow truck, and considering the night, it might've been a long wait. Can I pay you for your trouble?"

"Hell no." A grin took over his face, softening the craggy angles, which she could barely make out in the shadows. He shook his head and he threw out a snort. "I can't believe that guy just picked up and left like he did."

"You saw the other car?" So she hadn't been hallucinating. Instantly her unease returned full force.

"Yeah. It was odd. He had to have spotted you. Hell, he's the reason I stopped. From my vantage point, looked like he was the one who needed help, but when I slowed, he took off like the devil was after him."

"That is odd." Her gaze flew to the dark road ahead at the same moment DJ hopped in next to her. Like the stranger, a river dripped from him too. He quickly jacked up the heater and flipped all the vents in his direction. Her attention went back to the helpful stranger, who had to be just as cold. No sense detaining him further. "Well, at least you stopped. I *am* very thankful." She smiled. "Are you sure I can't pay you?"

"I wouldn't be able to call myself a man if I expected payment for doing the right thing when someone needed help." He added, "Just pass it on," before turning to make his way back to his car.

Her gaze rested on the rearview mirror until he climbed inside his car. The entire time she stared, the eeriness of the drenched fun-house scene increased, along with her unease. Her thoughts reverted to the earlier mystery man.

Who was he? Was the past returning to haunt her?

She spared a glance at DJ and engaged the door locks. Her heartbeat quickened at the thought of how vulnerable they'd been, something she hadn't felt since those first months after Jimmy's death. She pulled onto the road to start down the mountain. While she drove, maintaining a steady foot on the accelerator and slowing to a crawl only for turns, her resolve stiffened as a familiar fear resurfaced. She'd dedicated too many years to protecting DJ. He was her life and she'd never risk his safety. Not now. Not ever.

Cʘ

He scrambled inside the Mercedes, sliding into the seat and shutting out the driving rain, then opened the glove box and grabbed a few paper towels. After wiping most of the water off his hands and face, he reached for his cell phone.

"Yeah?" shot through the device after the second ring.

"I think we have a problem." Up ahead, Lauren Kane had already pulled onto the empty rain-swept road. He started his car and followed. Since the Honda was staying well below the speed limit, he was able to maneuver his car one-handed to catch up and talk on the phone at the same time, even with the gusting wind and pounding rain propelling the car sideways.

"What happened?"

"I don't know exactly. I'm still trying to figure it out." He broke off and stared at the taillights ahead of him, barely visible given the conditions.

"Go on. I'm listening," registered and he cleared his throat.

"A little earlier, the lady had a blowout and ran off the road after picking up her kid from camp. No one should be out driving in this shit, much less do it on a mountain road with all these twists and turns. It could be a coincidence, but the timing just feels wrong."

"Hmmm. You don't think it was an accident?"

"Gut instinct? No. I was too far behind to actually see the tire blow or see her Honda leave the road, but when I rounded a curve, another vehicle pulled off to the side caught my attention. Looked like he needed help. It's why I originally slowed. Anyway, I pulled over."

"Maybe he stopped to help."

"Maybe. The weird thing is, even though I was hanging back so as not to alert the lady to my presence, I never saw another car's headlights or taillights. From my vantage point, which wasn't great because of the conditions, I could've sworn he carried a high-powered rifle that he threw into his truck before jumping in and hauling ass out of there like he was going to a fire."

"Did you get a plate number?"

"Too dark and he had his headlights out, another red flag on a night like tonight. Once he left, I inched closer and caught the taillights further down the hill. I stopped to help. She's driving home as we speak."

The line was silent. A moment later, it crackled to life with, "Thanks for the update. I'm working on a long-term solution to my problem, so keep on 'em for now. Twenty-four/seven."

"Will do." He pushed the OFF button and threw the phone on the passenger seat where it would stay dry, cranked up the heat, and tried not to think about the long, miserable hour of driving ahead of him. His wet clothes clung to his body. Even the leather seat was saturated.

Able to devote his complete attention to driving, he sped to catch up with the other car. His mind churned with one thought. Since he'd made contact, following her from this point on would be a hundred times more difficult.

ೞ

Forty-five minutes after getting back on the road, Lauren pulled into her driveway at the end of the cul-de-sac. Streetlights lit the block in front of her three-bedroom house, but everything behind it was black.

"Looks spooky," DJ said.

"Yeah, it does," she agreed, peering into the rain-swept night. "The back porch light must be out. Makes it seem spookier." Almost eerie, she added mentally, then rolled her eyes. Lord, she was imagining things, but given the last two hours, she felt entitled.

Still, she couldn't help thinking she was overreacting. Nothing happened in Pemberton, North Carolina, situated in the foothills of the Smokies. The town was small enough for her to keep an eye on strangers, yet big enough for her to blend in. In other words, perfect for her purposes. After more than a decade, she was finally considered a "local," which had added another element of safety.

Pemberton was her home and she loved her house, especially the fact that her backyard bordered a national forest. On nights like tonight, forests were generally dark. That was the beauty of nature. Being isolated from neighbors was the biggest reason to love living here.

The garage door began opening when she hit the remote. Chancing a glance at DJ, she said, "It'd be nice if we had a connecting garage." Like the newer homes in the area. Their one-story ranch had been built in the early fifties when features like connecting garages hadn't become the norm yet.

Her son winked. "What? Afraid of melting?"

She laughed. Still smiling she drove forward, easing into the garage, then braked and switched off the ignition. "You should get out of those wet clothes. I'm betting a hot shower sounds pretty good about now." It certainly was her main goal.

"You said it," DJ said as both exited the car together.

Not bothering with the camping gear or bags, they ran, dodging raindrops, to the covered porch. She quickly unlocked the door and pushed it open, shaking water off before stepping inside.

"Shit, I'm cold," DJ said, rubbing his hands and coming in behind her. "Tonight's definitely a hot chocolate night, don't cha think?"

"Watch the mouth," she shot back automatically, shutting the door. "Great idea," she added about sharing hot cocoa, something that had become a ritual on cold nights. So was his dumping in oodles of those little marshmallows on top. She frowned. "But we're out of

9

marshmallows." This was the end of August and she was lucky to have a few packets of hot chocolate in the cupboard leftover from last winter. She shrugged and offered, "I can always make a trip to the store."

"That's okay, Mom. You're just as cold as me." His lips curled into a smile. "You should get out of your wet things too." That was DJ, always looking out for her. From her vantage point, his mouth held a blue tinge and he was shivering as he added, "I'll survive without marshmallows."

He might survive, but he looked as miserable as she felt. She nodded toward the hallway leading to his bedroom and second bathroom. "Hurry up and shower. I'll have it ready by the time you finish." Her shower could wait, but getting out of damp clothes couldn't.

"Sounds good," he said, planting a kiss on her cheek. "I'm just happy to be home." As he walked away, her heart swelled with love. She treasured any affection from him, which didn't come automatically these days, not like it had when he was a little boy. In two more years, he'd be off to college and wouldn't be here to offer hugs or kisses at all.

Lauren's eyes misted. Lately just the thought of him leaving was enough to make her weepy. And even more disturbing, the thought kept popping up at the worst times. "Quit worrying about something so far into the future," she scolded herself, blinking back tears while heading for her bedroom to change, unwilling to dwell on negatives in front of DJ.

Once in her master bath, she unsnapped her jeans and rolled wet denim down her legs. Next came her blouse. She hurriedly changed into the clean sweats she'd grabbed from her antique chest. Leaving her clothes in a heap on the white tile floor, she shrugged into a terrycloth robe and a pair of comfy slippers, then made her way to the kitchen to make hot chocolate.

She was just pouring the warm liquid into mugs when DJ appeared around the corner.

"It's all ready," she said, handing him his cup when he stopped in front of her.

"Thanks, Mom."

She picked up her mug and followed him to sit at the table.

Heat seeped into her fingers now wrapped around the mug. She took a drink. The hot liquid filled her with more warmth as she sipped. Sitting next to her son, both stared out the bay windows, the comfortable silence highlighted by the sound of rain hitting the roof.

"Can I spend the night at Joey's tomorrow night?" DJ asked a few minutes later, breaking into the quiet.

"Sure." Her son had tons of friends, but Joey had been his best friend since kindergarten. "Got any big plans?"

"Joey has to baby-sit, so we're going to play World of Warcraft."

"Sounds fun." She smiled. Thankfully she'd been able to provide him with a stable childhood that included lifelong friends, an experience very different from her own.

When he wiped a mustache of chocolate milk off his face, she resisted a sudden urge to hug him and never let go. She swallowed the last mouthful, then set the mug on the table as she stood. "Well, I've got bills to pay." Wouldn't do to go all emotional or sentimental. Teenage boys didn't quite know how to handle emotion or sentiment. Not that men were any better at it. Still, DJ tended to fret if she got upset. Fretting was a mother's job, not a son's.

"I'm doing a Sim Flight to Amsterdam," he announced, shoving his chair back.

"Got it." *DJ and his simulated airlines.* She grinned, only too happy to latch on to his obsession to keep from lingering on more distressing thoughts. He flew in the virtual world, where planes never really crashed. The computer-generated simulations were all pretend, which in her mind was a hell of a lot safer than what happened in the real world.

DJ picked up her mug along with his and took both to the sink. After placing them in the dishwasher, he came up behind her.

When she turned with eyebrows raised he only smiled, then wrapped her in a big bear hug and squeezed. "Thanks, Mom. That really hit the spot." He then let go before spinning around and sauntering out of the room, looking more like the lanky teen he was than the sweet boy who'd just hugged her.

Imagine that. Two PDAs in one evening. DJ rarely displayed affection, public or otherwise. "Are you feeling okay?" she shouted after he'd disappeared.

"Yeah," he yelled back from his room. "I feel fine. Why?"

"No reason." Shaking her head and holding on to her grin, she headed for the spare bedroom that doubled as her home office.

Like all the furniture in the house, the teakwood desk and file cabinets had been a splurge right after moving in. She'd wanted pieces that lasted a lifetime. If she couldn't have permanence with people, she could at least have it with things.

Spying the misshapen, ugly ashtray that doubled as a paper clip holder, she touched it as the memory of DJ presenting it to her came to mind. She'd never forget his proud smile. To this day, no store-bought gift could outdo this simple offering.

Despite all her hardships early on, she'd hit the jackpot with her son, she thought, sitting behind her desk and dismissing the past from her mind.

Jackpot or not, the quarterly invoices for the soup kitchen wouldn't pay themselves. She donated her time acting as finance director, also putting in two mornings a week, opening up on those days when her shift as a receptionist for Tilly's House of Beauty started later. As she dug through the drawer, she noticed a few misfiled folders. She quickly switched them around, then found her "to pay" file and thumbed through it, searching for the insurance bill.

Her fingers hit a letter, stopping her movement.

That's funny.

Perplexed, Lauren pulled it out, along with the invoice she originally sought. Why was this letter mixed in with the soup kitchen bills when she distinctly remembered placing it into her personal file?

Eyeing it, her mind raced back to the moment she'd first opened the missive from her dead husband's father some two months ago. She'd trembled as she'd read it back then, and rereading it now that same surge of anger erupted all over again. How dare the man?

Kicker Kane's attempt at reconciliation was laughable. The words on the page were a far cry from her definition.

Some reconciliation.

He'd obviously thought he could buy her acquiescence with the news that DJ had been added to his will. She'd struggled to find some solace in the fact that the guy was at least accepting his grandson as a Kane, rather than casting aspersions on the boy's parentage like he had right after her marriage to Jimmy. The old man had the gall to demand to spend time with DJ during the summer with no thought to the fact that he'd shoved her son out of his life when Jimmy had died. She hadn't known how to respond or how to bring up the subject with DJ, so she'd taken the easy way out and filed the letter away.

Selfish or not, she had precious few summers left with her son before he left for college and she darn well didn't want to share that time with a manipulative bastard who'd called her everything from a bimbo to a money-chasing whore.

Her thoughts shifted to the earlier menacing stranger and her gaze flew to the window. The light reflecting from the office lamps revealed no signs of the rain letting up. As water beaded on the glass panes, her mind spun.

Was there a connection? Had Kicker been stalking her because she'd ignored his demands?

The wind howled as she watched a single drop make its way from the top of the window, gathering more momentum and moisture as it slid to the bottom.

Jimmy had loved his father, but something hadn't been right between the two. Lauren had sensed that he'd been afraid of him or rather, afraid of losing his love, which played into her assessment of him as a master manipulator. She wouldn't put it past the elder Kane to be behind tonight's events.

The thought stopped her cold and didn't wash. A demanding letter was more Kicker's style. Plus, from what she knew of him, he wouldn't lurk in the shadows. So, if not him, then who?

Lauren jumped up and practically ran the distance to her son's room. "DJ?" She rapped on his closed door.

"It's open," came from the other side.

She turned the knob and entered. "Did you go through my files?"

"What?" He didn't even look up, keeping his focus on the screen as he played with the controls. "Why would I go through your files?"

"I don't know. Maybe you were looking for something?"

"No."

"Are you sure? Some of the files have been moved around."

"I already told you no. I don't know anything about moving any files." Finally he spared her a quick glance, his eyes flashing impatience. "Can we talk about this later? I'm right in the middle of taking off."

"Never mind," she said, backing down. She read her son like a book and his title page revealed in bold print that he had no clue what she was talking about. "I'm sorry I bugged you."

Lauren closed the door as fast as she'd opened it, wondering if her imagination had overtaken her common sense. As she continued down the hall toward her office, more memories of that horrible time in her life resurfaced, along with the old feelings. Call it instinct or a sixth sense for survival, but Jimmy's family hadn't been the only reason she'd run so far away from Tampa.

Was the past repeating itself?

Resuming her position at her desk, she rolled her shoulders in an attempt to alleviate the same threatening tension she'd felt earlier out in the rain. Despite being a lifetime ago, not to mention hundreds of miles from Tampa, she couldn't dismiss the idea that these recent happenstances were connected to her past.

Only now, she was no longer a scared nineteen-year-old girl on the verge of womanhood. Still, erring on the side of caution, she'd keep a more diligent watch over DJ, along with an open eye to anything unusual in town, just in case.

If a threat existed, contacting Jimmy's family was always an option. Not a great one, but an option nonetheless. Silas "Kicker" Kane may think her an undeserving pariah, someone unworthy and not woman enough to hold on to his son, but he'd protect what he considered his. Once the two met in person, he wouldn't be able to doubt DJ was a Kane.

Sighing, Lauren reached for the pen and the checkbook. Hopefully at that point DJ would be emotionally armed with the warmth and love she'd supplied to stand up to the old man and his demands better than his son had done all those years ago.

When that day came, she'd probably have to face Dillon Kane too. Except, she didn't want to think about what that really meant. Not now.

Chapter 2

Dillon Kane's rental car screeched to a halt in one of the visitors' parking spots. He switched off the ignition. Immediately muggy warmth began seeping inside the car, but Dillon made no move to open the car door, instead just peered out the window.

Florida had a smell all its own, he mused as that musty scent enveloped him along with the humidity. Funny how a smell could extract deep, forgotten memories, like turning on a switch and snap…there they were…in the spotlight.

In the lengthy moment he spent eyeing the ten-story mirrored, state-of-the-art building that housed Kane Aeronautics, more memories filled him. His heart raced, the thuds so loud they could have been drums beating at a rock concert. He took deep breaths of damp air and wiped his sweaty palms on his faded jeans to still a sudden onset of nerves, wondering why the hell he was so anxious.

He was no longer the naïve kid who could never measure up to Kicker's lofty standards. Dillon had made something of his life without his father's money or connections, and at this point he didn't give a damn what the old man thought. He'd stopped caring a lifetime ago, after wasting his youth attempting to win the asshole's approval—approval that might as well have been the bunny a greyhound chased in training, for all the good it had done him.

So, why would he even have a reaction now? Especially after all these years?

"Shit," he said under his breath and climbed out of the car, dismissing the disturbing thoughts. He hit the lock button on his key fob. The horn beeped and the locks snapped into place. In three long strides, he halved the distance to the walkway. Taking in the waterfalls, the lush greenery, and colorful gardens, he continued walking, using the splashes of reds, yellows, and purples on either side as a distraction to expel any and all ideas that this meeting affected him more than he'd anticipated.

He'd agreed to this reunion out of curiosity. Nothing more;

nothing less. Of course, he'd flown several hundred miles to satisfy that curiosity, but so what? He had other pressing business in Florida, so he wasn't going out of his way.

Once inside the lobby, cooler air chilled the light sheen of sweat on his arms and neck. The musty scent vanished. Translation? This was a new structure. It took years of mold and mildew buildup to invade and permeate the air-conditioners. Once it did, the odor never died.

Dillon's thoughts switched from smells to his surroundings. Money didn't play into his search for happiness, nor did it substantiate his success. He certainly didn't regard it in the same way his father did. Despite his unwavering sentiments, he couldn't deny a begrudging admiration. Kicker had obviously spared no expense on his building.

Money well spent that definitely made a powerful statement.

The exterior windows overlooked the flowery entrance, and beyond that, the view of Tampa Bay, a blue-green wall of water with the bridge to Clearwater in the background couldn't be ignored. Impressionist works of art graced the interior walls, and Dillon knew they were the real deal, neither reproductions nor prints.

Kicker wouldn't allow fakes in his world.

Both the inspiring view and the paintings added an elegant flair to the space. Extensive use of granite on the floors and on the countertop at the guard's station, along with etched glass and dark wood, didn't detract from that flair. Every square inch shouted the image Kicker wanted to convey. Success. Polish. Extravagance. The visible trappings of wealth were as important to his father as possessing the money in the first place. Hadn't his father proven that by marrying the daughter of his biggest and wealthiest client, only months after his wife's death?

Dillon stopped at the desk and nodded to the guard. "I have a two o'clock appointment with Silas Kane." Not particularly willing to divulge that he shared the same last name, he wasn't about to add more until asked.

But the guard, wearing an expensive suit that fit too well to be off the rack, already seemed aware of his identity. This was confirmed when he glanced down at his paperwork, then smiled a little too agreeably before making eye contact. "Yes sir, Mr. Kane. I'll inform them upstairs of your arrival."

The man raked a gaze over Dillon's attire, his expression smug as if he found the faded jeans, sport shirt, and deck shoes amusing. Then his attention went to punching numbers into a phone. Seconds later, he mumbled into the mouthpiece. After a short conversation, he disconnected and once again, his too-pleasant expression was back in

16

place as his glance landed on Dillon's face. "If you'll wait over there, Mr. Kane is sending someone down to meet you."

Determined not to react in front of one of his father's minions, Dillon tamped down irritation and said, "Thank you." After all, he wasn't here to impress anyone, especially a guy who was only following Kicker's orders and probably had no idea the small slight was a silent message—one Dillon caught. If he thought all was forgiven and forgotten, the mere fact that he wasn't trusted enough to travel upstairs on his own said otherwise.

Yep, he thought, crossing his arms and leaning against the desk. Kicker's methods hadn't changed. Not one goddamned bit in all these years. Then his glance landed on his feet, sporting the worn, frayed edges of denim over shoes worn without socks, and he grinned. Neither had his. Kicker considered jeans beneath him or low-class, the complete opposite of Dillon, who wasn't inclined to wear anything but without a good reason, especially when he knew it would piss Kicker off.

No more than thirty seconds had passed when another suit stepped out of the elevator on the other side of the security gates.

"Mr. Kane?" he said, staring straight at him.

When Dillon nodded, he offered the first guard's same too-pleasant smile. That smirk had to be part of their training, Dillon mused as the suit pushed a button and the metal gate opened.

"Right this way."

Following him inside the elevator, he mused that his father must be mellowing to not fully capitalize on his advantage. At the very least, he'd expected a five-minute wait.

Seconds later the elevator opened on the top floor and he remained a few feet behind the suit, who led him to a set of imposing twelve-foot double doors—the obvious entrance to Kicker Kane's inner sanctum.

Dillon continued inside, maintaining a neutral expression while eyeing the décor and secretly appreciating his father's knack for creating a dramatic sense of grandeur.

He halted in front of the overlarge dark walnut desk, a focal point in the spacious room that made the lobby look like the slums of Calcutta in comparison. And like the king he aspired to be, Kicker sat in a throne-like leather chair, framed on both sides with elaborate draperies opened to another killer view, which only added to the intimidating impression his father clearly knew how to exploit.

Still seated and absorbed in paperwork, Kicker nodded, the only acknowledgement of his presence. Dillon didn't move. After an awkward silence, Kicker pointed to a maroon upholstered chair to

Dillon's left. "Have a seat." But he never made eye contact.

Refusing to be ignored, Dillon waited. His father had requested this meeting and he could damn well afford him the same courtesy given to any business associate.

When Kicker finally glanced up, their stares connected for more lengthy seconds before he stood. Clearing his throat, he came out from behind the desk and offered his hand. "Thank you for coming."

They shook, then his nod indicated the same chair. "Please. Have a seat."

Without taking his eyes off his father, Dillon made himself comfortable and leaned back in the chair.

The two men studied each other.

After another prolonged moment of silence, one Dillon wasn't about to interrupt, his father smiled and proceeded to sit behind the desk. "You're looking fit, even if you're dressed like a homeless bum."

Dillon forced out a laugh that sounded more like a cynical snort. "Thanks." Then his smile became genuine. "I could say the same. About looking fit, I mean, not the homeless part."

Except he was a little taken aback by how much his father had aged, and even a two-thousand-dollar Armani couldn't disguise the fact that time had taken its toll. In the past, he'd always been invulnerable and invincible. His once larger-than-life demeanor seemed diminished somehow, the slight curve of his shoulders and loss of muscle mass revealing just how much. Wrinkles that had always enhanced his father's good looks with a certain ruggedness now spread out like a road map, too many side roads leading to the main interstates running along the sides of his face. Kicker Kane looked old…and worn…like he'd lived half a century since their last meeting, rather than only a decade.

Of course, his father *was* old if you went by chronological age. He'd married his first wife, Dillon's mother, in his late thirties, had his brother right away and then him two years later. After her death, Kicker hadn't wasted any time in replacing her with a stepmother. His last child had been born days before Kicker's fifty-fourth birthday. Since Rory, Dillon's half brother, was almost twenty-four, that put his dad well on the wrong side of seventy. Great genes or not, seeing this new vulnerability meant the old man wouldn't be around forever.

An uncomfortable rush of sentiment flooded his consciousness. He shook it off. Though age had ravaged his father's appearance, anyone staring into those cobalt eyes could see that his intelligence hadn't suffered. If anything, that gaze was more alert. More wary. An eagle searching for prey came to mind, emphasizing a shrewd awareness that never missed much.

Besides, Kicker wouldn't appreciate his pity…or caring…or whatever he'd felt just then, so it was wasted emotion. The old man viewed such sentiments as weaknesses, and he'd already jumped when his father had called out of the blue, asking to meet.

Resting an ankle on his knee, Dillon spent a long moment picking imaginary pieces of lint off his jeans as more memories of his father's harsh verbal lashings, along with his cruel comparisons that indicated he'd never measure up to his brother, surfaced and squeezed out the rest of his concern.

"So, now that I'm here, care to enlighten me?" Though Dillon feigned indifference, he couldn't quite convince himself that he really felt nothing. Nor could he continue with the belligerent bullshit he usually dished out when in his father's presence. He glanced his way and asked, still striving for nonchalance, "Why the urgency?"

From the moment he'd hung up the phone, his curiosity had been a constant companion. Now that curiosity was eating a hole in his gut. Being Kicker's son meant he was no one's fool, so his features revealed nothing of his thoughts. Kicker would seize any opportunity to exploit an advantage.

"It's time I met my grandson."

Dillon drew back, totally stunned, and struggled to keep his expression neutral. He certainly hadn't expected those words.

"But I need your help to do it." Kicker's steely gaze bored into his. "Have you been in touch with DJ or Lauren?"

Dillon held eye contact without flinching, his poker face remaining intact as complete understanding of why he'd been summoned registered. For some reason, he'd hoped Kicker might actually be softening toward him, but he should have known better than rely on false hopes. His dad only wanted to reconnect with Jimmy's kid.

Shoving disappointment aside, he waited a full ten seconds to show the old geezer how unaffected he was, then flashed a sardonic smile. "I know where they are." Dillon uncrossed his legs and planted his feet on the floor, stilling a sudden urge to get up and leave. "But after Jimmy died, I made a promise." He hesitated a heartbeat and added, "And so did you. In other words, you've wasted your time and mine." He stood, giving in to his need to escape.

"I've wasted nothing. Sit back down. We're still talking."

"You'll never change." Dillon threw the words out in a sneer. "Still think you can run people and manipulate outcomes?" He shook his head. Why was he even bothering to be nice? He should just leave and save himself some grief. Instead, he sat and said, "Didn't work then and it damn sure won't work now."

Kicker reached for a pipe resting near an ashtray in the center of his desk. After fingering it a long moment, he pulled out a bag of tobacco, holding it up. "You don't mind, do you?"

"No." Dillon chuckled and offered a more honest grin while his father busied himself with filling the pipe. The old coot certainly had a knack for stalling when he didn't get the sought-after response, he decided, watching him stick the pipe in his mouth and light it.

Kicker inhaled. "You shouldn't make hasty assumptions when you don't know all the particulars," he said, blowing the words out in puffs of smoke.

The rich scent of tobacco penetrated Dillon's nostrils. A freeze-frame from their past flitted through his brain. The déjà vu feeling was unsettling. It was eerie how smells could affect memory. Just as the one in the parking lot had, he thought, reliving their last fight in seconds flat—when his dad had hurled in ugly words what he really thought of his second son. Not a Kodak moment, that was for damned sure.

Did Kicker expect that time and distance would mitigate his offenses? Of course he did. And why wouldn't he? Hell, Dillon was here, wasn't he? Maybe it was time to realign the old man's thinking.

"I know enough," he said in response to the bit about particulars. "Enough to say you're delusional if you think I'd help you connect with them before DJ's twenty-first birthday."

After all, Kicker hadn't hurled hateful words only at him. No, he'd gone and forced his widowed daughter-in-law out of their lives by telling her she hadn't been woman enough to hold his son. Kicker had never approved of her during their short marriage, which had already driven a wedge between the couple. In response, Lauren wanted nothing to do with Kicker and, by virtue of their relationship, him. Yet Dillon couldn't lay the entire blame on his father. He'd cemented his fate the night Jimmy died, when he'd hurled a few hurtful, drunken words of his own.

Still, he'd kept tabs on his nephew and his brother's widow, with the help of a few people in the town. Of course, she knew nothing of his interest or of his reports. Otherwise, she might up and disappear with her son as she'd threatened, only to hide so well it would take years to find them. He'd recognized the resolve in her voice right after Jimmy's funeral, the last time they'd spoken to each other.

"Hutcheson's out of prison. Did you know that?"

The chilling statement froze his smile in place. "What? The murdering son of a bitch got twenty years. Ronald Hutcheson should still be rotting in a jail cell for second-degree murder." A jury had found him guilty of tampering with Jimmy's plane, the ultimate cause of the accident. The DA had proven beyond a reasonable doubt that Hutcheson had motive to kill Jimmy, but Dillon knew he'd been the real target. Only he'd been too drunk to make his scheduled flight. In the end, he'd lived and his older brother had died. A transgression his father would never forgive. For that matter, would he ever forgive himself? "How can he be out?"

"Hell if I know why. Politics, economics, crowded prisons. Take your pick." Kicker shrugged. He took another long puff and exhaled smoke along with his next words. "Does anyone really understand the criminal justice system in this country?"

"I figured he'd at least be out of commission for a long time." Dillon had many regrets concerning that night, but his main one was that the prosecutor hadn't felt confident enough with only circumstantial evidence to go after first-degree murder and the death penalty.

"Twelve years is a long time. Unfortunately that time was spent as a model prisoner. The parole board considers him a saint. Take a look." He reached for a thick file and threw it on the desk. Dillon picked it up and thumbed through it as Kicker added, "Apparently he's no longer a threat, and as you can see, a long time's been over for a while. Saint Hutcheson completed his parole eighteen months ago. I don't know why you weren't notified, but he is, for all intents and purposes, a free man."

"Okay," Dillon said, absorbing the news as well as the words in the file. "What has that to do with DJ or Lauren? They're safe. Out of his reach. If anything, I'm the one who should be watching my back, since his threats were aimed at me to begin with and I'm an easier target."

"What if you're wrong and she's the target?" When he started to object, Kicker held up a hand. "Hear me out. About a year ago, he headed north. Got a job in Chattanooga, close to the Georgia border. Lauren and DJ just happen to live an hour or so out of Asheville, North Carolina. A mountain town nestled in the Smokies." He hesitated. "A fact I've been aware of since weeks of her landing there. Of course, it may not mean anything, but the coincidence of him residing within a few hours' drive is disturbing. Add to that one recent event, and I'm damn near terrified."

"I thought felons had to check in with their parole officers." Chattanooga wasn't far from Atlanta, where Dillon lived, which put Hutcheson about the same distance from him and Lauren. As much as he'd like to walk away, that fact changed his mind about interfering. However, he'd play it his way. On his terms. Not Kicker's. "Can't you talk to someone? Keep an eye on him?"

"I have kept an eye on him. He's followed every rule. Quite frankly, I have no proof he's done anything wrong. Yet. Unfortunately I've been advised to waltz carefully around this, or I could face harassment charges."

A knock interrupted and both turned to the oversized doors that opened.

A darker-haired, wrinkle-free clone of his father peeked his head around one panel. "I don't frickin' believe it." He stepped inside and sauntered up to the desk. "Peters told me you were here, but I had to see for myself."

Dillon stood up to hug his younger brother, who'd only been a kid when he'd left Tampa. He released him and nodded at the rolled-up shirtsleeves, silk tie, expensive dress slacks and shoes. "You're looking good. Like an executive."

"Yeah. I appreciated all your advice," he said, alluding to a conversation when Rory was deciding whether or not to work for Kane Aeronautics after graduating from college two years ago. They'd mostly kept in touch through Facebook or e-mails, and when Dillon did come through Florida on business, he always made time for his half brother with lunch or dinner in a neutral city like Orlando. "Dad's cracking the whip. Making a man out of me, so he says." Rory laughed. "Think he can do it?"

Dillon threw out a disgusted snort. "It didn't work with me." And it damn sure hadn't worked on Jimmy, despite what Kicker thought about his oldest son. The old man had made snap judgments at birth regarding each of his sons. He'd certainly never taken the time to get to know either him or Jimmy, so why would his father be any different with Rory? "All I can say is the job must agree with you." Dillon moved to sit again.

Rory followed, plopping into the chair next to him. "So, what brings the prodigal son back to the fold?"

He laughed. Leave it to Rory to be so blunt. "I'm not back in the fold." Dillon glanced at Kicker with eyebrows raised. "You want to field that one, *Dad?*" he asked, unable to resist throwing a bit of belligerence into the last word.

Kicker cleared his throat. "I asked him to come," he said, skirting the issue and not adding any more than, "It's about time, don't you think?"

So, Rory didn't know. He mentally rolled his eyes. Same old Kicker, keeping everyone in the dark until he needed something.

"I texted Mom on my way up and she says I can't leave this office without extracting a promise that you'll come home for dinner." Rory looked at Kicker and his lips parted in a bigger smile. "Obviously she doesn't trust you to pull it off."

"Dinner's an excellent idea," Kicker said, returning the smile. "You'll have time to assimilate what I've told you. We can finish our talk after dinner." He stood. "Rory. Why don't you give Dillon a tour of the building."

"Awesome." Rory jumped up.

Dillon rose and pushed out annoyance. Not that he wouldn't enjoy Rory's company. He just didn't like being orchestrated into it or dismissed so readily when questions peppered his brain. Grudgingly he swallowed his frustration and nodded. After all, hadn't he promised himself he'd be on his best behavior for this reunion? "Lead on."

If only he wasn't so curious, he could just walk out those double doors and keep going. Instead, he dutifully followed Rory with Kicker saying behind him, "Think about our conversation and how it would be better if you handled things with Lauren rather than me."

His hands curled into a fist. Manipulative to the end. That was his father. When his fingernails dug in to the point of pain, he relaxed and flexed his fingers. He exhaled a resigned sigh, awarding this round to Kicker. But, he thought, smiling inwardly as they headed toward the bank of elevators, one round was all he'd hand over.

Half an hour later, Dillon and Rory stepped off the elevator together. The two had worked their way down from the top floor, having just completed a tour of the finance department.

At the end of the hallway, a man Dillon recognized noted their exit, and after obviously dismissing himself from the small group, he headed in their direction.

"Oh, there's Peters now," Rory said. "He was hoping he could break away to say hi."

Frank Peters slowed his stride, coming to stand a few feet from them and offering his hand. "It's good to see you, Dillon."

"Peters," Dillon acknowledged with a smile and a nod, while shaking hands. Though his first name was Frank, everyone called him Peters. He'd held the number two spot in the company since Kicker had promoted him soon after Jimmy had died and Dillon had left Tampa. "Looks like you and Dad have created some phenomenal growth in the last ten years."

"Well, Rory here hasn't been a slacker." Peters clapped his brother on the shoulder. "He's been busy bringing in new business."

Rory practically beamed.

The three then made small talk for a few minutes until the older man looked at his watch. "I'd love to stay and chat, but I have another meeting in ten minutes."

As Peters departed, Rory's head indicated the opposite direction. "This way."

Dillon followed behind his brother who stopped outside an office, obviously Rory's judging by the name on the door.

"Kane Aeronautics has a fleet of thirty planes. We do everything from providing aircraft for as few as four people to as many as a hundred." Rory opened the door and both men entered the extravagant room with wall-to-wall windows. "Some have their own pilots. Some request ours. Business is booming." His brother dropped into an expensive black leather chair in front of another million-dollar view of Tampa Bay. "Make yourself comfortable."

He nodded for Dillon to sit in one of the plush chairs flanking an oversized white oak desk, while he began typing on the computer keyboard in front of him. A moment later, he swiveled the large monitor around.

"Take a look." The three words were filled with pride and confidence.

Wearing an indulgent smile, Dillon read as Rory clicked through the roster of scheduled flights on the screen. Considering the contents, Kane Aeronautics was rolling in business. In direct contrast to his own struggling airplane parts and repair company. Money was tight right now. Most of his customers were everyday people who loved to fly and when the economy went south, so did their hobby, along with the need for the services his company usually provided. He was working on bringing in different revenues from companies possessing planes in need of maintenance, but that business was slow in coming in this soft market.

"I'm in charge of sales and marketing. I make things happen. Working on booking Blue Metal." Rory's chest pumped up with what Dillon could only call pride. "That'll net more than a few grand. If the rock band decides they like the way we handle their equipment and passengers, my year will be set because they'll hire us for all their gigs."

Dillon kept his smile in place, pleased his brother was so successful, yet wishing he could escape. Seeing Kicker's success only drove home the point of how little he'd accomplished in over a decade. He'd barely survived. Of course, he fully planned to continue surviving. He did possess a solid reputation in the industry and didn't have to cower to the old man. It was obvious he'd never out-do his dad. That fact, along with the realization that he'd actually been trying, was damned depressing.

After leaving Rory's office, he saw more of the same, going floor by floor until he'd explored them all, thanks to Rory and his enthusiasm.

The two finally made their way to the lobby and the suits. When the one behind the counter pressed the button, Dillon went through the gate behind Rory, thinking the kid definitely had a handle on Kicker's business.

"Thanks for the tour." He hit the keyless entry on his rental after Rory had escorted him to the parking lot.

"You're welcome. Got me out of the same boring meeting Peters was attending, so I should be thanking you." Rory's nod indicated the Camry. "Does Kicker know you're driving this Japanese piece of shit?"

"No." He grinned. Though it had been over ten long years since he and his father had shared more than a conversation before today, he could still envision Kicker's sneer about not renting a German brand, the only country that could engineer a solidly built car, in his father's opinion. "No doubt I'll get an earful if he sees it, but I sure as hell wasn't renting a Mercedes just to impress him." He didn't add that he hadn't wanted to spend the extra money.

"I decided early on the luxury knock-off battle wasn't worth fighting." Rory laughed, referencing Kicker's term for any high-end model not from Germany. When Dillon joined in, he added, "I drive a 528i," pointing to a silver one near the entrance. "But hell, the world's changed, even if the old man hasn't. Some of that German perfection comes straight off the line from Mexico."

"Yeah," he snorted, "and I'm sure if you offered him proof, he'd be too stubborn to believe it. He'd call it propaganda or deceptive marketing or some other shit." He reached for the door handle. "I'll catch up with you later, at dinner."

"I don't know how he did it, but I'm glad he got you to come home. It's well past time we were together again. As a family."

"Jesus, Rory." The heavy door slammed shut when he let go of it to rub the back of his neck, searching for the right words. "I've always tried to keep our relationship strong, but we'll never be a family again. Not in the way you want. Jimmy's death changed everything."

"Then why'd you return?" Rory's chin angled higher, his expression combative.

"The returning prodigal son has a sentimental ring to it." He shrugged. "Stick with that explanation, if it makes you feel better."

"That was an attempt at sarcasm," Rory said, his lips curling at the edges. "Aimed at Kicker, in case it went over your head."

He laughed. "There might also be a bit of truth to it, but it's short-term. A day or two at best." He wiped his face and concentrated on a car turning into the parking lot as all humor died. "Kicker and I don't do well together for longer than that. We'd kill each other."

"So, he didn't lure you back with the promise of revising his will? Or an infusion of cash?"

"No." He eyed his brother warily. "Why would you think that? You know I don't give a shit about his money. Kicker knows it too."

"That's what Mom thinks. She's had you investigated. I know your company's hurting."

Dillon held up a hand, palm out. "Back up just a bit. I'm not here because I need anything. I'm here at Kicker's request." At Rory's raised eyebrows, clearly asking, "Is that all?" he grunted. "I'll admit to feeling somewhat nostalgic, but the past doesn't just go away because time elapses and covers it with years of new memories. The old ones eventually resurface to remind us how little has changed. Nothing's resolved."

"Maybe it's time to come to terms with the bad memories, resolve some of those issues, and take part in your legacy."

"My legacy?" What was the kid thinking? "There is no legacy, other than one of sorrow."

"I disagree. Mom thinks you're here for what you can get out of Kicker. She's protective of Dad and me. She doesn't know you like I do. I told her she was wrong. Kane Aeronautics is your legacy. Just as much as it's mine. Hell, even more so. You and Jimmy helped start this." He made a sweeping motion with his hand toward the building. "And it wouldn't exist without either of you flying for free in the early years." His brother shook his head. "Kicker needs you. And I know you need Kicker."

"Shit," he murmured. He looked Rory straight in the eye. "Don't set your hopes on me returning to the company. Kane Aeronautics was never my legacy. If Kicker needs anyone, it's you." He threw out a half laugh. "Definitely not me. You understand him better than I ever could and unlike Jimmy, who was his favorite, you don't possess the same limitations." Kicker could never accept Jimmy's biggest flaw, so his father had pretended it hadn't existed.

Dillon reached for the door handle again, then slid inside once the hot air escaped. After starting the engine, he glanced up at Rory. "I'll see you at dinner, kid," he said, using the familiar nickname. Even though Rory was twenty-four and an imposing adult male to boot, he'd always think of him as his kid brother.

Rory nodded and shut the door, remaining in the same spot as Dillon backed out.

He drove out of the lot, eyeing the rearview mirror. His brother hadn't moved a muscle, just stood and watched his departure.

Dillon heaved a relieved sigh when he couldn't see him any

longer.

Meeting the old man to satisfy his curiosity hadn't been such a great idea, especially since appeasing Kicker meant he'd have to confront Lauren Kane.

Remembering a time gone by and seeing her in his mind's eye, he smiled.

He sped toward the interstate, wondering what her reaction would be if he showed up on her doorstep after all this time. Most of all, he wondered if he had the guts to find out.

Chapter 3

The second the school bus stopped, DJ jumped off and ran the two blocks to his house, taking the porch steps three at a time.

"Hey, Mom, I'm goin' with Joey."

"What about homework?" his mother yelled.

"Got it done on the bus. Monday, I got a quiz in Calc, but I'm solid on it. I'll give it a look a couple of times over the weekend. 'Kay?"

"Okay. Dinner's at six. Don't be late." He was almost out of the house when her shout, "And wear your helmet," hit his ears.

He groaned. If he'd gotten out sooner, he wouldn't have heard the shit about the helmet. When he entered the garage a minute later, he glanced at the plastic bubble resting on the nail over his bike. He reached for it, stuck it on his head, then grabbed his bike. He clipped the helmet in place. Safety. If he didn't show her he could be safety conscious, she'd never be cool with him flying. He already faced an uphill battle. Why make it harder with stupid stuff like not wearing a helmet? Besides, he knew she'd check. Since that flat in the rain a few weeks ago, she'd been super crazy about everything he did.

He took off down the street feeling as if he'd escaped some kind of prison. After all, he'd spent the last five days cajoling her into having some freedom this afternoon.

"Hey, Joey," he yelled, seeing his friend riding toward him after rounding Maple Street. DJ stopped and waited for him to catch up.

"Where're we goin' today?" Joey braked, then did a one-legged dismount off the bike right as a car with two girls, one driving and one hanging out the window, honked.

"Hey, guys," the window-hanger shouted. "Need a ride?"

DJ laughed and waved. "We're exercising." He turned back to Joey. "How 'bout the airfield?" It was a perfect day to watch planes take off and land, something he'd done almost daily during the summer. He hadn't had a chance to ride there lately, thanks to his mom's hovering because some of her papers were out of order the same night they'd had the flat tire. DJ suspected she moved the papers herself and forgot about it. It didn't make sense when nothing was disturbed. If someone had broken in, why go through her files and not take stuff? What kind of burglar moved files, for cripe's sake, and left big flat-screen TVs and laptops behind?

Leaning against his bike, Joey watched the car disappear. Sighing, he kicked a rock. "Man, riding a bike is lame. I can't wait to get my license. I hate it that Lindsay and Katie have theirs before us." Then he made eye contact with DJ and cocked a brow. "Why the airfield? Don't cha go there enough?"

"You got someplace better in mind?" DJ's chin went up, daring Joey to disagree, praying his best friend wouldn't because he was dying to see if his dad's half brother would make an appearance today. Hellraiser, the name he used on Mystic Airlines, the online game where the two had first become acquainted in a chat room, always showed up on Fridays. Or at least he had the last three in a row before his mom started keeping him on a short leash, thanks to her overactive imagination.

His mother would kill him if she knew he'd actually communicated with Rory Kane.

Just mentioning his father's family was enough to cause that sad expression he hated seeing on her face. Apparently Grandpa Kane had made her life a living hell right after his dad had died, so much so that she'd pushed him out of their lives. DJ didn't want to add to her pain by letting on that he and his uncle had formed an online relationship for months before meeting in person at the beginning of the summer.

Rory flew a really cool plane, and best of all, he'd taken him up in it for his first flight. His mother would shit bricks if she ever found out about that. Now that he'd been up in a real cockpit, rather than a virtual one, he damn sure had to figure out a way to get her okay to take lessons.

"I guess we can ride there," Joey said in a resigned voice, yanking DJ out of his thoughts. "I just wish we could drive there instead."

He grinned, relieved not to have to do any arm-twisting. "Don't worry about it." He offered a low five. "We'll have our licenses soon enough and we'll still ride bikes. For the exercise."

When he started pedaling, Joey hopped on his bike and followed.

"Who knows," he added, shouting over his shoulder. "We might even start a trend and we'll be considered cool, rather than lame. Besides, bikes or no bikes, you're looking at the honking all wrong. I prefer to think we caught their attention. Hell, they honked, didn't they?"

"You're the man." Joey laughed. "Always seeing the bright side."

"Yeah. And you're my wing man." There was only one thing DJ

liked looking at more than cool airplanes. Girls. Of course, Pemberton High wasn't a mecca for hot babes. There were only four hundred kids in the entire high school and half of them were boys, so that meant only fifty per class and the hottest two of those fifty were just driving by again as Lindsay and Katie honked after circling the block. He was now a junior and the dating pool had increased by one third this year, but it was still too little. What he wouldn't give to live anywhere but Pemberton, North Carolina. Like Atlanta, LA, or Dallas, where he was sure there were thousands of Lindsays and Katies just waiting for cool guys like him and Joey. College would be like that, but then he'd have to leave his mom all alone.

"Look out!"

DJ heard the yell and glanced behind him in time to see a pickup truck come out of nowhere, aimed straight at them like they had bull's-eyes on their shirts. Joey swiftly veered out of the way and narrowly missed an embankment on the other side of the road. Simultaneously DJ jumped the curb to pedal straight into a fence post, hitting it with force because he hadn't had a chance to brake before he realized what was in front of him. He lost his balance and dropped sideways. His left arm and shoulder took the brunt, meeting the concrete with a loud thunk, and his head bounced off the pavement.

Everything happened so fast he could barely think, but he was lucid enough to thank God for his mother's badgering about wearing a helmet and for Lindsay's warning. If not for both, he might not be able to stand and brush himself off so easily.

"Are you okay?" Lindsay asked.

He looked up to see that she'd parked her car, and now stood with Katie and Joey a few feet away with concern etched onto their expressions. Joey's "Jesus Christ, man, you're bleeding," filtered past his ears. He glanced down. Sure enough, blood oozed out of the skinned side of his knee and his elbow, also bleeding, hurt like a son of a bitch.

"Damn," he said, picking up his bike and rolling it back and forth. The tire wobbled, but it was rideable. He touched the gouge on his helmet, suddenly doubly thankful for his mom's reminder. "Didja see that? The jerk almost hit us." He refrained from calling him a more colorful name. After all, he was trying to clean up his language and his mom had a point. People who cussed were too lazy to use other descriptive words. But at times, like now, the word on the tip of his tongue described the pickup driver better than anything. "He didn't even slow down or stop to see if we were hurt."

"You guys are lucky. You could've been killed," Lindsay said. "He must've been texting or something."

"Yeah. Or something." DJ stared in the direction of the main highway, where the truck had disappeared. "Did anyone get a license number? Maybe we can report him."

"The guy was speeding so fast, I only got the first letter and one number," Katie said. She shook her head, frowning. "It was white and had Florida plates." She flashed an apologetic half smile. "Sorry, but by the time I processed the need to check, it was already too late."

"It's not your fault the guy's a frickin' idiot," he said.

"You're hurt." Lindsay nodded to his arm, eyeing his bleeding elbow. Plus, the fist-sized scrape on his leg looked like raw hamburger. She ran back to her car and returned seconds later with a bottle of water, paper napkins, and a couple of those wrapped towelettes that everyone carried thanks to threats of a swine flu epidemic awhile ago. She grabbed his wrist to lift up his arm, then began dabbing at the blood.

"Ow." He tried to jerk out of her hold after she hit a sensitive spot with her patting, but her grip only tightened.

"Sorry. I didn't mean to hurt you," she said, "but it needs cleaning, then disinfecting, so hold still."

"'Kay." DJ bit back a smile, realizing he could capitalize on a golden opportunity and milk some sympathy from "hot babes," especially these two. "I appreciate the TLC." He could also be tough now that the worst was over and the pain was ebbing along with the bleeding. Once Lindsay poured half the water over his leg, the scrape didn't appear so deep, and was in reality only a superficial wound.

"So, where're you guys off to?" Lindsay asked, shading her eyes from the sun. She'd finished washing away most of the blood and dirt and tossed the muddy, blood-soaked napkins and towelettes in one of the nearby trash cans that were placed sporadically along the town's streets to curb littering.

"Probably the airfield, stupid." Katie glanced first at him and then at Joey, where her gaze lingered. DJ noted the calculation forming in those aqua eyes. Oh, yeah. Hottie Katie Hughes had a thing for his friend and the moron had no clue, he realized, slanting a glance at Joey to take in his reaction.

"As a matter of fact, that's exactly where we're headed." He'd fought too hard for his freedom and had waited all week for Friday to come. No way was he going to abort his trip over a little pain. "Wanna meet us there?" If he had to hit his friend upside the head with a few facts about girls, he could do it while riding. That way, they'd both get something worthwhile out of this afternoon.

"We'd love to." Katie, now all smiles, turned to Lindsay.

"Wouldn't we?"

Yep, he thought, listening to Lindsay's agreement and plans to meet them in fifteen minutes. Besides actually being up in the air, there was nothing better than watching planes take off and land, except doing it with two hot babes, even if one of those babes liked his friend. She was still hot and no rule said he couldn't scope her out while waiting to scope out his favorite plane. Though Lindsay had never given him more than a "Hi, how are you," he might even have a chance at impressing her enough to sit together at the upcoming football game.

"You ready?" DJ asked Joey as the girls sped off. "We have to hustle if we want to make it there before them."

Joey nodded and they began pedaling.

When they could coast, DJ said, "Here's the deal, dumbass. Katie's eyeing you, so go with it."

"You're delusional." Joey snorted. "She's not eyeing me."

"Man, you're not payin' attention. She's interested." He shook his head at how clueless some guys could be. "At least smile at her and talk to her, but for God's sake, don't start going off about World of Warcraft. Girls hate WOW."

"Man." Joey frowned. "I'm not good at talkin' to hot girls. I never know what to say."

"Just be cool and go with the flow." He sighed, wondering why in the hell he was bothering when his friend was acting like a moron. Joey had to get over his fear of the opposite sex, otherwise he'd stay a virgin forever. As far as he knew, he hadn't even kissed a girl and that was a real tragedy.

"What if I screw up? And say something wrong?"

"Ask about her. Ya know? Her hobbies and classes," he encouraged. "Girls always like to talk about themselves."

"That's boring. Why do I want to hear about some stupid chick flick or what color nail polish she's using? That's all my sister talks about."

DJ rolled his eyes, deciding to give up for the moment. Minutes later he slowed, seeing the empty grassy area near the fence, where he usually sat, up ahead. The girls hadn't arrived yet. After dismounting and attaching the helmet he'd been wearing to the bike, he reached into his pocket for his iPhone to check the time.

Three fifty-five. Good. Plenty of time before the expected Saratoga landed, usually around five, and he knew that within forty-five minutes Joey would get bored enough to ride home. Alone. Plus, Joey's mom worked the dinner shift at Morey's Diner on Main and Mrs. Selby expected her oldest son to be home no later than five fifteen to watch his little sister while she worked. His dad, who'd been laid off at the quarry, was working a temp job out of town. According to Joey, he made a lot less and the Selbys needed the money.

Of course, once Joey left, so would the girls because Katie's thing for Joey was the only reason they'd given them the time of day in the first place. But hey, he lived in Pemberton, the most boring place on the planet, and he had to get his thrills where he could.

A minute later, Lindsay drove up and parked next to their bikes.

Smiling, DJ hit the application on his phone to begin playing a list of pre-arranged songs and set the device on the car's hood. As a concession to his guests, Taylor Swift's voice blared out as the two girls exited at the same time. Both bent at the waist and shook out their hair, drawing his and Joey's rapt attention.

The two then positioned themselves on the hood. Lindsay patted the spot next to her, peering over at him. "Have a seat."

"Okay." DJ didn't need to be asked twice. Using his arms for the extra leverage, he landed a few inches from her delectable ass. He hadn't really appreciated the full effect of her short shorts and bare midriff earlier when pain had fogged his brain, but he did now. Oh, yeah, he thought, leaning on his one good elbow, enjoying the view as Joey climbed onto the opposite side next to Katie. Music, hot babes, and sunshine. He heaved a contented sigh. What better way to spend the next hour while he waited for Hellraiser and his Saratoga?

Some time later, DJ glanced at his iPhone. Five forty-five, almost an hour after Joey and the girls had left, and time for him to start home if he was to make it in time for dinner. God knew if he showed up late, his mom would start in on her spiel about his safety. He'd already thought of the spin he'd put on his injuries. She didn't need to know all of the particulars, otherwise he'd become a prisoner again. No way he'd miss next Friday.

He gave one more furtive glance at the field and sighed, then skipped a rock at the street, swallowing his disappointment. Rory and his cool plane hadn't shown up, so he hadn't gotten to fly today. He chucked another rock. This one skipped half a dozen times, but DJ paid no attention, having lost interest in how many times he could make it skip. Dusting off his shorts, he bent to retrieve his bike. Pain flared from his leg and elbow, reminding him of his injuries. He waited for the pain to ease, then gingerly hopped onto his bike. Avoiding quick movement, he began the trip home, riding as fast as was possible without incurring more pain. While he rode, he decided to focus on the positive.

Though he hadn't scored another flight, he had scored the

opportunity to sit with Lindsay at the game tomorrow. True, it would be a major sausage fest, with ten or more of the hundred junior and senior guys also sitting nearby, all vying for her attention, but at least she now knew more than his name. Not a hell of a lot, but something to show for the afternoon.

☙

After noting caller ID, José Sanchez cut off the Latin music ring tone with the push of a button and brought the cell phone to his ear.

"What the hell are you thinking?" The angry sound burst into his ears. "Why not announce to the world you're trying to kill them?" The voice was distorted, same as always, most likely a computer-generated disguise. He had a number, but had no idea who the caller was. All he knew was that this person had already made good on one threat.

He wiped his face and looked around the crowded diner, but no one paid him any attention. Still, he lowered his voice. "No. They should've gone off that cliff."

"What? You mean that sloppy attempt? Sloppiness wasn't part of our agreement," the voice shot back. "One more screw-up and your son goes to jail. Do I make myself clear?"

"What more do you want?" Thank God no one knew about his latest attempt, especially the person at the other end of this conversation. Just his luck, he'd missed another shot at the brat only hours ago. "I've done everything you told me to do."

"No. You haven't. If you had, they'd already be dead." There was a slight hesitation, as if to emphasize the next words. "I was sure you were the right person for this job, but right now I have huge doubts. Not a good sign for your precious Carlos."

Though spoken a decibel louder than a whisper, the menacing sound caused a chill of unease to creep up his spine. "It's not easy in a town where everyone knows everyone." In Tampa, he was a phantom, nameless and faceless. Anyone snitching on a gang member, no matter the side, was a dead man and pretty much guaranteed he could do whatever needed doing with no finger-pointing. Here in Bumfuck, North Carolina, he felt like he had an X on his forehead, especially outside of the Latino neighborhood. He'd taken a big chance earlier, when an opportunity just presented itself. No way he'd get that lucky again.

"You've had a month. Plenty of time, not to mention plenty of my money, to blend in and become part of the scenery." The voice broke off. An instant later, it crackled to life again in his ear. "Our arrangement still stands. You kill them or Carlos goes back to jail. Society doesn't treat felons who've violated parole lightly, especially one like your son who's already had two strikes. A third and he'll go back to prison, a certainty if the law gets a hold of my *evidence*. This time they'll throw away the key."

He drew in a deep breath as the waitress walked toward him holding up a full pot of coffee with the question in her eyes. He nodded and clenched the fist that gripped the phone, subduing the impulse to send it flying across the room. "I get the friggin' message," he said through gritted teeth. Then he rolled his shoulders in an effort to relax and stuck out his cup as the voice added, "Good. Then we understand each other. You take care of business, make it look like an accident, and no one will be able to tie you to them. Carlos is safe and you'll disappear back into your gang a hundred grand richer. We'll each get something we want out of the deal."

"I'm working on it." He shouldn't have to listen to this garbage. He'd shot out the tire, exactly as instructed. Could he help it if the bitch got lucky and managed to gain control before going off the cliff? Hell no. With a tightened jaw, he remained silent until the waitress finished filling his cup. After offering him a CFM smile, she sashayed away, the swing of her hips an exclamation point to that do-me smile. His mouth twisted into a wry grin. That piece of tail would have to simmer until he got this monkey off his back.

"Since your *plan* didn't work, comin' up with another takes time," he ground out. That, in a nutshell, was the problem. If things had gone as planned, they'd be dead and he wouldn't be sitting in this lousy diner trying to figure out how to kill someone and make it look like an accident.

He wasn't a patient man who held back on anything he wanted. One more rash move like going for the brat on a bike might just send him to prison, something he'd avoided thus far. Still, he damned well wanted this over and done with. Now. Wanted the threats gone. The entire time his caller rambled on with more advice on how to kill, he stilled the urge to pound the crap out of someone—namely the asshole threatening him now with his son's incarceration.

No one messed with José Sanchez and got away with it. In Tampa, he'd just shoot his way out. He owned an arsenal of weapons…was a crack shot…loved firearms and explosives because they gave him power…that extra hard-on…especially after a kill. Doing it slow, or *accidentally*, was for pussies, like his caller. Gang-related slayings were nothing new and no one cared enough to figure out who or why. They just accepted.

Unfortunately the two he was supposed to kill, in exchange for his oldest son, just happened to have a connection with the sheriff, like every other citizen in this Pollyanna town. Understanding his adversaries, enemies and the law alike, was one concept he believed in. This sheriff wouldn't just roll over and accept, even if it looked like an accident.

"You're running out of time," the voice said, interrupting his train of thought. "Just do the job. Are we clear?"

"As glass." He smiled at the waitress and lifted his cup in a silent salute. He took a sip, holding his hot eyes on the bitch in heat as she touched her pen to her mouth and flicked it with her tongue before licking the full length of first her top lip and then that luscious pouty bottom one, her silent message shouting he'd definitely enjoy that tongue.

"Make it look like an accident and get it done. Soon."

The line went dead and he cut the connection, still focused on the eye candy. His tongue skimmed his lips in response to her silent teasing, craving more than a taste.

Suddenly he was in a hurry. He was much better at being macho and rushing in and getting out before the smoke cleared. To hell with making it look like an accident. He'd kill the bitch, then her brat, and have the waitress as a reward. He glanced at the caller ID and pressed the right app to stop the recording, swallowing a laugh over his foresight to tape the call. The number on caller ID referred to one of those disposable phones and made it harder to trace, but that wouldn't stop him. He'd figure out who was on the other end and then he'd get his revenge.

Blackmail worked both ways.

&#x03;

As Rory had stipulated, Dillon stood on his father's elaborate front porch precisely at seven and pressed the bell. The memory of the last time he'd done just that flashed. Too many years had passed, but in his mind's eye, it could have been yesterday or an hour ago, given the clarity.

"Dillon," Arletta exclaimed after opening the door.

Grinning, he wrapped the tiny black woman in a bear hug, lifted her off the ground, and twirled her around. "You don't look a day older than twenty-five."

"Get outta here." Laughing, she slapped at his arm when he let her go and he could have sworn she was blushing, given the dark tinge coloring her cinnamon cheeks. "Ya always were a kidder."

"It's true." He hadn't lied. Though no one really knew her exact age because she'd never revealed it, she had to be pushing sixty, but looked decades younger. He waited until she closed the door and followed the woman who'd been more than a housekeeper during his entire childhood. "You're ageless…an angel sent down from heaven to protect two clueless boys." The woman had been his and Jimmy's salvation after their mother had died, smoothing the transition to a new stepmother. Back then, the bumps were pretty damn big.

"Oh, hush. You two were the angels and I feel blessed to have had a hand in raising you."

Neither he nor Jimmy had dealt well with Sophie's arrival. Even after all this time, Dillon wasn't quite sure how he felt about his stepmother, except relief that his father had her in his life, especially now that Kicker was showing signs of aging. Took the pressure off him to fill what could easily turn into a necessary role, one he didn't think he had in him to fill. His father had killed all desire for maintaining a father-son relationship years ago, so why pretend to be a nurturing son now?

"A day doesn't go by I don't miss your brother," Arletta said, drawing his attention. She gave him a critical look and snorted. "'Course, the way you been hiding up there in Atlanta, y'all would think you'd died too."

Choosing to ignore her comment, he didn't reply. Age hadn't mellowed his surrogate mother's tongue one bit. She'd always said exactly what was on her mind.

Arletta stopped outside the formal living room. "Go right in. Sophie and Kicker are waiting on you before they have cocktails." Her ire forgotten as quickly as it had formed, she was suddenly all smiles and lovingly ran the back of her hand down his face. "Welcome home, baby-cakes," she said, using her pet name for him. "It's good to see you back where you belong."

Nodding and letting an unwelcome wave of nostalgia pass, he watched her head in the direction of the kitchen before turning to face Kicker and his stepmother. He shoved his hands into the pockets of his Dockers, a concession to Sophie. If he had his druthers, he'd be in jeans or shorts and a T-shirt. Clothes were clothes. Meant to cover the body, and the more comfortable the better. He certainly wasn't about to concede further and dress for dinner like Sophie always insisted on doing. Looking at his stepmother now, who stood to welcome him, he noted that hadn't changed either.

"It's so good to see you," she said in a voice as phony as her expression. Maintaining her frozen smile, she offered him a cheek, dressed to kill in a frothy red dress that looked to be right off the runway and probably cost a sum with three digits behind the first number. "Thank you for coming. It means a lot to Silas. And to me."

Her makeup was perfect, as was her ash-blonde hairdo. She could easily step out of a magazine cover, except for the telltale fine lines hidden within Botox and filler that somehow added a certain disproportionate element to her features. Even still, Sophie Kane was a gorgeous woman. Much more beautiful than his own mother had been. Another surge of the past welled up and he squelched the memory. Wouldn't do to rehash old wounds.

"It's good to see you too," he lied. He was here for two reasons, Rory and curiosity, but if she wanted to keep up pretenses, who was he to spoil her party?

"Would you like a glass?" Kicker held up a bottle of what had to be aged Kentucky bourbon, probably Woodford Reserve since that's all the man drank.

When he nodded, his father asked, "Straight up or on the rocks?"

"Straight up is fine," he said, knowing without a doubt that Kicker would pour a liberal amount, something he desperately needed to survive this ordeal.

He sat in the plush, dark blue upholstered chair Sophie indicated.

"Remember, only one drink." She glanced at Kicker, trying for what seemed like a concerned frown, except her botoxed forehead remained unnaturally wrinkle-free. "You promised."

"Ease up, woman," his father said. "This is a special occasion, and I'll be damned if I can't have a few drinks to celebrate my son's return."

"But the doctor said—"

"Screw the damned doctors," Kicker cut in loudly, adding a glacial stare that dared her to continue.

He could tell Sophie wanted to say more but after a quick glance in his direction, she backed down and remained silent.

No one spoke as his father walked toward him with two drinks and handed him one before moving to sit in the loveseat across from him—an uncomfortable thirty seconds, Dillon noted. He brought the glass to his lips and shot back more than a swallow, trying to ignore the tension.

Just then Rory breezed into the room. "You're looking beautiful tonight, Mom." He walked up to his mother and bent to plant a kiss on her forehead. "Is that a new dress?"

"Yes. You're a sight for sore eyes and so sweet to notice." The smile Sophie bestowed was no longer fake. In fact, she nearly beamed while patting the hand still gripping her shoulder. "Is that a new suit?"

"Yeah. You like?"

"Yes I do." Her smile widened. "You look successful, as you should."

"I aim to please." His face split into a grin and he winked. "It's why I wore it." Still grinning, Rory nodded first at Kicker, saying,

"Dad," then at him. "Glad you're here." He strode to the bar and made himself at home by pouring a drink, adding, "I wasn't sure you'd actually make an appearance."

"I said I'd come, didn't I?" Dillon chuckled. Leave it to Rory to ease the tension and lighten everyone's mood, something the kid had been born to do. Something Dillon would never attempt, since he'd been born to irritate. The warmth in Kicker's eyes as he watched Rory take a seat in the chair beside him threw light on their bond, also driving home the point that Dillon and his father had never shared such a bond and never would. Not in this lifetime.

Bringing the bourbon to his mouth, he chugged a large mouthful and pushed the disturbing thought aside, determined not to care. As the amber liquid slid down his throat, he luxuriated in its heat, also relishing its mellowing effect. Of course, he didn't care.

He concentrated on the idle chitchat the four then engaged in until Arletta, God bless her timing, stood at the door to announce dinner. Relieved, he jumped up with the group and filed into the dining room with one thought. This was turning out to be a long, *long* night.

Arletta pointed to a place setting. "I put you there, across from Rory."

Dillon pulled out a chair to sit as Sophie took a seat at one end of the table and Kicker did likewise at the other. Delicious scents rose up, again reminding him of the past, but these memories were good ones. The fried chicken, potato salad, green beans in a savory butter sauce, and biscuits all made his mouth water, especially when he spied the added sausage gravy. He realized she'd cooked his favorites. Foods he seldom ate. Not just because they were laden with fats, but also because no one else did them justice, not like Arletta.

He and Rory started passing around plates. When all the dishes had made a complete round, his stepmother got up from the table and picked up Kicker's full plate, one heavy on the biscuits and gravy. "You can't eat this." On her way to the kitchen, she said, "Arletta should remember your doctor's orders."

"It's what he likes, and once in a while won't kill him," Arletta groused from the doorway, shaking her head and rolling her eyes. "A man has to have some pleasure in his life, otherwise he might as well be dead." She glanced at Dillon. "I been cooking for this family almost forty years, and suddenly it's not good enough. I'm about ready to retire."

"Now, Arletta," Kicker crooned. "She's only trying to keep me healthy."

"Humph." She crossed her arms and her chin went up. "I don't see your health improvin' one damn bit. If y'ask me, eating that slop she shoves at you's killing you slowly. Got no flavor. What's the use o' eatin' if it don't taste good?" She left, still mumbling about tasteless food.

Rory laughed and shoved away from the table. "I think I'll go and try to smooth things over between them."

Dillon watched his younger brother walk out of the room, then turned back to his father and went for a smile. "Things seem a little strained." A little? What an understatement.

"There's always been friction between those two." Kicker's gaze flew to the doorway where Rory and the women had disappeared. "Sophie's been on me to get rid of her since the day we married."

Just then, Rory's joking voice floated into the room as well as both women's laughter.

Yep, he thought. His brother could charm a rattle off a rattler, and it seemed his charms were needed in more ways than one in this household.

Kicker sighed. "But you know I'd never let the woman who spent so long taking care of your mother go. Not until she wants to and then I'll miss her. I reckon almost as much as I miss your mother."

The last two sentences came out barely louder than a whisper, but Dillon caught them and quickly wished he hadn't. Considering the pain etched onto Kicker's face along with the torment in his words, one might actually believe he'd cared about his mother. Dillon knew differently. A grieving man didn't up and marry a woman less than half his age within weeks of burying his widow, or produce a child six months after that. Kicker had done both.

Dillon's attention went to the food on his plate. No way he could view his father with compassion. Like he was an ordinary guy with ordinary problems. Ordinary just didn't fit the Kicker residing in his memory.

Quiet in the room pervaded until the distinctive ding of the microwave rang from the kitchen. More time slipped by before Rory finally burst back into the room, interrupting another long, uncomfortable silence.

As Rory sat, his stepmother reappeared and proceeded to place a different full plate in front of Kicker. "There," she said, in a satisfied tone that matched her smile. "That's much more nutritious." Still smiling, she took her seat at the end of the table again. "If you'd only follow the doctor's advice about eating, I'm sure you'd feel better."

"Goddamn it all," Kicker grumbled. "Those doctors don't know squat."

After that no one spoke. Sterling silver utensils scraping against the fine china plates Sophie insisted on using was the only noise that marred the silence in the room.

No wonder his father had lost so much weight, Dillon thought, eyeing the food Kicker had scarcely touched after five minutes. The steamed vegetables might be palatable with a pat of butter or grated cheese, but from this angle, the plain overcooked broccoli and cauliflower appeared to be quite tasteless. Add in the colorless tofu casserole sitting next to it and you had something as unappetizing as dirt. He sided with Arletta on this one. Fried chicken with biscuits and sausage gravy were ten times more preferable.

Wanting the meal to be over as quickly as possible, if only to spare himself the misery of watching his father stir his unpalatable dinner around his plate, Dillon shoveled the food in without really enjoying the housekeeper's efforts.

A few minutes later, Kicker pushed his still full plate aside and threw his napkin on the table while rising. He turned to Dillon. "Now that you've finished eating, why don't we talk in my study where we won't be disturbed."

Dillon nodded and stood.

On the way to his father's study, he glanced at the front door, longing for escape.

Sighing, he followed Kicker into a more masculine-looking room than the living room, and sat in a black leather chair opposite Kicker's gigantic desk.

Satisfying his curiosity had turned into a painful mistake. He should have stayed away. His best strategy now would be to go and visit Lauren as quickly as possible, otherwise Kicker would never let up.

Dillon wiped his sweaty palms on his pants, quelling the nervous energy running amok inside his system at the thought of seeing her again. All afternoon he'd fought, and failed, to dismiss the idea that he was latching on to his father's demand as an excuse to see her.

Considering their history, he suddenly realized how damned glad he was to be able to justify the need. Unfortunately, having an excuse didn't ease his mind one bit as thoughts of visiting Lauren only opened a box in his heart he'd closed long ago.

Chapter 4

Dillon knocked on the door, then spent the idle minute taking a closer look at the neighborhood. The neat little ranch was nestled in the center of a cul-de-sac of seven houses, every one far enough away so as not to be right on top of each other.

He'd viewed pictures over the years, but nothing had prepared him for seeing the scenery firsthand. The dark greens and browns of the forest were set off in stark contrast to the deep blue of the sky. This area might be considered God's country. Even if the term hadn't already been attributed to half a dozen spots in the US, he could totally appreciate why Lauren lived here.

He spun around when the door opened and waited until recognition flashed in her eyes. When it did, he smiled. "Hello, Lauren," he said, catching a glimpse of that familiar connection in her gaze, the same one that had drawn him to her all those years ago. "It's been a long time."

But all too quickly it disappeared as she continued staring, her mouth changing from the *O* of surprise to a grim line.

"Can I come in?" he asked, going for broke before he lost any more of his surprise advantage. "We need to talk."

She stepped back to close the door in his face, saying at the same time, "I don't think we have anything to talk about." But the foot he stuck on the threshold stopped its momentum.

"Still running?" He knew better than to taunt, but her dismissing him so readily pissed him off.

She yanked the door open wider but not in welcome, considering the look she sent him. Her stare could freeze the rain forest. "I've never run. I left. There's a difference."

His smile remained intact and he let the comment pass. After all, he bore the brunt of responsibility for what had happened, taking his drunken outrage into account. But she'd owned some culpability, and he wasn't about to pretend ignorance of the real reason she left Tampa. She'd run away from feelings and was probably still running, afraid to slow down because the truth might catch up with her.

"Okay. You left. I promised to stay away." Hell, he couldn't judge her. Hadn't he slunk off to Atlanta because he couldn't face the truth? That she preferred his gay brother, who'd been in denial and could never really be there for her emotionally, to him? Even though there'd been a strong connection or attraction between them? Still was. At least on his part, he thought, noting that despite the anger snapping her eyes, her knack for stirring something within him with her gaze hadn't diminished. Not one dammed bit.

"I'm here now, which means I lied. So, sue me." He took his foot off the threshold and crossed his arms, daring her to slam the door in his face.

"You'll never change," she said, shaking her head.

"Doubt it. My irreverence was what you loved most about me, remember?"

To be fair, she hadn't known Jimmy's secret. Probably still didn't, he thought, watching more annoyance rise in her eyes. Otherwise she'd quit running from the guilt, as she'd taken her vows seriously. It was something he'd admired about her. He just wished her husband could have been as honest, which caused friction between brothers. Though Jimmy had loved his wife, as much as a gay man could love a woman in his opinion, he'd also kept her in the dark. Determined to make his marriage work, every bit as much for Lauren and DJ as for his fear of coming out of the closet, he refused to budge on the subject. A true tragedy. Despite possessing so many fine qualities that made him an exceptional human being, he'd struggled to change and go "straight," as if he'd had a choice. Having been born exactly as God had intended, Jimmy should never have felt compelled to change. Dillon had gone hoarse trying to convince Jimmy to accept himself as he was, also stating that by finding fault with the way God made him was to find fault with God.

Even more tragic, Jimmy Kane had felt driven to live this "lie" to please their father—a father who didn't deserve it in Dillon's opinion. The one flaw that Kicker would never accept was that his oldest son had been attracted to men, not women. In order to save face, Kicker spun his own story, one in which Jimmy was involved with Hutcheson's wife, not Hutcheson, and no one bothered to verify the facts. Who knows what Hutcheson's wife believed, but a divorce was a direct result.

Hutcheson was now out of prison. Free as a bird, according to Kicker, and causing problems from his Chattanooga hideaway. That thought brought him back to Lauren and his problem at hand.

"I'm sorry. That was uncalled for." Dillon swiped a hand over his face and reconnected with Lauren's gaze, letting the seriousness of the situation show in his eyes. "Look, give me five minutes. Please?"

Few had known the real truth about Hutcheson and Jimmy's relationship. They'd been lovers until Jimmy broke off their relationship just before Hutcheson left for an extended overseas assignment. During that time, Jimmy had rejected his true nature to marry and produce a baby right away, proving he *could* change. Then days before his brother's death, Dillon had overheard Hutcheson begging Jimmy to continue their relationship where it left off and no one would be the wiser, something Dillon knew tore him in two.

Remembering it all again still had the ability to anger him, even after fifteen years. Losing a mother to cancer during their teens had been hard on both of them, but more so on his older brother. Catherine Kane had always stood as a buffer between her two boys and their father. Dillon figured she'd known about Jimmy and had provided total acceptance…total love. If she'd lived, he had no doubt things would have been different. For all of them. But she hadn't, and at that point, Jimmy couldn't risk losing Kicker's approval by not living up to his father's expectations. Kicker, as he'd already demonstrated in his every action, would never accept the truth about his oldest son. Just another sin to add to the many his dad carried on his soul.

"Why should I?"

Lauren's question pulled him out of his thoughts.

"Ronald Hutcheson," he said, throwing the two words out in hopes of scaring her. Judging from her intake of breath and her spine out-stiffening a board, he'd succeeded.

She nodded, her head indicating her living room. "You have five minutes." Lauren waited until he'd pushed past her before closing the door.

Words suddenly failed him as she looked at him with raised eyebrows without speaking for too many seconds. Well, this is a little awkward, he thought.

Dillon cleared his throat. "I didn't think this would be so hard."

For something to do while figuring out how best to proceed, he glanced around the room. The words warm and cozy came to mind. A coffee table with a jigsaw puzzle in the middle sat in front of a slip-covered L-shaped sectional. Two oak tables matching the coffee table flanked the ends of the sofa. Ornate ceramic lamps were centered on each end table. Lauren may lack Sophie's sophisticated taste, but she definitely had a knack for putting blacks, beiges, and browns together. He utilized same color scheme, but had to admit that hers worked a hell of a lot better than his.

"What'd you expect? That I'd throw you a parade?"

"No." He laughed. "Nothing quite that drastic." He'd always enjoyed her twisted humor, something Jimmy never appreciated, mostly because half of her jokes went right over his head and the rest he took literally. "But I was hoping you'd at least be a little happy to see me. After all, it's been a long time."

For an instant the old Lauren peeked out in a spark of laughter in those green eyes, along with a glimmer of longing or remembrance. But whatever he'd caught dissipated much too quickly before she glanced at her watch.

"I'm not." Crossing her arms, she tapped her toe. "You've just wasted one of your five minutes. You have four left."

"Look, I've already tried to apologize for my behavior that night. I had no business butting in on your relationship like I did." Hell, glancing at her now and seeing her expression totally closed, he wondered if his interpretation of the way things were hadn't just been wishful thinking on his part, a manifestation created because he'd wanted her to feel something between them all those years ago.

"So you did." She shrugged, then spent an inordinate amount of time studying her hand. "But nothing's changed in how I felt back then or how I feel now."

"Okay, I can accept that." Real or imagined, apologies would never change what happened. She hadn't been free to feel anything for him and he'd forced the issue, resulting in Jimmy's ultimate death. Sure, he hadn't sabotaged the plane, but if he hadn't gotten drunk, his brother would still be alive.

He'd had no business getting drunk to begin with, nursing her rejection. He'd had no business judging Jimmy. Whether his brother had misrepresented himself or not, he'd had no business coveting his wife. No business whatsoever.

Still, he had to make her understand. "Kicker believes Hutcheson might be out for some kind of revenge, and you need to take precautions." The guy had already proven himself to be a crafty and dangerous man in his dad's opinion. Kicker also reminded him that Hutcheson had sworn to get even for Kane treachery. Time had a way of softening the memory of that day, a lifetime ago. Yet Dillon hadn't completely forgotten their last confrontation in the courtroom, this coming mere months after he'd first met with the man to beg him to leave Jimmy alone…just days before his death. Until his conversation with Kicker, he'd all but forgotten the angry, hate-filled look in Hutcheson's eyes when he'd voiced his threat.

"Look, Dillon," Lauren said, drawing his attention. "I was informed of Hutcheson's release. He's been out for almost two years, so why would he suddenly decide to act now?"

"That's true." He nodded, having said the exact same thing to Kicker a few nights ago. "But my dad thinks he's up to something. That he waited on purpose." Kicker could be persuasive. Or he thought, eyeing Lauren cautiously, his real motivations had nothing to do with his dad's concerns and everything to do with his own personal agenda. Her unyielding expression only made him realize he'd wasted his time.

"Hutcheson isn't a threat. You can go back to your father and tell him I don't need or want his help. While you're at it, make sure he understands that nothing has changed. He threw away his chance to include us in his life. All is not forgiven or forgotten. He won't be able to worm his way into my son's life until I'm satisfied it'll be in DJ's best interest." Her gaze hardened. "Do I make myself clear?"

"So, you're willing to take chances with DJ's life?" he said, throwing up the same argument Kicker had used.

She laughed. "That sounds like something Kicker would say to scare me into cooperating. I never expected you to start manipulating like your father."

Without glancing at her watch, she stated flatly, "Your time's up," at the same time a voice from the back of the house asked, "Hey, Mom, who're you talking to?"

That had to be DJ. Dillon glanced toward the hallway, wishing he could stay and meet his nephew.

Yet the resolve moving into Lauren's gaze squashed the wish, flattening it more as she said a little louder, "No one important. Besides, he was just leaving."

"'Kay. Mr. McCall's taking a break and we both need a drink before I ride to the airfield," the voice said again. "Do we have anything in the fridge?"

"Yes. I put some soft drinks in this morning," she said over her shoulder, before turning back to him and smiling. "To ease both your minds, you can tell Kicker I've hired a handyman. His presence should dissuade any lurking danger." Her nod indicated the exit. "Don't let the door hit you on the way out."

Dillon knew all about her handyman, Jeff McCall, AKA Kicker's investigator. According to his father, McCall had bumped into Lauren several times around town after the flat tire incident. Earlier, while keeping the lady under surveillance, he'd spotted more than a few repairs her older house needed. During one of his orchestrated "meetings," he admitted to being a handyman needing a job and promised to work for cheap. He eventually talked Lauren into hiring him with orders to remain close enough to protect while gaining more information at the same time.

She was in good hands, and still spotting resolve written in bold letters across that obstinate expression, Dillon had no choice but to leave. He'd simply have to wait until another day to meet DJ. Forcing an introduction now would be a huge mistake.

On the walk back to his car, he wondered why in the hell he'd made the trip in the first place. Well, he'd already admitted to why. She'd never ceased to stir up something inside him. Something he couldn't let go of and after five minutes of being in her company, the old memories charged back in and took over his good sense.

Her words about nothing changing spoke volumes. She hadn't wanted him then and she damn sure didn't want him now. Unfortunately, the biggest thing that hadn't changed was that, God help him, he still wanted her.

☙

The front door slammed. "Mom," DJ yelled at the top of his lungs. Both were sure signs of his excitement. "Wait 'til I put this on Facebook. It's a damned miracle."

"Watch your language, and what's a miracle?" Lauren shouted back, adding the remaining stuffing, consisting of chicken, cheese, sour cream sauce, and broccoli, to the last flour tortilla. Once she tore off a sheet of aluminum foil to cover the dish, her chicken enchiladas, DJ's favorite, were ready for the oven. She stuck the empty bowl into the sink and ran a bit of water over it.

Dillon's visit had rattled her, leaving her with too much to think about. Cooking was the best way to think. Unfortunately, unwanted thoughts kept intruding. Like memories of Dillon and the way he'd always had a ready ear when she'd needed to talk. He'd been a constant in Jimmy's life and she'd forgotten how much she'd come to depend on his steady companionship. Lauren didn't want to think of him or of the void he'd filled when her husband tended to shut her out emotionally. Or how the more she'd begged for Jimmy's attention, the more he'd shut her out. Yet instead of trying harder, or yanking Jimmy to a marriage counselor, she'd taken the easy way out and used the attraction she felt for his brother, along with his concern, to mollify her apprehension over her marriage. She'd simply been too timid, or maybe secretly she'd kept quiet on purpose, in order to hang on to Dillon's attentiveness. Either way, she was guilty. Guilty of not fighting hard enough and guilty of leaning on a man other than her husband.

Then there was Dillon's earlier warning about Hutcheson. Lord, she really didn't want to remember how threatened she'd felt back then. Especially when, after fifteen years, nothing bad had happened, making her fears seem overblown, that maybe she'd seen threats where none existed. It hadn't helped that Jimmy's death had left her totally alone in the world. After calling her aunt and being given a curt "Don't call me again," she'd just wanted to get away. Run somewhere. Anywhere but where she'd been. A place she could hide out and feel normal.

A month had passed since the flat tire without incident. She'd finally decided her worries over the moved files were unfounded. Lauren just couldn't see any connection between her disturbed papers and the mystery man, and imagining one seemed silly. Her son's bike accident had concerned her until DJ admitted the real cause—having his attention on a car full of girls at the time. Rather than feel sillier, she'd refrained from overreacting and forbidding him the freedom to spend his afternoons riding to the airfield.

DJ burst into view as she had the oven door open and was placing the rectangular glass dish inside to start baking. She wiped her hands on her apron when he danced up to her, wrapped his arms around her middle, and kissed her cheek.

"I got a job today," he said, lifting her off the ground and twirling her around. "A real job that pays eight bucks an hour."

"A job?" Lauren laughed. "That's great. When? Where? Doing what?"

He released her and charged for the refrigerator. "On the weekends and after school." He grabbed a bottled water, unscrewed the cap, and said before taking a swig, "At Stanley Field."

Her spine stiffened. Had Dillon somehow gone behind her back and met her son and offered him a job? She took deep breaths in order to remain calm and not go all crazy on him. "What kind of job?"

"A gofer for one of the pilots." He wiped his mouth with the back of his hand and stuck the water on the counter.

"Oh?" She searched his face, making sure he wasn't leaving anything out, but only noted excitement in his expression. "Who is this pilot?"

"Ralph Smith, just a regular guy who has his own plane and saw me watching him fly in and out during the summer. He tests maintenance on planes several times a week. He's cool."

"Hmm." Her gaze narrowed. She continued eyeing him thoughtfully, focusing on niggling red flags in DJ's manner…like quickly looking down instead of holding her gaze, and that spot of color pinking his cheeks.

Rather than articulate her suspicions, instead she prompted, "Just a regular guy, huh?"

He nodded.

"And what was his name again?"

"Ror—Ralph Smith."

"Ralph Smith?"

"Uh-huh."

Lauren had met a lot of regular guys at the airfield through DJ over the last few years, and most of those pilots seemed to enjoy DJ's enthusiasm. Lord knew at this point in his life, her son needed a father figure, someone he respected to show him how to be a man, so this could be a blessing.

He and Thaddeus Johnson didn't get along, which was reason enough to put up roadblocks with the sheriff when he'd shown interest. She wasn't into getting involved with anyone. They were friends. Period. Or as close to what Lauren allowed in a friendship.

"So, where does this pilot live? Tell me more about him." As DJ spent a few minutes talking about the pilot and how they'd met and become friends, some of her reservations faded. You'd have thought the guy walked on water, considering the glowing commentary and the fact that he flew a really cool plane.

"You didn't make a pest of yourself, did you?" When he wasn't riding his bike to the airfield, DJ followed her new handyman around and sometimes it seemed her son was more bother than actual help.

"Oh, Mom. I'm not some stupid-ass kid who can't think for himself or know how to act." He rolled his eyes, flashing an impatient glare he'd perfected, the same one that said she had no idea what she was talking about. "He's legit and I'm assisting him. With maintenance. Stuff like changing tires and cleaning the bugs off the wings and the windows after he lands."

"Maintenance, huh?" Still studying his face for deception, her mind spun. It sounded plausible. DJ knew a lot about planes. Besides hanging out at the airfield on a daily basis during his summers since his tenth birthday, he'd read anything and everything he could get his hands on for almost as long. As much as she liked their new handyman, she didn't know much about him. Not enough to consider him a decent role model. Pilots were of a higher caliber of people, at least those she'd met through Jimmy had seemed so. Her dad's flying buddies had all been top-notch Air Force officers, but that didn't mean she shouldn't be diligent or that this "job" couldn't backfire.

"Okay. As long as you don't get any ideas about flying. You know my rule. No flying. Not yet. In a couple of years, maybe." Then she'd have no control over what he did. But that was then and this was now. Which meant for a while longer, she did have control. "I expect you to abide by my rules."

"Ah, Mom. That sucks." His smile died. So did the excited gleam in his eyes. "The FAA lets students solo when they're sixteen and earn a pilot's license at seventeen. I can work and earn credit toward flying. Please?"

Realizing that had been his game plan all along, Lauren shook her head no. "I don't care what the government says. You're my responsibility, living in my house, and you'll follow my rules until you're on your own. Got it?"

His shoulders slumped. He nodded, but the remainder of his spark was stolen with a heavy sigh that came out in his, "Yeah."

"You can work at the airfield as long as you promise to obey my rules." In a heartbeat of time, he'd be off to college and until then, she meant to keep him safe. "Agreed?" Ignoring the twinge of guilt sneaking its way into her consciousness, she eyed his face closely.

Remaining silent, he nodded, but the petulant tilt of his head conveyed his real thoughts. He was agreeing, but he didn't like it. Not one little bit.

That was A-okay by her. She planned to delay the inevitable for as long as possible.

Of course, once he met Kicker that would change. God only knew how long she could postpone that inevitability, considering his demanding letter along with Dillon's untimely arrival on her doorstep just hours ago. All of the Kanes had learned to fly in their teens. Jimmy and Dillon had, and she had no reason to believe the youngest, she couldn't remember his name offhand, hadn't followed in his brothers' footsteps.

The timer buzzed, interrupting her train of thought. Lauren opened the oven door and grabbed a potholder before peeling the foil off the enchiladas. To keep DJ from arguing further, she nodded in the direction of the bathroom. "Go and wash up, then set the table. Dinner will be ready in another fifteen minutes."

Watching him storm out of the room, she closed the oven door and reset the timer. She wasn't really fooling herself. He had an iron will, too much like Jimmy's. He'd figure out a way even without meeting his grandfather. That thought brought her back to Kicker, his letter…and unfortunately the memory of Dillon standing on her front porch. How like the old man to send his son to do his dirty work. Lauren had to admit; he'd looked good. Too darned good for her liking, and seeing him had taken her back to a place she'd spent fifteen years avoiding—that last year with Jimmy.

Sighing, she shrugged, then grabbed a potholder and opened the oven, dismissing the Kanes from her mind. She had enough to contend with at the moment. Wouldn't do to continue reexamining the past. All she could do was move forward and learn from her mistakes so as not to repeat them.

Tomorrow would be an extra-long day of combining her volunteer work at the soup kitchen with her part-time job as a receptionist for Tilly's House of Beauty. Filling in two extra days a week for another volunteer out due to an emergency operation had left little time during the past month to worry over Kicker Kane's demands to meet DJ. Of course, Dillon's visit told her it was only a matter of time before the situation blew up in her face. She'd cross that emotional bridge when the time came and not a moment sooner.

As she washed and rinsed the bowl, then set it on the counter to dry, she sent up a little prayer that staying busy wouldn't allow too much time to dwell on Dillon Kane, even as the same question she'd discarded half a dozen times since his visit came ricocheting back in her head again.

What would have happened if she'd met him first?

Chapter 5

Ignoring the putrid stench of stale booze and perspiration, José grabbed the bum's greasy hair with a latex-glove-covered hand. He yanked his head back and, trying not to gag, he tipped the bottle, allowing more liquor to pour into his mouth. "There you go, *mi amigo*," he soothed, urging him to keep drinking. "Isn't this what you love?"

His patsy nodded, his glazed eyes revealing the drug had taken hold. When he continued gulping the liquid like a dehydrated man needing water, José smiled. "Soon you can drink as much as you want," he whispered. "All ya gotta do is kill 'er. Charge her with this knife and slice her throat the moment she enters the kitchen." He stuck the blade into his hands. "*Comprende?*"

The bum, half-demented from the PCP he'd laced the vodka with, nodded again, this time more enthusiastically. "Good."

A noise caught his attention and he listened, determining that the sound was a key being inserted into the keyhole. His smile broadened. *Showtime.* He'd set the stage for a quick death, which in his mind worked better than trying to figure out how to make it look like an accident.

"She's coming in to open up the kitchen." José indicated the front room of the soup kitchen the widow opened on Tuesdays and Thursdays. No one would interrupt for at least an hour, but he only needed a minute, maybe two, because once the drunken, drug-crazed fool started in on her she'd be dead, the desire for more shit overriding everything else. He'd timed it perfectly. Violence was his way of life and how he operated best. As soon as the bitch was dead, he'd take care of her brat using similar means.

"Remember, to get more," he said, holding up the half-full bottle, "you have to kill her." He backed up, slipping into the utility closet, and headed for the sink situated next to a window, his entry into the place—and soon to be his exit. He peered into the mirror over the sink. The reflection, via the two-inch crack in the door, provided a decent view of the doorway leading to the back room. A few seconds later, the woman appeared and then stopped, her expression of horror telling him the exact moment she caught sight of the intruder. She turned to run back out but the homeless man charged, grabbed her by the hair, and all but tackled her to the ground.

She screamed, a bloodcurdling yell that hurt his ears. He winced when she gained her balance, then spun around and kicked her attacker right in the *cojones*. He hadn't pegged her for a fighter, but fighting would do her little good. The drugs surging through the bum's system made him impervious to pain.

His instrument for death didn't disappoint as he lunged in her direction, now out of his view. A loud crash indicated more futile struggling. Unable to see it all, he willed the man to plunge the knife exactly where José had instructed when the alley door suddenly burst open.

He swore under his breath, staring in disbelief as her handyman charged in with gun drawn. Without even hesitating, after obviously sizing up the situation in a heartbeat, he fired.

Six times, by José's count.

Holding on to his breath, he waited to hear the final outcome, hoping against hope that the bum had at least gotten in one good slice.

"Please," the bitch cried out as the handyman rushed out of his line of vision in the direction of the voice. "Get him off me."

Taking advantage of their preoccupation, José silently retreated to the window and climbed out of it as fast as his big body allowed in the small space, his mind shouting every swear word he could think of the entire time.

That bitch's luck had just run out, he decided as he ran to his truck, parked on the next block. He was tired of taking orders over the phone, tired of living in this hellhole of a town. And most of all, he was tired of failing. Killing was a big part of his business, so he should be good at it. He'd figure out a way to off both the mother and her brat. He'd do it his way and he'd do it soon.

෫

"Are you okay?"

The words floated above her, and Lauren fought to understand them. Fear still fogged her brain, barely allowing her to register what had happened. DJ. Pictures of her son at various ages flashed in her mind, now and earlier as she'd fought for her life. Thank God he was safe. Along with images of DJ, memories of Dillon had also snuck into her brain. Right now she couldn't stop more of the same thoughts from forming. Like, what if she'd died? She'd never see her

53

son…or Dillon…again.

"Oh God," she whispered, sitting up and then looking down and spying blood. A lot of it, drenching her blouse. "I'm fine. But…" She'd been attacked. As hard as it was to grasp, the metallic scent filling her nostrils had the last minute hurling back with the force of a bucket of ice water, chilling her from the inside out and making it impossible not to comprehend her brush with death.

Lauren glanced up at her handyman and tried for a smile, but fell far short. "You saved my life. Thank you." Her gaze moved to her assailant, a body lying prone on the linoleum floor, blood still oozing out of several wounds. "Is he—" Tears broke free from the corners of her eyes, and she wiped them away before trying again. "Is he—" She couldn't say the word out loud.

"Yeah," Jeff McCall said abruptly after checking his pulse. "He's dead." His gaze went to the storeroom for a long moment. Then his attention went back to the dead guy.

As she sat upright, bile rose up. She placed her forehead on her knees, took deep breaths, and stilled an overwhelming urge to vomit. "I owe you my life," she said once she'd gained some control. "Thank you." She knew she was repeating herself, but those were the only words her mind seemed able to form.

"I heard you scream. I was on my way to pick up a few supplies. If I'd been a minute later or earlier…" His voice trailed off. He didn't need to finish the sentence. If he hadn't been there to hear her scream, she'd be dead right now and not the intruder. Another whiff of blood hit her nostrils. She shuddered, hugging herself tightly, suppressing another urge to lose her breakfast.

"Do you know who he is?" her handyman asked, carefully searching the bum's pockets for ID.

When the feeling passed, Lauren chanced a glance at the body again. More tears broke free when she recognized his face. "I only know him as Andy. He's one of the regulars here." Lauren wiped at the tears and closed her eyes, blocking the sight of his bullet-ridden body out of her mind.

"I'm sorry, I never learned his last name." Oh Lord, that wasn't all she'd never learned about him. Most of the people who came in here on a daily basis weren't open with their lives or with their stories. She accepted their silence because to do otherwise meant having to reciprocate with information she had no desire to share. They all coexisted and mingled, day in and day out, without learning a darn thing about each other.

What a way to live.

Now, more than a twinge of regret snuck into her consciousness.

Lauren could have at least found out something about him. Some little thing that could have tipped her off to his motivations, then she might have been able to stop him from doing such a heinous act in the first place...or might have even prevented his death. She hadn't bothered.

"He's got no ID." Jeff reached for his own cell phone. "Hopefully the law can determine his full name." He punched in numbers and then put the phone at his ear. "Yeah, I have an emergency. I just shot a man who was attacking Ms. Kane with a knife with intent to kill at the soup kitchen." After a brief pause, he answered a few more questions then said, "Thank you." He ended the call, then looked over at Lauren. "They'll be here momentarily. Also an ambulance and EMTs are on the way." He started for the storeroom, then paused, eyeing her intently. "Ms. Kane? Are you sure you're okay?"

"I'm fine," she said, lying through her teeth because, no, she wasn't okay. As he nodded before continuing his trek toward the storeroom, she wondered if she'd ever be okay again.

Suddenly unable to hold the bile down any longer, Lauren reached for a wastebasket. Emptying her stomach in violent retches did little to make her feel any better. A man had been shot and killed while trying to kill her.

But Jeff, who was now in the storeroom and couldn't see her hobbling over to the sink, didn't need to know these thoughts either. She reached for a glass and filled it with water to wash the putrid taste out of her mouth, then grabbed a towel and, after dampening it under the flow, wiped at the perspiration that had formed. Now that she felt more human, she was finally able to get out, "I've never seen anyone act like that. He was totally crazy. I could see it in his eyes."

Lauren had heard stories from some of the other volunteers about the dangers of working with people who had little hope of changing their situation anytime soon. Yet she'd blown off their concerns. She'd never in a million years believed they were dangerous. Desperate maybe, but not dangerous and certainly nothing like deranged killers. "How did he get in?"

The volunteers always took precautions. The doors were always locked until it was time to open when two or more people would be on hand, and there was an alarm system.

"Looks like he jimmied a window in here. Disabled the alarm," McCall shouted from the storeroom. In seconds he reappeared in the doorway. "I'm looking for a motive."

"Motive?" She stared at him, wondering about the guy. After all, he'd just shot a man, but he seemed so calm and unaffected. How was it that a handyman carried a gun in the first place? "What do you mean, motive?" she asked cautiously.

"Can you think of any reason he'd want to kill you?"

"No, other than I surprised him." She rubbed at her temples to ease a throbbing headache forming. "He had to be looking for money or drugs or something. I don't know why he'd be searching for those things here." She ran a hand through her hair and felt dried blood. Another shudder rose up her spine. "So, how is it you had a gun handy?" she asked, not wanting to think about Andy's motive. She had enough to deal with.

"I'm a Southerner," he said smoothly. Almost too smoothly. "My daddy taught me to never go anywhere without one."

Noting his closed expression, she nodded, deciding it wiser to accept his explanation, as any more questions would probably go unanswered. "I only hope the police hurry." After all, too many in the town held the same opinion, evident in all those pickups with rifles in the rearview windows. "I just want this ordeal to be over."

As if her wish had conjured them up, sirens filled the air and within thirty seconds, four squad cars lined the street in front of the soup kitchen. Just knowing help had responded so quickly added to her sense of well-being. Except that well-being was marred when, in seconds, the chaos of being attacked turned into a different chaos as one by one, bodies invaded her personal space, disrupting her well-constructed privacy with their questions and probing.

Ignoring her unease, Lauren answered their questions as best she could for over an hour. In that amount of time, the body had been removed and two deputies had fingerprinted every surface and had snapped pictures, while the one questioning her taped her responses in his little black recorder. Before starting his interview, the officer had assured her someone would notify her son, telling him she was okay and that she wanted him to remain at school. If DJ saw her like this, he'd worry.

Thankfully the deputy finally flipped off the small device, indicating their session had ended. At the same time, Sheriff Thaddeus Johnson emerged from the storeroom. He headed her way.

"I have a few questions to ask your handyman before I can finish my report," Thad said, moving to stand beside her. "But they can wait until after I take you home so you can shower and get out of those clothes."

"I can't leave until I clean up this mess and help the volunteers get ready for the breakfast rush." Her mind was still in a daze and Lauren couldn't think clearly. All she could focus on was how much work needed to be done and how short-staffed the kitchen was. Those needing food had already lined up outside and she knew they were hungry. "That is, if it's okay with you. I mean, I know this is a crime scene."

"My deputies are almost done." Thad's gaze followed her nod, indicating the mess her attacker had caused. "They'll help the volunteers get the place in shape ASAP." His sigh came out in one long exhale as his focus returned to her face and his hand raked through his hair. He rested it on the back of his neck and rubbed. "It's pretty open and shut. Come on. You look pretty bad." He nodded to the plate glass window. "They'll just have to wait a little longer. You're in no shape to stay here and work right now. I'll drive you home. One of my deputies can follow in your car."

"Thanks." She was too weary to argue and too numb to do anything but trail behind him to his squad car.

The short drive to her house was made in complete silence. Idle chitchat was beyond her ability, so why pretend otherwise, she thought as he turned into her driveway.

After following her out of the car to her front porch and waiting for her to unlock the door, Thad asked, "Do you know of any reason he'd attack you?"

"No. He always seemed pretty normal." Lauren realized what she'd just said and added, "I mean, for a homeless guy." She shook her head. "Sorry. I know I haven't been much help."

"Don't worry about it. You've been through a lot." His ringing cell phone cut off what he was about to ask. He threw her an apologetic glance. "Excuse me, I have to get this."

Too tired to nod, she murmured, "Sure."

By now the blood had dried and a faint coppery whiff only rose up every so often. It seemed she'd adjusted to the smell, although she didn't see how anyone ever really got used to the cloying scent. She pushed inside her safe haven of a house, thankful to be home. The split second she spied her sofa with DJ's sweatshirt and T-shirt tossed on it, along with his flip-flops, a football, and other teenage paraphernalia like iPods and ear buds strewn about the room, a sense of rationality returned and her fear began to subside.

Her glance hit the hallway leading to her office and Dillon's warning popped into her head. Her thoughts flew back to those moved files as the memory of the night in the rain resurfaced. Nothing, other than DJ falling off his bike, had happened since, so why did her instincts point to a connection between those incidents and a crazy homeless man's attack?

Oh, Lord. Lauren rubbed her temples to stop the throbbing ache. Was she overreacting?

Stay calm and remain rational. The mental command acted as a balm to her overactive imagination. Somehow, she mustn't allow her fear to consume her.

Protecting DJ had always been her main priority. So was ensuring he lived a normal life, in one spot until adulthood, without all of her dead husband's emotional baggage…or hers.

"That was Bob Miller. He showed up right after we left," Thad said as the screen door slammed behind him.

She nodded. Bob was the director of the food bank, including the soup kitchen, and in essence the person in charge.

"He said not to worry about coming in for the rest of your shift today or for the rest of the week. They'll cover for you." His eyebrows rose. "Want me to call the beauty salon to tell them you won't be in?"

"No. I'll be fine." Lauren was scheduled to work this afternoon. She'd always thought her job of answering phones and scheduling appointments, as well as running the payroll for the salon, was ideal because both the stylists and the customers did all of the talking while she quietly worked. No one expected her to provide any conversation, and she preferred it that way. Of course today would be different, as gossip at the salon would probably center on her ordeal. Still, she felt a strong need to be around the cheerful people she worked with. "I just want to take a shower, then I'll head over there."

Tilly Dickens, the owner, was always after her to increase her hours, so Lauren knew she wouldn't mind her going in early. "Could you just stay out here until I'm done?"

Oh heavens, listen to her.

She'd lived as a loner, leaning on no one but her son for all these years, and here she was practically begging the sheriff that she'd always kept at a distance for help. She didn't want to lead Thad on, but she didn't want to be totally alone either. Not right now.

"I'll wait out here." His nod indicated the hallway. "Go and shower. I have a few calls to make."

"Thank you." She turned and hurried toward her bedroom, hating the relief she caught in her voice. But so what? She'd never almost died before. After changing out of the bloody clothes, Lauren slid into a robe, then rolled the ruined, blood-soaked garments up in a ball and carried them out to Thad.

"Could you do something with these? I never want to see them again."

Nodding, he relieved her of the clothes. While he headed for the kitchen, she made her way to the shower, sending up a silent prayer of thanks that she didn't have to deal with them.

"I feel a hundred percent better," Lauren said, striding out of the hallway twenty minutes later, feeling refreshed despite a few bruises and sore muscles. "It's amazing what a hot shower can accomplish." So much so that she no longer felt the need to have Thad hang around. "I really appreciate your staying, but I'm sure you've got better things to do than baby-sit me."

"Trust me, you're more important than any paperwork or questioning waiting at the office." His face broke into an indulgent smile. "I could stay longer. Keep you company."

"No need. I'm heading over to Tilly's in a bit. Besides, you've already done enough and I'm grateful for your help, Thad." Unwilling to hurt his feelings, she threw out her best attempt at a smile. "And your patience." Remembering how his three deputies, practically the whole force, had treated her with kid gloves, Lauren added, "Oh, and please thank your deputies for all they've done to bring normalcy to an abnormal situation." She'd have to give her handyman a bonus, as mere words didn't seem enough to thank him for saving her life like he had. "I'm sure you have work to do, so I'll let you get back to it."

He hesitated, still making eye contact. "You sure you and DJ wouldn't be more comfortable at my place? It'd be no trouble."

Spying sincerity in his dark gaze, Lauren forced herself to continue smiling. "Thanks, but that's unnecessary. I feel much better." Thad's offer was all she needed to make this experience a total bust. Then she mentally groaned at the ungrateful thought, especially when he'd been so helpful.

Still, she really wasn't up to fielding his attention. Not today.

Over the last three years, they'd dated on and off, mostly off, except for those times when loneliness and the craving for adult companionship had overtaken good sense. Maybe if she hadn't buried three of the most important people in her life within a decade, she might be willing to open herself to love again.

"I really appreciate your help." He was kind, attractive, and well respected in the town, someone who deserved more than she could ever give. The reality of that always resurfaced to lay a guilt trip at her feet. She didn't need any more guilt in her life, thank you very much.

Thad shoved his hands in his pockets, rocked on the back of his heels, and continued to study her face. "I don't like you being out here all alone, given what's happened."

She could hug him for his concern, but refrained. "I'm not alone. I have DJ."

Sighing resignedly, he nodded. "Well, if you need me, I'm only a phone call away." He turned and pushed the screen door open.

"Don't worry," she yelled at his departing back. "I'll be fine." Holding her smile in place, she watched his retreat, continuing to inhale and exhale slowly, refusing to believe she wasn't fine. Hadn't she been fine for the last fifteen years, thanks to Jimmy's foresight?

Lauren's earnings at Tilly's augmented the interest from the million-dollar life insurance policy he'd left her. One could live quite comfortably on both in the middle of nowhere. She'd never wanted nor needed Kicker's money.

Her last conversation with Jimmy's dad and those hate-filled accusations—the main reason contacting Kicker had never been at the top of her to-do list—resurfaced. He might not have believed DJ was a Kane, but Lauren knew better. His demanding letter, along with Dillon's untimely arrival yesterday, meant the old man had finally realized his mistake. Yet he hadn't bothered apologizing. That would have been a good start if he were truly serious about seeing his grandson.

Her gaze made one last sweep of the neighborhood and everything seemed normal. She'd chosen well. Nothing ever happened in Pemberton, and living at the end of a cul-de-sac allowed her to notice any stranger.

No need to be paranoid, she reasoned, observing the sheriff climb inside his squad car. Thad had promised a deputy on patrol would drive by her house periodically. His favor added more security.

Lauren closed the door after he'd driven off and headed for her kitchen, still thinking of the past. For some reason, the danger of the day elicited more old feelings of fear, experienced so long ago. Unfortunately, along with the feelings came mental pictures of a few not-so-accidental accidents. One in particular came to mind, where DJ had almost been kidnapped out of his baby carriage.

If not for an eagle-eyed woman who'd seen what was about take place and had yelled a warning, DJ might not be here today. Since the attempt happened the day she'd left town, she'd kept that incident, along with the others to herself. None of them could be attributed to her husband's killer. He'd been behind bars and he didn't seem the type to conduct hired kidnappings from prison.

But what if? After all, Hutcheson had been released. Almost two years ago. No. That still didn't wash in her mind. Why would he wait so long for revenge?

Besides, he was a scrawny man, a younger Woody Allen look-alike. She could see him sabotaging a plane, which took more brains than brawn, but he didn't seem the type to lurk menacingly in the woods on a rainy night. Her mystery man had definitely seemed much bigger and scarier.

Nothing had happened that night. Just like nothing had happened in all these years and nothing was going to happen in the near future. Not if she had a say in the matter.

She made her way to her office. Sitting behind her desk, Lauren reread Kicker's letter, only to wonder if she'd made the wrong decision in keeping her son from his father's family.

Lauren shivered at the thought of not surviving Andy's brutal attack, but what terrified her more was that DJ would be on his own. All alone without a clue of his extended family.

Unwilling to allow that to happen, she set about rectifying the situation in a detailed letter. Just in case. Once done, she stapled the sealed envelope to the letter, then re-filed both. In seconds, she was heading out the door to the garage, satisfied with her effort.

The salon parking lot came into view after a short drive. She parked and stepped out of the car, striding toward one of Pemberton's biggest buildings. Tilly's House of Beauty was a mega salon, with a reputation of being the best place for women to get their hair cut in a ninety-mile radius.

Her footsteps crunched on the gravel. She marched up the stairs and into Tilly's. The little bell over the door tinkled as it closed. Every head in the place swung around to watch her entrance.

"There you are, sweet pea," Tilly Dickens cried, using her favorite tag for anyone she took under her wing. The woman, who reminded Lauren of a female Pillsbury Doughboy, threw her big arms around her, pulling Lauren into a bear hug. "My God, we heard what happened. We just can't believe it. Are you okay?"

A sense of well-being filled her the moment the familiar Southern accent hit her ears. She'd drawn out her *sweet*, her *can't* sounded like cain't, and her *are* was a combination of air and hour.

Lauren smiled, a genuine one that came from her heart, as Regina and Mary Ellen crowded around her, all clucking like hens. She hugged each woman separately, unable to refute one truth any longer. Coming to this town and distancing herself and her son from the Kanes hadn't been a mistake. She'd never be alone, not as long as these women were alive. And neither would DJ.

Although she'd done her best to keep these people at arm's length over the years, they'd proven mere strangers could sometimes become family, one more loving and accepting than her own had been. Even more surprising, considering every lady present was as nosy as all get-out, none had ever pushed for more than she could give. Her inability to talk about herself didn't seem to matter. They still accepted her without question, and at this moment, she loved them all the more for their silent understanding.

"Sit down, sweet pea, and tell us all about it. We're dying to know," Tilly said, her Southern accent soothing and comforting.

"It's too gruesome to talk about."

"Oh, honey, talking about it is therapeutic," Regina said, emptying her bowl of cuticle conditioner and washing it out. Once done, she dried the bowl then refilled it. "I like to think of myself as a shrink, but my manicures and my ready ear cost a lot less money."

"Yeah, sweet pea. You think all our customers come in just for a trim?" Tilly laughed. Even her laugh sounded Southern. For the first time since this morning, Lauren felt almost normal. She'd kept her vow made all those years ago. As long as she had breath in her body, her son would not suffer. Thank God he hadn't had to endure a childhood like hers.

Or Jimmy's.

In her mind, the elder Kane didn't know how to give. He only knew how to take, which was something she'd always believed caused her husband's inability for true intimacy. Sadly, with her failures and inabilities added into the mix of their marriage, they'd had the perfect ingredients for a dysfunctional relationship. Apparently she'd come to the right place.

The dysfunction of Tilly and company worked just fine for her.

Deciding not to worry about the past or the future, she spent a few moments reliving her nightmare, one that suddenly seemed less horrific in the retelling.

In a way, it was as if facing the fear by talking about it gave it less power.

Chapter 6

Frowning, Kicker dropped the phone in its cradle, cutting the connection once Dillon said his good-byes. He leaned back in his chair and scrubbed a hand over his face, reviewing the gist of the conversation.

His son had basically thrown back his original argument, echoing Lauren's assessment that Hutcheson had been out of jail too long for either of them to be worried. Even after fully explaining how dangerous the situation could become and offering Dillon a much-needed infusion of cash to go back to Lauren's and stick around, Kicker had been told exactly where to shove his money.

Hell, he'd already suspected bribery wouldn't work. His middle child certainly hadn't changed. Not one damned bit. He was too stubborn to take one measly cent from him, even if his paltry request was the only string attached to it.

Dillon's business might be hard up for cash, but that was only situational due to lousy timing, a downturn in revenue, and failing banks. Similar companies had already gone under, but Dillon's firm had a solid foundation. He had the smarts and, according to his sources, was taking all the right steps to survive the worst. More than that—his son's company would thrive and grow, despite a poor economic outlook for the next few years.

Kicker had always admired Dillon's business acumen and survivor instincts, which was part of why he wanted his middle son back on his team, working for Kane Aeronautics.

A knock pulled him out of his thoughts.

"Dad? Are you in here?" Rory opened the door and poked his head around.

"Oh good, Rory." He swallowed his annoyance and focused on another pressing problem. "Come in and close the door."

His youngest pushed into the room. "Arletta said you wanted to see me?" His nod indicated the empty plate on the tray at the edge of the desk. "I see she's fed you. You might want to get rid of the evidence before Mom sees it."

Kicker offered a semblance of a smile. "I will. Sit down. We need to talk."

"Oh?" Rory's eyebrows rose as he sauntered closer, then made himself comfortable in the same chair Dillon had sat in only days ago. "Sounds serious. Did something happen?"

"You might say that." He opened the middle drawer, grabbed a thick file, and tossed it across the oversized cherrywood desk. "Take a look."

"What am I looking at?" Rory reached for the file and spent a moment thumbing through it.

"You tell me." He observed his son's face closely, spotting the exact moment he spied the first picture.

"You had me followed?" Rory's voice was laced with indignation and when he made eye contact, surprise lurked in those blue eyes so like his own. "I can't believe this family. Mom's checking out Dillon and you're having me followed. Next, you'll be following Peters."

Kicker ignored the remark about Peters, not wanting to admit to already having his second-in-command thoroughly investigated, despite his outstanding job performance these past six months.

Rory's crack about Sophie didn't surprise him. She could investigate Dillon all she wanted. He could be drowning, and if Kicker possessed the only lifeline, his middle son wouldn't take it just on principle. He damn sure wasn't after his money, as Sophie believed. Hell, his son had laughed in his face when he'd mentioned the changes to his will that included him and DJ.

"I'm not concerned with anyone's whereabouts but Ronald Hutcheson's. I've had him monitored since his release from prison." He nodded to the file still in Rory's hand. "That report's the detailed accounting I just received of the last few months. I certainly hadn't expected to uncover the fact that you've met with him. Not once, but several times. I'm wondering why you'd meet with him, and more bothersome, why not mention the meetings."

"He called." Rory shrugged, ratcheting back his outraged attitude and seeming to mull his reasons over mentally before he added, "Said he's trying to exonerate himself. Overturn the conviction so he won't be a felon for the rest of his life. I thought I should at least hear him out."

Kicker's jaw dropped a good inch and he stared at him, too dumbfounded to speak. "Are you out of your mind?" he asked once he regained his wits. "You're aware that the man threatened Dillon," he added when Rory hadn't responded right away, "…threatened our family right after he was convicted of…of murdering your brother." His voice rose, becoming a heated outburst by the last word.

"It's okay, Dad. Don't get all bent out of shape before hearing my side," Rory said in a soothing voice, offering his confident smile. He waited while Kicker took a deep, calming breath before continuing. "He explained all that and actually apologized. Said he was angry at the time. Still is, but not at our family. At whoever set him up." He cleared his throat and his slight grin faded to an expression that wasn't so cocksure any longer. "In a weird way he made sense, and I decided to humor him. He asked me to do some checking before I totally blew him off. Which I did."

"Checking?" Kicker shook his head and snorted, absorbing Rory's words, still trying to make sense of them. "What kind of checking?"

"Flight records. Maintenance. That type of thing. He wanted me to examine the old records with a keener eye, which piqued my interest. I kept thinking, why? Why not just get on with his life? He's done his time and in my opinion, along with everyone else's, has gotten away with murder. But what if?" Rory threw him a sideways glance, his expression softening. "You have to understand, Dad. I wasn't as close to Jimmy, so his death didn't affect me the way it did you and Dillon." He shrugged. "I guess I just wanted to look at this from a more objective viewpoint. Anyway, I dug a little and found a few discrepancies that I plan to research further when I get the time, but I haven't met with him again."

"You didn't think to come to me with this?" he asked, locking gazes. "That I might be interested?"

Rory continued meeting his stare without flinching. "You were busy with more important issues."

Like my health, he thought, wincing and breaking eye contact. A sliver of guilt snuck into his consciousness. In other words, he hadn't been there for his youngest son, something he'd vowed to be since Jimmy died and Dillon left. It was why he'd promoted Frank Peters to be his right-hand man from outside the family in the first place. Catherine had always chided him for not spending more time with his boys…for not really knowing them.

"I didn't want to upset you until I had something concrete." Rory paused as if weighing his next words.

"I'm not dead yet," Kicker snapped, exasperation filling him when his son still hadn't continued a full moment later. Stilling more annoyance, he opened his desk drawer, pulled out another manila folder, and then slammed the drawer shut. "Just tell me the truth, goddamn it all."

"Whoa, Dad. Calm down." Rory held up a hand. "I'm not trying to upset you."

Kicker sighed. "I'm not upset, just finish your explanation."

"Sure." He nodded. "The couple of discrepancies I found made me think the sabotage was more widespread and went on months longer than what was originally uncovered, but proving my theory is taking some time." Rory's shoulders lifted in another shrug. "I'm slowly unraveling it all, but if I'm right, then it doesn't make sense that Hutcheson was involved. He was out of the country until two weeks before Jimmy died."

Sitting back in his chair, Kicker wiped all emotion from his face and let the words sink in. "Okay. Your reasoning's sound and your actions seem logical." Rory never lied. Plus he was always dependable, excessively so this past year, having never once failed to pick up the slack for his lack of energy and fatigue, something Kicker wished could be avoided, but he appreciated nonetheless. "But what about this?"

He tossed the second report toward him. "Why'd you contact my grandchild and not tell me you were friends, especially when you know I've already tried *and failed* to make a connection?"

After picking it up, Rory flipped through the file. Then his lips turned into a snarl and his head jerked up, his gaze full of fire. "You *are* having me followed."

"No." He shook his head. "Another odd coincidence. Hutcheson's moved closer to them and I needed to make sure he wouldn't harm them. Best way to do that was to have everyone's actions monitored." He pierced his son with another firm stare. "Apparently a full-time job's not enough to keep you busy, because you're suddenly showing up all over the place—while, I might add, you were supposed to be helping Peters man the helm. That's worrisome enough, but what really bothers me is that you're doing it all in secret."

Rory stiffened. "What I do on my own time is my business and no one else's." Then he leaned forward and stabbed a finger at the desk, red coloring his cheeks. "I put in my hours. If you or Peters have a problem with my performance, then fire me."

"Okay," Kicker said under his breath, swallowing a smile.

His youngest was not afraid to stand up to him, a combination of the best of Jimmy and Dillon and someone who'd make a fine CEO. When the time came.

Originally he'd planned on his eldest taking over his empire. Jimmy had been the easy son, gifted with his good looks, Dillon's brain, and Rory's glib tongue. He was an all-American who'd taken to flying like a bird, maintaining a four-point-zero GPA all while charming the sour right out of vinegar with his smile alone.

Rory's charm was like Jimmy's times a hundred. Yet Rory wasn't near ready to take complete control, and Peters might be competent, but he wasn't family—a fact Kicker just recently decided mattered. He wanted Dillon for the job. No, he *needed* Dillon for the job because, despite being as prickly as a cactus, his middle son's leadership was exactly what Kane Aeronautics needed to flourish.

Only God knew how much time Kicker had left to make amends for lashing out in anger all those years ago. Hell, since he was being honest with himself, he'd have to admit to always riding the boy hard. Didn't seem to matter any longer that the boy had rubbed him the wrong way and was always asking for a fight. What mattered more was that Kicker had to bring his family together before his time ran out.

Damn fatigue. And damn doctors who couldn't figure out what was wrong with him,
spouting off initials like CFS, CLL, and ALS, diseases he never knew existed, along with some he had heard of like mono, fibromyalgia, anemia, and any one of a dozen others. He'd been tested for all of them, all with the same inconclusive results. More tests were just a damn waste of money—and time. Time he didn't have. More than likely it was old age, but rather than just say that, it was easier—not to mention more profitable, in his opinion—to run batteries of tests.

Kicker didn't give a rat's ass whether his ailment was attributed to age or some rare disease not yet recognized. He refused to give up. Despite having no energy some days, he dragged himself out of bed and into the office, if only to get a decent meal when Arletta couldn't smuggle him real food at home. He hated that soy-based paste Sophie was always shoving down his throat. Goddamn it all, if he wanted to spend his last days eating hot dogs and French fries and drinking bourbon, then so be it. At least he'd go with a smile and a full stomach.

"Besides," Rory said, pulling his attention back to their conversation, "I meant it to be a surprise. I thought if DJ and I became friends, I could convince him to talk to his mom and get her permission to meet you. I mean, let's face it, you may not have the time to wait until he's old enough to make up his own mind."

Kicker flinched over his bluntness, but he had to admit to admiring that trait. He'd much rather know his son's honest thoughts rather than have him dancing around the truth with empty platitudes.

Rory relaxed and leaned back in his chair in an unconcerned fashion, his handsome features completely without guile. If he had ulterior motives, he was good at hiding them.

"I may have been too young back then to figure things out, but I wasn't stupid," Rory said. "I know there's a darker reason why she forced that promise on you, then left town with DJ and never returned. Mom won't talk about it except to say leave it alone." Then all nonchalance ceased as Rory's serious gaze probed his eyes' depths, as if he'd find some clue to the past in there. "Besides, I know you. I know the way you operate." He snorted. "Given current circumstances and health issues, I sense you're hell-bent on forging ahead, working to twist things your way, acting as if DJ's mother shouldn't get a say in her son's future without giving a thought about your part in what really happened after Jimmy died."

Kicker hesitated, searching for the right words. When none came to mind, he said, "You're mother's right. This isn't your concern."

"No." Rory leaned closer and pounded the desk. "I won't accept that answer. Not now when the stakes are too high. I only want to help and I can't do that unless you level with me and tell me the truth."

How easily the tide of suspicion turned, Kicker thought, scowling. He opened his mouth, his retort on the tip of his tongue, but Rory held up a hand.

"No. Don't give me any of your patronizing BS. I'm part of this family," he said hotly. "I deserve to be treated like an adult. I was only nine when Jimmy died, but I was old enough to recognize the emotions that filled this house. Grief was only part of it. Anger, disappointment, frustration were the norm and all the yelling you and Dillon did made it hard to ignore and made it my concern. I've been silently living with the results for too many years."

Kicker's heartbeat quickened, rushing heat to his face. "You think to swoop in and save the day when this is so damned complicated even the highest-paid shrink couldn't unravel the mess without years of therapy for all of us?" he yelled back, slapping the desk.

"That's bullshit, Dad. This all stems from the way you've treated those you can't control. Like Dillon. He's always been the outcast. The one everyone loves to hate. You've never once tried to understand him. Or made him feel welcome. I imagine that's exactly how you treated Jimmy's wife."

Controlling his rising temper, Kicker sucked in a deep breath. Once he achieved a decent level of calmness, his eyebrow cocked higher. "You have all the answers, I suppose?"

Rory only nodded, not backing down and added, "Arletta told me you even accused Lauren of foisting off a bastard on this family. It's no wonder she left."

Kicker stared at a spot on his desk, uncomfortable with the all-consuming guilt suddenly sneaking up his spine.

Too much honesty resided in his son's words, reminding him he had to make amends. For everyone's sake. Bad enough that

Catherine's sad face haunted his dreams, yet if she was watching from heaven, she wouldn't appreciate the way he'd mucked things up.

His shoulders slumped. He was tired of it all, or just plain tired and only wanted his sons and grandson home before he died. Not that his dying would be any time soon if he had a say, but he knew he was on the downward spiral of his life. Lately the spiral was spinning faster and faster.

"Maybe I should fill you in a little more." Kicker then spent a few minutes giving Rory a rundown on the report his son was flipping through, along with why he'd asked to meet with Dillon. "The latest incident happened the same day Dillon came to dinner," he said, ending his spiel. He waited a heartbeat, then asked, "So, what do you suggest I do?" With his options narrowing by the minute, he was suddenly desperate for another opinion.

"Since Dillon shot you down, why don't you let me take a stab at him."

"Save your breath." He waved his suggestion away with the flick of a wrist and frowned. "He has a will as tough as a rhino's backside. Hell, I've got a half century on you and I've tried to cut through his belligerence. For thirty-nine years. Nothing works with that hardheaded boy." He was too much like his mother. A flash of insight hit and more guilt overwhelmed him, filled him with more regret so fast his heart ached. When he looked at his middle child, he was looking at Catherine. Though she'd forgiven him for having an affair during her illness, he couldn't forgive himself. Even worse, he'd lived with the knowledge that he'd hurt the woman he'd loved more than life itself. Yet before he could make it up to her, she was gone.

Hell, he barely remembered that night, he'd been so wasted and full of grief, but his actions changed his relationship with Dillon forever.

And he sure as hell had never planned on marrying again, but an unexpected pregnancy altered his course.

Too late, he'd realized he should have had the good sense to keep from dipping his wick into that particular inkwell in the first place. He was lucky that his second wife was a decent sort. Over the years, he and Sophie had come to an understanding. He didn't love her, but he did care for her. After all, she'd given him Rory. It seemed a fair exchange at the time.

Still, his slip had in essence resulted in trading one son for another.

"Well?" Rory said, drawing him out of his thoughts and offering a smile that was much too knowing and much too old for his twenty-four years. Maybe he'd underestimated his youngest son. "I can still try, don't you think? I have managed to become friends with DJ, and now he's even working for me on some maintenance runs I've incorporated to put me into Pemberton a couple of times a week."

"Sure." He shrugged. "Why not?" It was better than doing nothing and might actually work. If not, he'd think of another plan. He spied the half-full bottle of bourbon, and since Sophie had gone to bed, reached to pour one more drink, then raised the bottle. When Rory nodded, he grabbed another glass. After pouring a liberal amount, he handed it to him before lifting his drink in a silent salute and swigging half the contents. Then he let out a contented sigh. "Your influence might be exactly what I need to bring my family back together."

The two sipped in companionable silence. Rory was good for that, Kicker mused as he swallowed the last bit of bourbon, relishing its fiery warmth filling his belly. He always seemed to know when to speak and when to keep his mouth shut.

Rory shot back the rest of his drink, then placed the glass on the desk. "Thanks for the nightcap." Rising, he said, "I'll let you know what I find out. On both counts." As he turned to leave, the phone rang.

Noting caller ID, Kicker waved his good-night and waited until his son was out of the room before picking it up. "Kane here," he said. "Whatcha got, McCall?"

"There was another more disturbing incident this morning." The PI spent a moment explaining about the break-in and the homeless man he'd had to kill.

"It's a good thing you were there," he responded, wondering if the attack had anything to do with the white pickup that had run the two kids off the road and then vanished without a trace. DJ had mentioned it in confidence when the PI had asked him about his banged-up helmet and slight limp. His grandson hadn't wanted his mom to know the entire story because she'd worry.

"My sentiments exactly," McCall said. "I'm just glad I had my focus on the mother at the time and was there to intervene."

Kicker nodded. After realizing his grandson was starving for male attention, the PI had bonded with the boy by taking DJ up on his offer to help rebuild Lauren's porch railing after school and on weekends.

He sighed. Another transgression Catherine would add to his long list. The picture of his dead wife shaking her head in sorrow formed in his mind's eye and was all the more reason to bring his family together. He should have been there for his grandson. Hell, he never should have shoved him out of his life in the first place.

"Do you think it was a deliberate attack or connected to the other two incidents?" he asked, glancing at McCall's report still resting where Rory had left it after reading it, open to the picture of his grandson and son together. According to that report, the guy on the night of Lauren's flat drove a white van or pickup truck with a shell. He felt there was a connection.

"It's anyone's guess. The point of entry was a utility closet. If you ask me, the man I killed was too wasted to have the smarts to figure out how to disable such an elaborate alarm to break in, but I could be wrong. No one knows about his past. I doubt he's military, or they'd have his prints on file. Tox screen results won't be back for at least a week. The sheriff says Andy Miller, the assailant I killed, had a history of alcohol and drug abuse, but he could find no history of violence. That doesn't mean one doesn't exist."

"Hmmm." Glancing back at the picture of Rory and DJ together, he sent up another prayer of thanks that his youngest had already made contact. Then Rory's words about Hutcheson resurfaced. Was Jimmy's killer trying to exonerate himself?

"Maybe there is no connection and we're worrying over nothing." But he didn't fully buy it. Gut instinct, something he relied on heavily and was rarely wrong, told him his grandson and Jimmy's widow were being threatened. No one except Hutcheson had a motive, a pesky little fact he couldn't ignore.

"Maybe," McCall said. "The papers Lauren thought moved could've been happenstance. The blown tire could've just been bad luck and some guy not wanting to get stuck helping in the rain, just as the pickup driver who almost hit DJ could've been texting or could've been distracted. White pickups *are* common. And more important, none of those incidents tie in to Lauren's attacker. The man I killed didn't own a car and he lived on the streets."

"Goddamn it all." Kicker sighed and wiped his face. "Not a lot to go on, is it?"

"No. I plan on checking out the area where Lauren had her flat, see if I can find something."

"What about Hutcheson?"

"According to my guy watching him, he's been traveling back and forth to Tampa." Which made sense, considering an ailing mother in a nursing home in Chattanooga and other familial ties in the Tampa area.

His exhale came out in another long sigh. "Well, keep working at protecting Lauren and DJ while I work on a way of getting them to come to Florida from this end." That was the surest way to keep the two safe.

They said their good-byes.

Kicker hung up the phone as a sudden burst of energy pulsed through his blood. With this new threat, Dillon wouldn't be able to ignore Lauren's vulnerability. His recalcitrant son cared far more for the lady than he'd let on, which was his ace in the hole. He rubbed his hands together in satisfaction and smiled, feeling renewed, almost stronger.

Funny how facing mortality put life…and eternity…into perspective. Kicker had no doubts he'd face his maker at some point, and when he looked him in the eye, he'd do it with few regrets. Facing Catherine wouldn't be so easy.

Dillon Kane would carry on his legacy to become CEO of Kane Aeronautics, by God, and Jimmy's kid would be part of that legacy.

He grabbed his stomach as a gut-wrenching pang hit, reminding him that his time was limited and increasing his determination. He'd damn well make sure of both or he'd die trying.

Otherwise, there was no way on God's green earth he could meet Catherine in the hereafter.

Chapter 7

"Dillon!" Maggie's shout from the front office drew his attention over the noise of several drills and compressors in the busy shop. "You have a call on line three. He says it's important."

He nodded to Steve, his head mechanic. "See what you can do about getting the part from Anderson in Nashville." The client would rather take a rebuilt nose-wheel strut to save on costs, if at all possible. "I'll be right back." Please Lord, let it be his banker with good news. Over thirty people and their families depended on his company for a paycheck, and he didn't want to let them down by having to lay anyone off.

Once inside, Dillon proceeded to his office manager's desk and grabbed the phone. "Thanks, Maggie," he said before putting the receiver to his ear. "Kane here."

"He's made another attempt."

He recognized his father's voice and disappointment surged through his system. A conversation with Kicker rarely elevated anyone's mood, but definitely not his and not this morning.

"Who's made another attempt?" he asked, purposefully misunderstanding his meaning. In his opinion, a near hit and miss with kids on bikes didn't qualify as an attempted murder. Nor did a guy standing in the rain. His dad's crazy suspicions were all he needed to send his day further into the toilet.

"Hutcheson, you moron. Didn't Rory fill you in? It's not enough that he strikes at my grandchild. The damned coward is now striking out at Lauren, using homeless bums to do his dirty work. I'm sure of it. McCall's doing his best to keep them safe, but he's undercover and his protection is limited, especially when she's ignoring the danger."

"Hold on a minute, Dad." With the beehive of activity going on around him, there was as much noise in here as there'd been in the hangar. "Let me get into my office." Dillon looked at Maggie and put the phone on hold. "Has Evan Jones called?" When she shook her head to indicate no, he said in a loud voice to be heard over the din, "If he does, interrupt me. Got it?"

Maggie nodded. "Got it."

"Thanks." He hurried inside and closed the door, wishing his banker would call to let him know if he was extending his loan. The uncertainty was killing him. He pressed the button and lifted the receiver to his ear. "Sorry, Dad. It's been a hell of a day."

"No problem. As I was saying, McCall had to kill a man yesterday to stave off an attack on Lauren. If he hadn't interrupted him in action, she would be dead right now."

That got his attention. "You're kidding. What happened?"

Kicker spent a moment updating Dillon on the attack at the soup kitchen, ending with, "You're the only one who can get through to her." He hesitated a heartbeat, then added, "Their lives are in danger and I need your help to protect them."

Of course the fact that Lauren was attacked bothered Dillon, but she'd made her wishes all too clear.

"You don't need anything of the sort for what sounds like a random attack, and blaming Hutcheson doesn't mean he's involved," he said quickly, focusing on her recent declaration about Kicker going for the dramatic and unwilling to allow his dad's manipulation to work on him. Not this time. Lauren was safe enough with McCall guarding her.

"Besides, you've got Rory," he reminded, rolling his eyes and wishing he had a cold beer to drown his troubles. Facing restructuring was bad enough, but a phone call from Kicker in and of itself was enough to drive anyone to drink.

"We've already had this conversation." Dillon had never been a hundred percent sure about the dire need for his intervention in the first place. Just look what his caving in and rushing to North Carolina had gotten him. Nothing but Lauren's disapproval, along with a lot of wasted time and money.

"Yes, but you didn't hear me, did you?" Kicker's voice interrupted his thoughts.

"There's nothing wrong with my hearing." Unfortunately, Kicker was increasing the pressure. The old codger wouldn't quit until he'd exhausted all resources.

Reaching in his in-box for the contract he prayed would get extended, Dillon bit his tongue to keep from saying what he was really thinking—that his father was wasting his precious time with more arguing. As much as he was dying to give in to Kicker's request, if only to ensure Lauren's safety himself, he knew it would be a big mistake. The lady wanted nothing more to do with him.

He flipped through the pages as Kicker added, "Oh? Then I'd have to say you're holding on to your stubborn pride. At her expense.

At my grandson's expense."

"You're blowing this way out of proportion." Dillon had made a few calls and had done a little research, and after his trip to North Carolina, had done some strong soul-searching. He'd also thoroughly read the investigator's file and it all seemed too circumstantial for his liking.

Why would Hutcheson seek revenge on Jimmy's wife when the guy was now spouting off to anyone who'd listen about being innocent? True, Lauren had testified at his trial about how he seemed to be stalking Jimmy, presumably because Jimmy was cheating with Hutcheson's wife. She'd noticed him several times in the weeks before Jimmy's death and had felt uneasy with his lurking. Yet her testimony wouldn't have incriminated him without all the other evidence the DA had. Though circumstantial, it had been enough to build a convincing case.

Only he and Kicker knew the real truth, that their fight was about more than cheating spouses. A hell of a lot more. Jimmy wasn't cheating with Hutcheson or his wife and had no plans to. Besides, Hutcheson's blanket threat was aimed at Kicker and him, rather than Lauren.

"I'm telling you…no, I'm begging you to go back to that little town in North Carolina and see what's what," Kicker said. "Protect her and DJ, goddamn it all. Better yet, talk her into coming to Florida for a spell. They're both in danger. He's out for blood. I just know it."

The unusual panic in Kicker's voice alerted him. The man never got upset, was always cool under the most intense pressure—so much so that Dillon swore he had ice water running through his veins rather than blood.

"Please, son!"

Dillon sighed. His father sounding scared to death was hard enough to handle, but the pleading that was so totally unlike the Kicker he knew rattled him to the core.

Plus, he'd called him *son*. That alone had the power to lure him into action, despite an inner voice warning him not to get involved.

Instead of his standard *go to hell* response, he ignored the niggling thoughts and said, "Calm down. I'll see what I can do."

"I knew I could count on you, which is why I put in a call to your banker. As of twenty minutes ago, your loan is being backed by Kane Aeronautics."

"What?" His hand itched to slam the receiver down. Dillon counted to ten in order to stem the rush of anger roaring inside his head. Once he could talk without emotion, he snorted. "You never know when to quit, do you?"

"Don't give me that affronted BS. I won't deny I've got my selfish reasons for not wanting you distracted with worries about going under right now, but basically it's tit for tat. Your company needs help and I need help. We each get something we want out of the deal."

Same old Kicker. Dillon sighed. How he wished to throw his offer back in his face. Unfortunately, because too many others depended on him for their livelihood, there was nothing he could do but go along. Besides, his dad had a point. If Lauren and DJ were really in trouble, and the jury was still out on that one, then he was the most likely candidate to get through to her. Not that she'd listen to him, but at least he had a better motive for pushing himself on her.

As Kicker talked, he turned to his monitor at the left of his cluttered desk, where his computer waited in hibernation. After moving the mouse, which brought the machine to life, he swiveled his chair and plopped down. While he clicked the mouse to go online, his thoughts shifted to a decade and a half ago and his brother's actions, which had started a chain of events with life-altering repercussions.

If only Jimmy had been honest with those he'd loved. If only his brother hadn't feared losing Kicker's love with revealing the truth. If only Dillon had stayed the hell out of it. All he had were *if onlys*…and if onlys caused a ton of regret.

Jimmy wasn't the only one affected by their mom's death. Dillon had suffered just as much. Worse, in fact, because a few days before dying she'd confided in him about Kicker's affair.

Dillon's world had collapsed and Sophie had wielded the driving force. The way he saw it, his stepmother had wanted his dad and hadn't even had the decency to wait until he was a widower. He hated the woman for stealing his father at a time when his mom had needed him most…when Dillon had needed him most…and in the years since, he'd hated Kicker for being so weak.

"It would mean a lot to me, son."

He sighed, quickly discovering it was a love/hate relationship as the word *son* rolled over him like a blanket of warmth, heating him from the inside out. In a flash, the old yearning returned full force. Imagine! After all this time and after all that had happened, he still craved his father's love. That alone told him he could never completely hate the old man.

"I'll see what I can do." Even more disconcerting, considering his first try with Lauren had been a complete bust. What if he didn't succeed?

Somehow he wouldn't think about failure with winning Lauren over…or with Kicker.

☙

Dillon slid into the cockpit of his Beechcraft Sundowner behind Rory. Once seated with the door latched, he concentrated on all of the necessary tasks to prepare for departure rather than dwell on his impending reconnection with Lauren. Still, nervous energy filled him as he finished his run-up before takeoff out of Tampa Executive Airport.

After checking his gauges, he glanced over at his brother, who flashed him an encouraging, sunny smile and asked, "Ready, bro?"

"Yeah. I'm ready." Or as ready as he'd ever be, considering that up until actually climbing inside the plane, he'd swung back and forth over his decision to fly to North Carolina this afternoon to meet DJ. And Lauren, who he hoped would see reason, he added mentally. Thankfully his brother had offered to tag along.

Dillon's attention shifted to the business of flying when Rory, handling radio communications for their flight, said into his mic, "Tampa Executive, X-ray-six-six-seven-nine, departing runway two-three, to the northeast."

Now clear, he pressed the throttle and eased the Sundowner off the ground in a flawless takeoff.

Once at the proper altitude and out of any dangerous airspace, he set the autopilot before turning his focus on Rory.

As if sensing his gaze, he glanced his way. "Am I doing something wrong?"

"No. As a matter of fact, I'm impressed with your attention to detail." He meant the words. Rory, who rode in the copilot's chair today, was a damned good pilot. "I don't know. I guess you remind me a little of Jimmy."

"I barely remember him, other than through pictures. I wish I'd known him better."

Dillon nodded. Jimmy had been sixteen when DJ was born. Two years later he went off to college, after which he never returned to live in Kicker's household, only visiting for holidays and such until he died. "I miss him. A lot. I'm glad you figured out a way to get through to his boy." He hesitated, and because the question was on his mind, he asked, "So, what do you think is going on? Do you think Kicker's gone bonkers in hiring investigators and seeing danger around every corner?"

Rory laughed. "I like your description. Kicker going bonkers says it all."

He smiled. Then his smile faded and his seriousness took over all humor. "I thought so at first, but after his phone call yesterday, I don't know what to believe."

"He's definitely worried about Hutcheson. I just don't buy the guy's a threat."

"I go back and forth on that one," Dillon stated honestly. "But if not him, then who? I spent the night pondering that exact question. Who else would benefit the most from the decisions Kicker's recently made?"

"You mean like changing his will?"

"There is that." He glanced over to make eye contact with Rory. "What do you think about it?"

"I'm the only person it really affects, so…" He broke off and shrugged. "What's there to think about?"

"Thirty-three percent of half, rather than the full fifty percent, is a lot of motivation."

Rory tossed out another laugh. "You're joking, right?" He continued staring at him, his expression saying much the same. Then he sobered. "Hell, you're serious, aren't you?" He shook his head, breaking their visual connection, but not quick enough to hide the hurt Dillon spied.

"Okay, I'm off base there," he said in a rush, feeling like an ass for entertaining the thought, even if for a heartbeat. "But what about your mother?"

"What about her?" Rory drew back, almost affronted. Then he snorted. "Jeez, man, I feel sorry for you. You've got a hell of a cynical outlook on life."

Dillon shrugged. "So, sue me. I was born that way." When Rory just continued shaking his head with an expression stating he'd become a bigger ass, he threw out an apologetic grin. "Hey, I'm not trying to insult anyone here. I'm simply asking the tough questions, that's all."

"Yeah, sure," he said, sighing, his head still moving slowly from side to side. "I used to think it was all Kicker. That he drove you away. Now I'm positive you share some part of the blame."

Dillon stiffened and bit back a snide retort. Once the burst of annoyance faded, he peered over at Rory and smiled. "Touché, little bro." His younger brother had hit upon something he hated admitting. As much as he'd love to lay the entire responsibility for the way things turned out at Kicker's feet, he couldn't. Not after their earlier phone conversation. It was past time to make his own amends and try to bridge a few gaps between them. After all, his father wouldn't be around forever. "We're not blaming anyone here. We're just trying to get to the facts, remember? If Lauren and DJ are being threatened, as Kicker and his investigator believe, who stands to gain the most with them out of the picture?"

"Well, it's not my mom," Rory stated emphatically. "Her fifty percent hasn't changed. Besides, she's an heiress in her own right. Hell, she's bailed Dad out monetarily. More than once, according to her, but the biggest infusion of cash was sorely needed when the company was in a real bind due to Jimmy's death and your sudden departure."

"I didn't know that."

"Yeah, well, it almost went under. If not for her money and Kicker and Peters working their asses off, it would have."

He'd figured his exodus had put a strain on Kicker, but he hadn't thought the company had been in any true danger of going under. At one time, he might have derived some sick sense of satisfaction over this news, considering the anger he'd harbored toward his father, but now it only made him regret his actions all the more.

"So, lay off my mom, will ya?"

"Sorry. I stand corrected." Dillon nodded. His smile added to the apology.

"Yeah, well, just so you know, she's never needed Dad's money and she's always doted on him. Probably too much, if you really want to know the truth, because sometimes their relationship seems a little one-sided."

"I hear you on that one, kid." Hadn't Kicker treated his mother much the same way?

"Quit calling me kid." Rory's back went ramrod stiff. "I'm not a kid anymore." He glared, daring Dillon to deny the statement.

"I know." He laughed and clapped him on the shoulder. "I'm sorry. It's just that you're my kid brother, which is how I've always thought of you, but you're definitely not a kid."

When Rory seemed to accept his apology, Dillon smiled. "Okay, so we can rule out money as motivation. Tell me what you think about Peters," he said, completely dismissing the idea that Rory had looked up his nephew in order to get close enough to harm him. He wasn't even going there. Nothing led to that conclusion, so it was better to focus on the one other logical person besides Hutcheson who had any kind of motive.

Rory shrugged. "Peters is Peters." A frown marred his face and he scrunched up his nose. "But come to think of it, he has been acting a little weird lately."

"Weird? How so?"

"He's aloof at times and at others he has little tolerance for everyday shit. Short-tempered might better describe him." Rory's gaze moved to the passenger window and he spent a long time mulling over his next words. "He normally has the patience of a saint. I mean, heck, he's dealt with me all these years, running to him behind my dad's back and asking for help when I was overwhelmed with being a Kane and not wanting to fail." He broke off and continued staring. "He's always been indulgent toward me and loyal to the company. As far as I know, he's always gone the extra mile for Kicker and Kane Aeronautics."

"But what if he doesn't like Kicker's changes?" Dillon said more to himself than to his brother. He focused on the instruments, checking his ground speed, the altimeter, and his GPS, making sure they were still on course, until he felt Rory's gaze. He glanced over. "What?"

"You don't think he's behind all this, do you?"

"I don't know what to think. Something's going on."

"Jeez, Dillon, you're way off base again. Dad had him checked out. According to his report, there's nothing to indicate any dissention…in fact, his record is sterling. Why would he jeopardize his job when he's given his life for the company?"

"I can think of one reason. Did you know Kicker made me an offer to be CEO?"

"He did?"

"Yeah. He wants me to take over, like yesterday." He could tell his revelation was news to Rory. "Listening to what Kicker didn't say when he gave me his pitch, I got the impression Peters had always assumed he'd take over." He waved his hand. "So, you can see where I'm going with this, can't you?"

"Yeah." Rory whistled. "That's a definite slap in the face to any loyal employee, but to Peters? He'd take it more like a sucker punch to the gut. Maybe he does have motivation. It sure could explain some of his behavior."

"Exactly. None of these incidents started before Kicker decided to bring me back on board."

"Then why not target you, rather than Lauren and DJ, or me for that matter, since I'm right behind you in terms of company leadership. Dad's never made it a secret that he's been grooming me for the top job at some point."

"Those are the kinks I haven't worked out yet. I can't help feeling that Lauren and DJ are targets because of their relationship with Jimmy, and I was just trying to determine if someone other than Hutcheson's involved as Kicker believes."

"Dad's got tunnel vision where Hutcheson's concerned. He's convinced the guy is on the warpath."

"You obviously don't think so?" He peered over at Rory, snaring his gaze. When he shook his head no, Dillon added, "Tell me why."

"I read the investigator's report, and I already told Dad my feelings about the man when I spoke with him. I'll tell you the same thing. I think he's on the up-and-up. He seemed to be genuine."

"You met with him?" He was taken aback by the news.

"Yeah." His brother then recounted those meetings, along with some other interesting details about Rory's checking into old maintenance records and what he'd found at the guy's urging.

"Well, that all could be a cover," Dillon said after Rory had finished his spiel. "I'm glad Kicker's at least watching him. I mean, if you're going out for revenge, you don't broadcast it." That was another decision he'd come to at three in the morning. He'd reviewed this from all angles and decided to just make a list of pros and cons for any and all involved. Hutcheson scored the highest, with Peters trailing a few points behind, even if the whys were a bit murky. Both were at the top of his suspects list. His thoughts shifted to Rory's discovery concerning the maintenance records. "So who, besides Hutcheson, would sabotage our planes back then? And why?"

"I hate to say it out loud, but what if Peters didn't like the way Dad was grooming Jimmy to take over?"

"Hmmm." Dillon rolled that idea around in his brain, not liking the conclusion forming. Peters knew Jimmy would be taking Dillon's place that night. Hell, just about everyone in the company knew of his earlier outburst in Kicker's office, including Sophie, who'd called to give him a tongue-lashing for upsetting his father. "You might be on to something, Rory, so stick with it. If you need any help with digging, just let me know."

"Sure thing."

"Okay, now that we have that out of the way, tell me about DJ."

Rory grinned. "What do you want to know?"

"Everything you do."

Dillon lined up in the pattern for an approach to runway two-six after radioing his position. Suddenly gratitude filled him. Thank God his father had coerced him into making this trip. As Kicker had pointed out, it was time to reconnect with the boy. Promise or no promise, he should have done this years ago. For everyone's sake.

He cut back the throttle and eased the Beechcraft Sundowner to the ground. He steered the plane off the main runway, then taxied to the fueling station a ways from the terminal.

After coming to a complete stop, Rory pointed. "See?"

Dillon glanced to the left and smiled. Sure enough, DJ Kane sat on a bike, his rapt attention on their plane, just as Rory said it'd be.

With that shock of black hair and tall, lanky build, the kid was definitely Kicker's grandson, so much so, he'd recognize him anywhere. If he could see his eyes, from what he remembered were so like Jimmy's eyes, he'd bet big money that yearning would be bursting from those blue depths.

"DJ is nothing if not predictable," Rory noted. "Hell, it's understandable. Flying's in his blood, much to our good fortune, because flying was how I found him."

"Yeah," Dillon said, jumping out to pump the gas. "I know just how he feels. Jimmy and I used to spend hours just watching…and dreaming…of when one of those pilots would be us. 'Course, back then, there were no simulated flight games or Internet websites like Mysticairlines.com." Which was how Rory and DJ had become online friends. Then the two had met at the airfield, and Rory had eventually taken him flying, hoping to solidify their friendship before mentioning their familial relationship, even though it had to have been obvious from the very beginning they were related.

During his last visit, Rory had talked DJ into meeting Dillon.

He glanced at Rory, still sitting in the cockpit sporting his usual happy-go-lucky expression. Seemed his brother had learned a few things from Kicker, namely Manipulation 101, to gain what he wanted. That disarming smile made it hard to believe the wearer could be so crafty. But hey, he understood his motivations and under similar circumstances, he'd do exactly the same thing. After all, hadn't they both learned from the master?

With the fuel pumped and paid for and the other incidentals out of the way, he and Rory taxied to the parking area just outside the terminal. Once the engines died, they jumped out of the plane together and headed in the direction of their flight-hungry nephew.

"Hey, DJ," Rory shouted as they neared the fence, close enough to be heard over the drone of a Baron doing a run-up at the end of the runway before taking off. "As promised, I brought my brother to meet you."

"Hey." Nodding, his nephew turned his head, giving him a full view of his face.

Though he'd been prepared for a familial likeness, Dillon was stunned over how much DJ resembled Jimmy. It was like peering into his dead brother's face.

"Hey?" He tried to laugh off the unsettling sensation rising in the pit of his stomach. Putting up his hands palms out, he joked, "That's all you have to say for a long-lost uncle?"

DJ rolled his eyes, totally unimpressed. "You're lucky I'm even talking to you at all."

"Oh?" Unable to think of a quick comeback, he flashed a smile in an attempt to charm, except DJ wasn't buying it.

"Yeah. Took you long enough to make an appearance." His chin rose a belligerent inch. "Why'd it take my whole life for you to finally decide to meet me?"

"What? I don't rate more than a hello before you start busting my balls for what I didn't do?" Squinting in the late afternoon sun, Dillon studied his nephew's face, glimpsing a bit of hurt, almost a wounded look that he hadn't expected. Nor had he been prepared for the sudden burst of guilt exploding in his own gut. His nod indicated the plane they'd just flown in on. "Rory says you're interested in planes."

"I might be."

He swallowed his smile, catching a lot of an attitude that was too similar to his own. This DJ he completely understood. "Would you like to go up in her?"

The kid glanced over at the Sundowner and practically salivated. "Now?"

"Yeah," he said, this time giving in to the urge to grin. DJ was family. Why had he stayed away so long? He mentally grunted. He knew why. Acquiescing to Lauren's ultimatum had been easier. On everyone involved.

"Oh, I get it." DJ's eyes narrowed into skeptical slits that didn't mix with his sixteen-year-old image. That baby face seemed much too young to possess such cynicism, yet he couldn't think of a better word to describe his expression. Cynical. "You think you can bribe me?"

"Why not? You've gone up with Rory, haven't you?"

DJ snorted. "You think one measly flight will make up for you being an absent asshole my entire life?"

"So, sue me." He bit back a laugh when the boy's dubious expression hadn't budged one inch from the quip. The kid's distrust made him one tough nut to crack. Fortunately he was the worst kind of cynic himself, so he knew exactly where to position the nutcracker for a clean break. How he wished to God things could be different between them, that he hadn't waited so long to make a connection. Admitting that to the lanky teen standing in front of him, one on the verge of manhood, didn't seem like a wise move. He might misconstrue the words as empty platitudes.

"Look," he said, taking another tack. "The way I see it, we've wasted too much time already. You can either tell me to fuck off, or you can go up with me and have the ride of a lifetime." He caught DJ's gaze and winked. "After all, I'm a better pilot than Rory."

"That's debatable," Rory chimed in, a grin sweeping over his face.

"No it's not." Dillon's focus then went to his hand, where he spent an inordinate amount of attention on wiping a tiny smudge of grease off his finger. "But it doesn't matter because to tell you the truth, I've never needed a reason to fly. Neither has Rory, and when your dad was alive, you couldn't keep him out of an airplane," he said, snaring DJ's gaze again. "I'd find it hard to believe you don't feel the same way. You're a Kane and Jimmy's kid, for crissake." He hesitated, then smiled encouragingly. "What do you say to a quick flight? I guarantee you won't be sorry, and I might even let you take the controls."

Disbelief flashed in DJ's eyes. "You would?" He frowned. "Even though I'm being a jerk to you?"

"Sure. Besides, you're entitled to being a little bit of a jerk. I'm just glad you like the idea of taking the controls because you're right about my intentions. It's bribery, plain and simple." Hell, he'd use whatever worked to connect with his nephew. It was the least he could do and maybe, just maybe, they could become a family again, like Rory wanted. Like he wanted, he suddenly realized.

"Okay, you're on. I'll go up with you." DJ smiled, a mischievous one that reminded him all too much of Jimmy. "You should know, I plan on wringing out every bit I can get from your guilty conscience."

He laughed. "Touché, DJ."

"Another thing you should know," DJ said, beaming, "I'm a decent pilot. You don't have to worry that I won't know what to do with the controls. Besides going up with Rory, I've flown a ton on Mystic Airlines, huh, Rory?"

"That he has." Rory nodded. "He's been flying online for almost as long as me. I can attest to too many chats after all those long flights DJ took to places like Tokyo or Amsterdam."

Until this moment, Dillon hadn't appreciated what a gift Rory had given him by somehow connecting with DJ doing something they both loved—flying in cyberspace. Rory had told him a bunch of pilots who loved flying created the simulated airlines to fly and used the online chat room to promote something that was more than a hobby.

"It's a great way to get a feel for flying without actually leaving the ground," Rory added.

"Well, then. Why are we standing around talking?" Dillon indicated his plane with a slight jerk of his head. "Come on. Let's go see what you got."

"Sure thing." DJ nodded gravely, all skepticism now gone from his expression as excitement shone in those blue eyes once again.

In seconds, the two headed toward the Sundowner. Rory remained behind with DJ's bike.

DJ buckled himself in, then studied the instrument panel and most likely had a good idea, considering the simulated games he'd played, which dials did what. Except using instruments and playing at flying on a computer was nothing like actually being airborne.

After snapping his seat belt in place, Dillon glanced out the window to see Rory wave from his perch near the fence. He waved back, then turned to DJ. "You want to start her up?"

"Really? You'd let me?" he asked, touching the yoke with reverence.

Something in the way the boy said the words and the look on his face took him back fifteen years. A priest holding the communion tray couldn't give more respect to what was in his hands, the same way his brother used to view a plane. So much so that if Dillon closed his eyes, he could have sworn he was with Jimmy again.

Clearing his throat, he lined up for takeoff and tried to think of something to say that wouldn't sound stupid.

He glanced at DJ once they were airborne and soaring over the Smokies. The kid was family. Period. He'd owed it to Jimmy to be part of his life, if only to repay him for covering for him on that last flight. The flight that killed the wrong man. It didn't matter what Rory had mentioned about discrepancies in the maintenance records. If he hadn't been drunk in the first place, Jimmy would still be alive.

At the very least Dillon could take Jimmy's boy under his wing and teach him all he knew. "How about taking the controls for a bit?"

"Sure."

Dillon grinned at DJ's enthusiastic voice and observed his progress for several minutes. He was a sharp kid and accurate with his flying, but he tended to pay more attention to inside the cockpit. "You're a pro at watching the instruments and keeping them in sync, but you also need to notice your surroundings. When you work on obtaining your private pilot's license, you'll be using visual flight rules and that means maintaining your bearings at all times without instruments." It was like walking before crawling. Dillon's nod indicated the windshield. "Can you figure out where you are?

"Yeah, I know exactly where we are," he said, pointing out a couple of landmarks. A few minutes later, he pointed to his house. "It's right at the edge of the forest."

He smiled. "Okay, besides being aware of where he is at all times, a good pilot should always have a field in mind in case of engine failure."

DJ nodded. "Sounds reasonable."

Dillon's eyebrows lifted as he asked, "Do you have a spot in mind?"

Nodding a second time, DJ aimed a finger at a wide grassy area near the base of the mountain. "How about that field to the left?"

Dillon's gaze followed his hand, noting a perfect spot to land in case of an emergency. "Good job."

Suddenly a loud *ka-chunk* erupted from the front of the plane, the noise overpowering the drone of the engine for a split second.

"What was that?" DJ asked, turning to him with an anxious expression.

Though his heart was doing somersaults inside his chest, Dillon remained calm and met DJ's gaze without letting any concern show on his face. "I don't know," he said, moving his attention to the instrument panel. A noise like that could be any number of things. After a few seconds, he relaxed. "We're okay. Nothing appears to be wrong. I'll check it out when we land, just to make sure. If something did happen and we lost power, we have our landing site below us." He glanced at DJ. "Right?"

"Right." A huge grin appeared, shoving out DJ's concern.

Dillon checked his watch. They'd been up in the air for fifteen minutes. "Let's make a wide turn and circle back," he said to DJ, who still had the controls. He didn't want to land just yet. A few minutes later he added, "You didn't exaggerate, DJ. You are a pretty decent pilot."

"You think so?" Holding his rapt attention on the altimeter, DJ practically glowed.

"I know so." Like all beginners, focusing on his outside surroundings was his biggest hurdle. He definitely had a knack for keeping the plane level and staying on target without the autopilot. "It's obvious you belong in the cockpit."

"I love to fly and this is a really cool plane." DJ slanted a glance in his direction and a grin split his face. "Thanks for taking me up."

"You're welcome." Dillon flashed an answering smile. "It's time to start back." His eyebrows rose as he asked, "Want to try your hand at landing?"

His nephew's eyes lit up. "Are you serious?"

Dillon nodded. Rory had told him ahead of time DJ had already landed his plane a few times, handling it like a pro, so Dillon felt confident the teen could do it. Still, he kept a vigilant eye on everything he did.

After notifying aircraft in the area they were landing, DJ lined up for an approach. The entire time, Dillon realized his actions weren't even close to those of a novice, attributing some of his skills to the online games. Yet some was pure inherited talent. DJ just seemed to have an innate ability to maneuver the plane properly.

In other words, the kid was a natural.

As a CFI, certified flight instructor, he'd seen just about every type out there, and DJ was one out of a thousand. Just like him…and Jimmy. At that moment, he knew his brother had to be watching from heaven and smiling. Even more incredible, as he observed his nephew land with so little effort, Dillon could barely feel the exact moment the wheels actually touched the ground.

He looked to the skies and expelled a contented sigh. This was the first time since Jimmy's death Dillon was able to think of his brother without feeling guilt.

He took back the controls and taxied to the terminal.

Both shoved out of the plane once he'd shut off the engine and the propeller stopped spinning.

"Go and get Rory while I lock up the plane. Then you can help with the paperwork." He raked a hand through his hair and swallowed hard. "That is, if you have time."

"Cool." DJ ran to where Rory waited.

"You know, DJ," he said, when he rejoined Rory and their nephew, "I'd like to spend time with you, and I was thinking since you love to fly so much, why don't I give you flying lessons toward earning your private?"

"Wow." A spark lit DJ's eyes before it vanished and a frown chased away his excited smile. His shoulders slumped and his head dropped. "Nah," he said on a long sigh. "I've already pushed my luck too much. My mom won't let me. Says it's too dangerous. She'd kill me if she knew about today's flight or the flights I've already taken with Rory."

Dillon's eyes opened wide with shock. "Your mom doesn't know?" When DJ shook his head, he added, "So, outside of flying with me just now and Rory, you've never flown before or taken a lesson?" He hadn't expected that, but it just strengthened his belief that the kid was a natural.

"No." DJ shook his head then glanced at Rory, whose surprised expression said it all. His brother had obviously assumed DJ had his mother's permission.

"With all your simulated experience, it's hard to believe you haven't pushed for a lesson," Dillon said, trying to think of a backup plan. His brow furrowed. He might have a tiny problem with his plan to use lessons to reconnect if Lauren was dead set against flying, but how could she be against it? "Maybe if you approach it in the right way, you can get her to change her mind. It seems a shame not to at least try when flying's obviously your thing."

"I've been working on it, but she's not easy to convince." DJ kicked a rock and shrugged. "I don't blame her. Her dad was killed in a plane crash, and that's how my dad died. In a plane crash, you know?" He lifted his head, making eye contact, his expression again reminding him too much of Jimmy. "She's worried that the same thing could happen to me. Hell, I'm all she's got."

"Ah. I see the dilemma." He hadn't known about Lauren's dad. Two such deaths could cause a lot of anxiety. "Well, you can't fault her for worrying. That's what moms do. You shouldn't have lied to her, though."

Still her fear was irrational and DJ shouldn't have had to lie in order to fly. Jimmy's plane had been sabotaged and that sabotage had been meant for him, not Jimmy. Hutcheson could have easily cut the brakes on his car and if Jimmy had been driving on a steep, winding road, he still could have died, only in a car. If so, would she have kept DJ out of cars? Hell no.

In his opinion, flying was much safer than driving. True, taking off and landing posed the most danger, and a pilot had limitations once up in the air, but he also had only himself to worry about. If a pilot was safety conscious, followed all the set rules, and had enough experience to circumvent emergencies, then he was better off in the air in a plane than on the ground in a car. In a car, you always had to watch out for the other guy. Lately there were too many crazies on the road for him to like driving at all. It was an unavoidable means of transportation.

"I didn't lie, exactly," DJ said, pulling him out of his thoughts. "I just didn't mention it."

He recaptured his glance and shook his head. "Omission's as good as a lie and it always comes back to haunt you. You know that, don't you?"

"Yeah, DJ. At the very least you should've told me," Rory interjected, tsk-tsking. "Shit, man, I could've gotten into a lot of trouble."

"I'm sorry." DJ's contrite tone added to his apology. "But I didn't have any choice."

"There's always a choice," Dillon said. "Takes being a man to make the right one."

DJ dropped his head, breaking eye contact. "I couldn't," he mumbled. "When Rory asked me if I wanted to go up, I was dying to go. If I told my mom, I already knew what she'd say."

"I understand." Dillon smiled, then his smile faded. "Still, it was still wrong and we'll have to tell her."

"I know." He kicked another rock. "I expected the shit to hit the fan eventually."

"If she says no, you have to abide by her rules until we can convince her otherwise," Rory said. "Do we have an agreement?"

Remaining silent, his nephew turned his attention to a Cessna 172 taxiing onto the runway for a takeoff.

"DJ?" Dillon said after several seconds had passed. "Did you hear Rory?"

DJ glanced his way again and nodded.

"Then you agree?" he asked, ignoring the teen's petulant frown.

"Yeah." His chin angled higher. "But I don't like it."

Another smile snuck up on him. "Don't worry. She'll come around," he promised, adding a silent *eventually*. He'd figure out some way to change her mind. DJ had been Jimmy's son too and Jimmy would have wanted his son to fly. He was probably turning over in his grave right now over Lauren's fears.

"How 'bout this," Dillon said. "Rory and I will meet with her and explain a few things to try and gain her permission before we mention any of the flights you've already taken." Lauren was simply misguided. He smiled, thinking of his own mom, who'd encouraged her boys to follow their dreams and had never tried to keep them out of a cockpit, but she died too soon to see either of them earn their wings. "Of course, we won't mention anything about the noise we heard earlier, okay? No need to spook her more."

"But wouldn't that be a lie of omission?" DJ's eyes narrowed in confusion.

"Not in this case, since nothing really happened. Mentioning it will only add to her worries, which is a completely different reason for keeping it between us. It'll be our secret, okay?"

Their gazes locked and a silent communication passed back and forth before DJ nodded and said, "Okay."

"Once she understands what this means to you, she'll come around." Though Dillon spoke with conviction, he had no clue what would happen once Lauren found out he'd broken his promise. She'd be pissed, more so with what she might consider the additional crime of aiding and abetting something she was against. Now that he'd met DJ, there was no way in hell he could just walk away without more contact, and no way he could *not* introduce him to more of the wonders of the skies. Making sure his kid followed in Jimmy's footsteps was the least he could do in his brother's memory.

Rory bobbed his head in agreement. "Yeah, she'll come around once we talk to her."

Kicker was right, Dillon decided. Too much time had already passed and DJ needed to know that there were others who cared about him. And about her.

Dillon squelched a sudden burst of pleasure at the idea of actually seeing Lauren again. Hell, he wondered how she'd react. "How's that for a plan?" he said, making eye contact with DJ again and pushing out that thought too. No sense getting ahead of himself. "Here." He nodded to the blocks. "Help me finish chocking the wheels and tying her off."

Once done with securing the Sundowner, the two then followed him into the terminal. As Dillon made his way across the tarmac, he wondered what would happen when he came face-to-face with Lauren. Even more disturbing? How in the hell was he ever going to get her on his side?

Chapter 8

Lauren had halted in the middle of reaching for a shirt in the laundry basket to say good-bye, but the screen door had slammed before she'd uttered the first syllable. After folding a few T-shirts, she'd then set the basket aside and had stood, advancing to the window. Thirty minutes later, she was still staring out at the street, suddenly filled with questions about this "new job."

DJ's parting words, "I finished my homework and I'm riding to the airfield, Mom," danced through her brain. Something in the evasive way he'd rushed out the door bothered her.

Three days without incident had flown by since her attack, and life had reverted to normal, or as normal as it could after almost dying. Still, she'd tried to relax her guard a bit so as not to appear totally paranoid to DJ, but in the last half hour her protective instincts had returned full force.

Usually her son was talkative about his activities, but last night he'd seemed closed and uncommunicative, as if he had something to hide. She shifted her gaze in the direction of the airstrip, and unable to ignore nagging questions, more apprehension rolled over her.

What did she know about this pilot? What if DJ had spun the truth?

He wouldn't lie. Would he?

Why hadn't she asked him for more clarification before agreeing to allow him to go off in the afternoons?

Lauren rubbed her temple, easing her rising fears as reality hit her like a slap in the face over her biggest question. Why had she agreed to let him work at the airfield in the first place?

In a heartbeat, she grabbed her keys, almost running on her way to the garage.

After backing into the street, she hit the button to bring the garage door down, shifted into first, and sped off toward the airfield, slowing only for lights and when she had to turn.

The moment she pulled into the terminal parking lot, she spotted DJ's bike near the chain-link fence. Her gaze swept the field, but he was nowhere around.

Now out of the car, she rushed through the terminal door and up to the counter where a kid not much older than DJ sat.

"Can I help you?" he asked, glancing at her as if she was a little nuts, which judging from the utter panic swamping her senses, she could easily be. Slowing, she pressed her hands over her pleated pants to work out the wrinkles, using the act as a balm while searching for the right words. She couldn't understand why this weird sensation filled her, but it was there nonetheless.

Once she could talk calmly, she said, "I'm looking for my son. Tall, slender, dark-haired kid."

"Oh, yeah. DJ, right?" he asked, suddenly all smiles. "You must be his mom?"

At her nod, his head indicated the wall of windows behind him where a few parked planes were in view. "They just landed, so they're probably filling out the paperwork. Should be in the pilot's lounge. Through that hallway, beyond the door. Third door on your left." He then pointed to the glass door revealing a hallway in between the window and the counter.

"Landed?" The sinking feeling in the pit of her stomach wrapped itself into a tiny little ball. "As in airplanes?"

"Well, yeah." His incredulous expression was back. The kid shook his head and rolled his eyes, whether due to impatience or disgust or because he found her just plain stupid, she wasn't sure. "What else would you use a landing strip for?"

Save the sarcasm, sweetie, Lauren thought, subduing an urge to wipe that smirk off his face. Her own impatience and disgust filled her when she realized that her instincts were spot-on. DJ *had* lied to her. Her baby had gone up in a damned airplane.

"DJ's lucky," the kid offered. When she glanced at him, he added, "Mr. Kane's a really cool guy. I'd give anything to go up with a pilot like him."

"Go up with a pilot like him?" she repeated, not sure she heard him correctly. *Mr. Kane?* Heat flushed her face, warming it. "Just how long has this been going on?"

"I dunno." The kid shrugged and scratched his head. "A month or so. Before that, I'm not sure."

She offered her best attempt at a smile. "Thank you." Holding on tightly to her frozen smile, she turned and marched in the direction of the hallway. Considering her state of mind, if she stayed in the office another second, she'd likely hit the kid.

Lauren flung the door wide enough to hit the stopper and stormed toward the pilot's lounge, fuming the entire time. How could he? DJ knew what this meant. How could he go behind her back? And what about the pilot who gave him the job? The kid had called him Mr. Kane.

Oh Lord, she prayed, please don't let it be Dillon.

Her prayers went unanswered because the minute she peered through the glass partition on the door marked PILOT'S LOUNGE, she spotted him standing next to her son in front of a computer screen. Both were too engrossed in something on the monitor to notice her in the doorway.

She gripped the doorknob and took a deep breath, working to subdue a sudden surge of panic. Her hands clenched into fists and her resolve stiffened, along with her spine. She would not be cowed. The man had blatantly disregarded their agreement. Not once, but twice. Anger rose, replacing some of the doubt, and grabbing on to that anger with gusto, she let it build. With every step her temper simmered, just waiting for something to set it off.

Watching for her son's reaction, and *his*, she noted the exact moment recognition hit both.

"Go get your bike and wait in the car," Lauren ground out the moment DJ's gaze connected with hers. Though fury consumed her, she controlled her temper so that none of her anger showed. But there was no mistaking the seriousness of her tone.

DJ complied without comment, something she didn't expect. She waited until he was clear of the lounge and out of earshot before she whirled on Dillon, her finger stabbing at his chest.

"I expected something like this from Kicker, but never you." Though she continued to modulate her voice, heat sparked in the words. Still, she couldn't excise the surge of disappointment rising from her midsection when their stares connected. "How could you?" Not wanting him to know exactly how much his actions had hurt, she quickly added, "I should've known better than to think you were different. You Kanes are all alike. Always messing with other people's lives, thinking you know best. None of you seem to understand promises or simple directives."

"I understand plenty."

"Oh?" Lauren crossed her arms, her hot gaze searching his. "Then why are you here? I remember quite clearly our last conversation just days ago when I told you to stay away from us. I meant it then as much as I meant it fifteen years ago."

"DJ needs me. He wants his uncles in his life again." He nodded to the door that was opening. "Both Rory and me. He was as eager to meet us as we were to meet him."

That's when she noticed another person coming into the room.

Of course, Rory Kane, the younger half brother. She snorted. She should have recognized the name when DJ had tried to cover up his mistake. "What? You mean after you baited him." Her arm made a sweeping motion indicating the huge window behind the desk showing the airfield and three small planes that were secured to the ground. "With all this. Then lured him in with the promise of flying, all in the most underhanded, sneaky way possible?"

"It's not what you think."

"Then what is it?" Lauren angled her head, her glare accusing. "Why not be up front about it when you came knocking on my door?"

"Shit," Dillon blew out as he wiped his face, impatience stamped on his rugged features, features that she'd never forgotten. Features that sometimes invaded her dreams. "For the same damned reason you're yelling at me now. It wouldn't have done a bit of good. You'd have told me to go to hell."

"You got that right." Her spine stiffened. "Go to hell!" she yelled. "And leave my son alone. All of you." Ignoring whatever reply Dillon was about to make, she presented her straight back and strode with purpose out of the lounge, through the hallway, past the kid at the counter, all the way across the parking lot to the car without looking back. After hurriedly climbing inside, she slammed the door, stabbed the key into the ignition, and started the engine. That's when she turned and caught Dillon's gaze as he stood at the entrance staring after her.

Anger flared in her eyes and Lauren flashed him a silent message. If he thought that his appearance, both last week and today, would sway her resolve, he had another think coming. She hadn't forgotten the past or her threat of so long ago. He'd better stay away from her and her son, or she'd disappear so fast and go so deep no one would be able to find her.

Then she glanced at her son and her anger flared up all over again. "I can't believe you lied to me and disregarded my orders, DJ."

"Yeah? Well, we're even because I can't believe you lied to me about my family. If you ask me, that's a hell of a lot worse."

"I didn't lie."

"A lie of omission's lying. Dillon said so."

Lauren sighed and her stance softened somewhat. Swallowing regret over his condemning stare, she sent up a silent prayer, begging for the strength to get through this. If she hadn't been prepared to see Dillon Kane again last week, she certainly hadn't been prepared to catch him with her son just moments ago. "I know you don't understand my actions but trust me, I have my reasons for keeping you away from them."

"You're right. I don't understand." DJ crossed his arms and looked out the window. "They're family." When he met her gaze again, the accusation deepened to hurt. "Why keep me from them?"

"I can't talk about it." Lord, how could she explain her fears when sometimes she didn't even comprehend them?

"Oh, like that's an excuse?" He turned back to her, still glaring. "If I don't get to use it, then neither do you."

She jerked the gearshift into reverse in an angry motion. Just like her son to go on the offense with past arguments. She'd always prodded him to talk and had never let him off the hook without at least stating what was wrong. "It's different with adults," she said, backing out of the space before shifting into drive. "I'm the mom and you're the kid." Okay, it was a stupid-ass thing to say, she thought, borrowing one of DJ's phrases, but her mind was still trying to twist around Dillon's arrival. "When you have kids of your own, maybe you'll understand," she added, not caring that that excuse sounded just as inane.

Lauren stomped on the gas and burned rubber, peeling out of the parking lot.

⚃

Dillon stood mesmerized as Lauren's fuming glare dared him to follow her…dared him to keep away…dared him to do exactly what was on his mind…chase her down and shake some sense into her and then kiss her until she couldn't ignore what was between them any longer.

He snorted, discarding the last as part of a delusional stunned reaction. Hell, he'd experienced the same reaction a few days ago, so that had to be it. Just as then, seeing her had definitely sent another jolt to his gut. He hadn't expected the wrecking ball of her temper to knock him senseless, which had kept him from responding and saying what needed to be said.

She *was* holding back his nephew from being the man he was supposed to be, and attraction, promises, and threats notwithstanding, he damned sure wasn't going to let her get away with it. If Jimmy were here, he wouldn't approve. Of either of their actions. Dillon never should have stayed away like a coward all these years. Right now, that was the only thing he was sure of.

For an instant, he was glad his brother was dead so he couldn't see the depths of how low he'd sunk. Two wrongs never made a right. Here he'd been disappointed in his brother and had chastised him for not being honest, and he was basically doing the same thing.

"Come on," he said to Rory, who'd followed him out of the pilot's lounge. Clutching Rory's shirtsleeve, he dragged him toward a loaner car the airstrip provided for users. He let go and nodded at the faded and dented Ford Tempo that had to be at least two decades old and looked barely drivable. Once inside, he ignored the gagging odor of stale tobacco, and trying not to touch anything he didn't have to in the grimy interior, he cranked the handle with two fingers to open a window that hadn't seen Windex in at least ten years. Once the window was down, he turned the key, sending up a silent thank-you that the car actually started.

"Where are we going?" Rory asked, cranking his own window, which allowed a burst of cooler air into the car. A good thing, too. Besides not having automatic window openers, the stripped-down Ford had no air conditioner.

"We're following her." Dillon shifted into gear and backed out of the parking space.

"But didn't you hear what she just said—"

"I don't care what she said. She's bluffing." Once on the surface street, he gunned the motor in an effort to catch up with Lauren's Honda SUV. "She's held her cards close to her chest all these years, it's time to see what she's really got."

"What if she takes off like she's threatened?"

"We'll track her down and find her." Then knock some sense into her, he mentally added, wishing it could be that easy. Lauren wasn't running out of fear. Well, she was, but she was afraid of him and of her feelings for him. He knew it now as sure as he breathed. Otherwise she wouldn't have reacted so violently. Wasn't it the same reason Dillon had run? Fear. Fear of acting on his feelings? Fear of what their attraction meant?

It was time for the two of them to face their fears because if they didn't, and if his father was right about their lives being in danger, then whoever was threatening her and his nephew just might succeed in killing them both. That was one fear Dillon couldn't outrun.

Having made the drive days ago, he was familiar with the road. The rural town, a few miles from the airstrip, complete with a public square and city hall in the middle, took less than two minutes to traverse from end to end. He sped past several residential-looking streets, which all veered off the main road. He'd almost caught up with Lauren when she turned onto her street, a quarter of a mile past the town's outer limits.

She drove to the end of the rural cul-de-sac, passing the few houses on each side, and pulled into her driveway. By this point, he was right behind her. She screeched to a halt so unexpectedly, he had to stomp on the Tempo's brakes, which weren't that good to begin with. Pressing as hard as he could, he almost plowed into the CRV, eventually stopping with only inches separating the two cars.

Lauren must have hit the garage door opener because it slowly began to rise, but instead of waiting to pull in, she emerged from her car and ran for the house.

Rory jumped out. At the same time, Dillon jerked open his car door and sprinted after her, reaching her in seconds. His hand shot out, connecting with her elbow.

"Don't touch me," she cried, stopping and turning abruptly, her chin rising. Again, he had to put on the brakes to his approach or he'd have mowed her down with his body.

He halted inside her personal space and didn't retreat. "Oh, no," he said, ignoring those hot eyes aiming daggers directly at him. "We're not done here. Not until we talk this out. We're not running any longer."

"Yes we are. I told you everything I had to say at Jimmy's funeral. I reinforced my sentiments only days ago, and nothing has changed since then."

"Mom, please. Just listen to him," DJ begged. He'd gotten out of the car and now stood a foot away, his expression pleading. "You can't keep him out, he's family."

Lauren was about to respond when a blast erupted. The earth shook, almost knocking them down as both cars, closer to the detonation site, literally jumped backward. Stunned, they all stared at the garage, watching flames shoot from what was left of the walls and ceiling.

"Shit," all three guys said at once, their voices drowning out Lauren's, "Oh my God."

For long seconds, every gaze remained glued to the burning embers.

Dillon was the first to recover from his shock. His first thought was that his father hadn't been far off the mark after all. One glance at a now-shaking Lauren, whose complexion had gone completely white, strengthened his resolve.

"Let's go." Brooking no argument, he grabbed her arm and started up the porch steps, wondering how in the hell someone had slipped past Kicker's investigator. Where in the hell was McCall, anyway? The guy had done a piss-poor job of protecting. On the top step, he glanced at DJ, who had his iPhone out. "Call 911. This is no accident." He glanced at Lauren, determination burning in his gaze, so she'd understand he meant his words. "You and DJ need to pack a bag. You aren't staying here."

"Wait!" Still trembling, Lauren resisted, slowing him further by trying to jerk out of his hold.

He halted his movements and glared down at her.

She stared at him for a long moment with a confused expression. Finally the confusion cleared. She stiffened and fought harder to free her hand from his firm grip. "This is none of your concern." Her chin lifted and the fire in those green eyes suddenly shouted she didn't give a damn what he thought. "I don't want you here."

"This is serious, Lauren." His nod indicated the burning pile of rubble that was once a garage. Thank God it was detached and quite a ways from the house. "Considering the timing of the blast, you were lucky." He didn't want to think about what could have happened if she hadn't stopped short, gotten out of the car, and run. If anything had happened to her or DJ, he wasn't sure he could live with the outcome.

"It's still my problem, not yours." She pulled out of his grasp, hurried to the front door, and shoved a key into the lock. Once open, she turned back to him. "And I'll deal with it."

"You'll deal with it?" Was she nuts? "I'll tell you how you'll deal with it. You and DJ are packing a bag and going to Florida, where we can protect you."

She was about to throw out another retort, but the pings from rapid gunfire interrupted and wood splintered nearby.

"Get down!" He didn't hesitate, just shoved her to the ground and covered her as bullets ricocheted over them. "Get inside," he yelled to Rory and DJ, who'd also taken cover. While they scurried on all fours through the open doorway, he lifted up as much as he dared to scoot on his hands and knees, pulling her inside with him as quickly as he could. He kicked the door shut behind him. A split second later, more bullets sounded.

"Stay down," Dillon warned, not hesitating to shield Lauren with his body.

As of this moment, she and DJ were under his protection. There was no way he'd leave here without her now, even if he had to hog-tie her, pack her stuff, and throw her into the plane himself.

Eventually all noise ceased. For long seconds there was only silence, during which time he felt her rapid heartbeat. Or was it his? No matter, he thought, shoving aside the idea of how soft she was, all woman, lying underneath his hard angles. He struggled to keep his breathing even.

From a distance, a car in desperate need of a muffler interrupted the quiet. Soon the rumbles faded as the sound of sirens built.

Chapter 9

Still lying prone over Lauren, Dillon closed his eyes and fought to slow his ragged breathing as adrenaline pumped through his veins. The thought of death wasn't all that kept his heart rate soaring, he realized, inhaling a whiff of her flowery essence. Part of it was awareness. Right now he was utterly aware of Lauren's softness beneath him He outweighed her by at least fifty pounds. She seemed so tiny, so needing of protection, and unfortunately, so unyielding. If anything had happened to her, he honest to God wasn't sure how he'd handle it.

He tightened his hold, which brought her closer.

Big mistake.

More of her delicate scent invaded his nostrils, unleashing a ton of memories…and a ton of emotion. Dillon wanted to hold on to her and protect her forever, just as he had back then.

If only he could pretend she hadn't been married to his brother. Images of Jimmy flashed one right after the other, eventually leading to darker recollections. Recollections better off left buried, like the words he'd hurled at his brother that last night, criticizing him for not manning up. For hiding the truth behind a woman.

As the sirens grew louder, he struggled to subdue the mental pictures. No amount of regret would change the past.

Now that the threat had abated, he pushed up on his elbows and noted a blush of red burning her cheeks. In a heartbeat, more unwanted images invaded his brain, taking him back to when they'd shared a friendship. To those times when he'd say something outrageous to put a smile on her face, or sadder times, when he'd offer words of encouragement to lift her spirits because Jimmy had said or done something to distance himself from her.

It had been awkward to sit on the periphery of their relationship, to see both sides, yet helpless to alter the situation. His mind then switched frames to their last encounter only days ago. A wave of yearning hit. Damn. He tamped it down, knowing she wouldn't appreciate being the center of his fantasies.

"Now are you satisfied?" he snarled, using the explosion of words like a release valve to alleviate his building anger over the whole damned situation. He'd felt this exact frustration all those years ago and he didn't like the feeling. Not one little bit. "Get a clue, lady. Someone, most likely Hutcheson, wants you dead. You are not staying here to continue being a target for him to aim at. You understand?"

When Lauren simply stared at him, her eyes glinting with unadulterated fear, he bit back a strong expletive. Swearing wouldn't produce the outcome he wanted; neither would letting her witness his frustration over seeing her again.

Dillon ignored the gut-gnawing desire to kiss her fears away. At the very least, he wanted to shake some sense into her with the truth. Instead he stood, taking several deep breaths, reaching for calm. Once he achieved a modicum of control, he turned back to her.

"Think about what just happened," he urged, while extending a hand to help her rise. "You and DJ were almost killed."

More color drained from her face as full realization set in. She sat up and scooted too quickly away from him, as if his nearness affected her in exactly the same way her nearness always affected him.

He should probably be glad for the distance, but her reaction only irritated him further. Swallowing what he wanted to yell, he stoically bent to help her up instead, forcing the issue by grabbing her arm and refusing to back off this time.

"Please, Lauren." He was so damned tired of playing her game, so tired of dealing with the polite façade of indifference she'd always hidden behind back then. Still did, considering her reaction toward him the other day. Her pretending their attraction didn't exist only seemed to shine a spotlight on it. "If you don't care about your safety, think of DJ's. The explosion was a near miss and those bullets—real bullets, I might add—came too damn close, and neither can be ignored."

Lauren's face went a little whiter before she finally nodded and allowed his help to stand upright.

"I'll help you pack a bag," Dillon added in a terse tone, dropping the hand she'd eased out of to his side. He made a fist and released it, suppressing the desire to draw her closer.

"That won't be necessary." She dusted off her slacks. "I have other friends I can stay with until this dies down."

"Until this dies down?" He could barely get the words out. Why was she being so obtuse? Sighing, Dillon wiped his face and raked fingers through his hair, resting them on the back of his neck. He rubbed to ease more of the building tension, struggling to remain calm in order to think of the best approach in persuading her to leave with him. "Lauren, you're right in the middle of it. And now you want to put other people's lives in danger?" he asked, deciding on appealing to her tender heart.

Her answer was cut off when two big fire engines and three police cars screeched to a stop in front of the house, their sirens blaring. All eyes in the room focused out the picture window. That's when Dillon noticed a Mercedes that hadn't been there when he drove up.

McCall, a man he recognized as Kicker's investigator, emerged and jogged up the walkway. By the time he hit the porch steps, pandemonium had broken out in the form of Pemberton's finest piling out of their trucks and cars. Like ants whose habitat is disturbed, they'd swarmed both the house and the yard. As police officers set up a perimeter, firemen worked to get the hydrant flowing.

McCall charged through the front door. "I'm a private investigator," he said, flipping open an ID to two officers denying him access.

"That's Jeff." Confusion filled Lauren's features as she eyed the badge.

"It's okay, he's working for Mrs. Kane," Dillon said.

The deputy nodded and let him pass.

He rushed toward them, saying, "Damn, I wasn't expecting him to make such a bold move."

Lauren glanced at McCall, her brow furrowing, and searched his face. Then her attention went back to the badge. "Oh my God," she said, awareness dawning in her green gaze. "Are you investigating me? Is that why you wormed your way into my home?" Next her focus landed on Dillon. "Did you send him?" Her tone added to the accusation.

He swallowed hard, even as a knot of tension in the pit of his stomach tightened. The PI's inconvenient arrival meant he was screwed. The Lauren he remembered wouldn't like McCall's involvement any better than she did his.

"He didn't send me. Dillon and I have never met," McCall interjected. "And in reply to your first question? No. I'm not investigating you. Silas Kane hired me to protect you."

"What?" Her eyes narrowed into angry slits and her spine stiffened, along with every cell in her body. Even her hair looked stiff, which didn't bode well for Dillon's cause. "Take a look around." Her sweeping hand indicated a yard full of cops and EMTs through the picture window. "As you can see, I have plenty of men who are here to keep me safe, the sheriff included. Which means I don't need your *protection*." She then turned back to Dillon and stabbed his chest with a finger. "And certainly not yours."

Dillon glanced down and wondered what she'd do if he grabbed that hand and started kissing his way up her arm. He smiled. God only knew this was not the time for such thoughts, but hell, he had to think of something that would keep him from plowing a fist into a brick wall.

"You find this amusing?" Lauren's outraged question nabbed his attention and his gaze moved to her face.

He almost laughed outright and answered in the affirmative, until she froze him on the spot with a glacial glare. Biting his tongue to keep from laughing, he couldn't help wondering how in the hell she managed to throw off so much cold with a look, when the heat from the burning garage had warmed the air considerably.

To keep from saying something stupid while strategizing the best course of action, he glanced around the living room and noted the same warm, cozy atmosphere he'd picked up on earlier. Lauren's house was definitely a home, something he didn't want to see destroyed. Shifting his focus back to the problem at hand, he decided to just go with cold, hard facts and get them out as quickly as he could. "Can we go somewhere to talk? You need to know why Kicker sent McCall."

"We do need to talk, Mrs. Kane," McCall said with a nod. "I followed you to the airfield. I saw Dillon chase after you, and figuring you were safe enough, I hung back, which turned into a blessing because I may have spotted the shooter. Driving a white pickup. I'm pretty sure it's the same truck—"

"My God, Lauren, are you okay?" A police officer stormed into the room and up to their group, cutting McCall off. With a protective, almost territorial air, he clasped Lauren's shoulders. His gaze slowly traveled down the length of her and then back up before ending at her face.

Lauren offered a small smile. "Yes, Thad. I'm fine." She then looked Dillon in the eye and added, "These two were just leaving."

"No one's leaving," the officer said, straightening and flashing his badge, which identified him as Sheriff Thaddeus Johnson. "Not until I say so."

"Weren't you supposed to have a deputy watching the house?" McCall asked, his tone slightly critical.

Johnson's body went rigid, adding another inch to his tall frame. "Look, McCall, I don't tell you how to saw a board, so I don't expect you to tell me how to run my deputies." He then returned his full attention to Lauren.

Dillon clenched his hand into a fist, stilling a sudden urge to hit Johnson for his possessive stance toward Lauren. But he had no say in her life. No right to this sudden jealousy. However much it annoyed Dillon, there wasn't much he could do about it if the two were involved.

He sighed. What irony! Or maybe it was divine justice that now, after finally finding the guts to overcome his cowardice and force the issue, he'd lost his chance with her.

McCall's snort drew his gaze. "I'm a private investigator, and I know exactly how to run your business. This woman was attacked only days ago. I haven't let her out of my sight until a few minutes ago, but that was because I expected you to be watching her house like you promised."

"I don't have the manpower to watch her house every moment of every day."

"Which means you didn't take the earlier incident seriously enough," he accused further, icicles shooting from his stare.

As the sheriff fired back a retort, Dillon's jaw tightened. He redoubled his effort to refrain from throwing out a snide remark about both men's ineptness in letting someone blow up her garage and then spray the porch with bullets. Didn't matter that he felt McCall was more at fault, since he'd been paid to protect Lauren.

While McCall and the sheriff continued arguing over who was to blame, Dillon nodded to the front door. "Like I said, we need to talk." He reached for Lauren's hand. Gripping her fingers tightly, not giving her any choice but to follow, he started walking. "Let's go outside where we won't have to shout."

The investigator could handle things with Johnson and he'd handle things with Lauren. For safety's sake, he damn sure wasn't leaving without her or DJ. "Give me a chance to explain." He led her down the porch steps. At the bottom, he added, "Please." A gentler approach might be more effective.

They walked to the far left side of the house, near the street and away from the fire. He let go of her hand and turned so that they were face-to-face. "We can talk here."

Her posture still stiff, she eyed him warily. "Last time I gave you five minutes. This time you only get two." She crossed her arms and her chin lifted with such impatience, he had no doubt she'd be tapping her foot in seconds. "So, start talking."

He pursed his lips to keep from smiling, which would only piss her off more and he wasn't about to push his luck. "I know you're upset with our interference. Kicker—"

"Ya think?" Now she did tap her foot. "I told you to leave me alone. What part of that did you not understand? Hiring an investigator to spy on me is a direct violation of my privacy and one I

103

resent."

"I had no part in Kicker hiring an investigator. You should be damned glad he did."

"Well, I'm not happy. I'm quite unhappy. You're guilty by association so you can just go right back and tell your father it didn't work. I'm not budging on this."

Dillon cleared his throat, then caught her angry gaze with his pleading one. "I understand you're not happy, but in all fairness to my dad, he was only doing what he thought necessary, given Hutcheson's original threats."

"Exaggerated the threats, if you ask me." She shook her head and snorted. "More likely he's the one behind it all, using them as a means to take my son away from me."

"You can't believe Kicker had anything to do with this?" He made a sweeping motion with his hand to indicate the burning garage the firemen were trying to put out and the bullet holes in the porch columns.

"I wouldn't put it past the man to throw out a little mayhem in order to manipulate me into turning tail and cowering. After all, that's the way he operates and stuff didn't start happening until after I received the letter he sent demanding to see his grandchild."

"That's bullshit and you know it," he blurted out. "Yes, Kicker wants to see DJ, but he'd never put his grandson at risk." He wiped his face and took a calming breath. Once he had his frustration under control, he lowered his voice. "He's getting old, Lauren." Softening his tone a little more and snaring her gaze again, he held it with his now serious one and said, "I honestly believe he's seen the error of his ways and just wants to make amends." Funny how, by saying the words out loud, he recognized them for what they were. The truth.

"Yeah, right," she grumbled, crossing her arms and looking away. "The man has a lot to make up for after what he insinuated about my child. About Jimmy's child."

"At least give him a chance to rectify his mistakes. DJ can only benefit from having Kicker in his life. He's trying. Hell, he's already taken a gigantic step." Another truth he absolutely bought, he realized just then.

"Oh, you mean by adding DJ to the will?" Lauren laughed in his face. "Trust me, we don't need his guilt money."

This wasn't getting them anywhere. Dillon took another deep breath, resisting the urge to pull out his hair. He glanced around the yard. The firemen almost had the fire out and they continued spraying water onto flames that were slowly fading to smoldering embers. Other deputies were inspecting her front porch, taking pictures and looking for clues as to the shooter. The sheriff and McCall had come out of the house and stood on the porch by the front door, still arguing. His gaze wandered back to Lauren, taking in the resolute line of her mouth. He had to figure out a way to get through to her.

"Okay. Let's back up." He looked her square in the eye and said, "Let's just cut to the chase and put this into simpler terms. You say your goal is to protect DJ, right?" When she nodded, he added, "My dad has good reason to believe your lives are in jeopardy. Someone wants you dead." Before she could interrupt with what he knew was an objection, he held up a hand. "You don't seem to understand how close you came to dying. Are you willing to take another chance with DJ's life?" He could tell those details registered so he went for broke. "You've been selfish all these years, hiding from life and keeping your son away from those who care about him. He needs his family. You don't have the right to deny him his roots and thanks to our visit today, you can no longer pretend we don't exist."

That got her dander up. "Why should I believe a damn thing you or Kicker have to say?"

"Because Kicker's been monitoring Hutcheson since he was released from prison. A few months ago, when he moved within a couple of hours of Pemberton, my dad began paying McCall to watch over you and DJ." He hesitated. "McCall was following you the night your tire blew and he's positive someone shot it out. McCall went back to the site and found a spent bullet in your shredded tire. From a Barrett M82, a sniper rifle. Both he and Kicker believe you were meant to go off that ridge. If McCall hadn't scared the guy off, we might not be having this conversation."

His voice had gotten louder, and after looking in her face, he realized the news had taken some of the wind out of her sails.

"No," she said, her expression eventually reverting to one of denial. "Why would someone shoot out my tire to try and run me off a cliff?" She threw him a skeptical glare. "Kicker's obviously gotten to you. You're starting to see threats where none exist. If you're trying to scare me, it's working."

"Good. I want you to be scared. Because this," he said, waving his hand toward the now smoldering garage, "started long before my untimely visit, long before a pickup almost ran DJ down, and long before a homeless guy tried to kill you. Think, Lauren. Does stuff like that usually happen in your sleepy town?"

"What? DJ was almost run down?" Her stunned expression said it all and much more vividly than any additional words ever could. She hadn't known the full extent of DJ's near miss. She shook her head slowly. "He told me that accident was his fault. If he hadn't been watching a car full of girls, he'd have never hit that pole."

He bit back a snide comment, fighting the impulse to roll his eyes. "That's because if DJ had told you the truth, he'd lose his freedom and wouldn't be able to see Rory."

"So, he lied to me about that too?" Her gaze sought out her son. He stood off to the same side of the yard, yet closer to the house and under an oak tree, deep in conversation with Rory.

Dillon prayed his brother was doing his own convincing. DJ was Lauren's Achilles' heel, and she'd be more apt to agree to their leaving with him if her son wanted to go.

"He's growing up, Lauren. You can't keep him a kid forever. You can't alter who or what he's supposed to become and you can't shield him from harm." His tone softened. "Whether you want to accept DJ's close call with a pickup that tried to run him down as a threat or not is your choice, but you heard what McCall said about a white pickup, before the sheriff cut him off. I'm betting it means something. What if it's the same one? What if it's Hutcheson's?"

As Thad had done only moments ago, Dillon grasped her upper arms with both hands and turned her in the direction of what had once been her garage, now a smoking pile of ashes. "Think about what would've happened if you or DJ had been in there when it blew. Something is going on here, and until McCall can figure out what that is, you and your son are in danger."

Lauren glanced back at him, worry taking over her features and replacing all skepticism. "You really think Hutcheson's involved?" In seconds flat, fear eclipsed the worry in the depths of her gaze that now appeared as dark and turbulent as the ocean during a thunderstorm. "That he'd try to have me or DJ killed?"

"I'm not one hundred percent certain," he said, blowing the honest words out in a heavy sigh. "But why take any chances? Not with this. Your best bet is to accept Kicker's help. He's already done plenty to keep you two safe. He hired McCall. His reasoning makes sense and I'm damned glad he was paying attention. I damn sure wouldn't be here if he hadn't convinced me. And you know what else? I'm damned glad I ignored your wishes."

"It doesn't make any sense." She slowly shook her head, absorbing his revelations. "Why would he go after me now when he's been out more than a year?" She stared at something in the distant woods behind her house for an extended moment. The wind had shifted, blowing some of the smoke in their direction. Lauren made eye contact. Tears filled those emerald eyes he'd always thought were so beautiful. "Why would DJ or I suddenly become a target?"

"I wish I knew. I'm just relieved you're finally realizing the danger you're in." He spent a moment updating her on everything he knew about the investigator's report, leaving out the part about what Rory had told him concerning his brother's interactions with Hutcheson. He ended with, "After the blown tire, Kicker wasn't willing to leave it alone."

Just then, Dillon noted the sheriff and McCall veer toward the porch steps, barely visible through the haze. Shouts from the yard drew the sheriff's attention. A few seconds later, he spotted the two of them and started down the steps, heading in their direction.

Dillon's focus landed back on Lauren as McCall followed Sheriff Johnson, who was closing in fast. Realizing his time alone with her was about to end, he said, "Those were real bullets and next time he might not miss." His nod indicated the two men. "Why not take a trip to Florida for a few days to give McCall and your sheriff time to see what they can find out. Now that he's come out in the open, he'll be easier to catch."

She weighed his words as her mind obviously spun, then produced a wan smile. "I'm still really angry at you for going behind my back with DJ, but I'm willing to think about your offer."

He nodded. "Well, think fast. I'd like to leave in an hour."

By this time, Johnson stood next to Lauren. "I'm ready to take your statement." He placed an arm around her shoulders and said to Dillon before leading her back toward the house, "I'll need yours too, but one of my deputies can get it."

Dillon gritted his teeth and tamped down the irritation over the sheriff shooing him away like an annoying gnat.

"Patience," he muttered. He just needed to be patient. After all, she hadn't totally brushed him off. Too bad patience wasn't exactly one of his virtues, and he didn't appreciate the way the sheriff had just whisked her off so easily.

His gaze lingered on the two, and he fought another surge of jealousy over their obvious familiarity. Why should he care that the two were an item? He shouldn't. He didn't. Period.

Yeah, keep telling yourself that, Kane, and eventually you'll believe it.

He discarded the thought. His inner voice was wrong.

Oh yeah? Nice try.

Even his conscience saw through the ruse, also telling him if that were the case, then why was he still eyeing the two of them and wishing she'd look at him like she did Thad?

Swearing under his breath, he mopped a hand over his mouth and jaw. Hell, she'd been a widow for a good fifteen years and she was a gorgeous woman, having become more so since the last time he saw her, in the courtroom at Hutcheson's trial. Back then, her face held the roundness of a twenty-year-old woman. Now, maturity had muted the softness, refining her beauty as only age could do.

He shoved aside thoughts of smashing Thad's face into a wall and reached for his cell phone to update Kicker.

❧

"Who is he?" Thad demanded. He lowered his voice and said, almost in a snarl, "Don't you think it's a little convenient that he suddenly shows up right before your garage explodes? And then he wants you to pack a bag and leave?"

"Please, Thad." Lauren sighed and rubbed her temple to ease the vice of tension his ranting was causing. "Don't make this harder." She wished she hadn't said anything about Dillon or what he wanted. First, it was none of Thad's business, and second, he had no more right to tell her what to do than Dillon had. At least Dillon was family and someone she cared about.

"You don't need to do a damn thing but stay put, or better yet, come home with me," he stated harshly for the second time in less than a minute. "This is my county and I'll make sure nothing happens to you. I'll sure as hell get to the bottom of the explosion."

Noting a scowl that had turned darker, Lauren placed a reassuring hand on his forearm and squeezed. "Don't worry. We'll be okay." He meant well. Her gaze then drifted to where Dillon paced like a caged tiger as he talked on a cell phone, probably to Kicker. She glanced back at Thad and offered, "DJ's grandfather has the means to keep him safe, which is my main concern." In that moment, she fully grasped the truth in that statement. If someone wanted to harm her son, the Kanes *would* keep him safe. She knew it as sure as she knew night followed day.

She glanced beyond Thad's shoulder at the exact second her son laughed at something Rory had said. Instantly she grasped something else too. Seeing this through another perspective, primarily DJ's, had her reassessing her long-held motives. Maybe she had been somewhat selfish, as Dillon had mentioned, in keeping her son away from his uncles. Which meant it was time for him to finally meet his grandfather.

Her focus remained on her son until, sensing her attention, he glanced her way and his smile thinned into a frown. He didn't look too happy with her. Heck, at the moment she wasn't exactly happy with herself or her motives either.

"So, I think I'll take him up on his offer of a trip to Florida," she said, glancing back at Thad. She doubted she had a choice, considering DJ's accusing stare as he continued to talk to Rory, listening to God only knew what. Nothing good about her role in keeping them apart for all these years, that was for sure.

She'd never really thought about the repercussions of her actions, of how her son might feel once he discovered his long-lost relatives. Would he ever forgive her? Lord, she hoped so, but didn't see how. Not when total honesty demanded that she own up to her sin of concentrating more on how her decision affected her life, rather than DJ's.

Lauren swallowed a lump of regret. Keeping him away from his only family meant she'd acted no better than Kicker.

DJ turned away from her and continued talking with Rory, and another realization set in. She might not possess the ability to make things right.

ଔ

After disconnecting from his father, Dillon started in Rory and DJ's direction. McCall, who'd been talking with deputies, noted his movement and headed the same way.

As Dillon stepped within hearing distance, Rory clapped DJ on the back and said, "DJ says he's ready to fly to Tampa with us for the weekend." He made eye contact and his eyebrows rose. "That is, if Lauren approves. What's the verdict with her?"

"I don't know yet. Depends on how influential that guy is." Dillon's thumb indicated the spot near the door where Lauren and Thad stood talking, in full view. As much as he'd made her see reason and had pretty much convinced her of the need to leave with him, he knew the sheriff was doing his damnedest to talk her into staying and letting him protect her. It's what he'd do, if she were his.

"Don't worry about him," DJ said. "He doesn't rate more than a date now and then." He snorted. "I don't even know why he keeps trying when it's obvious to anyone who's got twenty-twenty eyesight my mom's not interested."

By that point, McCall had joined them. Dillon wanted to ask DJ more questions about Lauren and Thad, but mentally filed the information away for a later conversation. Instead, he asked DJ if he could go and get him a bottle of water. He wanted to talk to the PI without the teen overhearing.

"Sure thing." DJ nodded, then glanced first at Rory and then at McCall. "Does anyone else want water?" Both Rory and McCall shook their heads.

The minute his nephew was out of earshot, Dillon's attention returned to McCall. "So, how'd it go with *the sheriff*?"

"We understand each other." McCall's lips curled into a sneer.

109

"He thinks he's in charge and I didn't disabuse him of the opinion."

Dillon smiled. "You were mentioning something about a pickup when we were so rudely interrupted. You think it's the same one that tried to run over DJ?"

"What's this?" Rory asked, looking at the PI for more information.

"I'd stake my PI license on it," McCall said. He updated Rory on the bike accident, then spent a moment filling them in on the white pickup he spotted peeling onto the main street just as a light turned green a block from the cul-de-sac. He'd already arrived late, having gotten stuck behind an emergency vehicle. "It's too much of a coincidence for me not to put two and two together." He grinned. "His license plate was obscured, so I didn't get it, but I got a good look at the driver. He had to be the drive-by shooter. Considering the way the bullets sprayed after the explosion, it reminds me of some kind of gang-type warfare."

The entire time McCall spoke, Dillon had surreptitiously kept his attention on Lauren, who continued talking with Johnson, wishing his thoughts weren't so similar to that last night. Nothing had changed in the fact that he had no claim to her. Yet everything had changed with the threats.

"Of course, when I mentioned my observations to the sheriff, he shut me down with 'Pemberton doesn't have gangs.'" McCall shrugged, drawing his attention. "An advantageous difference of opinion, considering my preference is to follow this lead alone." He caught Dillon's gaze and certainty blazed in his eyes as he said, "Something about the pickup and the driver seemed familiar. I'm positive he was up on that mountain and shot her tire out. That blowout was no more an accident than what happened here today. Someone wants them dead."

McCall broke off. Dillon nodded with full understanding. If Lauren now gave him any sass about leaving, he now had more ammunition to reinforce the idea that her safety and DJ's depended on trusting him.

Just then he saw DJ rushing toward them with two bottles of water in his hands and determination in his expression, reminding him of Jimmy. Dillon wasn't sure how it happened, but in less than two hours, his nephew had become an important part of his life. As important as Rory. He had to make Lauren see that DJ needed them in his life just as much they needed him. In order to do both, he'd have to keep his emotions in check.

DJ joined them. Dillon took the offered bottle of water, wishing not for the first time that he'd tried harder to get along with his father and stepmother back then, if only to save Jimmy more grief. Like Rory, his older brother had been the peacemaker in the family and only wanted everyone to get along.

A white-haired lady wearing a tiger-striped spandex top and black spandex pants suddenly entered his peripheral vision. She marched across the street and up to the front porch, apparently to stop to chat with Lauren and the sheriff.

"That's Mrs. Meyer," DJ said, noting where his focus had drifted. "She gets her hair done at the salon where my mom works." As the lady talked nonstop, he added, "Mom helps maintain her place for her. She's a little off." He grinned. "Actually, she's a lot off. She walks the perimeter around her yard along with her dog, looking as if she's counting each step every single morning and every single evening, no matter if it's ninety-five degrees or twenty-five degrees."

Dillon nodded and opened the bottled water, then took a swig.

"Why would anybody count their steps?" Rory asked, staring at her, while her nasally, irritating voice asking about the garage, the bullets, and the firemen's progress carried in the wind along with the smoke. Her tirade grew louder and more grating on the senses as she went on and on about the crime rate in Pemberton rising since undesirables from the bigger cities, like Atlanta, Raleigh, and Chattanooga continued to move into the area. Grinning, Rory caught Dillon's gaze. "You gotta admit it is a little weird."

"Yeah, weird," DJ said. "I've always wanted to know why she does it, but I've never had the balls to ask her." He broke off, then groaned. "Uh-oh. Here she comes." Mrs. Meyer, having obviously not gotten any satisfaction from Lauren or the sheriff, started marching in their direction, wearing a purposeful expression. "She can be a little long-winded, so don't say I didn't warn you."

Dillon laughed. Here they were, in the middle of a yard after surviving a drive-by shooting and an exploding garage that almost killed two people he cared about but hadn't seen before today in over a decade, and they were discussing some lunatic who hated outsiders and had weird habits.

"Excuse me," the older woman shouted when she got within earshot, stopping a couple of feet from the four men. "Which one of you is Lauren's PI?"

"Unfortunately, that would be me," McCall admitted, turning to Mrs. Meyer.

"Oh my." She put her hand to her mouth and eyed him more carefully. "Aren't you Jeff-McCall-the-handyman?" she asked, enunciating the entire sentence as one word.

"Surprise." McCall rolled his eyes. "I was undercover, after all."

"Yes, but I still should have guessed. I pretty much stay on top of stuff in this neighborhood. I mean, goodness me, with all these undesirables taking over, you can't be too careful."

"Of course not," McCall agreed. "I'm sure those residing on Mountain Ridge Court appreciate having such a vigilant neighbor."

"Yes, my thoughts exactly."

It looked to Dillon as if she wanted to say more but suddenly seemed hesitant. Hell if he knew why, since she hadn't been afraid to stick her nose in thus far. "Is there something you'd like to tell us?" he asked. Just because she was weird didn't mean she wouldn't have useful information to offer. In his opinion, not much got by nosy neighbors. Thank God, there seemed to be one on every street

"Well. Since you asked." A spot of red colored her wrinkled cheeks. Patting her white hair done in a neat little bun, she cleared her throat. "The sheriff wasn't interested in hearing anything I have to say."

"We're very interested, Mrs. Meyers," McCall said. "So please, tell us."

"Well, aren't you a smart young man." A smile spread across her face, taking a good ten years off what had to be at least seventy. "Since you're an investigator and all, I was wondering if you took note of the white pickup that has recently been parked on the next street over? I passed him half a dozen times in the past week when I walked my Buffy. She needs her exercise, you know. So do I. Walking is great for that."

"I'm sure it is." McCall nodded. "You were saying about the pickup?"

"Oh, yes, the white pickup. Well, he had a lawn mower in the bed, but he was no gardener. At least none that I'd ever seen, considering he didn't do any yard work. Just sat in the cab. I used my dog's preoccupation for sniffing to get a better look at him and what he was looking at. At the time I thought he was casing my place, but now that I think about it, Lauren's garage was also in his direct view."

"You didn't happen to get a license number?" McCall asked, cutting her off.

She shook her head. "Oh, good gracious, no. Not with my memory. But I did snap a few pictures pretending to make a call on the cell phone my granddaughter gave me. Never use it for making calls, but I love taking pictures of strange goings-on in the neighborhood. You just never know when they might come in handy." She then pulled out a phone, and with the dexterity of a teenager, clicked away. In seconds, she held the small device out. "See for yourself. I even got a picture of him."

"This is too unbelievable," Dillon said, huddling around the phone with the rest of them and noting clear pictures of both the pickup with full license plate in view and a side view of the driver, with his focus appearing to be on Lauren's garage, just as the lady had said.

"Can you e-mail those pictures to this address," McCall said, indicating her cell phone. He tore a page off his notebook after scribbling something on it.

"Sure thing, Jeff." Her genuine smile brought a thousand more wrinkles out of hiding, making her appear her age, but the spark in those sharp blue eyes said her brain still had a lot of mileage left to burn. "In fact, I'll do it right now. So I don't forget." She lowered her voice to a conspiratorial whisper and winked. "You know, considering my memory and all."

"Thank you for being so observant." McCall smiled.

"I'm only too glad to be of help." After typing away on her phone, she put it back in her pocket. Then she said her good-byes.

Dillon watched her march away with the same sense of purpose she'd displayed on her way to talk to them. "Thank God for nosy neighbors."

"My sentiments exactly," McCall agreed. "I'll put a call in to my connection with Tampa PD to find out who owns the license plate," he added as he prepared to leave. "Once I have all the particulars, I'll fill Johnson in. If my suspicions are confirmed, the sheriff won't be cawing quite so loudly. I'm even looking forward to him eating a little crow."

Dillon nodded and looked around the yard. The firemen had the fire completely out and were now cleaning up, rolling their heavy hoses and putting away equipment. He watched them work for a few more seconds, until a tingling sensation pricked the back of his neck. His gaze swept the area one more time. There were too many places in the jungle of green beyond Lauren's back door for a person to hide and wait for another chance to do more harm.

"Come on," he said to DJ. He just wanted to be gone, to get DJ and Lauren the hell away from here, away from any more threats, and the sooner the better. "Let's go find your mother. I need to talk to her." To persuade her to fly to Florida with him. He doubted she'd stay behind once he informed her of all he'd learned in the last half hour.

Chapter 10

"Do you have all your books?" Lauren asked DJ as Dillon loaded bags packed in record time into the plane. She sent up a little prayer of thanks, totally relieved that Thad hadn't made a huge production out of her traveling to Florida. She just didn't have the energy to argue with him. Dealing with her fear of flying, along with her attraction to Dillon, was enough to handle.

It didn't help that Dillon was being very agreeable. As he added the last suitcase, she couldn't help but notice his ease in lifting it, like it weighed next to nothing rather than thirty pounds. She knew this because he'd asked for an accurate weight and she'd stuck the bag on the scale to be sure. He probably worked out a lot.

Trying not to gawk at his gorgeous, well-developed upper body, Lauren had to admit that maintaining a safe distance might be more difficult than she'd anticipated. His physical presence was hard enough to ignore. It was near impossible when he flashed that understanding smile directly at her. Instantly she felt the warmth all the way to her core, which only melted more of her resolve.

Lauren quickly dropped her gaze, eyeing an ant crawling on the ground near her feet.

"Yes, Mom. I have all my books." DJ's voice brought her attention back to her question. Happy for the diversion from the ditch her thoughts had drifted into, she glanced at his face and spied a facial gesture that implied her fussing was totally unnecessary. Except, she knew better. DJ still had a tendency to skip important details. Monitoring simply gave her peace of mind.

"Mr. Miller told me what I needed to do, and I have all weekend to do it. So, will you quit with the twenty questions?"

"Okay." Lauren wasn't sure how long they'd be gone and in order to make sure he stayed up with his studies, she'd called the principal of the high school who'd been very helpful on short notice. DJ could do his assignments online. Thank God the virtual world was finally good for something useful.

"Bags are loaded, guys. Time to hop in," Dillon said.

With one less thing to worry over, Lauren wiped her sweaty palms on her jeans and now focused on following DJ and Rory into the cockpit of Dillon's plane. Moving slowly, she had to mentally urge her feet to work, one step at a time. A prisoner on the way to an execution came to mind.

Finally she was seated. Dillon helped her latch the shoulder harness and seat belt. Then he handed her a pair of earphones. She stuck them on her head and adjusted the mouthpiece.

About to start the plane, Dillon halted with his hand on the key and glanced at her. "Are you okay?"

"I'm fine." The words sounded weak and came out much too rushed for her liking, and when her gaze scanned his face, she caught him studying her with a skeptical expression.

"You don't look fine." His nod indicated her tense posture. "Just relax. You'll be okay." He looked away and busied himself with departing. A moment later, he yelled, "Clear." He turned over the engine and the propeller began spinning.

The plane inched forward.

"I'm just anxious to get there," Lauren admitted, looking out the window as he taxied in the direction of the airstrip.

"Well, I'll try to make the trip as uneventful as I can," Dillon said, slowing and then stopping at the runway's edge.

"Did you ever figure out what that—"

DJ was cut off when Dillon shook his head, saying curtly, "I did, but this isn't the time to discuss it, as I doubt it's something your mother wants to hear right now."

"Oh, yeah." DJ nodded. "You're right. I wasn't thinking."

"What are you two talking about?" she asked.

Dillon eyed her for a long moment. "Just procedures pilots need to follow. You know, aviation stuff. You'd probably find it boring." He smiled and shrugged. "I'd be happy to give you the details if you'd like, but can it wait until after I finish my run-up and get up in the air?"

Lauren snorted. "That's okay." DJ was bad enough when he went on and on about a topic that only God and someone with the patience of a saint could listen to for more than ten seconds without his or her eyes glazing over. She hated flying, hated anything to do with airplanes, and preferred talking about any other subject but that one, even with Dillon. "I'd rather remain ignorant."

Sitting back with mounting trepidation, she let her gaze wander to the pavement outside the window. Why oh why had she allowed him to talk her into climbing into this claustrophobic, rattle heap, tin can of an airplane anyway, rather than drive to Ashville for a commercial flight? Yet, here she was. Stuck, with no idea of why or how. All she knew was that she'd never wanted to sit in a flying death trap like Dillon's small plane again. Ever. Not after Jimmy's horrible accident.

As the reality of an imminent departure loomed in front of her, she grabbed the handgrip above the door. In those few minutes of his final safety check before takeoff, her fingernails dug into the leather padding.

Dillon radioed to any nearby planes overhead that he was taking off. Within seconds, they were speeding down the runway and she inhaled deeply. She hadn't realized she was still holding her breath until her relieved exhale came out in one huge puff of air once the plane was off the ground and began climbing.

"You can let go now," Dillon said, nodding to her white-knuckled grip. "We're past the most dangerous part of takeoff."

Lauren let go, then flexed her fingers before taking another deep breath. No need to freak out. Millions do this every day and don't crash. Yet even as she tried to calm herself with similar thoughts, fear wouldn't let her relax. From the moment she'd read the NTSB's report and discovered that Jimmy's plane had crashed during takeoff, she was terrified of takeoffs, so much so that she halfway expected something to go wrong now, just as it had that night.

Thankfully, as Dillon eased back on the throttle once they'd climbed high enough, she experienced nothing more ominous than a smooth ride. Eventually he set the autopilot and slanted her a sideways glance.

"You *are* aware that planes're actually safer than most other forms of transportation?"

"Yeah, Mom," DJ chimed in from the backseat, drawing her attention. Casting his perfected impatient eye roll again, he added in his sixteen-year-old, know-it-all manner that indicated her cluelessness as to what was going on in the world, "I've told you that a gazillion times, but you never listen to me."

"So, sue your mother for having well-founded and understandable fears given her experiences," Dillon shot back. He threw Lauren an apologetic smile. "I can appreciate your reservations, but I promised you an uneventful flight to Tampa. As God is my witness, as long as you're in my care I won't let anything happen to you."

"Yeah, Lauren. You're in good hands," Rory said from his perch in the seat behind Dillon and next to DJ. "Dillon is the best pilot I know and that's saying a lot, since I know a lot of pilots. You can barely tell there's a stiff crosswind."

"A stiff crosswind?" Oh Lord. She knew what that meant, thanks to Jimmy's insistence that she take a Pinch Hitter course for spouses on flying, in case of emergency. Turbulence. Clutching her seat, she looked at Dillon for verification and he nodded.

"It's a little windy. I'll try to find smoother air." He gently pulled the yoke back and they started climbing again. "Once we're high enough, it should even out."

As soon as the plane leveled, Dillon reset the autopilot, then glanced over at her and winked. "See. No problem."

She gave him a brief nod, her ghost of a smile spreading and erasing some of her fears.

Rory hadn't exaggerated, she decided as Dillon returned her smile. He was an excellent pilot, demonstrated in his ease of keeping the plane from bouncing around while finding the best altitude. Besides that class and having gone up with Jimmy too many times to count, she'd also spent years listening to her dad discuss flying with his Air Force pals, all from which she'd acquired more than enough knowledge to judge his ability. Certainly more than she ever wanted to learn.

"What'd I tell you?" Rory asked, drawing her attention. "Is he smooth or what?"

"Did you hear that, DJ? My number one fan has spoken." Dillon increased the wattage of his smile, a smile that always made her knees go weak at the most inopportune times, like now, when she'd had no business letting it happen. "As I recall," Dillon added, "you used to say much the same thing about me…and Jimmy."

"How could I forget," she said, remembering the way the two brothers would always try to one-up each other, then ask her to determine the superior pilot. "I also recall knowing better than to pick between the two of you." Both knew their way around airplanes and could pretty much fly anything with a propeller, making it an impossible choice when Jimmy and Dillon were equally skilled.

"The three musketeers! Remember? We had a lot of fun." Dillon was silent for an extended moment before sighing. "Some of the best times of my life."

Lauren had forgotten the label that Jimmy had used to describe the trio back then.

"I remember a few fun flights." Her smile widened as more memories of the three of them laughing together filled her mind. "'All for one and one for all,'" she whispered, too softly for anyone to hear, feeling a pang of regret. Leave it to Dillon to take her back mentally. That, quite simply, was why she ought not be here, sitting so close to him, wishing for the same things she never should have wished for in the first place. She tossed a furtive glance his way to study his face, careful to block the attraction she'd always felt for him from her eyes.

Why, after all these years, did this strong reaction to him still exist? What was it about him that drew her?

That was easy to answer, she quickly realized when he turned and their eyes met for an extended moment as that same familiarity engulfed her. Like two kindred spirits who've known each other forever, they'd always had a connection. From the very first moment they'd met.

Back when Jimmy was alive, Dillon always seemed available, offering a sympathetic ear and his same ready smile. He never once failed to be there when she needed a friend, when her husband would zone out emotionally, especially during those last weeks of their fifteen-month marriage. She hadn't known how or why, but soon after DJ's birth, he changed. Drifted away, which was the best way to describe the disconnect. The more she tried to pull her husband back, the more he seemed to withdraw. Toward the end, they'd lived like roommates, rarely talking. At which point, having been young and naïve, she just quit trying and accepted, even while sensing, the same way she knew the sky was blue, that that had been the wrong way to handle things. Unfortunately, Dillon's presence made it easier to accept.

Lauren purposely looked out the window again.

"It must've been awesome to fly with my dad," DJ said from the backseat. "Mom said he was a good pilot. I wish he were still alive so that I could fly with him. I was a baby when he died. I can't even remember him." Lauren didn't know what to say to that, but he didn't seem to require an answer. DJ just reached forward so that his head was close to hers, and asked in a curious and amused tone, "The three musketeers, huh?"

She glanced at her son and nodded, letting another smile form.

"So, does that mean you used to fly a lot, Mom?" he asked. "With Dad and Uncle Dillon?"

"Yes, as a matter of fact I did. It was fun."

"Get outta here!" Grinning, DJ shook his head. "I just can't picture you flying for fun."

"Don't look so shocked," Lauren said, laughing.

"I'm sure there are many things your mom used to do that you have no clue about, DJ," Rory added. "Just as there are things you keep from her."

"Exactly." Lauren sobered, meeting her son's eyes. "Some things are meant to be a secret and some things aren't."

He caught her message and sighed as spots of pink colored his cheeks. "I know. I'm sorry. I should've said something."

"Yes, you should've. Now that we've passed over that bridge, we won't dwell on it, okay?" Her focus returned to the window.

"Sounds like a plan," DJ said agreeably. He and Rory then carried on a separate conversation. Since it was about planes, something DJ never tired of discussing, Lauren tuned them out and continued staring at the view of the mountains below.

"Did you know I was named after my dad and Uncle Dillon?" DJ asked a few minutes later, drawing her out of her lost thoughts. "Dillon James Kane. Mom said my dad wanted it that way, huh, Mom?"

Lauren blinked and glanced at Dillon, who'd been concentrating on flying. For another long second, their stares reconnected before she turned her attention to the backseat. "Yes." She nodded slowly, ignoring the butterflies flapping in her stomach such a stare always generated, as well as dismissing that same sensation of familiarity. "Your father always said Dillon James Kane sounded much better than James Dillon Kane. Plus, then we could call him DJ, which he also preferred to JD."

"I always thought that's what DJ stood for, but I wasn't completely sure, and I never had the guts to ask," Rory answered. "That is so cool, dude."

"Yeah, I've always thought it was cool to be named after two pilots. Now that I've met the uncle I'm named after, I think it's cooler."

"Did ya hear that, Dillon?" Rory nudged his seat. "He's glad he's finally met his namesake."

"I heard," Dillon grunted.

"Yeah," Rory added. "And if it hadn't been for me and Mystic Airlines, you might still be strangers." Though he'd obviously spoken in jest, Dillon stiffened, indicating his comment had struck a nerve.

"Better late than never." Dillon broke off for a moment. "Besides, I'm not the computer geek you are, Rory."

"Don't fret, big bro. It only means you're not cool. Not like us. After all, we fly for Mystic Airlines and you don't."

"Who knew there was a website devoted to virtual flying?" Dillon asked at the same time DJ exclaimed, "You said it."

Rory chuckled and gave DJ a high five, saying, "I can tell he's annoyed that I didn't include him. I tried to interest him in checking out the website a million times and he always gave me his stock answer. He was too busy."

Considering the look that passed between DJ and Rory next, Lauren was certain some kind of secret bonded the two—probably something to do with flying or the online game.

Dillon didn't offer anything else. The discussion in the backseat turned to other topics.

Lauren's gaze moved to Dillon's face. His strained expression told her the earlier exchange had bothered him even more than she'd suspected.

"Is everything okay?" she asked, still scrutinizing his features.

He glanced her way and smiled. "Sure. Everything's fine." Only he didn't sound convincing and his eyes were devoid of the warmth in all those other smiles.

"I know you're well aware of Jimmy's version of how your name came first on DJ's birth certificate, but I don't think Jimmy told you the entire story." She glanced behind her to see if Rory and DJ were listening. They were immersed in their own conversation. Still, she lowered her voice and said, "The placement of the names or the way the two initials sounded together had nothing to do with the decision." She shrugged when Dillon's eyebrows shot up. "I mean, Dillon James, James Dillon, DJ or JD. There's not that much difference between any of them. Or at least that's what Jimmy really thought." She broke off.

When Lauren remained silent for one too many seconds, Dillon prodded, "Well? Are you going to finish?"

Now that she had his undivided attention, she smiled. "Jimmy named him Dillon James because he wanted to honor someone he loved." After another pause, she placed a tentative hand on his arm, hoping to comfort him because he seemed to need comforting just then. "He did love you, you know."

Dillon swallowed hard. Then he nodded and blinked at the moisture gathering in his eyes. "Yes," he whispered, covering her hand and giving it a gentle squeeze. "I loved him too."

"So did I," Lauren said. Who didn't love Jimmy? And he'd loved her too. In the beginning. In the beginning, everything had been perfect. And then it wasn't.

DJ and Rory's voices behind her indicated they were still talking, so the moment Dillon let go of her hand, Lauren placed hers on her lap. She then refocused on the scenery outside her window without noticing the horizon this time. She closed her eyes in an effort to block the memories, mainly those concerning the night of his fatal crash. But Dillon's return, her conversation with him only moments ago, along with recent events culminating in today's bombing and shooting, hit her at once. All those things together had finally cracked the mental dam she'd built to hold the images back. A river of guilt washed over her. Fast and furious. Leaving her soul bare with no room to hide.

When news of the fatal crash had reached her ears, Lauren had never forgotten her complete devastation over the thought of losing Dillon. Her world had gone black. Blacker than black. Then after hearing that he hadn't been the pilot flying that night, the light returned full force. Unfortunately, her joy was short-lived as within moments, she'd also discovered his replacement.

Jimmy.

Just weeks before her twentieth birthday, she'd become a widow and a single mother. She'd never see her laughing, fun-loving husband again. She'd never get the chance to make things right between them. She'd never be rid of her guilt either—not when she couldn't deny the end result—the irrefutable truth. Jimmy was dead, while Dillon still lived.

In essence, her original and unequivocal exhilaration over Dillon not flying might have really meant that maybe some small part of her was also relieved that Jimmy had taken his place. Lauren remembered thanking the Lord for saving Dillon. For that prayer she'd rot in hell, because she'd known, deep down inside, if given a choice right then, she honest to God wasn't sure if she could pick Jimmy over Dillon. What kind of wife did that make her? Worse, she couldn't excise the memory of all those prayers, too many to count before the accident, where she'd begged God to let her husband be more like his brother.

Dillon had been so right when he'd accused her of running. It was time to stop and face her guilt. For all their sakes, especially DJ's.

"If I can get through this flight, everything will be perfect," she said to herself.

"What was that?" Dillon asked.

"I said, I hope I can survive the rest of this flight." Of course, then the real roller coaster ride would begin and she'd come face-to-face with Kicker Kane again. Not a pleasant thought.

"Just relax and enjoy the trip," Dillon said, placing his hand on her knee. Warmth flowed from his fingers when he squeezed gently, spreading contentment all the way to her core. "We'll be there in no time."

It didn't help that his calming baritone caused the warm sensation of well-being to swirl inside her, even as her guilt increased.

"I'll try," she murmured, concentrating on the terrain and forcing herself to ignore the lack of heat on her leg the second his hand returned to the yoke. After a moment of deep breathing, she was composed enough to focus on the green treetops, along with the late evening haze that gave the Smokies their name, also noting Dillon's competence in maneuvering the small plane above the mountains.

"So, what's he like now?" Lauren finally asked, more for something different to talk about that would keep from her dwelling on guilt.

"What's who like?" Dillon asked, turning to her.

"Kicker. You said he'd mellowed. I find that hard to believe." She didn't add the rest of her sentence—*considering he always reminded me of a charging bull.*

"He has. But that's only due to the physical restrictions of age."

"Really?" She shrugged. "I guess he is getting up in years." Even still, he'd had the stamina of a bull, which tended to negate the idea of him slowing down any due to something as human as aging.

"He is." Dillon smiled, accentuating fine lines around his eyes and highlighting his strong, handsome features. Though striking in his own way, he didn't look anything like Rory or DJ, who both favored Kicker. Maybe that was what made him so approachable.

"I think he finally realizes he's mortal, just like the rest of us," he said.

She nodded, but couldn't help thinking of the last time they'd been in the same room with each other and Kicker had been so cruel. "Do you think he'll be nice to me?" she blurted out, quickly wishing she hadn't given so much of her anxieties away in the question.

"He's not stupid, Lauren. He wants to see his grandson, and to do that he needs your support." Dillon nodded. "So, yes. He'll be nice to you and if he doesn't, I'll beat him up for you. How's that?"

There was that smile again and his hand was back to squeezing her knee.

"Sounds good," she could barely get out as a jolt of awareness engulfed her. For the hundredth time in less than an hour, Lauren had to look away and concentrate on the scenery rather than on their timeless mental bond. Why couldn't she have met Dillon first?

Heat swamped her face, which meant she was blushing, which also meant she ought not think such thoughts. Jeez, the years had been good to him and he was just as attractive now as he'd ever been. Actually more so because the few wrinkles that framed his eyes, along with the mature angles of his features, gave him a more rugged look.

Why did Jimmy have to die before she could demand an explanation? Demand changes in their relationship, giving him a choice to work toward a better marriage? Or not. If her suspicions that he wasn't interested in changing had been confirmed, then she could have extricated herself from her vows. Now she'd never know. Besides, guilt wouldn't allow a relationship with Dillon, which considering that familial connection seemed impossible.

Once her face quit burning, she reached into her bag for a book. Needing to place some distance between them, she opened the paperback and concentrated on the words on the page. Thankfully the story soon absorbed her attention and she continued reading until the setting sun made it too dark to read.

At that point, she closed her eyes and leaned her head against the window, supporting it with her hand. All too soon, thoughts of the past, of all those wonderful times spent with the man sitting next to her, ping-ponged through her mind once again. Unfortunately, along with the memories came the feelings, and hers for Dillon all those years ago hadn't diminished one little bit, she suddenly realized with a guilty twinge. She'd loved him. Almost as much as Jimmy. Definitely way more than a married woman should love any man not her husband. Lauren would probably always love Dillon, which only made her feel guiltier.

Lauren crossed her arms, deciding right then and there to never reveal the truth. She'd never act on her feelings and her love would remain a secret forever.

CB

"Wake up, Lauren. We're here."

Dillon's rich voice invaded her dreams.

"Come on. Time to wake up."

"What?" Groggily Lauren opened her eyes and sat up straight. She blinked, then looked around. They were on the ground. She held her arm up to the light coming into the cockpit from a nearby lamppost and squinted to view the time. Over an hour had gone by since she'd last glanced at her watch. She must have slept through what in her mind was the worst part of flying after the takeoff—the landing.

Dillon, who'd already exited the plane with Rory, opened the door on her side. She climbed out, grasped his outstretched hand. As he guided her to the ground, DJ followed close behind. Solid concrete never felt so good.

She then turned and spotted Kicker, who stood a few feet away.

He started toward her. "Hello, Lauren. It's been awhile," he said, holding out a bony hand.

She was taken aback, totally unprepared for the shock of seeing such drastic changes in him. She'd expected him to age. After all, it had been fifteen years since their last meeting. But even in the shadows, which obscured her full vision, he seemed frailer…and old.

"I'm only too happy you've honored my request." Kicker offered a semblance of a smile. "As I told you in my letter, you're welcome in my house any time."

"Thanks," she said, connecting with his hand and politely shaking it, all the while taking in his shrunken appearance. Surely she hadn't been afraid of this man? "I appreciate your hospitality, considering…"

She cleared her throat. Oh, Lord…what if she'd made a terrible mistake by staying away all these years? "Considering all that's happened." Had she done it out of spite?

"If you can forgive me for my past transgressions, then I can certainly forgive yours." His smile broadened slightly and warmth emanated from his eyes as he clasped their handshake with his other hand and gave a reassuring squeeze. His grip was firm and steady as he added, "For now, let's just concentrate on the future."

"Of course," Lauren murmured, awed by this new demeanor. Apparently Dillon hadn't lied about his intentions.

Kicker then turned to DJ and pure joy erupted from the grin that totally took over his face, replacing some of the visible strain in his features. "You must be DJ. Let me get a good look at you, boy!" As if DJ were a cool stream on a hot summer day, he drank in the sight of his grandson. At that moment, Lauren could swear his eyes welled up, even though the dim surroundings made it impossible to really know for sure. "You look just like your dad did at your age."

"Yes, sir." Standing tall with shoulders back, DJ held out his hand.

"What's this 'sir' shit? Call me Grandpa. Or Kicker."

Lauren couldn't be more proud of DJ when he only nodded with a serious expression and said, "I'm pleased to meet you, Grandpa Kicker."

Kicker laughed, waved away his outstretched hand, and wrapped him in a bear hug instead. Then glancing over DJ's shoulder, he caught Dillon's eye. "And thank you for bringing them here."

"What about me, Dad?" In the act of helping Dillon unload the bags, Rory hefted the last one out of the compartment and said in an affronted voice, "Don't I rate? After all, he couldn't have done it without my help." Except the smile negated his insulted tone.

"I owe you both more than you know. I say this calls for a celebratory drink once we get home." Kicker let go of DJ with one hand to indicate a stretch limo, at the same time keeping an arm around him. "Well, shall we?" he asked, urging DJ with a nudge and the group in that direction with a nod.

In silence, they proceeded to the car and waited for the driver to open the door. Then they clambered in one by one.

During the ride to Kicker's mansion, Lauren listened to Rory and DJ chat about flying and airplanes. Every once in a while, Kicker would add a comment. It didn't help that too many times over the last twenty minutes she'd look up to see Dillon staring at her, his expression unreadable. He'd taken the seat directly across from her. Unfortunately, her expression wasn't as unreadable and she had to glance away, otherwise he'd guess where her mind kept wandering.

Since he'd always been nothing but the best friend a person could have, she doubted he'd appreciate the direction. Her thoughts were definitely not the thoughts a friend should have toward another friend.

Thank God, the car finally eased to a crawl before turning into a long paved driveway. The minute the limo came to a complete stop, Lauren opened the door without waiting for the driver, only too relieved to have occupied a window seat, which allowed for the quick exit.

Once out, she slowly pivoted, taking in the lighted ten-foot stucco wall surrounding the property on the street side of the house at the end of the lengthy driveway. A fragrant humid breeze ruffled her hair and felt good on her skin after being inside the air-conditioned limo. Rubbing her arms and exhaling a long sigh, she glanced around further.

Her gaze ended at the imposing house, flanked on each side with lush tropical greens of elephant ear philodendron, Japanese boxwood, and scrub palms, all filling in as ground cover below, and royal palms and live oaks touching the sky above. Lights illuminated the foliage that blended with riotous colors of yellow clematis, pink hibiscus, purple bougainvillea, and orange bird of paradise. The thick plants paralleled the winding paved road all the way to the iron gates that were now closing. These were the colors of Florida. A twinge of homesickness invaded her thoughts. Until this moment, Lauren hadn't realized how much she missed the Bay Area. The warmth, the water, the white sand beaches. Everything that this part of the state had to offer and was so different from the mountains she now called home. The dark purple and navy shades of Tampa Bay on the back side of the property seemed to go on forever until they met the twinkling lights of Clearwater. The view was impressive by day. So much so, that the magnificence of it had always made her feel less than significant. At night it was as lonely as it was vast. That loneliness, along with the reminder of how imperfect she was, pervaded her senses.

"Go on up and ring the bell while I see to your bags," Kicker said. "Sophie's waiting."

Sophie. Frowning, Lauren nodded, having forgotten all about his wife.

Kicker paid her disapproving expression no heed, just spun back around to talk to the driver.

Coming up behind her, Dillon said so that only she could hear, "I'm not so sure having my stepmother awaiting our arrival is a plus."

Her sentiments exactly. Lauren's gaze swept the spotlighted house once again, this time its shadows casting a menacing presence.

Suddenly too many memories rushed out, none of them good and all of them reinforcing one point. This was a mistake. Except, her mistake wasn't in agreeing to come to Florida. No, her mistake was in agreeing to come *here*, to Kicker's palace, as she'd coined it all those years ago. She'd vowed back then never set foot in there again, yet somehow here she stood, as placid as ever.

"Don't tell me. Let me guess," Dillon whispered. "You're suddenly having second thoughts about seeing Sophie again, aren't you?"

"How'd you know?" Were her thoughts that transparent?

"Kindred spirits think alike. Besides, it's written on your face."

"Ha, ha!" Was it really so obvious? "I'm not sure I'll ever be ready to face that woman again," she stated honestly. What if he could see other, more personal thoughts as easily?

"I know the feeling." He grinned. "Don't worry. If she tries anything, I'll beat her up too."

Lauren smiled, unable to hold it back because his grin was too contagious. Dillon could always do that. Make a joke that enabled her to perceive her fears in a more humorous vein, so they weren't as daunting. "What happened to Arletta?" she asked, purposely changing the subject.

"She's still around, which means I wouldn't worry about Sophie if I were you. If I'm not here, Arletta will keep her in line. Plus, I doubt Kicker will allow her to make you feel unwelcome now."

"Thanks." Lauren eyed the warm smile still brightening his face and her tummy did a backflip. Note to self: Be more cautious around Dillon, especially when he smiles. He was much too attractive for her liking. Not only that, he was much too perceptive where she was concerned.

DJ suddenly appeared at Dillon's right and whistled his appreciation. "Get a load of this place, Mom," he said in a low voice. "Grandpa Kicker must be rich."

Lauren nodded. "He's definitely not poor."

Rory joined them as they converged at the bottom of the veranda steps.

"Just remember, DJ, money isn't the sum of a man. How he earns it and what he does with it all factor in," Dillon said. He turned and called to Kicker, "You need any help, Dad?"

"Thanks for the offer, son, but I've got everything taken care of. I may not be as fast as I once was," he said, starting toward them, holding up a cane. "But I've got this, which keeps me steady on my feet when I get tired."

"Dillon's right about money," Lauren said to DJ. "It doesn't buy happiness." All the money in the world hadn't made Jimmy happy. She wondered if all that money made Kicker and Sophie happy.

As Kicker joined the small group, Dillon glanced at her with raised eyebrows. "Want me to go in first and see which way the wind blows?"

Lauren offered a half laugh. "Thanks, but I have to face her sometime. Besides, she'll probably be on her best behavior in front of Kicker, if only to make me look bad." She mentally shook her head. No, the woman would most likely wait until they were alone before she spewed her venom.

More unpleasant recollections of her few confrontations with Sophie filled her mind just then, somehow replacing the confident woman she'd become with images of the scared girl she'd been. She dragged behind everyone up the stairs, wishing DJ had come by himself.

On the veranda she caught up with everyone just as the huge front door opened wide. "You finally made it," Sophie said, greeting them with a brittle smile. "Your rooms are all made up."

Then staring right at her, obviously singling her out, Sophie added, "I'm sure you're all tired, especially you, Lauren, considering the dark circles under your eyes."

"Hello, Sophie." Lauren held her head high, refusing to cower as she'd once done. "You're looking good." She smiled and added in the sweetest, most sugary tone she could muster, " Have you met DJ?" She nodded to her son, who smiled and held out his hand.

Sophie turned, pretending not to see the hand, but Lauren knew better. Unable to ignore the small slight, she held on to her smile and said, "I doubt anyone would ever suspect you of having a sixteen-year-old grandchild." Sophie had always hated any reference to looking her true age, and maybe it was cruel of her to point it out now, but considering her venomous glare and her behavior, the woman had it coming.

"And of course you're rude enough to point it out," she almost hissed.

"Was I?" Lauren asked, adding a bit more honey to her voice and increasing the wattage of her smile. She didn't like fighting fire with fire, but drastic times had called for drastic measures. If she hadn't provided a courageous front to begin with, the viper would continue striking. This way, she'd at least slither away, giving Lauren some time to shore up her courage for their next round. There was always a next round.

"I see little has changed in all these years." After throwing out her little barb, Sophie presented her back and retraced her steps, leaving the door wide open.

"Not so fast, Lauren," Kicker said, coming up behind her and grabbing her elbow. When Lauren spun around and looked up, a sad smile crossed his face. "I'd like to apologize for Sophie. I'd hoped the two of you would get along better, if only for DJ's sake." He shrugged. "She isn't particularly happy that I didn't give her much notice of your arrival."

"That's okay. I should probably apologize to her too," she mumbled. His confession made her feel two feet tall. She should have just ignored Sophie. That's what both Dillon and Jimmy had always done. Yet having endured Aunt Dory's cruel jabs for most of her teen years, she was a little sensitive to Sophie's digs. A little? Ha! That was an understatement, like calling the Grand Canyon a hole in the ground. Still, if she'd just quit reacting, then Sophie might not bother. It was definitely food for thought.

"Anyway, I sincerely hope you're not too tired for a drink," Kicker added. "As I mentioned earlier, I'm in the mood to celebrate. After all, it's not every night I get to meet my grandson."

Lauren nodded and said, "I'd like that," at the same time Dillon said, "I second the idea."

"Good." Kicker let go of her elbow and continued through the door his wife had left open.

Lauren sighed. Hanging around a woman who'd always treated her like a classless nobody who had no business infiltrating her circle was so not on her to-do list.

Dillon leaned in and whispered, "Remember, don't let Sophie intimidate you. Just ignore her and if you can't, just imagine her without makeup or the expensive clothes and you'll see what I see. Nothing special." He then winked and added, giving her shoulder an encouraging squeeze, "Always works for me to bring her down to our level."

"I'll have to remember that." Lauren laughed, but this time it was too forced and probably sounded as fake as Sophie's smile. She and Dillon trailed after DJ and Rory, who'd followed Kicker into the house. Once in the large foyer, Lauren spotted Sophie standing sentinel at the library's double doors.

"Since Silas wants drinks, why don't you all make yourself comfortable in here?" Sophie said, sending her a calculating stare, all the while holding that Stepford wife smile in place. She looked as if she were gritting her teeth, and Lauren decided to imagine her naked, sans that Armani, the three-hundred-dollar shoes, and no makeup. In her mind's eye she saw a short, bitter woman whose skin was starting to sag. Not much different than what Aunt Dory probably looked like.

Lauren offered a more genuine smile. Funny how Dillon's tip had done the trick, proving once and for all that no one could make her feel less without her permission. She threw her shoulders back to stand taller and walked steadier. She *was* stronger now and had a sense of herself. So what if the woman had accused her of being a gold digger? Judging from that glare, Sophie still believed her one. It really didn't change the truth.

Just then, an ornate cherrywood grandfather clock that stood ten feet tall began bonging the hour. Ten o'clock. Listening to the bongs, Lauren's focus roamed across the spacious entryway. At every beat, she'd notice something different and more impressive than the previous item. It seemed her entire house could fit into this room. By the last bong, she was staring at the chandelier, which hung from a two-story ceiling. The fixture had been shipped from Austria. Lauren knew this because Jimmy and Dillon had cracked a million jokes about it right after Sophie had ordered it, thinking her pretentious and snobbish when the chandelier looked exactly like the one it had replaced.

She continued walking toward the library and her purpose wavered a bit. This house, by its very grandeur, had always made her feel inadequate and that sensation wasn't as easily dismissed. How in the hell was she going to endure spending time in this mausoleum?

Remember, Lauren, she urged herself silently. *This is DJ's family and he needs them.* Yet as her heels clicked loudly on the marble floor, her mind spun for a way to escape.

Chapter 11

"When can you make it back?"

"Damn," Dillon said under his breath as Steve's question registered. Several of his company's bids had been accepted and his head mechanic needed his help with scheduling some of the maintenance. Steve rarely asked for help, so when he did, Dillon couldn't say no. He raked a hand through his hair, then rubbed his neck. "I'm not sure."

Thinking of what his departure might mean in terms of Lauren, his gaze settled on two blue herons making use of Kicker's backyard beyond the pool. They skirted the water, searching for bugs or fish. Whatever it was, they were intent on their mission. The peaceful scene did nothing to ease the anxiety he felt over deserting her.

He checked his watch and sighed, wishing he hadn't let too many things slide already. "I'll try to get there by late this afternoon or early evening."

Dillon turned his back on the million-dollar view and paced back and forth, unable to focus on anything but the way Sophie had treated Lauren upon their arrival last night, and then afterward as they'd celebrated with drinks. A niggling inside his gut told him Sophie might try something to ruin this visit, which was important to his father. He couldn't help thinking the worst was yet to come. His stepmother was so good at disguising her insults in a fake smile. Few had ever grasped how devious she could be. Dillon wasn't even sure Kicker or Rory were aware of that aspect of her personality. She'd always shown a different, softer side to them, and taken at face value, most of her comments seemed harmless. Yet after spending his formative years parrying her outwardly innocent, yet carefully worded verbal attacks, Dillon knew better than to drop his guard around her. He'd damn sure been astute enough to catch every veiled slur the night before, and most had been aimed at Lauren.

Unwilling to make a scene and destroy Kicker's happiness, he'd held his tongue. A next to impossible feat when he'd sat next to Lauren, listening to her clipped, one-word answers. Nor had her stiff posture set his mind at ease any. He'd wanted to hug her close and protect her. More than that, he'd wanted to see that same relaxed smile she'd granted to him during their flight. The one pasted on her face last night had seemed strained and all he'd been able to do was silently watch her withdraw even further.

He shook off the familiar edge of frustration and headed for the bathroom to grab his shaving kit. Once his overnight bag was packed, he slipped it over his shoulder and started for the door, wishing he could hang around a few more days. Just to muzzle Sophie so that Lauren could relax a bit. She definitely hadn't appeared relaxed at breakfast, subdued was a better word, thanks to Sophie's digs. In fact, Lauren hadn't spoken a word from the moment Sophie mentioned some snide comment about Jimmy and their short marriage.

His stepmother had a lot of nerve; he'd give her that.

Too bad she hadn't gotten one of her famous headaches. Then Arletta would have greeted the group so they could have at least enjoyed their drinks. That Sophie had even bothered to be social surprised him, considering she'd never been hesitant to speak her mind—out of Kicker's earshot, of course—on what she thought of Jimmy's family, or of him, for that matter. Still, he'd tried to be cordial, just like always. For his father's sake. Hell, if she'd met him somewhere near the middle all those years ago, he might have even come to like her.

In his mind, Sophie shared the greater responsibility for their lousy relationship, and still did. Hadn't she been the adult in the mix back then? From the beginning, she hadn't liked him, which had played into his feelings for her. Rory had it let slip that she'd had him investigated. He shook his head and descended the stairs two at a time, wondering if she'd paid someone to check out Lauren.

Obviously she still felt a need to protect her turf. He snorted, dropping his shoulder bag at the bottom of the stairs. Both he and Jimmy had spent too many years trying to please their stepmother, trying to let her know neither of them were a threat—which hadn't made a damned bit of difference in the long run.

Sophie would never change. Her world only included Rory and Kicker. A world no one else could penetrate.

Dillon treaded lightly over the marble entryway, his Sperry deck shoes making no noise to announce his arrival. Near the library, Kicker's stern voice alerted him. He stopped short. It sounded as if he was giving Sophie a tongue-lashing. He stood silently at the door and listened. Not to eavesdrop, just to time his entry, waiting until after his dad had had his say, so as not to embarrass anyone, especially Sophie.

Why he was still trying to be nice to her, he had no clue. Maybe it had to do with wanting to please his father.

Kicker had always urged his wife to be friends with his sons, but now, as his voice grew louder, there was no doubt he was totally annoyed with Sophie.

"Lauren and her son are guests in my house and I'll thank you to treat them with courtesy."

"Courtesy?" Sophie sneered the word. "After the way she treated you for all those years? She hasn't bothered to call or write, or send pictures of your grandson."

"That was more my fault than hers."

Damned straight it was more Kicker's fault, Dillon thought, leaning in to hear more and to view the two through the crack in the door, totally unconcerned that he'd crossed into the rude zone by doing both.

"Have you forgotten what she is?" his stepmother asked in a clipped tone. "That she trapped your son into marriage?"

"Bah." His father waved the statements away. "That's in the past."

Dumbfounded, Sophie just stared at him. "You weren't even sure he was your grandchild," she said after a moment's hesitation. "How can you forget?"

"As I recall, you were the one who put that idea into my head. He's the splitting image of his father…" He pierced her with a look. "…and Rory and me, for that matter. There's no question in my mind who fathered him."

Dead silence followed Kicker's last statement, one that had him reeling. Had Sophie's dislike caused the rift between Lauren and Kicker? Dillon had just assumed Lauren had run away out of fear of her feelings for him.

"And because he's my grandson," Kicker went on, "I expect you to treat him as such. Otherwise, you can move out of *my* house. Are we clear?"

The blood left Sophie's face. Even her makeup couldn't hide her ashen complexion. "You wouldn't dare?" she said, lowering her voice and visibly trembling. "After all I've done for you?"

"I appreciate your loyalty, as always. We've done well together over the years and will continue to do so, as long as you don't try my patience. The way I see it, you've come between my family and me once too often. I'm warning you. Back off." Kicker then turned his back, and started for his desk.

"Is that a threat?"

"It is what it is. I'm absolutely serious, Sophie. I won't allow you to treat him like you did Jimmy or Dillon."

Dillon stared, too stunned to move. His dad had known of her mistreatment? Anger flooded his system, causing his heartbeat to soar and his ears to start ringing. As Sophie warily eyed Kicker for long seconds, he counted to ten, stilling an urge to storm into the room and demand answers to questions suddenly besieging him. Why hadn't his father done something if he'd known? Why had he allowed her to get away with emotionally abusing his sons? Dillon meant to find out, but now was not the time for that confrontation. Nor was it the time to lament the fact that a relationship between them seemed more out of reach than ever.

"I'm sorry I came across so rudely, but you have to admit, I had good cause." Sophie's contrived backpedaling yanked him out of his thoughts. He recognized her insincerity. "I simply wasn't expecting them last night." She offered a smile that appeared too well-timed to be genuine. "You could have at least warned me, especially since it seems as if you've planned this reunion for weeks, if not months."

Dillon remained glued to the spot. Polite or not, he was learning far too much information to regret eavesdropping

"Deal with it," Kicker said in a firm tone. "I'm not losing this chance to spend time with my grandson."

"Of course. I didn't realize how much it meant to you…" Sophie's words trailed off again.

The break in their exchange was a perfect opportunity to knock on the door. "I hope I'm not interrupting anything," Dillon said, knowing full well he was, and judging by the hateful glare Sophie threw his way, she hadn't liked his untimely arrival. Not one little bit. Well, too bad. It was time to ruffle those perfectly coiffed feathers. "I couldn't help overhearing your conversation."

The displeased thin line of Sophie's lips grew into an all-out grimace. "Eavesdropping, no doubt."

He shrugged and offered a smile that said maybe he was and maybe he wasn't. Then he glanced at Kicker. "I need to talk to you." His gaze reverted to Sophie, whose nose was going further out of joint. That was her problem. He hadn't intended to aggravate her, but if he had, he damn sure wasn't sorry.

His smile broadened. Stirring the Sophie pot and instigating her aggravation might not even their score, not by a long shot, but at least it made him feel better. "Why give Lauren such a hard time?" Dillon had already determined there was no way he'd leave Lauren to fend for herself against the woman's viciousness. But how to get her to agree to go with him? That was the million-dollar question.

"I'm only trying to protect Silas."

"Really?" His gaze bored into hers and he waited. Not that he didn't believe her, he just liked watching her squirm.

Her chin lifted. "Her slinking off to North Carolina ripped Silas' heart in two. I won't allow her to do it again." Her expression dared him to refute her assessment.

He didn't. Just continued to stare with his eyebrows raised. Eventually she backed down and looked away. Oh yeah. The Sophie pot was starting to boil and it felt great to be the one increasing the temperature for a change. He couldn't help adding, "What about what Dad just said only minutes ago when he admitted it wasn't one-sided?"

Angry eyes met his again and she stiffened, clenching her teeth into a semblance of a smile. "As far as I'm concerned, the responsibility to keep in contact was on her." Her gaze never faltered, nor did her chin lower when she added, "It's a little too suspicious that she didn't call him or let him know anything about her life until Silas included her in his will. Tells me I was right all along."

"It tells you no such thing, goddamn it all." Kicker slammed his fist onto his desk, exasperation evident in both his expression and his voice as he added, "Have you not heard a flipping word I've said?"

"Calm down, Dad." Kicker looked ready to explode, which probably wasn't good for his blood pressure. The last thing Dillon wanted to do was cause him to have a heart attack or a stroke. "I've come up with a solution that Sophie may like. I have to fly back to Atlanta. Lauren can go with me. That is, if I can persuade her to leave."

"You don't want to do that."

"She'll be safe with me," Dillon said. "I'll make sure of it."

"I don't think so." Kicker shook his head. "She's safer here. I got a call from McCall and this is getting crazier and crazier."

Sophie brows furrowed. "What are you two talking about?" Her gaze roamed from Kicker's to Dillon's, then back to Kicker's. "Why would Lauren be safer here? She hasn't brought trouble with her, has she?"

"No," Kicker said. "Nothing like that."

"Well, what then?" she demanded, placing her hands on her hips and glaring at Kicker. "I have a right to know what's going on in my own house, don't you think?"

The two locked stares for more than a few seconds. Then Kicker sighed in resignation. "There have been a few incidents over the past month or so that make me question DJ and his mother's safety. I'm worried about them, which is why I brought them here. No one would dare infiltrate this estate."

"I hope you're right." Her tone changed from demanding to anxious. "I mean, Rory and DJ are as thick as thieves. If anything should happen to Rory, I'd never forgive myself."

"Oh, for God's sake, Sophie, quit worrying about Rory and yourself for one damned minute."

She faced Kicker, no longer contrite or worried about her position in the house, her expression turning mother bear ferocious.

"If anything happens to my boy, you'll have me to deal with and it won't be pleasant, I'll guarantee you," she said, almost hissing her threat. She then swung her attention to him. "I'd very much appreciate your taking Lauren with you when you leave. You're right, it will solve everyone's problem." She did an about-face and stalked out of the room.

Loud clicks from her heels hitting the marble slowly faded. In seconds, the clock in the hallway pealed. Counting the chimes, Dillon waited, eyeing Kicker and assessing his reaction. In all the time he'd known her, he'd never seen his stepmother raise her voice to his father.

His gaze moved to the double doors Sophie had just exited. He'd always thought she'd idolized his father, almost held him in what he could only describe as awe. The actions and words of the woman who just stormed out weren't those of the Sophie he thought he knew.

"She seemed upset," he finally said.

"Bah." Kicker waved his observation aside. "She's a hoverer and worries too much about things that will never happen. Sophie's always fussed over the two of us and quite frankly, it's cloying as well as annoying, especially for Rory. He's an adult, not an idiot, and he can take care of himself." He eyed him intently. "So, what's this about you leaving?"

"There are some problems in the shop that need my attention."

"Isn't that what you pay employees for? To handle shit like that?"

Dillon smiled because in the early days of Kane Aeronautics, Kicker would never let his paid employees handle *shit like that*. "I use a hands-on approach. I learned from you, Dad."

Kicker sighed. "I don't like the thought of you whisking her away. I'd hoped you'd stay here for at least a couple of days and help me keep her safe, until McCall can locate the guy who blew up her house. It's taking more time than he'd first thought, since the guy has all but disappeared."

"So, he knows who did it?"

℘

Lauren pressed the CALL END button on her cell phone, cutting the connection with Thad. He offered no answers to her questions as to who blew up her garage, simply saying he was still investigating. At this point, she had more faith in McCall. Thank God Kicker had hired him.

She plopped into a chair in the sumptuous guest room and set the phone on the table next to her before rubbing her temples, easing one mother of a tension headache. The day had gone from the toilet into the sewer. Dodging Sophie's well-aimed verbal darts was bad enough, but now she'd had to placate Thad and his distrust of McCall. Both took just too much energy.

"Mom?" A tap on the door followed.

"Come in." She eyed the bed where she'd barely gotten a few hours of rest last night, knowing that tonight would be no different. She couldn't sleep when she couldn't relax and she'd never relax in Sophie's house.

DJ entered wearing one of his favorite T-shirts and a pair of baggy shorts, his tanned feet bare. "Grandpa Kicker says he'll show me his company airplanes and then Rory is taking me to his condo to grab some of his games and a few videos." He shoved his hands in the big pockets and rocked back and forth on the balls of his bare feet. "I was wondering if there's anything you need? We can stop at the store while we're out."

Lauren subdued an urge to push the lock of hair off his forehead that always seemed to block his bluer-than-blue eyes, so like his father's and Kicker's. Instead, her brow furrowed in concern.

"Do you think it's safe to go out?"

"Grandpa's got a man guarding the house. He doesn't see a problem." DJ shrugged. "I kind of agree with him. I mean, who knows we're here?"

He had a point. He probably was safe enough here in Tampa. "Just make sure you mind your grandfather." If Kicker thought it unsafe he wouldn't allow it, so no need to freak out and refuse DJ's request.

"Don't worry, Mom." DJ leaned down to give her one of his infrequent hugs. "I'll be fine with Grandpa and Rory. I doubt anyone would dare attack them. Not in broad daylight."

Their place blew up in broad daylight and someone sprayed her front porch with bullets in broad daylight. However she refrained from saying so. DJ already had enough to contend with. Why scare him needlessly. She hugged him tightly for a few seconds too long. Then not wanting to get too mushy for his sake, she dropped her arms so he could step away. She nodded. "Okay. Just be careful."

"Thanks, Mom." He flashed her a quick smile and within seconds disappeared.

She stared at the closed door. Nothing was going the way she'd planned. For one thing, she hadn't expected Dillon's quiet support last night. There was no question in her mind that his presence had tempered Sophie's tongue. Even Kicker had sent a few fierce glares in his wife's direction every so often. Jimmy's dad had never bothered to mitigate the digs all those years ago, so why would he do so now?

Dillon's comment about mellowing came to mind. She wasn't sure if that was the reason he'd changed or not. What she was certain of was that the desire to flee kept growing throughout the night and now it was a burgeoning need.

She stood, then paced back and forth, rubbing her arms. She had to escape, but returning to Pemberton wasn't an option. Even though Thad thought it safe enough, she knew better. Maybe she could rent a cheap apartment of her own for just a month or two. October was off-season and she'd be vacating the place before the snowbirds flew south for the winter. Of course, renting would probably require a deposit and two months' payment, which would eat into her savings—savings she'd already allocated for DJ's college and her safety net. Yet what was a safety net for, if not for times like now?

She sighed and pulled her hair back, tying it with a scrunchie. After giving her face a cursory once-over in the mirror, she added a dab of lipstick, then threw her shoulders back and headed downstairs.

At Kicker's study door, she knocked, then poked her head inside.

"Ah, Lauren," Kicker said from behind his desk. "Come on in. We were just chatting about something that involves you." His outstretched hand indicated an empty upholstered wingback chair in front of the desk.

She entered and her gaze swept the masculine room. Like most of the rooms in the house, this one faced the ocean, and the open plantation shutters let in sunlight that brightened the dark oak paneling. On the opposite side of the large study was a separate seating area they'd used last night. Tables matching the paneled walls flanked two sofas and a similar coffee table separated two more upholstered chairs.

Out of the corner of her eye, she caught movement when Dillon stood and watched her approach. Heat flooded her cheeks as she sat in the chair next to him. She hadn't noticed him at first. They'd obviously been discussing her.

All the more reason to make a quick exit from this house. His concern couldn't be more noticeable than if he'd waved a flag with the words "I care" emblazoned on it in big letters.

Lauren cleared her throat and glanced back at Kicker. "So, what is it you were talking about that involves me?" Maybe Sophie had said something and she wasn't welcome any longer. She could only hope.

"I was just telling Dillon what McCall's dug up." He indicated the bar behind him with a nod. "Before we get into that, would you like something to drink?"

"No. Thank you." She waited a moment for him to continue. When he didn't, she lifted her eyebrows and prodded, "You were saying?"

"I'll get to that. First I want to make sure you're comfortable. I hope your room is satisfactory?"

"Yes," she lied. "Everything is perfect." She smiled, working up the nerve to reveal her desire to leave. "This reunion seems to be going well. I mean you and DJ seem to be bonding. I'm grateful for that."

"I'm the grateful one." Kicker's face split into a grin as wide as the Mississippi River. "I want to thank you for giving me this chance, Lauren. I wish his visit had come under better circumstances, but I don't regret the end result."

"That's something I wanted to talk to you about." Breaking eye contact, she pushed a few strands of errant hair behind her ears and allowed her gaze to wander around the room. "I realize it's important for DJ to be here." She cleared her throat again. "But I feel like I'm imposing and was thinking of leaving."

"Why?" His gaze narrowed and he spent a moment searching her face. "No need to answer. I think I have a good idea." He smiled indulgently. "I should apologize for Sophie. She's overprotective of me and doesn't mean to be rude. As you can see, we have plenty of room." He broke off, not saying what she figured he really meant. The place is big enough that you can avoid her. "Besides, where would you go?"

"Hotel? Rent a condo for a month or so?" Both would provide more security than a cheap apartment, which she didn't think Kicker would go for judging from the disapproval now creeping into his expression, but going that route would be way more expensive. Not that she could afford either, but desperate times called for desperate measures and suddenly spying the same disapproval on Dillon's face, it seemed she'd never felt more desperate.

"I'd rather you remained here," Kicker said. "Where you're protected."

Lauren couldn't just blurt out the main two reasons. Sophie was his wife and Dillon was his son. Admitting to a desire for avoiding both would only invite more speculation.

Kicker reached for his pipe and pulled a bag of tobacco out of a desk drawer, then glanced first at her and then at Dillon, holding up the pouch. "Do you mind?" When both she and Dillon shook their heads, he began filling it while continuing to speak. "You might want to reconsider leaving. I was recounting McCall's report to Dillon just before you walked in." Once tamped, he lit the pipe.

The scent of some flavored tobacco wafted under her nose. Cherry, she thought, recognizing it from those days when Jimmy would buy his father tobacco for a gift. The smell unleashed other memories best forgotten. And none were of her dead husband. All were of the man whose body heat now permeated her arm and shoulder, he sat that close.

"He's zeroed in on the person who blew up your garage."

"He did? So quickly?" Distracted with the comment, she re-aimed her focus on him and smiled. "Good. Then Thad can arrest him and I can go home."

"It's not that cut and dried," Kicker said before taking another puff on his pipe. "The sheriff isn't buying McCall's theory, mainly because the guy's upset about jurisdiction and protocol." That sounded like Thad, she mused as he added, "Says McCall went behind his back when he sent the picture your neighbor provided to his friend at Tampa PD, who was able to identify the guy through facial recognition on TPD's database. Sanchez was dumb enough to use his own van, but the sheriff wants to investigate further."

"That's his name?" Dillon asked.

"Yeah. José Sanchez." Kicker exhaled the words in puffs of smoke. "According to the TPD detective, he's the head of the Warmongers, a small gang that operates near the university. Got a rap sheet a mile long, but has evaded prison for the last twenty years. His son, Carlos Sanchez, wasn't so lucky. The younger Sanchez spent four years in Florida's Hillsborough Correctional Institution and has been out about six months. What's more, he was Hutcheson's cell mate in prison. McCall figures that Hutcheson has paid this gangbanger to do his dirty work for him."

"Then it should be easy to arrest him," she said. *And I wouldn't have to rent anything.*

"They have to find him first and even if they do, Johnson's not convinced enough to put out an arrest warrant without completing his own investigation."

"They don't know where he is?" Dillon asked, drawing her gaze. She had to break the connection when he glanced at her and their gazes locked for too many seconds. The understanding spilling from his eyes unnerved her. Made her want to chuck her resolve to escape and stay. To discover what, if anything, was between them. She was too much of a coward to risk engaging her heart again. Besides, he was just being nice. Just as he'd always been.

"McCall has a good idea." Kicker leaned back in his chair and stuck the pipe in his mouth. He inhaled deeply and said on the exhale, "Less than three hours ago, papa Sanchez's van was spotted at a rest stop off I-75 near Macon, Georgia. At about the same time, Hutcheson, who's driving a different vehicle, gave my investigator the slip. He thinks both are headed for Tampa in separate cars, so it'll take several hours before either get close enough to be a threat. McCall's still trying to get a flight out. The airlines are booked until tomorrow and freak thunderstorms in the area have grounded the smaller charter planes for the time being. He's hoping to make it before nightfall. Just in case he can't, he's sending an investigator, which means you and DJ will be much safer staying put."

Staring at a spot on the carpet, she frowned. Not what she wanted to hear.

"Or she could stay with me."

ജ

DJ craned his neck to get a better look at his grandfather's building. Now that his mom, after some urging, had gone off with Uncle Dillon, he intended to enjoy himself to the fullest. He sensed she hadn't liked being in Kicker's house. Probably brought back memories of his father. Stuff like that always made her sad. Thank God she didn't have to stay sad for his sake. He'd never liked making her sad with too many questions about his dead dad. With Uncle Dillon protecting her, she'd be safe enough.

DJ climbed out of the limo and met Kicker at the curb, still eyeing the mirrored building. He whistled, totally impressed, and started walking with his grandfather to the main entrance.

"So, this is Kane Aeronautics?" Mom was right. Grandpa Kicker was rich. Richer than rich. "Wow." Even though Uncle Dillon had said money wasn't everything, the idea of having it was fun to bounce around. Not that DJ would have cared if his grandpa were broke. He liked Kicker, as he was told to call him. Though ancient, he seemed to understand his desire to fly. They'd spent hours talking into the night about planes and stuff.

"It wasn't always like this," Kicker said, opening the glass door. "The building is fairly new, built in the last ten years. We started out in an old hangar out at Tampa Executive. In fact, we still own the hangar and use it for housing spare parts. I'll have to show it to you. I've collected a lot of memorabilia over the years. According to Rory, the place could stand as a museum, except I may need the parts at some time or another." He chuckled as if the idea amused him. "Kane Aeronautics still has a few relics in the fleet. Mostly out of nostalgia. Your dad and Dillon used to fly those two planes, so of course I can't sell them."

"I'd love to see what my dad flew." He'd learned more about his dad from his uncles and grandfather in the last twenty-four hours than in all of his sixteen years and ten months of living with his mother. Of course, talking about him in any form had been too hard for her, so he couldn't blame her. He was just glad for the opportunity to finally get to know his dad through their memories.

Kicker opened the glass door and waited for him to go in first, then followed.

DJ glanced around. The inside of the building was even more impressive than the outside.

"Peters?" Kicker's loud voice drew his attention. He glanced first at Kicker, then at a gray-haired guy up ahead.

The man stopped and spun around. "Good morning, Kicker. I didn't expect to see you here, especially on a Saturday."

"I came to show my grandson around. Let me introduce you two. This is DJ." He turned to him and indicated the other man with the tilt of his head. "DJ, this is Mr. Peters, my right-hand man."

DJ held out his hand. "Nice to meet you." Rory had told him a little about Mr. Peters, who'd been with Kicker since the early days. They shook. This close up, the guy didn't appear as old as Kicker.

"So, what brings you in today?" Kicker asked. He smiled and added, "Although, I shouldn't be surprised. We've both put in too many weekends in the past." He turned to DJ and winked. "I just don't get in the office as much any more without an excuse."

"Mr. Kane, Mr. Peters," the guard said, interrupting what Peters was about to say.

"This is my grandson." Kicker patted his shoulder, almost beaming with pride, which caused him to stand taller and throw back his shoulders. DJ rather liked having a doting grandfather who seemed proud of him; made him feel proud too. Especially when his grandpa seemed like such a powerful man. "We can dispense with signing him in, since he's with me."

The guard nodded and hit the button to release the security gates and they strode past them toward a bank of elevators.

"So, you're staying with your grandfather?" Mr. Peters asked as they waited for a car.

"Yep." DJ nodded, uncomfortable with the way the guy was studying him. Like he had a dab of catsup on his nose or something.

Resisting the urge to wipe his face, he said, "I'm excited that I finally got to meet Kicker."

"How long are you staying?" Peters pressed the button, then continued his silent scrutiny.

DJ shrugged, deciding not to let Kicker's number one man bug him. He was probably just weird. "A week or so," he said, focusing on the man's question. "Maybe more." Staying longer would be way cooler. As far as he was concerned, he hoped once his mom came back from Atlanta, she'd want to live here full-time. Tampa was a shitload better than Pemberton.

They'd driven past a beach with hot-looking babes. It was as if he'd died and gone to heaven. He'd bet the local high school was a hundred times cooler than Pemberton High. He'd already done research and pulled in some facts about the closest schools, praying the statistics would convince his mom that graduating from one here in Tampa would help him get into a better university. DJ had always planned on going to a more prominent school like Duke or the University of North Carolina. Now, he was thinking more along the lines of a university somewhere closer to Rory and Grandpa Kicker.

"I'm surprised to see you in Tampa, DJ."

He threw Mr. Peters a questioning stare, but the man only shook his head and offered a stiff smile, saying, "I was around back when your mom left town. Sad business, all that." He waved his hand as if he was waving the sadness away. "We never expected to see her again."

"Lauren and I have come to an understanding," Kicker interjected, saving DJ from having to come up with an answer. Hell, he had no idea what to say, so he mimicked Mr. Peters' polite smile and nodded. Thank God the guy wasn't his right-hand man. He seemed a little too left-brain for his liking.

As the two men talked business, DJ glanced around, willing the elevator to hurry.

Kicker's question about old maintenance records dating from almost twenty years ago yanked him out of his thoughts. That was back when his dad flew with the company. His attention moved first to his grandfather and then Peters. He could tell Mr. Peters seemed put out by the question and that seemed odd.

The light above the elevator dinged, interrupting what Peters was about to reply.

No one spoke as they stepped into the car.

Once the doors closed, Kicker pushed the number ten button, then turned to Peters. "Well? Have you checked into them?"

The forceful way he asked the question made DJ glad he wasn't in that particular hot seat. He smiled at Peters' deft verbal footwork at dancing around the subject with a few excuses about time and being busy and all that. The same dancing he'd do whenever he'd evade something his mom wanted done.

Grandpa Kicker didn't seem to buy the evasive tactics any more than his mother had.

The guy should just own up to not doing whatever Kicker had wanted him to do because he could tell his grandfather was also just as tenacious as his mother. He recognized the stubborn gene when he saw it. Kicker clearly wasn't about to back down until he got results.

"Well, it was nice meeting you," Mr. Peters said, once the elevator doors opened on his floor. He didn't waste any time stepping out of the car. "I've still got to analyze Accounting's month-end report. Like I said, I've been busy."

"Wait," Kicker said.

Peters halted and turned back, his face expressionless. "Yes?" he prodded, after a few seconds of silence.

Kicker only smiled in the same way his mother always smiled when DJ thought he'd gotten away scot-free. A patient, indulgent smile that a cat waiting to spring on a mouse might use if a cat could smile. "I'm feeling much better this week and plan on being in the office bright and early Monday morning so we can finish discussing those old maintenance records."

"Yes, sir." Nodding, Peters fished a handkerchief out of his pocket and dabbed at his brow. "That'll give me time to delve into them." He then nodded good-bye and began walking in the opposite direction. Again, it seemed to DJ that he couldn't get away fast enough.

"Humph. Should've done it sixteen years ago," Kicker mumbled under his breath. "That's what I've been paying you the big bucks for all these years," he said in a louder voice to Peters departing back just before the doors closed again. "To delve into shit like that without me having to point it out."

Silence descended until the whirr of the elevator rising filled the air.

"Is everything okay, Grandpa?" DJ asked after a few seconds.

He glanced over at him, grinning. "Everything's just dandy, son. Remember, you were supposed to call me Kicker like everyone else." He clapped him on the back, keeping his arm in place as the doors opened. "Calling me Grandpa makes me feel old, and when I look at you I feel fifty years younger." He released him to indicate up ahead. "Come on. We have lots to do today."

"Right. Kicker." He trailed after him, looking around at all the offices. "So, I take it you're the big kahuna around this place?"

Kicker laughed. "You got that right. I call the shots." He sobered, and added as if he was thinking out loud, "Except when I've been a little under the weather, which is why I let Peters handle things. He's my VP and he's always been an exemplary member of Kane Aeronautics. He's not a Kane, though. Maybe that's why he wasn't as thorough as he should have been."

"You mean with the maintenance records?" When Kicker nodded, DJ's gaze narrowed. "What's up with them?"

"Nothing much. Just checking some old records that should've been dealt with years ago and have become a little glitch that I need to smooth out—you know—since I'm the big kahuna." Then his expression lit up again. "If I've succeeded in talking your Uncle Dillon into coming back, I may just let him become the big kahuna so I can retire completely. Then I'd have time to teach you to fly."

A thrill went through DJ at the suggestion. God, he hoped his mom would let him stay in Tampa. If he had both his uncles' and Kicker's support, he just knew he could talk her into letting him learn to fly sooner rather than later.

"You were telling me my dad and Uncle Dillon used to work for you when they were my age. Do you think I can get a job here?" A job would pretty much guarantee his mother's approval, especially with a big company like this one. She leaned toward a career that focused on an engineering background. Except he'd always known what he wanted to do. Once he got his private pilot's license, he intended to rack up the miles any way he could, eventually earning his instrument rating, then multi-engine rating, and maybe even eventually becoming an instructor like his grandpa and uncles. And just like his dad.

Kicker chuckled. "I'd hire you in a minute, son. First we have to make sure your mom approves." He stopped at huge pair of double doors and took out a keycard. This place was like a palace. "Maybe you can spend summers and vacations from school in Tampa. If so, we'll work something out." He smiled then swiped the card to unlock the double door.

"Sounds like a plan." DJ decided then and there that he was working for Kane Aeronautics.

"This is my office. Tell me what you think of the view."

He happily followed Kicker inside.

There was no way in hell he was going back to Podunk Pemberton. Not if he could help it.

Chapter 12

José Sanchez pulled into the motel parking lot fingering his AK-47, the preferred weapon among his fellow Warmongers. He'd driven most of the night and was dead tired. Taking care of the brat and her kid would just have to wait until he got some shut-eye so he could figure out a new plan. His cell phone rang. He glanced at the caller ID and whispered his favorite expletive before answering it.

"Yeah?"

"Where are you?"

"Heading to Tampa, as instructed," he said belligerently, stilling the urge to ram the cell phone into something, preferably the caller's throat. The monkey on his back wasn't here. Instead, he was checking up on him and pointing out the obvious, which pissed him off more. Those two had more lives than cats. They'd definitely been lucky to escape his assault. An assault done his way.

He'd taken his time and planned it right. Cased her place; sat outside timing her departures and arrivals for days. Set the explosives to go off exactly forty-five seconds after the garage door began its upward slide, allowing just enough time for her to drive in and park, and maybe exit the car, but not enough time to escape the blast zone. He'd activated it from his cell phone when he'd seen the two together in her car. Then in a heartbeat his perfect plan had nosedived. How in the hell was he to know that she'd stop short after tripping the timer and then run for the house with her kid following?

José shouldn't be subjected to this shit. At least his efforts forced them to run to Tampa—his turf—where others could take them down for the right incentive. There was always some *hombre* needing to prove himself capable of becoming a Warmonger.

"When will you get there?" the voice asked, pulling him out of his thoughts.

"I'm not sure," he said, stalling.

"Maybe I should rephrase. When will you get the goddamned job done?"

"Should've been done by now," he said, clenching his jaw in

frustrated fury as the muscles in his back went rigid with tension. He took a deep breath and rolled his shoulders, then flexed his fingers. "Those two have had some luck, is all. They should've died in that explosion."

"Well, they didn't. Nor did they die when you botched your next attempt, which, by the way, pointed a finger at you."

"What?" *No fucking way.* Bystanders were totally useless as witnesses when chaos erupted. He'd made damn sure there was chaos. "How?"

"Because you were sloppy and they have a picture of you. I'm sure you'll skate past an investigation, same as you always have." The voice hesitated. "Your son won't be so lucky. I'd hate to have to turn over my evidence to the DA. Understand?"

"Yeah, I understand." In hindsight, finishing the job gang-style hadn't been his brightest idea. At the time, he'd just wanted it done and decided to hell with finesse. What had always worked in Tampa should have worked in Pemberton. Now thanks to his stupidity, he was probably a wanted man.

Good thing he'd ditched the van at the Macon airport. After scratching off the VIN, he'd removed the tags and had stolen another vehicle from the same lot in hopes that the owner would be out of town for a while and not miss it.

"I should be there by this afternoon to finish the job," he lied. He climbed out of the car and started for the motel office. "Once I do, I don't want to hear from you again, except to tell me you've delivered my money. Are we clear?" he asked, repeating the same question his caller continually used just to irritate the bastard because he was past irritation. He then slammed the phone shut. A twinge of satisfaction that he disconnected first filled him. He reopened the cover to shut the damned thing off before shoving it into his pocket and grabbing the door.

Damn, his eyes burned and his head throbbed, both from lack of sleep. José wasn't stupid enough to be awakened by another phone call.

"You got a room for the night?" he said to the cute little thing behind the desk. If he wasn't so tired, he might have spent the time trying to get some of her.

She nodded.

"How much?"

He paid in cash and walked back to his car, driving it around to the back, in case someone reported it stolen. He was counting on the fact that the owner would be gone for days. Once he made it to Tampa and connected with his homies, he'd ditch it.

The air conditioner rattled as he opened the door. The cool air felt good, but it took a while before he got used to the smell of mold. He threw his quickly packed bag aside, and sat on the springy mattress. The side sunk in deep, nearly collapsing under his weight.

Damn the bitch and her kid! Damn the frickin' monkey on his back!

Despite being dead tired, this bed might just keep him from sleeping, it was so cheap.

He reached for his cell phone.

Screw this shit!

Why wait until he got to Tampa to finish the job?

ଔ

"Clear prop," Dillon yelled, then started the Beechcraft Sundowner's engine. He glanced at Lauren. "You okay?" he asked through the mic.

She bestowed a brave smile and nodded, but her tight grip on the grab bar above the door gave away her real thoughts.

He smiled, admiring her pluck. After convincing her to fly home with him, she hadn't grumbled one complaint.

"Despite not liking to fly, I do like your plane. It's cute."

His smile died. "Cute?" The word hung in his ears through his headset. "It's a classic."

"Does that mean it's old?"

"It's not new, but considering all the FAA requirements, just about everything but the structure has been replaced at one time or another, so it might as well be."

"I thought someone like you would fly a King Air."

"Nah! They're nice, but a hell of a lot of money to operate." He couldn't stop the grin from forming as he taxied to the edge of the runway to do a safety run-up. "Besides, I love the way this baby flies. If something ever happened to me, I sometimes wonder if she might stay in the air until she ran out of fuel, she's so easy to handle."

"Nice to know," she said over the revving of the engine. After that, she remained silent while he finished going through his checklist and then finally cleared the plane for departure.

"We'll be there in no time," he said, just before pushing in the throttle. "Try to relax and enjoy the ride."

"It's not as bad the second time around," she said under her breath, still clutching the handle. "Besides, according to the pilot, I'm riding in a classic that pretty much flies by itself." Her attention moved to the window as the wheels left the ground and the plane started climbing.

Dillon laughed, not expecting her to joke so readily. Nor had he expected to win the argument about flying back with him so easily, especially considering her fear of flying. This was Lauren he was talking about, so he should have expected the unexpected. "Should be a smooth ride all the way to Atlanta," he said to ease her mind further, once they'd leveled out. "The storms that kept McCall in North Carolina are further north. Everything south of Chattanooga is clear and they're predicting light winds in southern Georgia."

Earlier, he'd taken her aside to plead his case soon after DJ had barged into the room, intent on urging Kicker to hurry. He was excited to visit Kane Aeronautics. After that, talk of Hutcheson and Sanchez had halted, shifting to their plans for the day.

During that hour, Dillon had never seen his father so animated. Even with Rory, whom Kicker had idolized since birth, he'd never seemed so at ease and full of fun. Hell, he'd almost fallen off his chair when Kicker had cracked a few jokes with the boy.

Apparently aging really did have a mellowing effect.

"I can't believe how quickly my son and your father have bonded. They're like two peas in a pod."

"Yeah." Thank God for miracles, Dillon thought, nodding and remembering DJ's hero-worship-like gaze as he hung on Kicker's every word. "Dad always loved telling stories of the good old days," he replied, not adding *back when Jimmy had been alive*.

"Do you think DJ will be okay with him?"

"Yes." He hesitated. "I think they'll be good for each other." His dad certainly looked more robust and healthy than the last time he'd seen him. Clearly, having his grandson under his roof had worked wonders. In more ways than one.

Imagine, Kicker actually inquiring about him, his life, and his company.

The old man had never given him or his ideas any significance in the past. Yet today, he'd asked all kinds of questions and then had acted impressed and interested in the answers. Dillon realized he'd enjoyed receiving his rapt attention. In response, he'd asked about Kane Aeronautics and been given the lowdown.

Right now, he couldn't honestly deny he wasn't thinking about his father's offer more favorably. Especially if Kicker, as he'd mentioned in passing, bought his company out with the stipulation that he could continue running that one too.

Once Dillon set the autopilot, his focus centered on Lauren's hand still glued to the handle over the door. Too bad their morning successes were at her expense. He knew her well enough to understand why she'd jumped at his suggestion. To escape Sophie. He didn't blame her. After all, if Steve hadn't called him with an excuse to leave, he'd have invented another reason.

Even though he and Kicker still had unfinished business between them concerning Sophie's emotional bullying for all those years, he'd wanted to exit on good terms with his dad. If he'd stayed longer, he had a feeling that his stepmother would somehow spoil their progress. That's what she'd always done in the past.

"I'm glad you talked me into coming." Lauren's voice broke into his thoughts and his attention slid to her face. He was glad too, but he felt a hell of a lot more than gratitude. Unfortunately, he couldn't keep it from showing in his eyes as their stares locked. Instantly sensation struck—the same one that always knocked him for a loop whenever he was with her. Frowning, he shook it off. He didn't want to find her attractive, not now when she might misinterpret his intent. What exactly was his intent? He honest to God wasn't quite sure.

"Yeah," he said, searching for a way to evade his disturbing thoughts. Then he grinned, deciding to fall back on his old ploys to lighten the air around them that suddenly seemed as charged as an electrical current. "I'm surprised my persuasive skills still work with you."

"Is that what you were doing?" Her gaze slanted sideways and she perused him with half-lidded eyes. "Being persuasive?"

Damn! Dillon could have sworn she was flirting rather than teasing. Had to be wishful thinking on his part because he knew better. Even still, another blast from the past erupted so fast to slap him upside the face and make him want her all the more. He couldn't continue holding her stare and glanced away. Wouldn't do to scare her away, now that he had her right where he'd wanted her for over fifteen years.

"I guess I was," he teased back, once he'd regained some equilibrium. He didn't dare glance her way again. Then, unable to stop himself from riding closer to the emotional edge, he added, "I can be even more persuasive, if need be, but I don't want to overdo it on the first day."

"I'm not sure if that's a good thing or a bad thing," she said, giving him what had to be her confusing stare, a look she'd used far too often in the past. It was something he sensed but knew better than to confirm with a peek. If he did, he'd reveal too much of this thoughts in his expression.

That déjà-vu feeling hit. How many times had he had these exact same thoughts back then? Too many to count, that was for damn sure, he realized as a myriad of emotions swamped him. Only two stood out to make his life miserable.

Funny, how just being in Lauren's company for a short while had him reverting to the frustrated and needy bastard he'd been all those years ago. Yep. Frustrated and needy about summed it up, all right. The same two emotions had driven him to confront his brother in the first place.

He scrubbed a hand over his face, so tired of feeling this way around her. Why couldn't he just be the friend she needed? Both then and now? "I'm sorry. I don't know where that came from. I'll try to be on my best behavior from here on out."

The attraction between them had always been totally unwelcome. She'd been his brother's wife, for crissake. A crucial factor in his decision to move to Atlanta and establish his own business, something already in the works when Jimmy died. Their untimely confrontation was a last-ditch attempt to change things.

Whether it had been to change them for his betterment or theirs, Dillon wasn't sure, which kept him from blurting out the truth now. Lauren deserved better than either him or Jimmy.

"I could've done without all the threatening stuff, but as Kicker pointed out, it turned out okay. I mean, DJ has found his family and he's no longer angry with me for keeping them apart. Plus, I've made some peace with my past."

Like a magnet, her soft words drew his gaze again. He smiled and said in his most heartfelt tone, "Yeah. You did good, allowing DJ to meet Kicker. I know you didn't have much choice in the matter, but I don't think you'll be sorry they met." He believed what he said. Seeing Kicker show so much enthusiasm for Jimmy's kid took away some of the hurt his brother's death had caused. At least something worthwhile had come out of this reunion.

Dillon could finally view Kicker in more human terms and maybe, just maybe, he could find some way to forgive him for being exactly what he was. Human. Since he was thinking about forgiving, maybe it was past time to forgive himself. Only he didn't see that as a possibility.

Self-forgiveness seemed a stretch. The least he could do was make sure Jimmy's wife was safe. He glanced to the heavens and sent up a prayer to his brother.

I'll watch after her and make sure nothing bad happens. To her or your son.

∞

Dillon opened the door of Lauren's side of the plane after a smooth landing.

"This flight didn't seem as terrifying," she admitted, grabbing his offered hand.

Once out of the plane he let go, hopefully without realizing how fast her heart was pounding.

To cover nerves that had nothing to do with a fear of flying and more to do with his close proximity, she stretched and drifted away from him, feigning a calmness she didn't feel.

A few planes were taxiing to the runway of the busy regional airport outside Atlanta. Watching them, she felt almost at home…or like she'd come home. Shaking off the surprising thought, she let her gaze travel to the front of a huge hangar with massive doors slowly opening.

A solitary man emerged as Dillon approached him.

Lauren followed.

A few words passed between them, mostly indistinguishable until she got closer and stopped beside Dillon. He nodded at her and placed his hand on the small of her back. "This is Lauren."

Instantly the scent of sweat, deodorant, and the cologne he wore permeated her senses.

To make matters worse, she was too aware of his touch, warm and steady, too aware of his masculinity, all six feet of it, dwarfing her five feet seven inches. Both made her wonder if she'd ever feel normal around him. *Just be cool, as DJ would say.* Unfortunately, remaining cool around Dillon seemed an impossibility.

"You remember?" he asked, yanking her thoughts back to the introduction. "Jimmy's wife?"

"My God." The man squinted, a grin taking over his face. "I can't believe it. It's me, Steve. Steve Wyatt."

Lauren shaded her eyes, then offered her own smile as recognition set in. More intent on trying to ignore her attraction to Dillon, she hadn't paid much attention to the man in front of her. "Hello, Steve."

He had a wiry frame and wore grease-stained, though clean, coveralls. His face sported a few grease stains too. Neither detracted from his easy, friendly demeanor as he wiped his hands on a towel, then held one out.

"I can't believe I didn't recognize you at first," she said, taking it. Steve then surprised her, pulling her into a bear hug. When he released her, Lauren cleared her throat, uncomfortable that he acted as if no time had passed since their last meeting rather than a decade and a half, and here she'd never even once thought about him or how he'd suffered due to Jimmy's death. "Guess it's been awhile."

"You can say that again." Steve tsk-tsked. "You've been a stranger for way too long."

She wasn't quite sure how to respond, so she did the next best thing. Changed the subject. "I didn't know you were working with Dillon." Steve was one of Kicker's mechanics until he quit soon after the plane crash. He'd taken it hard and had felt somehow responsible.

"I should've guessed as much since you guys go way back." Dillon always used to joke about how they'd survived college together. He and Steve had been almost as close as he and Jimmy. "I'm glad you two have stayed such good friends."

Her focus landed on Dillon. "So, this is your company?" she asked, nodding at the one-story building just to the left of the hangar. "Impressive."

"Yep. I'm really sorry about this, but I need to check on something with Steve before we head out to my condo. Once I'm done, it's only a twenty-minute drive."

"I don't mind waiting." Smiling, she held up a book, reminded of all those years ago. "I came prepared." Back then, either Jimmy or Dillon was always checking on something to do with the plane, which always took more time than anticipated. A book came in handy. At least he wasn't doing a pre-flight for a trip. That took forever. "I can just read. Remember? Like in the old days?"

Steve laughed. "I see not much has changed in all these years," he said at the same time Dillon said, "Good."

Dillon then heaved a relieved sigh. "This way I can assess the situation and then come back later if I need to." His right hand indicated the open hangar before returning to the small of her back. "There's an employees' lounge inside."

Nodding, Lauren once again felt the heat of Dillon's fingers through her shirt. Struggling for a normalcy that eluded her, she fell into step with him as he led her into the hangar.

"Make yourself comfortable." He guided her to a seating area behind closed doors that resembled someone's living and dining room combined, rather than a lunchroom. "I'll hurry."

She sat and pulled out her phone. "No worries. I can entertain myself. In fact, this is a good time to call DJ and see how he's doing."

As he trailed behind Steve into the main part of the hangar, she brought DJ's number up and hit the SEND button.

After a brief conversation, Lauren disconnected the call. Wrapping an arm around her head, she leaned into the plush cushion and opened her book. Unable to concentrate on the words, she struggled to keep thoughts of spending the entire evening ahead with Dillon Kane from overwhelming her. Was dodging Sophie her only reason for agreeing to this idiocy?

Thinking back on their conversation hours earlier, she wondered.

"I have a two-bedroom condo with full guest bath, so it'll be no problem," he'd said, sporting his customary grin and capturing her gaze with those laughing eyes. Both had done strange things to her insides, pushing Sophie and her harsh treatment totally out of her mind.

"I don't know," she remembered saying. Hedging, her gaze had taken a trip around Kicker's huge hallway. Dillon had easily guessed she was seriously considering his suggestion before he went in for the kill, showing her his crossed fingers while saying, "Don't keep me in suspense. I'm holding my breath, dying for you to say yes."

"Do I have to fly again?" she'd asked, knowing the answer.

"Yeah," he'd said on his exhale, still grinning so enticingly and nodding slowly, maintaining eye contact. "It's a lot quicker, and safer, than driving. I can have us there within a couple of hours." That grin, which had spread all the way to his eyes, caused invisible tentacles to reach deep down into her soul. In those few seconds, the yearning to be with him had mushroomed. At that point, she hadn't possessed the willpower to resist. "Come on. You can't hate flying that much. Don't you take trips?"

As she shook her head, he only increased the wattage of that smile. Maybe that was why she'd caved after only putting up a half-assed argument—because she was under some kind of spell. Or maybe it was just that she'd wanted to find out what would happen once they were alone.

"Really?" His smile died and he gave her a curious look.

"Why is that so hard to believe?"

"I don't know. I guess you always struck me as being too adventurous—game for anything—to develop a fear of flying."

Remembering his words now, she snorted and concentrated on her book. Yeah, she was adventurous, all right. So much so that she'd hidden herself from life for fifteen years. It was well beyond the time to take a few adventurous risks, especially if it included Dillon. Suddenly she wanted more. In his presence, that old Lauren was dying to break out.

Even DJ had encouraged her, presenting too good of argument to dismiss. It was as if her son knew flying to Atlanta was the best thing for both of them. This way, he'd have a better chance to get to know his grandfather. In fact, now that it was a done deal, she wondered what she'd feared all those years. DJ's forgiving nature didn't ease her regret, considering what she'd taken away from her son.

She shoved the thoughts aside and went back to reading. It was too late to change the past but she intended to change the future. The first step would be to follow DJ's cue and give forgiveness a try.

When Lauren next glanced at her watch, another thirty minutes had gone by since she'd last checked. Not that she'd expected anything less, but one hour was turning into two.

The door burst open. Startled, Lauren turned to see Dillon charge through it, his energy filling the room.

"I'm sorry. This is taking longer than I'd planned. I can drive you to my condo and get you tucked in, then come back."

"How much longer do you think you'll be?"

"At least forty-five minutes to an hour, possibly more."

"Don't worry about me." Her nod indicated the book in her lap. "I'll be fine. I'm just getting to the good stuff." As he turned to go, a thought struck and she quickly added, "If you let me drive your car and point me to the nearest store, I can pick up something for dinner." She shrugged. "This sitting around has worked up my appetite." *For more than food!* Shocked at how fast the thought had formed, she felt her face flame.

He stopped and spun around. "Now there's a brilliant idea."

Their gazes connected. Judging from what flashed in his eyes just then, they were remembering the same thing. She threw out a nervous laugh, using amusement to cover any residual embarrassment for wanting to share more than a mere meal with this man. "It's survival. Saturday nights usually mean an hour's wait for a table at any decent restaurant, which leads to eating in. The odds are you haven't changed. You probably don't have much more than beer and spoiled milk in your fridge."

"Definitely beer. It never goes bad before I get around to drinking it." His eyes, crinkling at the edges, lit up his entire face. "But no sour milk. I quit buying the shit after throwing out so many gallons." She had to look away from that warm gaze, or risk him seeing too much in hers as he added, "Although, I think I have a carton of leftover lo mein." He shook his head, still grinning. "But I can't remember when I picked it up."

She tucked a stray hair behind her ear, her focus staying clear of his eyes. "So, you still eat out a lot?"

"Yeah. Especially since you weren't around to cook." Then, as if his words brought up the memory of Jimmy, he sobered. "Not that I blame you for leaving." He cleared his throat. "Eating out gets old fast, but since I can't boil water, it's a necessity."

"Like I said, I'd be happy to cook."

Lauren stood and set the book down, thankful for something other than Dillon to occupy her thoughts. "It's the least I can do for all you've done for DJ and me." Smiling, she added, "Just point me to the nearest store and I'll shop while you finish up."

"Since I never turn down a home-cooked meal, it's what I call a win-win solution." He took out a pen. "There's a shopping center not far from here, but you'll need directions on how to get there." After retrieving a piece of paper from the desk situated in the corner, he started writing. "Take a left out of the parking lot," he said, handing her the instructions.

He pulled out a set of keys, then placed his other hand on her back, gently guiding her toward the door. When she reached for the keys, their hands connected. Their stares locked again. A current of something she couldn't describe passed through her, one so strong she had to stifle an urge to run and never look back. Instead, she wrapped her fingers around the keys.

"I'm glad you're here," he said. Then he did something she hadn't expected. Leaned in to kiss her cheek. For those few seconds, she closed her eyes and forgot to breathe, just relishing in having him so close. The impulse to wrap her arms around him and bring him closer was more than a passing thought. Suddenly the old Lauren returned and she refrained.

He took a step back, breaking the spell entirely. Eventually his hand left her waist to open the door. Once outside again, she could finally take a deep breath.

Lord, this was going to be a long night, she thought, striding beside him to his car, unable to subdue the excitement strumming through her.

Being with Dillon both excited her and terrified her. But mostly she felt giddy…like a lovesick teenager. She didn't remember feeling this way around Jimmy. Heck, she doubted she'd ever felt this young…or this happy. So, why not enjoy it?

Yeah, why not enjoy his company? And why not take a few risks?

With her thoughts still on Dillon and the hours ahead, Lauren left the Winn-Dixie, loaded down with two large bags. She hit the clicker to unlock his Toyota Camry. Just then a shape suddenly loomed out of her peripheral vision. If she'd paid more attention to her surroundings, she would have been better prepared when a man grabbed her elbow. Reacting out of instinct, she yanked out of his grasp and shrieked, "Help! Call 911! I don't know this man."

Flustered, the guy took a step back, looking at her as if she'd lost all of her marbles.

Recognition set in and her voice faltered at the same time Hutcheson yelled, "Stop." There was nothing menacing in the command. Only panic, which confused her, as did his next statement. "I just want to talk." More of her fear evaporated when he added, "Please."

Someone intent on harm didn't stop to ask for permission.

Shouts from the parking lot drew Hutcheson's attention. Realizing the commotion she'd created, he said, his voice hardening, "Take a message to Kane and tell him I need to talk to him. Tell him…shit…"

"Hey, you," said one of two burly guys now hurrying to help her. Hutcheson backed up slowly, then pivoted and took off running in the opposite direction, calling over his shoulder, "Tell him nothing has changed. I'm still—" but Lauren couldn't make out the rest of his words.

"I'll go after him," the first one called out as his speed increased to an all-out sprint. "You tend to the lady."

"Are you okay?" the second one asked, giving her a cursory once-over. "Did he hurt you?"

"No. I'm fine." Hutcheson had seemed too focused on talking to inflict harm before her overreaction had scared him off. As a result, she might never know what he had to say.

When the helpful stranger's expression still seemed doubtful, she offered a wan smile. "It was a case of mistaken identity," she said, hoping to reassure him. "He thought I was someone else."

The first man returned while the second was helping her put the groceries she'd dropped into Dillon's car.

"He got away," he said, pulling a cell phone from its holder clipped to his waist. "You should at least report it."

She calmly brushed imaginary debris off her slacks, doing her best to maintain a smile. "I was just explaining to this gentleman. I don't think he meant me any harm." For some reason, as she repeated her spiel about mistaken identity, she believed the statement, so why restrain himself now? If Hutcheson were behind everything, why give her a message instead of killing her?

Both men now stood beside her with the driver's side door open.

Before sliding inside, she turned back to them. "Thanks for your help. I'll stop by the police station and file a report," she lied as the sudden urge to get back to Dillon encompassed her. Once she relayed all that had happened, he could then contact Kicker to pass on the information to McCall.

Hopefully between the four of them, they'd figure out what Ronald Hutcheson was up to.

Chapter 13

Midway through DJ's tour of Grandpa Kicker's old hangar, Rory showed up.

"I like the newer models, myself." Rory winked at DJ, his teasing grin saying *watch this*. "The junk in here is archaic and worthless." His smile faded, his expression becoming deadpan. "No GPS, no autopilot. I don't know how pilots flew in the Dark Ages."

"Humph," Kicker said, a scowl darkening his face. "In the Dark Ages pilots were pilots, not glorified computer operators."

Rory laughed. "Why don't you tell us what you really think, Dad?"

"Some of these ADFs, Loran Cs, and DMEs still work and will continue to work when maintained properly," Kicker stated proudly.

DJ flashed him a questioning glance. "I know that an ADF is an automatic direction finder that uses a radio signal and DME stands for distance measuring equipment, but what's a Loran C?"

His grandfather explained that it was a locating system using three signals to triangulate a position.

"Yeah," Rory chimed in. "And Global Positioning Satellites replaced those systems years ago because they are so far superior to any of them."

"What happens if your GPS navigational shit goes out of whack?" Kicker snorted. "I'll tell you what. You'll be screwed."

"Dad, the Loran C is so outdated I doubt the signals are still being transmitted. And without a signal, the technology is useless."

"My point exactly. A pilot should always be prepared for the worst-case scenario. In my day, we didn't depend on a namby-pamby GPS or Loran. We used charts and markings. A pilot should at least maintain a decent knowledge of dead reckoning and sextants and make more use of charts."

"How does a chart help you when you're in the clouds or when there are thunderstorms all around? Having a GPS on board makes flying much safer during those times. You can't tell me you'd fly without one."

"Of course not. I'm well aware the old methods had limitations. I know too many pilots who lost their lives to unexpected bad weather, but the really good pilots could outrun or outmaneuver it."

"In other words, most were just damned lucky."

"Maybe so." His grandfather shrugged. "Still, I miss the good old days." He turned to DJ, his wink letting him know that he'd been egging Rory on. DJ laughed as Kicker added, sighing, "Planes have gone through too many changes, DJ. No challenge in flying any more."

"But, Grandpa, it's just as challenging now with faster, computerized planes and the need to understand the software in them."

"Bah." He waved the statement away. "All that shit makes you lazy, depending on technology that can fail. In my day, we depended on our brains and experience."

"Stop while you're ahead, DJ," Rory chimed in. "Otherwise he'll have us all flying without GPS to prove his point."

"No harm in keeping skills sharp."

Rory leaned in and whispered, "What he's really saying is he just can't accept the fact that technology has advanced and he hates anything he doesn't understand right away."

"It's all gobbledygook. Give me a sextant, a map, a few ground points, and a speed indicator with a watch, and I can find my way anywhere in the world."

"It's a damn good thing you don't fly our customers around any longer." He pointed to an ancient biplane. "There sits Dad's favorite toy, a Beech Staggerwing that he flies to stay current."

"Wow." It was the coolest thing DJ had ever seen. "Can I ride in it sometime?"

"Sure thing, son." Kicker turned to Rory, still smiling. "Just because I have trouble accepting advances for myself, doesn't mean I'll let the competition get the drop on Kane Aeronautics. All the planes we charter have glass cockpits with state-of-the-art technology installed."

Rory grinned and turned to him. "He's got a point there."

As DJ continued the tour, bantering back and forth with the two, he felt like he'd died and gone to heaven. Everything he'd seen today had made him wish he'd known about his extended family earlier. The past may have made his mom sad, but her decision to keep him in the dark made him feel sadder…and even a little bit angry.

"We're ready to head out, Dad," Rory said, rising some twenty minutes later. They'd ended up in the back of the hanger sitting at a table after Kicker had sprung for Cokes from one of the vending machines.

"I'm stopping by my place to pick up my game system along with a few games before we hit the video store." Rory looked at Kicker with the question in his eyes. "Are you sure you don't wanna tag along?"

"Nah! You two go ahead and have fun, but don't be gone too long." He then turned to DJ and said, "Don't forget, you promised your mother you'd spend some time on schoolwork tonight."

"Yeah, I know. At least an hour today and two tomorrow." DJ sighed. In the last twenty-four hours, he'd already spent more time on the computer doing busywork than if he'd actually gone to school for a week.

"I plan on reading right before bed." He wished his mom wouldn't have said anything. Jeez, he had a whole ten days to finish *To Kill A Mockingbird*. He was already halfway through it, thanks to her stupid outline. She'd written out what needed doing after talking to each of his teachers and viewing the school's websites that contained the lesson plans. He was damned glad he wasn't being homeschooled because she was a gazillion times tougher than Mrs. Clarkson, his hardest teacher.

"I'll make sure he studies some," Rory said.

"I appreciate that." Kicker nodded. "I'll see you both back at the house. I shouldn't be too much longer."

Rory glanced at him. "You ready, bro?"

"Cool," DJ said, jumping up and tossing his empty Coke can in the trash can marked RECYCLE.

"Just be careful." Kicker's focus landed on Rory once again. "Though McCall's man isn't here yet, I don't expect trouble. Still, you never know if trouble has made it here from North Carolina this quickly."

"Don't worry, Dad. I'll be on the lookout for anything unusual."

"Good." He stood. "I'm feeling so much better since you've come to stay. I might just be able to play some of those games with you guys."

"Sure thing, Grandpa." DJ stepped in to give him a hug. "I can even help you with quests in WOW."

Kicker laughed. "I'm not sure that's a good thing. What are quests? They sound hard."

"No. A quest is a small mission that's really easy, and working on them is how you get ahead." He stopped short of saying that there were so many guys wracking up quests in World of Warcraft that Kicker wouldn't get very far without putting in a lot of time at the game.

"I'll take your word for it."

DJ nodded, then headed out with Rory to the parking lot. His grandfather might not stand a chance of going anywhere, but he'd have fun trying.

"I like your car," he said when Rory hit his key fob. The lights on the late model BMW blinked and the locks snapped open. "Someday, I'm going to own one just like this."

"You want to drive?"

DJ eyed the car with longing. He'd only had his permit for a few months and driving around Tampa seemed like driving at the Indy 500 compared to Pemberton. Finally he shook his head. "Nah. Maybe later, once I know the area a little better."

Rory chuckled. "Never thought you'd turn down an offer like that. I sure as hell wouldn't."

"I'm doing you a favor." He grinned. "I want to get used to the local traffic before I take this baby for a spin."

"No time like the present." He tossed him the keys.

DJ reached out and caught them, staring at his hand in wide-eyed wonder. "You're kidding? You'd let me drive knowing I'm nervous about it? What if I do something stupid?"

"Like what?" Rory shrugged and nodded to the car. "Besides, if you do, it's insured." He grabbed the passenger door handle and opened it. "Come on. Hop in and I'll tell you where to go."

Needing no other encouragement, DJ climbed inside and started the engine. He ran his hands lovingly over the steering wheel. This baby purred. As he backed out of the space, feeling the power of such a prime car at the touch of his foot, he wasn't sure what he liked more. Airplanes or BMWs.

"Turn right and drive for about a mile," Rory said when he reached the street. "Then turn left on University."

He followed Rory's directions. After a few blocks, he started to enjoy the car, mainly the responsive way it picked up speed when he tapped on the accelerator. Hell, who wouldn't love this baby's tight wheelbase and suspension system that let him corner like a racecar driver.

"Turn right at the corner. My place is on this street."

He pulled into the complex Rory had indicated, parked, and the two emerged from the car.

Thirty minutes later, Rory threw DJ the keys again.

He hit the keyless entry. Within seconds, he was backing out of the space. According to Rory's instructions, the video store was on the way to Kicker's house.

"I don't want to scare you, but someone's following us," Rory said when he slowed for a red light.

"Where?" DJ peered into the rearview mirror. When he didn't see anything out of the ordinary, just a bunch of cars, he glanced back at Rory, whose focus now centered on his side mirror. "Which one?"

"Yellow, late eighties Dodge Charger. Two cars back in the far right lane."

DJ studied the scene behind him more closely. "Shit. I see it," he finally said, spotting the car and the scruffy-looking driver. Reflective sunglasses hid his eyes. "He has a passenger." That guy looked meaner, like he ate nails for breakfast. Neither man appeared to be on their way to church.

"Yeah," Rory agreed. "Maybe it's nothing. I don't like generalizing about people. But I have this weird feeling, and considering all the shit that's happened and that McCall's man isn't with us yet, I say better to err on the side of caution. Forget the video store and drive straight home as fast as you can."

When the light changed, DJ floored the pedal. The BMW accelerated quickly. He wove in and out of cars for the next few intersections, even running a yellow light. The Charger got stuck behind a truck that had stopped, but it was definitely chasing them.

Exhaling a relieved sigh, he maintained a speed well above the limit. One glance in the rearview mirror seconds later had him swearing under his breath. The Charger was drawing closer. Fast. When it eventually caught up with them, he was doing more than sixty. This time when he ran a yellow light, the car in the rearview mirror didn't slow, just kept going despite the light turning red by the time DJ had made it into the intersection. Not worrying about a ticket, he stomped harder on the gas. The 728i shot forward.

Man, the car was responsive. Getting into the role, he tested his newly learned skill by driving faster and cutting in and out of cars to gain some breathing room. The Charger was now several car lengths behind but was still clearly intent on narrowing the gap.

"Damn!" he said. "I feel as I've stepped into a TV crime show." Considering the tropical locale, *CSI: Miami* came to mind. "Man, how cool is that?"

"It's not cool if their main objective is to kill us rather than chase us." Rory pulled down the visor and concentrated on the view in the vanity mirror.

"Shit." The thugs and gangs on TV were exciting to watch, and until his near miss on the bike, he'd never experienced anything so harrowing. Hell, Pemberton still existed in Opie Taylor land. In fact, *The Andy Griffith Show*, one of his favorite oldies on cable, could have been filmed in his town, it was so dead. It died back in the sixties along with the sitcom. "You don't think they'd really try to kill us, do you?"

"God, I hope not, but I'm not willing to find out." Maintaining his vigilance on the mirror, he added, "When you stop at the red light up ahead, let's change places."

DJ nodded.

The second he came to a full stop, Rory didn't hesitate, just shoved right underneath him.

Moving as fast as he could, DJ hadn't even had a chance to slide into the passenger seat or to buckle up before the light changed and Rory shot off. Veering in between and around slower cars, they now had to be doing more than seventy miles per hour.

The light up ahead turned yellow, but the Bimmer was too far back to run it. Rory slowed, just as the Charger cut off the guy in a gray Honda who'd braked right behind them. From the angle in the passenger side mirror, the two seated in the yellow Dodge appeared even more menacing than he'd first thought. Just then DJ saw one of them lean out the window, aiming... "Look out, Rory! He's got an assault rifle!"

Rory looked left then right, and without wavering gunned the motor, saying, "Hold on, while I put the tactical driving course I took to good use." He peeled into traffic that came at them from both directions, at the same second bullets pinged past their heads.

"They *are* shooting at us." DJ stared wide-eyed at a bullet hole on the right edge of the hood. "In broad daylight."

"No shit, Sherlock," Rory yelled. "Will you get down?"

Complying, he dropped to the floor as the car swerved left then right. If he hadn't seen it with his own eyes, he'd have never believed it.

"You can relax, they won't catch us now." Rory's head indicated the mirror. "They just got sideswiped and it's their fault." He snorted. "Let them explain that to Tampa's finest along with why they're shooting an illegal weapon."

DJ climbed up into the seat and glanced back. Sure enough, the Charger was wedged between two other cars. As they sped further away from their attackers, a siren filled the air.

"You think there are more like those two guys coming? That we're still in danger?" DJ asked when Rory repeatedly checked the rearview mirror.

"No. I don't see anyone behind us. But it never hurts to be cautious."

DJ nodded and, like Rory, didn't relax his guard until the 728i turned into Kicker's fancy driveway. When Rory stopped briefly to punch in the code, only then was he able to take a normal breath.

"Man, you sure can handle this Bimmer." DJ couldn't keep the awe out of his voice. "Those were some badass corners back there." Not to mention some badasses shooting at them. "I thought we were going to flip any minute, but this baby just held it together."

Rory shrugged. "I knew that class would pay off someday. Skill aside, I have to admit some of it can only be attributed to German engineering." He shook his head and added with a grim expression, "I'm not sure Dillon's Camry could've taken some of those turns doing ninety."

⚃

Still shaking, Lauren pressed the gas pedal to back out of the Winn-Dixie parking lot. Once on the road, she sped back to Dillon's company in half the time the trip to the store had taken.

When she pulled into a parking space, leftover adrenaline had her heart pumping much too fast. The last half hour was a jumbled whirl of cascading thoughts. She switched off the ignition and sat for a moment, breathing deeply.

As much as she struggled to make sense of Hutcheson's behavior, too many other questions peppered her brain to answer anything coherently without Dillon's feedback. Yet, if she didn't calm down, she'd go inside and spill her guts, sounding like an idiot in the process.

Eventually her breathing evened out and she felt confident enough to hop out of the car and head for the main entrance.

Dillon was coming out of the hangar just as she stepped inside.

"Oh, good. Your timing is perfect." He started toward her wearing a lopsided grin that did strange things to her insides, even causing her to lose her train of thought. "Ready to go whenever you are. I'm sure glad you're cooking because I'm starved."

Nodding, she smiled and cleared her throat. "Um…I…um." Oh Lord, she'd been somewhat prepared and now that her mind had gone blank, she couldn't do anything but look at the ground. Even worse, once rational thought finally re-formed, she suddenly was no longer sure of the best way to broach the subject. Should she just blurt it out or start slowly? She mentally rolled her eyes. Yeah, start slowly and say what? *Oh, by the way, I almost scared the hell out of Hutcheson when he tried to accost me outside the Winn-Dixie.* No way could she say that.

"Is something wrong?"

She jumped at the sound of Dillon's voice. Immediately heat rose up her face. She let her hair fall in front of it, then nervously tucked the strand behind her ear a moment later. "Um…there's no easy way to begin, so I guess I'll just speak bluntly. Hutcheson stopped me on my way out of the store and gave me a message. Said he needed to talk to you."

"What? You're kidding?" Dillon's gaze snared hers. He held the connection, adding a moment later, "You're not kidding." He wiped his face. "Shit," he said under his breath, reaching out to grip her shoulders, then giving her a slow once-over. "Are you okay?"

"I'm fine now, but at the time I was terrified," she admitted. "I yelled at the top of my lungs. Something I'd always told DJ to do if threatened." Then she shrugged and offered a thin smile. "Who knew it'd work so well." Her attempt to lighten the moment fell flat. "If you really want to know the truth, at that point I wasn't sure who was more scared. Me or him. Which doesn't make a heck of a lot of sense, does it?"

"Wait a minute." He shook his head, staring at her with a confused expression...or confusion now mixed with concern was a more apt description. "Start from the top."

Her shoulders slumped from fatigue. "I'm beat." Suddenly lack of sleep and the events of the last week were catching up with her. After her ordeal in the store parking lot, she barely had any energy left. She was certainly too tired to stand here talking about Hutcheson. "Can we just go to your place?" She glanced at him, pleading with her eyes. "I promise to fill you in on the drive."

He nodded, then wrapped an arm around her waist and drew her nearer, this time touching her with a purpose that warmed her insides as well as her heart. Strength flowed from those firm fingers now guiding her through the door. All she wanted to do at this point was sink into his tall, comforting frame. Somehow, she just knew he'd make everything better—just as he'd done all those years ago. With one difference. This time she wasn't going to allow guilt to stop her from enjoying it.

CB

Dillon adjusted the groceries along with Lauren's bag, freeing up a hand to open the condo's outer garage door. After listening to the complete accounting of her ordeal, he couldn't believe Hutcheson had had the balls to confront her. The guy had to have followed her from the hangar, which meant he'd most likely been watching it.

He waited for Lauren to go ahead of him and fell into step behind thinking that if the bastard had been out to harm her, he could have easily succeeded. Under his watch. That thought almost brought him to his knees. It certainly didn't ease the guilt he felt over leaving her completely vulnerable. Added to his troubling thoughts, the guy had had a perfect opportunity and purposefully didn't use it. Said he only wanted to relay a message...that he only wanted to talk. To him, specifically. So, it stood to reason that Hutcheson wasn't the person threatening Lauren and DJ. If not him, then who?

Once inside, he let the heavy door slam shut.

None of the scenarios floating inside his brain eased his tension. A tension made worse by the fact that in less than five minutes, he'd be sequestered with Lauren inside his house. Have her all to himself. No amount of worry or guilt could shake the pleasure the idea generated. Nor could he contain the anticipation strumming through his veins. The more he thought about being alone with her, the more eager he was to clear up that last argument, which would hopefully lead to a new relationship. It was past time. Jimmy had been dead too long to be a factor at this point.

At the elevator, he set the groceries on a nearby bench and let the shoulder bag drop to the floor.

"Let me get my mail," he said, remembering the check for the needed funds his banker had promised to send out by overnight mail. "I've been gone a couple of days and am expecting something."

Dillon started for the rows of boxes on the other side of the main entrance. Immediately his thoughts reverted to her and the evening ahead. Since she had nowhere to run, she'd have no choice but to listen to the truth about Jimmy. He should have told her the news long ago.

Uncertain of how she'd react, he sure as hell wasn't looking forward to the conversation. Instead, he focused on what *could* follow.

Everything about Lauren Kane attracted him. Her smile. Her wit. Her spunk. Her lithe, athletic body with just enough curves in all the right places. He loved them all.

More importantly, he loved her. That thought stopped him and he shot a quick glance in her direction. A surge of tenderness rushed through him when she noticed his attention and offered a tired smile. Dillon smiled back, unable to brush the emotion off as a reaction caused by her close call.

He did love her. Always had, he suddenly realized. He closed his eyes as the full impact of what that meant washed over him. In a heartbeat, his resolve hardened. No way he'd botch this chance to have her. Not when the outcome was too important. He also realized in a flash of insight, he'd been waiting for her return. Rather than wait fifteen long, lonely years, he should have gone looking for her and forced the issue right after the trial.

So much wasted time. But no more.

Done with making mistakes where she was concerned, he quickly opened his mailbox and grabbed a bunch of letters, spotting the express mail envelope and heaving a relieved sigh. He'd make his payroll for the week and also pay off several pressing accounts coming due. The extra money would definitely get him through this slump now that several large maintenance contracts were suddenly in the final stages. The very reason Steve had needed his help today. Two of the companies had wanted a more concrete time frame before committing to a contract. The extra business might even mean he'd be able to pay it back sooner rather than later, which would have pleased him a week ago. Now it didn't seem that big of deal. Especially considering that while he and Steve had been working out a rough schedule, Hutcheson had accosted Lauren.

Dillon swallowed hard. All the more reason to tell her how he felt. Tonight. What if something else happened and he never got the chance?

After making his way to Lauren's side again, he resisted the urge to pull her into his arms and never let go. Instead, he punched the UP button, acting as if his heart wasn't pounding a million beats per minute due to her nearness and praying she couldn't hear it.

Get a grip, Kane. You're not some horny teenager on hormone overload.

Mentally snorting, he slid the strap of Lauren's overnight bag over his shoulder and tossed the mail into one of the grocery bags, before bending to retrieve them.

The elevator doors opened.

"I can carry one of the bags of groceries," she said, reaching out a hand. For a split second their fingers connected. She immediately dropped her arm.

He wasn't sure who was more surprised by the jolt the contact created. It was if lightning had struck, zinging him all the way to his groin. A damned uncomfortable feeling, to be sure. And one he tried to hide as they simultaneously stepped inside the elevator.

The doors closed.

Instantly the small space shrank. Awareness buzzed through his system even as the citrus scent from the lotion she'd smoothed on during the car ride permeated his nostrils.

For the entire trip to the top floor, Dillon stared straight ahead, wishing he didn't feel the heat her body generated despite being a few feet apart. The plane ride with her hadn't seemed as bad because he'd had the flight to Atlanta to occupy his mind. During the twenty-minute drive from the airfield his thoughts had been on Hutcheson. Until he'd parked the car. At that point, he hadn't been able to think of anything but having her rapt attention for the rest of the evening. Now that he was mere seconds from actually being alone in his condo with her, he realized his palms were sweating.

"Why would he want to talk to you?"

"Hmmm?" Her question threw him for a minute. "Who?"

"Hutcheson." She offered a token smile before tucking hair behind her ear and rocking back on the heels of her feet. "He seemed intent on making sure I got the message."

A flash from the past filled his thoughts and he smiled. He was just as nervous. Only for different reasons.

"Like it was a life or death matter."

"I don't know, but there are a few things about Hutcheson that I need to clear up with you," he finally admitted. No time like the present to start the emotional ball rolling. "I'll fill you in during dinner."

Her smiled brightened and sent a signal straight to his heart, one so strong he had to look away. Given their chemistry and the desire he caught in her eyes all those times she assumed he wasn't paying attention, making love with her would happen. Just not tonight. Tonight was for talking, which meant he had to quit thinking lustful thoughts.

Sex wasn't all he wanted. He wanted a lifetime. Another shocking revelation. This was certainly a day for them, he thought, wondering why the idea of a lifetime with her didn't scare the shit out of him.

Dillon already knew the answer, he realized. Lauren was worth a lifetime. He just needed to slow down this urgency to tell her.

Thankfully the elevator doors opened.

Lauren strode ahead of him and he could finally breathe again without the faint smell of lemons tantalizing his senses. Clutching the groceries tighter, he followed behind her until they'd neared the end of the hallway.

"It's this one," he said, indicating his condo with a nod. He shifted the bag, reached into his pocket for the key. After unlocking the door, she scooted in front of him. Once inside, he kicked the door shut, then hurried toward the kitchen and set the groceries down on the dining room table.

"I'll show you to the guest bedroom." He glanced at her. "It's right through here."

Along the way, Dillon grabbed a sweatshirt carelessly tossed on the back of a chair. The maid hadn't cleaned in his absence, which usually wasn't a big deal because he never had guests. Spying running shoes he'd stepped out of three days earlier after a long run, he bent to add them to the several other items he'd picked up, wishing he weren't such a slob.

Outside the guest room Dillon stopped. Waiting for Lauren to catch up, he tossed the items into a hall closet.

"This is nice," she said, coming up behind him and peering inside the room.

He smiled and did a mental inspection of the space. Not a thing out of order.

"That sounds like a polite spin." Her place was nice. His wasn't, he thought, looking back at the living room, eyeing his boring and serviceable furniture, a black TV on a brown table across from a black leather sofa without pillows. Now that he'd gathered up and hidden the evidence, it was neat and tidy too. Not a whole lot ever got out of place here, he noted dismally, walking further into the bedroom.

Every room in his condo was sterile, without warmth. Without color. A stark contrast to the colorful flowers Arletta placed all over his father's house or the vibrant hues Sophie used in redecorating, along with all her extra props, like pillows and pictures and knick-knacks. Lauren's decorating might never make the cover of a magazine like Sophie's would, but her home had been warm and inviting, which seemed to match her personality.

He shrugged. "Nice or not, you'll be safe here. Safer than in North Carolina." He dropped her bag on the bed and retraced his steps to the door.

Funny, he'd never noticed how bare his place was before staying with Kicker and Sophie or visiting Lauren. "Just like my life," he murmured. He was chasing forty and all he had to show for his life was a three-bedroom condo devoid of warmth, and a struggling company.

"What was that?" Lauren asked, glancing at him expectantly.

"Nothing." He sighed and pointed across the hall. "Guest bath is right over there. My room is at the other end of the hallway." Hesitating, he cleared his throat, making no move to leave. "You might want to freshen up before you start cooking."

"Thanks." A wan smile worked its way across her face. "I think I will."

"Me too," he said, forcing himself to step away from her. "Meet you in the kitchen in ten?"

Her smile widened into an ear-to-ear grin. "I won't be late."

Dillon nodded. "Good." Then purposefully ignoring the urge to hug her again, he turned and walked the length of the hallway, all the way to the master bedroom. Once inside, he tried not to notice the brown bedspread and light oak floors that matched the bare nightstand and dresser. Lamps were centered on both pieces, but all they did was spotlight the emptiness.

The phone rang.

He grabbed it. "Yeah," he said, tossing the morose thoughts of his living space aside. His life might be colorless, but it was also unencumbered. Totally free. Of commitments. Of clutter. Of people. Just the way he'd been living for over a decade and the way he liked it—until that moment he'd spied Lauren—when his world had filled with color again.

"Dillon, it's Dad." The words drew him out of thoughts. A good thing too, because, he didn't want to think about how colorless and empty it would remain if he couldn't talk her into a relationship.

"Hey, Dad." Listening to the water running in the guest bath, he kicked off his shoes and added, "What's up?"

Barefoot, he padded toward the bathroom.

Chapter 14

Dillon disconnected the call with Kicker and headed for the kitchen, suddenly in need of a beer. The news that a couple of thugs had shot at Rory and DJ while on their way back to Kicker's house sent his cheerful mood plummeting. If anything had happened to DJ after he'd insisted Lauren fly to Atlanta, she might never forgive him. Hell, he'd never forgive himself.

Beer in hand, he gazed out the sliding glass door and studied the view. Every condo in the complex faced the central park-like setting below. It was the reason he'd bought this place. Even though he lived in a box, he considered the green space with tons of trees and grassy areas as his backyard. Staring at it usually made him feel better. The natural beauty in front of him did nothing to ease his gnawing in his gut. Right now he just wanted to know what the hell was going on. Hutcheson claimed to want to talk and Rory, and DJ had been attacked. Why?

Trying to make sense of recent events, he continued sipping the Budweiser until he sensed Lauren's presence.

"Hey." The one word confirmed the thought. In the past twenty-four hours, he seemed to have acquired a sixth sense where the lady was concerned.

"Hey back." Dillon kept his attention on a couple of birds chasing each other. He sighed then slugged back another mouthful of beer, having no idea how to tell her. All he knew was that he couldn't let her leave. He was too fearful for her life. Now more than ever, he couldn't handle the thought of losing her. Not again, after finally finding her.

"Are you okay?"

He turned at the question and saw that she'd walked toward him, in fact was only a few feet away. Her footsteps hadn't made a sound.

As she moved to stand beside him, Dillon glanced down at her feet, which were bare except for red toenail polish, which was sexy as hell. He'd never thought feet could be so alluring. Attached to those long legs, hers were.

His gaze wandered the length of her and ended at a face devoid of makeup. A smile broke free. Lauren wore shorts and a T-shirt, just like him. Only she looked adorably young—like some teenybopper—rather than a thirty-four-year-old mother of a sixteen-year-old son.

"I'm fine, now that you're here to share the view with me."

"This is a great view." She then indicated the table and two chairs on the patio balcony with the toss of her head. "What an awesome spot to have coffee in the morning."

"Yeah, it is." Problem was, he couldn't remember when he'd last taken the time to sit out there with coffee and newspaper in hand. Not wanting to dwell on how the thought spotlighted his empty life, Dillon focused on making some changes. A leisurely breakfast out on the balcony with Lauren, hopefully after a wonderful night of making love, would be his first step. But he was jumping ahead of himself. He still had to get through tonight.

"Dinner on the patio's also nice," he added. "But the angle of the setting sun this time of year makes it a little too hot." Late-night meals by candlelight came to mind and he prayed she'd be around to share them with him. "Speaking of dinner, you promised to cook. How about I show you where things are." Smile still intact, he nodded toward the kitchen, then placed his hand on the small of her back. For some reason, he needed to touch her. "That way you can get busy because I'm famished." While guiding her across the room, he decided to postpone the news about DJ's near miss. He had plenty of time to ruin their evening with Kicker's report.

"Wow!" Lauren's wide-eyed gaze landed at the rounder of hanging pans centered over the island. "Those're pretty fancy pots for someone who never cooks."

"I thought I might learn at some point, so I bought them." He shrugged. "That was right after I moved in. Ten years ago. I almost feel guilty for never having tried them out. Not even to boil water."

"You mean they've never been used?"

Dillon shook his head as his smile spread into a wide grin. "Outside of the maid cleaning them every so often, no."

"That's pathetic." She scrunched up her nose.

"So, sue me."

She snorted. "Pans like these shouldn't be ornaments."

"Then I'm doubly glad you're cooking," he said as she moved past him to the counter.

Lauren began emptying the grocery bags, extracting pasta, tomatoes, garlic, and mushrooms along with other assorted vegetables, placing the items on the counter.

"Just keep in mind that this will be their first time on a burner, so be gentle."

She spun around and glanced at him with a startled expression.

Still grinning, he winked. "I can't think of a better person to introduce them to heat," he added, too caught up in the moment to care that he was being suggestive. Plus, he could tell by the gleam in her eyes she liked his teasing.

"So, I gather your top-of-the-line stove is also untried?" She snared his gaze and offered what could only be called a wicked smile as he nodded, unable to look away. "Well then, rest assured your pans and stove will receive a good workout."

Damn, at that point, all he wanted to do was kiss that irreverent smile and make her squeal with laughter. At least she'd derive some pleasure out of the evening. So would he. Hell, after his confessions tonight, he'd be lucky if she didn't walk back to Tampa.

"Just think," Lauren added conspiratorially. "After tonight, they'll no longer be virgins."

Dillon laughed. "Glad to know they're in such good hands." If only she could be handling him instead of the pots and pans. He'd always wondered what kissing her would be like.

He had to glance down or risk making a complete fool of himself by allowing her to see exactly where his thoughts had drifted. Judging by that smile, she'd welcome his lips. He sighed. "So, what're you cooking?"

"Chicken parmigiana with angel hair pasta and sautéed vegetables. I make my marinara sauce from scratch, so this recipe is to die for." Lauren lifted a frying pan and one of the bigger pans off the holder above her head. "I texted DJ, but he's obviously too busy to answer." She set the fryer on the stove and started filling the other with water. "I wonder what he's doing. I hope he's okay."

Wishing for more time, Dillon cleared his throat. "I just got a call from Kicker."

"Oh?" She waited until the pot filled with water, then placed it on the stove and turned it on. When done she glanced at him, her gaze now curious. "And?"

"First things first. Would you like a beer?" Alcohol would definitely soften the news and, if he were lucky, keep her mood mellow.

"A beer sounds perfect." She started inspecting drawers. "Where are the knives?"

"That one." He pointed on his way to the fridge.

"So, why'd Kicker call?" She opened the drawer and searched through it, eventually finding the knife she sought, and placed it on the counter next to the chopping board. "What happened?"

"Fortification first, then answers." He reached into the back of the refrigerator and grabbed a beer. "Would you like a glass?"

"Bottle's fine."

When he handed it to her, she twisted off the cap and took a long swig, then wiped her mouth with the back of her hand. "Okay, now that I've had *fortifications*, tell me why Kicker called."

Lauren then unwrapped the chicken and set it on a sheet of wax paper next to the flour she'd located in the cupboard, along with a shallow bowl.

"Well…" He paused. Studying his beer, he trailed his finger along the path of a water droplet. He wiped his damp hand on his shorts. He'd stalled as long as he could.

"Seems when Rory and DJ were driving back to Kicker's house after their visit to Kane Aeronautics, someone fired shots at them while they sat at a red light. They ran the light to get away."

"What?" She stopped in the middle of cracking an egg. "Why didn't you tell me this the minute I walked into the room?" She set the egg down. "Is DJ okay?"

"He's fine. I promise you."

"Rory?"

"Fine too. I know I should've said something, but I didn't want you to be upset."

"Be upset? Of course I'd be upset." She flipped on the water. There was a ton of annoyance in that quick turn of her wrist. Briskly she washed and dried her hands. "How could you think I'd not be upset?" she asked, her voice rising an octave She started pacing. "I should get back there. I should never have left." She stopped and spun around, her eyes snapping fire. "I want you to fly me back to Tampa!"

"Wait a minute. Back up. There's no reason for you to put yourself in danger by going back there."

"Of course there is. My son's been attacked and he needs me."

"No, he doesn't. In case you haven't noticed, he's growing up and he doesn't need you hovering."

She glared at him. "What do you know about sixteen-year-old boys?" Everything about her demeanor shouted skepticism, especially her tone.

"I was one myself and I damn sure was old enough by then to think for myself and make my own decisions."

"DJ's safety has nothing to do with that."

"Yes, it does. Your main objective is to protect him, right?" When Lauren nodded, he added, "Kicker will protect him. With his life. My dad even mentioned that DJ is handling this in a mature manner. He's promised to stay inside the compound, and you saw how safe that was. Your rushing back will only send DJ a silent message. That you believe he can't take care of himself." He could see her contemplate his reasoning. "DJ will be fine. Trust me."

"I should at least give him a call to make sure." She pulled her phone out of her pocket.

Dillon stilled her hand as she started pushing buttons. "Just put it away until you hear everything." She was about to disagree. He gripped her shoulders to gain her attention. Once he had it, he then placed one hand under her chin and lifted her head, forcing her to look into his eyes. His breath hitched a bit over how beautiful she appeared. So feminine. So fierce. And so fearful.

Her turbulent gaze drew him closer. "It's okay," he whispered, kissing her forehead. In an attempt to ease her fears, he continued kissing her face, his mouth moving lower until their lips touched. The short, reassuring kiss left him wanting more. A hell of a lot more. Now was not the time or place.

He leaned back, eyeing her closely. "Overreacting at this point will only upset DJ."

A thousand emotions played across her features and he couldn't resist giving in to impulse once again. What could it hurt? Only this time his mouth lingered for much longer than a second before he murmured in between kisses, "I promise you, he's fine. Rory's fine." Dillon never meant to take the kiss further, but he'd been dying to taste her lips since that first moment he set eyes on her again. Kissing Lauren was a cross between heaven and hell. Heaven because she was right where he'd dreamed of having her all those years ago, and hell because the willpower to stop had deserted him.

When he did lift his head, what he saw took his breath away. She'd closed her eyes and was just opening them, her gaze speaking everything that was in his heart and more.

Dillon was also aware of the precise moment lucid thought returned, at which point he wasn't sure if he'd imagined the earlier look, as it had all but vanished.

Then her eyes narrowed. "You're sure he's fine?"

Not exactly the words of love he wanted to hear, but at least she'd calmed down. "Yes, I'm sure." He forced himself to drop his hands to his side and take a step back to avoid temptation. "And Kicker will make sure he'll remain fine."

"I still need to hear his voice." She brought up DJ's phone number on her cell phone. "So I'll know he's okay."

"Can you talk to him without going all crazy?" His eyebrows shot up. "If not, wait. Going crazy will only make the situation worse. It certainly won't help anything."

"You're right. I am prone to overreacting. I'll text him instead." She typed in a quick message, then pressed SEND and stuck her phone back in her pocket. "I'll call him later." She brushed the hair out of her eyes and picked up the egg again, now totally absorbed in the task of cracking it.

"You won't be sorry. Trust me to know about sixteen-year-old boys and their pride." How could she appear so cool and detached, acting as if their shared kiss hadn't taken place only minutes ago, when he was dying to have her? Was it nerves, or had he overstepped his bounds? "I'll fill you in while you cook." Unsure of anything at the moment, Dillon made an effort to mirror her nonchalant manner. "Then we can eat. Once you've had a chance to digest your food, as well as what happened, you can call DJ."

It wasn't easy to blather on so inanely, given the uncomfortable swelling in his shorts, even though it was no longer noticeable. Still, he was surprised he could even speak, much less think coherently.

"Fine." Lauren cracked another egg, dropped the contents into a shallow bowl, and tossed the shells into the sink with the garbage disposal. "But don't think that tactic will keep me from calling him if he texts me in the meantime because, kisses or no kisses, I need to make sure he's okay," she warned, vigorously whipping them. "So, keep your hands to yourself."

"Don't worry." He grinned as she reached for the knife and made quick work of an onion. Judging by those covert glances and the safe distance she maintained while chopping, she was suddenly wary of him. "I never kiss women who are armed." Or was she wary of kissing him? Maybe she wasn't as unaffected as she pretended.

Dillon watched her dump the chopped onions and minced garlic into olive oil heating in the fryer then add the canned tomatoes, and decided to let the matter drop. For now. After all, the two of them had too much to talk about and treading into the attraction pond would only muddy his task.

As she worked, the room filled with delectable scents that took him back to the days he used to watch Arletta cook.

"Well?" She stuck the lid on her sauce and set it to simmer, then turned to face him, hands on hips. Her eyebrows rose a solid inch.

"Well what?" He couldn't help smiling.

"I'm obviously cooking and you promised to fill me in, so start talking." Lauren was adorable. Dillon wanted to kiss her again to see if he could wipe that demanding expression off her face as she added, "What happened?"

"No patience," he said under his breath and shaking the thought.

"Not where my son's safety is concerned."

"Got it." Nodding, he straightened and his smile died. "Like I said, Rory evaded the bad guys by running the red light." He opted to forgo the details of the two bullets that hit his Bimmer. The important fact was that they'd come out of the attack unharmed. "The two chasing him weren't so lucky. Got sideswiped and ended up in jail."

"In jail? So, they were captured?"

He nodded and relief swamped his senses when she visibly relaxed. "Kicker swears he won't let either Rory or DJ out of his sight until Sanchez is captured."

"He thinks Sanchez is behind this?" Her body tensed once again. "I thought he was still on his way to Tampa."

"As far as I know, he is. McCall thinks he ordered the hit. The driver of the car and the shooter are Warmongers."

"Oh my God." Her expression filled with horror. "Isn't Sanchez the head of the Warmongers?"

"Yes." Sharp mind, he thought. She'd obviously been paying attention this morning. "Both have records for petty theft and illegal drug possession. Nothing violent. Until now."

"So, why order the attack on DJ and Rory?"

"Question of the year. It's hard to figure out why they'd attack without knowing Sanchez's motivations." Dillon was realizing that when it came to protecting her child, she never missed a beat. Which meant she wasn't going to like the rest of Kicker's news. He inhaled, stalling and wondering at the best way to tell her. Deciding on just throwing it out there and dealing with the fallout afterward, he blurted out, "There's a connection to Hutcheson. McCall's guy did some digging at the prison. Sanchez's son was Hutcheson's cell mate for three of the years he spent at Hillsborough. McCall ordered the same PI to investigate further. It may be a long shot, but the guy is planning on visiting the prison in hopes of learning something from one of the guards."

"Really?" Her complexion paled as he nodded. After a long moment of reflection, she went back to the chicken, dipping it first into the egg mixture and then tossing it into the flour.

Lauren didn't speak for several minutes, just continued to work.

Dillon's eyes narrowed warily. "You don't seem so upset any longer."

"Oh, I'm plenty upset, which is why I'm glad I'm cooking." She glanced at him and lifted a shoulder attempting a half-assed shrug. "It helps me think, and right now I really need to think." She then offered a wan smile. "Thanks for insisting I not call DJ just yet. You weren't off base. Overreacting is a mother's prerogative. However, doing so wouldn't help keep my son safe because it more than likely would cause him to blow off my concern."

"Kicker won't allow him to blow this off. He's really worried. The best place for DJ right now is with the old man. Besides, they need this time to get to know each other, which means the best place for you is right here."

"I can't argue with that logic." Lauren blinked as moisture misted her eyes. "I just don't want him to think he can live without me, because I can't live without him."

"Shush." Dillon wrapped his arms around her and drew her close as a tear slid down her face. He then leaned back and wiped it away with the pad of his thumb. "Trust me as one who lost his mother way too early. I'd give my right arm to have my mom with me. There isn't a day that goes by that I don't miss her. I need her now, just as much as I needed her when I was sixteen. I've just learned to do without." He peered into her tear-filled gaze and smiled. "Trust me when I say we Kanes never forget who nurtured us."

❧

Enveloped in Dillon's strong arms, Lauren relaxed as fears over DJ subsided and a sense of well-being never before experienced washed over her. His hands slid up and down her arms. Though the act was obviously meant to soothe, his actions stirred something else also missing from her life. Excitement.

His soft touch sent exquisite tingles throughout her system. The rarely felt sensation of pleasure traveled all the way to her core when his arms once again pulled her closer. Luxuriating in his warmth, she almost forgot to breathe. Her pulse quickened at the discernible pounding of his heart so close to hers as he continued hugging her.

Lauren closed her eyes, inhaled the male scent of him, and decided to enjoy the moment, wishing it could go on and on and on and on.

Unfortunately reality intruded in the form of one disturbing thought—how strange it felt to be in the arms of her husband's brother, even if he was the man she'd daydreamed about for years. Because it felt so strange, she pulled away.

Dillon immediately released his hold. A sense of loss followed, which also seemed strange. She'd done without having anyone in her life for all these years. Why would it bother her now?

He moved to lean against the counter, a few feet away thankfully, so she could finally relax and return to her cooking...and thinking. Lauren sensed him watching her, which made it all the harder to slow her still-racing pulse. She fought to ignore his unsettling presence and concentrated instead on his earlier words.

We Kanes never forget who nurtured us.

The entire time she breaded chicken, Lauren mulled the statement over in her mind. Then her thoughts shifted to her husband and Dillon's loss of their mother at an early age. Which had to have affected them. Maybe that's why Jimmy had been so distant. According to articles on the subject she'd read over the years in an attempt to understand her failed relationship, a traumatic incident could cause an inability to be truly intimate. Which also meant the likelihood of Dillon suffering the same dysfunction was pretty much a foregone conclusion, despite her always sensing a significant difference between the two brothers. After that kiss, she was more confused than ever.

"I need another beer." Dillon shoved away from the counter and headed for the refrigerator. "Would you like another?"

"Sure." She nodded. "Sounds perfect."

As he reached for the beers, she used the opportunity to study him. His hunter green polo shirt was tucked into cargo shorts, which along with bare feet in deck shoes highlighted a lean, well-muscled body. Besides being sexy as all get-out to look at, he seemed normal.

Yet even if he were, she wasn't, thanks to Aunt Dory's mistreatment and the loss of her parents. Both had to have also played a big part in why her relationship with Jimmy didn't work, so it stood to reason her dysfunction might hamper any new relationship.

Lauren opened the bottle he handed her, took a long drink, and refocused on the chicken.

Still working on autopilot, she mentally reviewed the last fifteen minutes. The powerful connection she'd felt during their kiss touched all the way to her soul. Jimmy's kisses had never generated such strong feelings. She'd always chalked it up to her own inability to connect, but that kiss wiped that idea away.

So much to think about. With all the attacks against them to worry over, the most recent against DJ the scariest, she wasn't sure if she could handle any more emotional fallout. Even if nerves weren't on full alert and even if she did come to terms with her guilt, that didn't answer her biggest question. Was Dillon *like* Jimmy?

"If that tastes one tenth as good as it smells, I'm doubly glad you're cooking."

Dillon's voice infiltrated her thoughts. She opened the oven and placed the chicken inside to bake, then started grating Parmesan cheese. "It'll taste as good as it smells." She glanced up at him and pasted a smile on her face. "Trust me."

"I do."

Lauren couldn't hold his gaze because it seemed as if he was talking about something deeper. As much as she'd like to see exactly where their attraction led, more doubts suddenly rushed in to paralyze her further.

For one thing, she wasn't exactly an experienced woman. She'd only made love with Jimmy, and had enjoyed a decent sex life in the beginning. But after several months, sex with him had become…disappointing. And somehow she'd felt responsible, that she'd been a big disappointment to her husband. Kicker wasn't far off the mark in accusing her of not being woman enough to hold Jimmy's interest.

That was just the tip of the iceberg of her secret fears. She had a ton more, a few centered on no longer possessing the body of a nineteen-year-old. No amount of hours spent at Curves classes would turn back the clock a decade and a half or change the effects of childbirth.

Jimmy hadn't found her exciting in the bedroom back when she'd had youthful beauty on her side. What would his brother think if he saw her naked now?

She snuck a peek in his direction to see him fiddling with his cell phone. He looked up and noticed her attention. "I had my phone on vibrate by mistake. I got Hutcheson's number from Kicker and called the guy. I was just checking to see if he's responded."

Lauren nodded, not caring one whit about Hutcheson at the moment, much more interested in observing Dillon.

He shrugged. "No message yet." He placed the phone on the counter, grabbed his beer, and leaned back in his previous position.

Of course, he'd aged too, she thought, still surreptitiously studying him. While he didn't share the Kane classic male beauty, his rugged features and forceful personality more than compensated for it. The years had been good to him. Laugh lines on men only made them more interesting and attractive. Dillon was no exception.

Then again, he'd definitely been into their kiss. Maybe she was looking at this from the wrong perspective.

If Dillon were any other man, it might be fun to figure out how to get him into bed.

She grinned. Imagine, her seducing anyone. *You're forgetting that kiss,* the little voice inside her head shouted, also telling her that based on the effects she was halfway there. Her grin expanded. Lauren rather liked the idea of herself as a seductress. It would certainly take Dillon by surprise and, considering his previous arousal, she doubted he'd think her unexciting.

"What?"

The one word reminded her that he'd caught her daydreaming again. Her gaze lifted, taking in Dillon's questioning expression.

"What's so funny?"

Her smile died. "Nothing." For the second time in less than ten minutes, she couldn't meet his eyes and had to look down.

"It's not nothing to have put a grin as wide as the ocean on your face."

Lord, if he only knew. Her cheeks flamed. She let her hair fall from behind her ears and turned back to the stove. "I was just remembering when DJ was a little boy and was a lot easier to parent."

Lauren kept her attention on cooking, feeling his gaze on her movements. Once she was sure her complexion wasn't beet red, she risked another glance at him. He was still eyeing her far too closely for comfort, so her focus drifted lower. To his hands. His fingers weren't delicate. They were masculine fingers, with his nails cut short and a few scrapes and scars from working with machinery, but his touch was gentle. He was gentle. And witty and caring and dependable and…all of the things she thought a mate should be. Funny, that's how she'd described Jimmy when she'd first met him. The thought brought her full circle. Back to her biggest fear, that a relationship with Dillon would be no different from with Jimmy.

Of course, she could just have sex and leave it there. A lot of people did these days. Unfortunately, that just didn't fit her moral code. Besides, even without desiring some semblance of a relationship first, she knew that sex with Dillon would never be the same as sex with Jimmy. No. Sex with Dillon would leave her wanting more than just one night with a good friend.

Lauren didn't just want a night in bed. She wanted what she hadn't had with Jimmy.

Now that they'd kissed, she had to consider the consequences of going further.

By Dillon's own admission, Kanes never forgot who nurtured them. Did Kanes also have trouble making an emotional connection? She was pretty sure Dillon didn't. To be fair, she wasn't sure she possessed the ability either. Worse, she didn't have the nerve to find out.

Oh Lord. She rubbed her temples, working to forget any ideas of having sex with Dillon. He already owned her heart. Had for all these years and if they slept together, he just might own her soul.

"So, why would Hutcheson need to talk to you?" she asked, referring to Dillon's call to the man. "I don't get that." Lauren set the timer on the oven, then reached for her beer and said before bringing the bottle to her mouth, "If Hutcheson and Sanchez are connected, it doesn't make sense that he'd stop in the middle of extracting his revenge to chat." She took several gulps.

"I don't know. I've been wondering the same thing myself. Kicker believes he's out for some kind of retribution against us for pointing the finger at him in the first place." Dillon's heavy sigh filled the air. "After speaking to Rory earlier, along with the guy's strange request to talk, I'm not sure of anything anymore, which is why I called him." He broke off a moment, deep in thought. "Maybe we've all been wrong about this all along." Leaning against the counter, he crossed his legs and glanced at her, his expression grave. "What if an innocent man went to jail? What if he's not responsible for sabotaging the plane?"

"But he was convicted." Her gaze narrowed. "If not him, then who?"

"Good question." His contemplating gaze shifted to his beer. "If we knew the answer to that, the rest might just fall into place." He took a sip, then caught her stare.

"The DA's case hinged on several witnesses who claimed to overhear Jimmy and Hutcheson arguing, which is why the prosecutor believed Jimmy was the target, that Hutcheson switched the control cables on the twin engines so that the plane wouldn't respond properly during takeoff. I've always secretly believed there was more to it. That Hutcheson meant to kill me. Yet he had no clue I wasn't in any condition to fly and couldn't undo what he'd done."

"Well, I never believed Hutcheson did it in a fit of jealousy," Lauren said, stating a fact that had always troubled her.

"Oh?" Dillon's eyebrows shot up. "Why not?"

"Well, first off, I don't see how Jimmy could've had an affair with his wife." Her husband might have been distant, but he was always home when he wasn't working. When would he have found the time for an affair? Back then Lauren had been too shocked to fully question details. Lately those details kept contradicting what she'd always believed as reality. "He was a wonderful father and spent most of his time off bonding with DJ." She shrugged. "I figured there had to be some other reason Hutcheson would want him dead. After all, he *was* there that night."

Dillon nodded. "Yeah, he was. Yet in light of all that's happened, maybe the DA was wrong about motive and maybe the crash had nothing to do with Hutcheson or Jimmy."

"Hmmm, you could be on to something." At least about the part where it had nothing to do with Hutcheson. Yet somehow, she still had this underlying suspicion that Jimmy was the target, especially if she considered the threats against DJ back then as real rather than imagined. "I mean, he really seemed desperate to talk to you and was afraid of drawing attention to himself. Maybe he's figured something out that everyone involved has overlooked."

The last statement was barely a whisper as she tried to understand the man's motivations. God, what if the DA put an innocent man in jail for killing her husband? During the trial Hutcheson had never stopped denying his innocence. According to what she'd read at the time, he and his wife had separated. She'd later learned through the Internet that they had later divorced. Had Jimmy really cheated? If so, then had that cheating caused the man to kill? She looked at Dillon and voiced her biggest question. "What's with Hutcheson and Jimmy? He didn't seem like he hated Jimmy during the trial." Between that and his never-ending denial of guilt, she'd often wondered.

"He didn't. His real beef was with me and I always thought I was the original target. I just kept the opinion to myself. Mentioning it wouldn't bring Jimmy back. If Hutcheson is really innocent, then it means Kicker was wrong, and by remaining silent back then, I may have done the man a grave injustice." The words slowly faded at the realization and his expression took on a note of regret as he added in a soft voice, "I need to figure out who else would've benefited from my death. It won't give him back the time he served, but it might help exonerate him."

"Wait a minute." She put up her hand, palm out. "Back up. Why would you originally think Hutcheson would've benefited from your death?"

"Because he didn't like my interference."

"Interference? I don't understand."

Dillon sighed. His focus returned to his beer, where he spent several seconds following the beads of condensation with his finger.

A full minute ticked by before Lauren prodded, "Dillon? Answer the question. What interference?"

"It had to do with you and Jimmy."

"What's that got to do with Hutcheson?" Her gaze narrowed in confusion. "You're not making any sense."

"God help me, I hate doing this." He closed his eyes, then rested the palm of his hand on the back of his neck and rubbed. "I never wanted you to find out this way."

"Find out what?" Her stomach did backflips at the torment she saw in his eyes when he opened them and looked directly at her. "Now you're starting to scare me."

Dillon hesitated for more seconds. "It's not an easy thing to verbalize."

"Then just spit it out. Tell me," she demanded.

"Okay, here goes." He inhaled deeply, then said on the exhale,

"Lauren, Jimmy was gay."

"What?" Stunned, she stared at him, wide-eyed and open-mouthed as he quickly added, "He was involved with Hutcheson before the two of you married."

She shook her head as realization of what he just revealed set in. "No… You're lying." Of all the things she might have expected to come out of his mouth, that wasn't one of them. "Why would you lie to me?"

"It's true." Dillon wouldn't meet her gaze, instead focused on a point on the carpet. His cell phone chimed just then, indicating a text message. He ignored it and continued staring at the floor.

"Take it back," Lauren said in an attempt to get his attention, grabbing his shirt and shaking him. "It's not true. I was his wife. I would've known." She started pounding his chest until his hand covered her fists, stilling them.

"It's okay," he said in a soothing voice, which only enraged her more.

"Don't tell me it's okay," she yelled. "It's not okay." As far as she was concerned, it would never be okay. Ever. "Jimmy was not gay," she shouted as his cell phone chimed again. "I would've known something like that. I would've…" Lauren choked on a sob, tears streaming down her cheeks. "I don't believe it," she whispered. She wiped the tears away and stepped out of his encircling arms, refusing to be comforted, refusing to listen to his lies, refusing to let them destroy what few good memories she had left of Jimmy. Her chin lifted higher. "I won't believe it." More tears trickled out, sliding down the sides of her face. She let them fall and added, "I can't believe it."

"It's the truth, I swear it. I never wanted to see you hurt." Honesty shone in his eyes. "Why do you think I was so upset during our last meeting? Why do you think I got drunk that night?" She couldn't keep looking at the pain in his eyes. His heart wasn't being ripped in two. Hers was, so why was he acting like it?

"I confronted Jimmy about it, told him he wasn't being fair to you. I wanted to tell you. So many times, but Jimmy swore me to silence."

"Don't! Don't you dare lay all the blame on a dead man who's not here to defend himself." Lord, she would know if Jimmy were gay, wouldn't she? Oh please, God. Please let it be anything but that. It would mean he'd lied to her, which would only make her out to be a bigger fool for believing his lies, for falling in love with him and marrying him in the first place.

No. Dillon was wrong. He had to be. Her husband couldn't have been gay. He hadn't acted like any gay person she'd ever met. He was an all-American in college. Quarterback of USF's football team. He had hundreds of girlfriends during high school, according to the signatures in his yearbook, and back when they dated, he got tons of female attention. Women fawned all over him. But he was only interested in her. Or so she thought. She closed her eyes as doubt suddenly filled her mind. Oh God! What if it were true?

The chiming began again, pulling her gaze to the spot on the counter where Dillon's cell phone rested. "Will you answer that damned phone or turn it off?" she snapped, tired of the stupid ring tone going off every few seconds while her whole world was collapsing.

"Sorry." Dillon glanced at the small screen, frowned, then looked at her, and said, "You're not going to believe this. It's Hutcheson. He got my message and wants to meet. He's downstairs."

Chapter 15

Give me a minute, Dillon typed in response to Hutcheson's messages and hit SEND as Lauren said, "You need to go and talk to him. Find out what he wants." There was a slight pause before she added, "I need to be alone right now." Though her voice was barely audible, her resolve rang out loud and clear.

"Will you be okay?" He set the phone aside and stepped forward, wanting to extinguish that stricken, lost look from her face, but she only shook her head and veered out of his reach.

"Don't touch me. If you do, I may just fall apart." She picked up her beer and then moved toward the sliding glass door.

Studying her stiff posture, he wondered if Lauren would ever smile or joke with him again. She appeared so vulnerable. Dillon sighed and wished he hadn't had to drop the verbal bombshell in the first place. Had the news destroyed their chances at some kind of a relationship?

Renewed anger washed over him. He hated his brother for not being honest. He hated himself for enabling Jimmy and allowing him the wherewithal to get away with not speaking up. Worse, he hated himself for loving her back then and failing her now.

She obviously wanted solitude, so he should just abide by her wishes. Only he couldn't seem to move and was rooted to the same spot a minute later when she glanced back at him.

"I'll be fine, I promise," she said, offering a wan smile. He could only continue to stare at her, his heart breaking for her and the need to comfort her far surpassing any other thought. "So, will you please go and see what Hutcheson wants. Then, once this is over, I can go back to my life."

Dillon nodded. He owed it to Hutcheson to at least talk to him, but he dreaded deserting her. Pangs of regret pierced his soul. She stood in his living room, so close physically, but a million miles away mentally. He recognized her MO. She was distancing herself from him just as she used to do, and if he left now, he doubted he possessed the ability to pull her back.

With no other choice but to do as she asked, Dillon quickly punched up Hutcheson's number and pressed the CALL button. Waiting for the connection to go through, he prayed the meeting wouldn't take long, but that just made him feel worse. How did one go about talking to a man you believed was guilty as sin when there was a slight chance the guy could be innocent?

"It's about damn time I heard from you," a male voice said, pulling him out of his thoughts.

"Are you still in the condo parking lot?"

"Yeah," Hutcheson replied. "Just waiting for your call back so we can talk."

"I'll be right down to let you in." There was a decent seating area in the lobby off to the side of the elevator that would provide some privacy. Meeting him downstairs would also give Lauren some space.

Ending the call, he headed for the front door. Once there he paused and looked back. Lauren hadn't so much as moved a muscle, just continued gazing out at the park below.

He sighed. "I'm sorry, Lauren." What else could he say? *Love me?* She'd never do that. Not when he was just as much at fault in the deception as Jimmy.

As Dillon strode through the hallway, his mind switched gears. To the past. The entire trip in the elevator, he mentally rehashed the days and weeks right after Jimmy's death. Considering recent events, he began to view the trial and Hutcheson in a different light, which in turn caused him to wonder about his own perceptions back then. Kicker's tactics came to mind. What if his dad's spin on Jimmy's relationship with Hutcheson's wife had ultimately hurt Hutcheson? But a court of law found the man guilty of sabotage.

Would it have mattered if the prosecutor had known about the prior relationship between his brother and Hutcheson? Or had that spin, one his silence had perpetuated, changed the outcome?

Dillon was saved from dwelling on the answer when the elevator doors opened at the lobby level. He shot out and hurried to the locked glass entrance, where Hutcheson paced on the other side.

He pushed the door to release the lock.

Once inside, the guy nodded. "Thanks for meeting me." He spoke in a subservient tone and appeared nothing like the angry man who'd threatened Kicker and him on that last day right after the bailiff had announced the verdict. "I know we've had our differences, but I want you to know I've had a change of heart and no longer hold you responsible."

Interesting how that *you* didn't seem to include Kicker, Dillon thought, nodding to a seating area consisting of several leather chairs and a few tables with lamps.

"We can talk over there," he said, leading Hutcheson to a chair and waiting until he sat before taking a seat across from him, one that provided an unobstructed view of his face. He wasn't a fool. Regardless of the doubts swimming around in his mind, he still didn't trust the man and decided to keep him in full sight.

Dillon leaned back, pulled his elbows in, and brought his hands together in a prayer-like position. He then rested his chin on his fingertips, eyeing the man while remaining silent. When thirty seconds ticked by, he said, "Well, you have my full attention."

"I don't know where to start." Hutcheson dragged a hand through his hair. "After I finish, you might think I'm crazy."

"I doubt that. As to the other, start at the beginning."

"Which one? The one where I was hauled away in handcuffs after the man I'd loved for five years was killed and I was accused of his murder? Or the one where I was convicted of the crime despite half-assed evidence, meaning I was set up hook, line, and sinker?"

Dillon cocked a brow. His flair for the dramatic could be a ploy to manipulate. Kicker was quick to use drama when manipulating. Dillon was well acquainted with the technique and wouldn't let himself get sidetracked by it. "Doesn't sound like you've had much of a change of heart."

Hutcheson met his gaze without flinching. "The change of heart comes from the fact that I no longer believe you're the Kane responsible for setting me up." He held eye contact for several long seconds before adding with conviction, "But someone did."

"Okay." Dillon nodded. "You're consistent. I'll give you that." The guy either was a good liar or wholeheartedly believed the statement, which coincided with Lauren's assessment. And Rory's. The jury was still out on his final take until after hearing what Hutcheson had to say. "So, tell me why you think all this."

"I've already told you why I believe it. I'm innocent, but someone went to a lot of trouble to make sure I'd be found guilty. I have a good idea who that someone is." Hutcheson crossed one leg, placed his ankle on his knee, and leaned forward. "I didn't realize how good I was railroaded until the day the bailiff read the jury's findings out loud."

"The DA did his job."

"With a little help from others, if you ask me. Considering the weak evidence."

"Help?"

"The judge was biased as hell. It wasn't exactly what he said on record, it was in the way he said it in the courtroom. Shit, I was too stupid to pick up on it. God only knows why my lawyer didn't, but he didn't." Hutcheson chuckled in a way that portrayed anything but amusement. "Hell, I was ripe for the picking. I believed my lawyer had to act in my best interest. I believed in the system. I believed that because I was innocent and the evidence was so circumstantial, no jury on earth would convict me."

He sighed, shaking his head. "I'd risked my life reporting on stories in countries where citizens are put in prison for no good reason, other than being at someone's mercy. I certainly never dreamed an innocent man could be convicted in this country. Besides being young and naïve, I was flat out wrong. I've paid for my naïveté. For more than a decade, and Lord knows I've learned a valuable lesson."

Dillon cringed inside and struggled to keep a straight face. The pain etched onto the man's expression as well as the anguish in his tone had him once again questioning his long-held beliefs. He'd been so convinced of Hutcheson's guilt. God help him, but what if he'd been wrong? "What do you mean?"

"I mean an innocent man can go to prison for something he didn't do because the system's fucking corrupt."

"Isn't that one of the biggest clichés in the prison system?" Though he didn't want to buy Hutcheson's claim, it was hard not to be moved with his vehemence. He offered a halfhearted laugh, covering the sick feeling churning inside his gut. "I bet everyone you met in prison swore they were innocent."

"Perhaps. But most of them are liars. I'm not." His gaze bored into Dillon's and something in those eyes told him Hutcheson spoke the truth.

Dillon certainly hadn't expected to feel any sympathy for the guy. He swallowed hard and nodded. "Go on. I'm listening."

"The moment I was convicted, I realized my lawyer did a lousy job. Hiring him was my first mistake, but my boss recommended him, so I assumed he was the best. He had a good reputation for winning even the most difficult cases."

"Why didn't he get you off if he was so good?"

Hutcheson snorted. "Now there's a million-dollar question." He paused as if weighing his words. Finally he added on an exhale, "I believe someone paid him to do a lousy job."

"That's a bold statement."

He shrugged. "My problem is proving it. That, and making sure I'm not railroaded a second time for the shit going on."

"You came to me because you think someone is railroading you?" Hutcheson's words sent another pang of guilt through his system. The more the man talked, the more Dillon couldn't continue believing his silence hadn't mattered. Damn. He'd acted no better than Kicker back then. Made assumptions based on an opinion and then orchestrated an outcome based on the lie he'd allowed Kicker to get away with telling.

"You tell me." Hutcheson's voice drew his focus. Yet, he couldn't keep meeting that intense gaze and had to look away as the truth hit him like a punch to the gut. He'd somehow become his father, something he'd vowed never to do. He had no clue as to how it had happened, nor was the realization easy to accept.

"I've been busy taking care of my mother." As Hutcheson continued speaking, Dillon fought to remain seated when the urge to flee from the room like a coward overwhelmed him. It took every ounce of willpower he possessed to glance back at a man he'd most likely wronged and act as if his silence hadn't played a part in ruining the man's life. "She was in an assisted living facility outside of Chattanooga. She's now in the final stages of Alzheimer's. A few months ago, I finally had to put her in a full-time nursing home, which is when I was able to get back to trying to clear my record. I started by asking questions about the maintenance records. Lo and behold, only days later I get a phone call out of the blue from my old prison bunkmate."

"Sanchez called you?" That was interesting, Dillon thought, relieved to focus on something other than guilt as Hutcheson nodded.

"A real *nice* fellow, if you know what I mean. Yet one I'd hoped never to have to sleep in the same room with again, let alone have contact with." He grunted. "But I digress. He called as a favor. To warn me. Someone's blackmailing his father into killing your dead brother's wife and kid. I'm damn sure not taking the heat for killing anyone this time."

"Someone is blackmailing Sanchez's father?" Dillon's head began to swim at the implications.

"Yeah. I couldn't make this stuff up if I wanted to. My parole stipulates I'm not supposed to talk to known felons, but I'm thankful the guy reached out to help an old cell mate."

Dillon rolled the information around in his brain, trying to see it from all angles. "Let's get back to your earlier accusation about being railroaded. Something tells me there's more to the story."

"Jimmy always said you were the brains in the family. A fellow inmate showed me how to access bank accounts from prison." Hutcheson snorted. "Can you imagine that? It's amazing how creative those guys can be, especially with a computer and access to the Internet. Jeez, they have all the time in the world and some of them become pretty adept at manipulating the system. Anyway, what I was able to discern following their advice made me dig further. Seems Reynolds, my esteemed attorney, had a deposit of one hundred thousand dollars over and above my paltry fifty grand into his account on the day I signed on with him, and another hundred on the day I was convicted. Both could be chalked up to retainers, except that according to him, he had no pending cases, nor did he take on any new cases before or during the trial and none for six weeks after. In fact, he told me not to worry and made a big deal about mine being his only case. Someone paid him off. The bastard wiped out my savings and came out a quarter of a million dollars richer. All for losing."

"I have a difficult time buying that a hard-nosed defense attorney took money to lose."

"Money I tracked back to Kane Aeronautics."

Dillon's gaze snapped to Hutcheson's, where he stared dumbfounded. Several moments ticked by before the buzz in his brain quieted enough for him to form a clear sentence. "You think Kicker paid Reynolds to lose?"

Hutcheson nodded. "He hated me enough to make sure I'd suffer. Plus, look at how he lied to save face with his own made-up version of our relationship. He knew I wouldn't refute it or do anything to hurt my ex-wife or my two children. Time in prison makes a man realize what's important in life." He pounded his knee with a fist. "I should've never tried to hide what I was. Your old man may not have wanted to believe his son was gay, but he was astute enough to know Jimmy meant something to me and me to him. Hell, setting me up for something he did was right up Kane's alley—"

"Wait…" Dillon put up a hand. "My dad wasn't involved in what happened that night. He'd never kill his own sons." He believed Kicker capable of a lot of things, even paying an attorney to lose, but not that.

"You're sure?"

"Yes, I'm sure, so let's cut to the chase. I lost a brother that night and I'll be honest, until I found out you wanted to talk, I'd always assumed you sabotaged the plane. One," he said, using his fingers to count, "you had the access. Two, you had the means, and three, you had the motive."

"There was no motive," Hutcheson ground out. "I loved Jimmy."

"That may be true, but you had no love for me. Admit it. Despite what the DA thought about your argument with Jimmy, I was your real target and that fight had nothing to do with his death. No one but you and me knew the true reasons behind it. You had no idea I was in no shape to fly that night. Peters said you—"

"Peters?" Hutcheson started laughing. "You can't be serious?" When Dillon nodded, he snorted. "He'd already left the hangar, so he couldn't have overheard shit. But I did overhear him arguing with Kicker's head mechanic earlier that day."

"You mean Steve?" When he nodded, Dillon asked, "What were they arguing about?" That was news to him.

"The mechanic wanted to ground the plane but Peters kept on him, saying Kicker felt he was being too cautious, that Kane Aeronautics was in the business of keeping planes in the air, not grounding them to recheck stuff that had already been checked."

Dillon shook his head. "Those two always argued like that. It was Peters' job to worry about the bottom line." What if Steve had done something and realized his mistake? What if Peters' harping had kept him from checking it out? He didn't really believe Steve could be guilty of negligence, but he couldn't discount the idea either. Not if Hutcheson was innocent. That meant someone else had switched the controls and that someone had to have access along with the means. Maybe there was more to why Steve quit so suddenly. Dillon definitely intended to have a word with him. At the very least, to rule him out as a suspect.

"Yeah, well, I still think your dad sabotaged the plane and Peters was just following his orders."

"No," Dillon said firmly. Peters was probably following Kicker's orders, all right. Just not in the way Hutcheson thought. "I've already told you you're wrong on that count, so figure out another scenario or this conversation is over. Are we clear?"

Nodding, Hutcheson sat back and focused on a point beyond Dillon's shoulder. After several seconds, he glanced up at him. "Then why would they argue? I know that means something. Maybe Kicker was cutting corners."

"No. He'd never cut corners. My dad's always maintained his planes following strict FAA guidelines. He's a registered airplane mechanic and had tons more experience under his belt before Steve came on board. Steve's overcautious by nature and too nitpicky. Works for my business, but not Kicker's. He can't afford planes to be down over a hunch." His dad had an instinct for determining the difference between real problems versus minor engine noises that meant nothing. It was an ongoing balancing act, even more so in the early years. "He'd never take chances when it came to his pilots or his planes." Eyeing Hutcheson, he asked, "Why didn't you say something about it back then if you thought it so important?"

"I did, and the investigators on the case wrote it all down in their little notebooks, but none of them paid much attention to anything I said. They probably figured they already had a patsy, so why make their job harder? My guess is the information got buried and my lawyer let it stay buried."

"What do you want from me?" He didn't want to believe Kicker had a hand in paying off the defense, but the niggling feeling inside his gut wouldn't subside.

"I want you to make sure nothing happens to Jimmy's son and widow."

"Okay." Dillon nodded. "What else?"

"If your dad and Peters were on the up-and-up, then I want to talk to your head mechanic and ask him why he felt the need to ground the plane that night." Hutcheson leaned forward. "Maybe he stumbled on something without knowing it."

"I can arrange a meeting." But not until he'd already had his own meeting, Dillon added mentally.

"Thanks."

"Yeah, well, don't thank me yet. I'm only doing it to prove that Kicker wasn't involved." And to do something that should have been done years ago. Find out what really happened. If Hutcheson *was* innocent, he probably wanted to plow a fist into his gut right now. Yet, here the man was thanking him for looking into something that had been overlooked. Dillon should be thanking him, but he was too much of a coward to say the words out loud and said instead, "I want to get to the bottom of this just as much as you do. Maybe more so."

"You have my number."

They both stood at the same time.

Hutcheson sighed as an agonizing look crossed his face. "You want to know the saddest part of all this?" He offered a rueful smile. "Jimmy said he'd leave his wife and come out if I'd do the same. That's what we were really arguing about. I urged Jimmy to live a double life, but he didn't want that. He couldn't stomach cheating. He respected his family more than he loved me and said he couldn't have it both ways, not like I'd had for years." His eyes misted as he added, "I couldn't stomach the thought of coming out. Hell, I was terrified of it. Thought doing so would only cause heartache. I was too afraid of the negative stigma that would follow. I was sure the plum assignments would dry up. I mean, even straight men who aren't homophobic don't want to be in the trenches with a proclaimed gay man. They might deny it, but deep down there is an underlying sense of fear. I fully understand fear. It's big part of being human. Plus, I convinced myself I had a family to protect, but really I was terrified of losing my kids." He shrugged. "In the end, I lost them anyway, along with Jimmy. Hell, I lost everything. If I can save Jimmy's son by telling you what I know, then I've done something noble…something Jimmy would be proud of."

Dillon swallowed hard and nodded as the two headed for the main entrance. He hadn't wanted to feel any sympathy for Hutcheson, but understanding how he felt made it hard not to feel even more shame for the way his silence allowed the events to play out. "I'll make sure nothing happens to them."

Hutcheson's voice was thick with regret as he added, "How foolish I was to think so naïvely. I've caused more heartache by going to prison. I've endured more heartache than a man should, that's for damn sure." He shook his head. "I keep thinking how much I'd still have if only I had been honest or if I hadn't confronted Jimmy that night."

They'd reached the condo entrance.

Before he pushed the door open, Hutcheson stopped and turned to him. His face broke into another smile that wasn't quite so sad. "Since I did end up behind bars, I try to look at the bright side. Every day I thank God I'd stayed in the closet. Prison would've been a living hell if I hadn't. Most of the men are afraid of murderers and I played up on that, so they left me alone. Still, if it brought Jimmy back and I had a do-over, I'd come out in a New York minute and be proud of what I am."

Dillon cleared his throat. "I'm sorry, man." Seemed *I'm sorry* was fast becoming his motto for the day, but what else could he say? He was sorry. He couldn't fault Hutcheson for wanting to fit in any more than he could fault Jimmy for trying to go straight.

Yeah, he was sorry, all right. Sorry that he hadn't taken the time to listen to Jimmy's side. He suddenly realized that deep down, he'd wanted his brother to end things, leaving him with the task of picking up the pieces. How could he throw stones at anyone for dishonesty when he'd lived that lie with Lauren all those years ago? Maybe she and Jimmy could have worked it out. His brother was obviously willing to try. Dillon should have done more to help, rather than just criticize.

He held the door open. As Hutcheson strode past him Dillon said with much emotion, "I never thought about what you might be going through." He never thought about what Jimmy had gone through either. The realizations only made him feel even guiltier.

"Yep," Dillon murmured, watching the man he'd judged so readily get into an old Honda Civic.

Like father, like son.

Chapter 16

The buzzer on the stove blared, jarring Lauren out of her stupor.

My dinner! She'd stared out the sliding glass door without noticing the world around her for so long, she'd forgotten all about it. Moving in slow motion, she veered toward the annoying sound.

Cooking had always soothed her soul and made her forget her troubles. Hopefully finishing the meal would provide some kind of solace, even though eating was the last thing on her mind. Once the noise was shut off, she reached for a hot pad to open the oven. It would take more than cooking to ease what troubled her this time.

Jimmy had been gay! Her face flamed and not just from the heat escaping the oven.

How had she not known? The entire time spent peering out at nothing, she'd replayed her relationship with her husband and their marriage in her mind's eye. The signs had all been there. Oh, yeah! Hindsight was twenty-twenty, all right. Which only made her feel foolish for believing someone as polished as Jimmy could love someone like her in the first place.

The chicken breasts were done. She turned off the oven. The food would keep warm and maybe Dillon could salvage the meal later. Lauren doubted she'd ever be hungry again, but couldn't bring herself to throw food away, thanks to a mother who'd grown up poor. Seemed even sillier to remember those long-ago stories her mom had told about going to bed hungry now, when Lauren was dying inside. Suddenly she felt ten years old again, enduring the loss of her mother all over again.

Oh, Mama, she prayed, blinking back tears. *How will I ever get past this?*

Despite her best efforts, a few drops escaped. What would she tell DJ? Honesty was required, but how did a mother go about telling a son something like that? Would her baby feel as bad as she did right now? Lord, she hoped not. No mother wanted to see her child suffer, nor should any child be privy to such an intimate fact about his parent.

What about Dillon, who had always known? Here she'd thought there might have been some kind of attraction between them, when in reality he'd only felt sorry for her and had used kindness to compensate for his brother's lack of attention.

Fresh tears sprang free. She wiped them away. He probably thought her pathetic and gullible, which only made her feel twice as stupid for secretly loving him all these years…and for waiting for him to come charging in on his white horse and save her from a life of loneliness.

More tears made the trek down her face, only she didn't bother wiping them away. She saw it so clearly now—the real reason she'd remained single all this time. Dillon had always remained her litmus test for a hero. No one she'd met over the years, including Thad, had ever come close to him in comparison. Yet, he'd stayed away until Kicker sent him to her. Of course, she'd made him promise to leave her alone, but that was asked and given in the heat of an argument.

Her face burned hotter over how she'd misread his concern for something deeper. A man like Dillon wouldn't let words stop him from going after what he wanted.

Lauren replaced the lid on the pan filled with water and turned on the burner under it. She then went for another beer, hoping to drown her misery. She popped the cap off and swigged several gulps as one question registered. How would she ever be able to look him in the eye again?

03

Dillon gazed distractedly out the plate glass entrance until well after Hutcheson's car had disappeared from view. Dread clenched in his gut as he stalled for time.

Finally he punched up Kicker's number. As much as he hated making this call, he needed to get to the bottom of Hutcheson's claim before he went back upstairs to face Lauren.

"Hey, son." The warmth in his father's voice reverberated through the connection and the knot in his gut twisted tighter. "I didn't expect to hear from you so soon after our last phone call."

"Yeah, well…" Dillon cleared his throat, even more hesitant to destroy the tentative friendship that had developed between them since his trip to Tampa over a month ago. He rather liked having Kicker for a friend. The thought surprised him and made him wonder how such a change had been possible in so short a time.

"Is something wrong?" Kicker said, his warm tone quickly switching to one of concern.

"I don't know." If someone had asked him six months ago if he and his father could be friends, his answer would have been an unequivocal no. He took a deep breath and decided to just blurt it out. "I called Hutcheson and met with him."

"What?" After a slight pause, his dad added, "Are you nuts?" All warmth or concern had vanished. "The man's dangerous. He's a convicted killer."

"What if he didn't do it?" The more he thought about it, the more he believed it.

"What do you mean what if he didn't do it?" Kicker asked heatedly. "Of course he did it. A jury found him guilty."

Dillon rubbed his eyes and sighed. He'd known this conversation would be hard. "I don't think he killed Jimmy. At least, not any longer after talking to him."

The line went silent for so long Dillon thought maybe he'd hung up. "Dad? You still there?"

"Yes, I'm still here. I'm dumbstruck is all, and trying to understand your change of heart."

Considering Kicker's stunned reaction, he realized sugarcoating would only prolong his chore. Nothing short of blunt honesty would get his point across in a way that let his dad know he was tired of dancing around Jimmy's homosexuality. "I was wrong to keep quiet about your spin on their relationship and I'm admitting it now."

"What are you talking about—my spin?" He clearly sounded perplexed. "I spun nothing."

"You flat-out lied, Dad. Jimmy wasn't having an affair with Hutcheson's wife and you damn well knew it."

"I told the police what I thought," he ground out. "It was their job to verify my statement."

"That's just it. You manipulated the system. You knew those in charge might never check, considering who made the claim. Hutcheson says he was railroaded, that he didn't get a fair shake."

"Then he should've spoken up and set the record straight."

"Yeah, right!" Dillon snorted. "He had his own reasons for not revealing the complete truth and setting the record straight. Just as you were hoping for, I'm sure."

"Exactly what are you insinuating?" Kicker's voice held an edge of warning.

"You know exactly what I'm insinuating, Dad," he said, exhaling the accusation on another long sigh and shaking his head. "Jimmy and Hutcheson were lovers before he married Lauren."

Again, silence permeated the line—a deafening silence.

"No. I refuse to believe that." That softly spoken denial came long seconds later and tore at Dillon's gut, as did the next words, which were much louder and angrier. "It's bullshit, goddamn it all. Total bullshit."

"It's the truth," Dillon shot back just as loud. "And if Mom were still here, you'd have accepted it long ago," he added, seeing the veracity in the allegation for the first time since her death.

"I…I…" Kicker broke off, clearly too choked up to refute his assertion.

Utilizing his dad's loss for words to his advantage, before losing the courage to speak up further, he interjected, "A lot of things changed after she died, the biggest being that disagreeing with you always ended badly for the person disagreeing." For the first time in his life, he told Kicker exactly what was on his mind. As a result, his spirit felt lighter. Freer.

"Now wait a minute, goddamn it—"

He cringed, preparing for the worst, and got in quickly, "It's true." *Please, Mom,* he silently begged, glancing briefly at the heavens. *Give me the strength to continue.*

As if his mom heard his pleas, renewed confidence washed over him and he was able to add, "No one, least of all me, ever wanted to confront you. Not when it's a losing proposition from the start." Insight filled his soul. The two of them would never have the relationship Dillon craved if he couldn't go one-on-one with his dad. The truth was on his side. He just needed to be capable of emerging victorious. "If I hadn't felt so guilty because the wrong son died, I might have questioned things a little more, which might have prevented an innocent man from going to prison for something he didn't do," Dillon said with newfound conviction.

For the third time in minutes, he'd left his father speechless. Finally Kicker asked, "You really believe that shit? That the wrong son died? Did you think that I wouldn't grieve if you'd been the pilot that night?"

"I know so."

"You're wrong," his father said on a heavy sigh. Another extended moment of silence followed until a pained voice shot through the connection. "I'm sorry if that's the way you felt."

"It was. It is," Dillon said, unwilling to back down, yet wishing he hadn't had to be so direct when Kicker sounded so old and defeated and worn out…and truly contrite.

"I'm so sorry, son. Can you ever forgive me?"

Dillon sucked in a deep breath and let it out slowly as his eyes welled up. He hadn't expected an apology, much less a plea for forgiveness. It was so unlike the man he thought he knew to beg for anything. "I already have." Blinking, he smiled into the phone, knowing without a doubt he spoke the truth. He sent up a quick thanks to his mom. "I already have."

"Then you're a better man than me, son." The sentiment spoken so fervently caused his eyes to water more. Dillon wiped the moisture away as his dad added, "I just didn't know how to deal with Jimmy, so I pretended he wasn't different. I knew something was up when he brought home a pregnant wife not long after we argued, when I told him to grow up and act like a Kane. I really screwed up and I've been trying to fix things." His father broke off again. Seconds later he asked, "You really don't think Hutcheson sabotaged the plane?" When Dillon answered in the negative, he added, "Care to tell me why? I gather that's also why you called."

"Yeah. It's just hard to get out."

"Well, I've always thought the direct approach the best. You've done an outstanding job thus far. So, don't stop now. Do your worst."

Dillon chuckled. His dad seldom joked with him this easily. He'd been so sure that after this phone call, Kicker might never speak to him again. "Okay, direct approach! Here goes." He took a deep breath and said on the exhale, "He told me someone paid off his lawyer to lose."

"That's quite a claim."

"That's what I told him and he countered, saying he traced the money back to Kane Aeronautics."

"What!" There was another long pause. "That's impossible! No one from my company would do something like that."

"I haven't seen the electronic trail, but the man assured me there is one."

"How much money are we talking about?"

"Two hundred grand."

"No." He shook his head. "Couldn't happen. I would've known if two dollars came from one of my accounts, so you can damn sure believe I'd have known about such a large amount."

Somehow he figured Kicker would deny culpability, but not so quickly or succinctly, without even thinking about it. "What if someone else did, without your knowledge?"

"In the past six months maybe, even with the accounting department's fail-safes in place. But back then?" He hesitated a moment. "I doubt it could happen. Which means he's either misinformed or trying to besmirch my character. I gotta tell you, my gut tells me to go with the latter."

"You doubt it could happen, but you're not sure," Dillon said, taking another tack. "What if someone figured out a way to do it without your knowledge?"

The silence on the other end indicated his father was considering the words. "It would be difficult, but not impossible."

"Okay, so let's just say, hypothetically of course, that it's true. How? What would it take for something like that to slide past your scrutiny?"

"Well, I need to think about that." He broke off. "Any funds going out over five hundred dollars needed a second signature. Besides that, I used to review our month-end accounts. A withdrawal of two hundred thousand would have stood out. I would have noticed it."

"Can you check it out anyway? Go back to the records for the week Jimmy was killed and the week the trial ended."

"Yes, I can access those records. I'll get right on it. May take a day or so."

Relieved over his dad's easy cooperation, Dillon spent the next few minutes updating him on the rest of his conversation with Hutcheson, including the part about his cell mate being blackmailed into killing Lauren and DJ, and last, the argument between Steve and Peters.

"You've given me a lot to think about and discuss with McCall. I'll get back with you," Kicker said with an icy remoteness that contrasted sharply with the camaraderie of the last few minutes of conversation. Then he abruptly ended the call, not even bothering to say good-bye.

Stunned, Dillon pushed the OFF button and stared at the phone, totally blindsided. He strode toward the elevator banks, wondering about his father's brusqueness. Earlier it seemed as if a barrier had been removed and suddenly the wall was back in place as tall as ever. He prayed he hadn't misread Kicker's changing attitude. Being on Kicker's good side felt a hell of a lot better than being on his bad side.

CB

After cutting the connection with Dillon, Kicker looked over at Sophie, who stood in the doorway. "I take it you heard the gist of the conversation?" he asked, not bothering to pretend she hadn't. Sophie had an instinct for when problems escalated, and he sensed she grasped that all was not well. Which had to be the reason she'd stoop to eavesdropping now.

"What was that all about?" She walked further into the room and sat across from him. She then picked up a decorating magazine and began thumbing through it, acting bored. "Sounded like you were asking the prodigal son for forgiveness."

Kicker shrugged. "Yes. That was Dillon." Judging from the

comment, he knew she was anything but bored. "I'd like to think we've mended some fences."

Sophie nodded. After a slight pause, she asked, "Is something wrong with Peters?"

"I don't know, but I definitely need to talk to him. There're a lot of inconsistencies in what supposedly went on right before Jimmy died." He didn't feel compelled to explain further about his son's relationship with Hutcheson. Shrewd as she was, she'd probably already guessed, considering her attempts to discredit Lauren all those years ago, claiming DJ wasn't a Kane. Lucky for him his daughter-in-law was more forgiving for his shoddy treatment of her, insinuating she was little better than a money-grubbing whore. Although he'd denied it at the time, he'd known from the beginning DJ was Jimmy's kid. Hell, the infant was the mirror image of his son at the same age. He'd just thought Lauren had gotten her hooks into Jimmy and had planned to use the kid to bleed them dry.

Seems they were both wrong. Only his *wrong* gave him much more to atone for than his wife's.

"You don't think it's associated with the attack on Rory today?" About to flip the page, her hand stilled, and she looked up. "You mentioned something about a hit?"

Yep! Sophie never missed a beat, not if it involved him or her son. "There's nothing to worry about," he said to ease her fears. "McCall's on it. Tampa PD has a BOLO out on Sanchez, who supposedly is being blackmailed into it. He won't get far once he's inside city limits. Rory's safe. DJ's safe. As long as they stay in the compound, they'll both be fine."

"What kind of inconsistencies would involve Peters?" Her attention went back to the magazine. "Why all of a sudden are you worried about him when he's been your right-hand man for all these years?" She was silent for a moment. "I told you not to trust him," she added in that acerbic, know-it-all tone he'd grown to hate. "He isn't family and Rory is more than capable of taking his place."

"I don't know what's going on. In fact, it could be nothing," he said, brushing the topic aside, not wanting to get into another argument about Rory filling the number two spot. Peters had been too loyal an employee to just toss aside, especially when Rory was still a little wet behind the ears. He could just imagine her reaction when she discovered he'd offered Dillon his job. "I won't know until I talk to Peters, when I can look him in the eye to gauge his honesty. Dillon thinks Hutcheson may be innocent." He spent a moment updating her on the argument between Steve and Peters, leaving out the part about the money.

"Hmmm. Seems you should talk to your ex-mechanic too." She flipped a page. "Didn't he quit—like the next day?"

Kicker nodded. "Yes. But Peters didn't mention anything about his wanting to ground the plane," he said. He didn't add that in the weeks before the fatal accident, Steve had discovered a few problems and had gone over Peters' head to get Kicker's opinion. Nothing major, just engines sounding too rough or some other part that intuitively didn't seem right, things that were easily corrected. What if Steve had found something back then? He specifically remembered telling Peters to stop discounting Steve and his hunches. Why hadn't Peters followed his orders that night? Had he been so obsessed with the bottom line, he'd ignored them? Only Peters could answer that question, and goddamn it all, he definitely planned on asking.

"Well, I don't care about Peters or your ex-mechanic," Sophie said, her razor-sharp voice cutting into his thoughts. "It's in the past. Rory is my main concern." She peered over the top of her magazine and eyed him intently. "Can you assure me he'll be okay?"

"What could possibly happen when I've taken so many precautions?" he snapped, annoyed that she was so tunnel-visioned.

She flinched and he bit back the next retort on the tip of his tongue, wishing Sophie could be more like Catherine. His first wife had cared about much more than just her immediate family. Everyone had loved her. There hadn't been a dry eye at her funeral. Yet, Sophie was Rory's mother and a damn good one at that. Digging deep for patience, he said, "No one can breach the property from the water because McCall's man will be watching. And so far, no one has ever scaled the eighteen-foot stucco wall, and no one can get through the iron gates without the right password."

Chapter 17

A noise from the front door drew Lauren's focus. She looked over to glimpse Dillon stepping into the condo hallway and glancing around, most likely searching for her. She turned up the burner under the pan filled with near-boiling water, then moved to the sink to run cold water on a paper towel and used it to blot her face. She prayed her eyes weren't all puffy.

His footsteps grew louder until they stopped behind her. "Are you okay?"

Am I okay? God! How could he ask such an inane question? She spun around and squared her shoulders. "What do you think? You've just dropped a bombshell on me that blew to bits any and all fond memories of my deceased husband and you ask me if I'm okay." She couldn't control her rising voice. "Just in case there's any doubt, let me assure you that NO, I am not okay." Too angry to continue meeting his gaze, she grabbed a fistful of pasta, broke it in two, and tossed into the now-boiling water.

"If I could make it better I would. I never wanted to see you hurt."

"Oh, that's rich," she said on a forced laugh. At this point, laughing in front of him was better than crying. "What bugs me the most is you couldn't tell me back then when it's obviously something you've known all along." She reached for a fork to separate the bubbling noodles. Thank God she had something to do. Once the meal was cooked, she'd force the food down, just to show him it didn't matter.

"I've already told you why."

"Yeah?" Lauren slammed the fork on the counter so hard her knuckles took the brunt, but the surge of anger muffled any pain. "Then why did you wait fifteen years? Knowing something like that sooner definitely would've answered a lot of questions."

"You know why. You were very clear during our last conversation about never wanting to lay eyes on me again. So, what was I supposed to do? Make it worse?"

"Yes! I thought you were my friend. This just tells me you care nothing for my feelings."

"So, sue me for being a heartless bastard," he said with a clenched jaw, struggling for control. Swearing softly, he ran a hand through his hair and rubbed the back of his neck.

Her ranting was definitely driving him crazy, but damn it all, she felt entitled.

"I've already said I was sorry." His voice rose slightly. "What more do you want?"

"The same thing I've always wanted. To never lay eyes on you again." She shouted the words—it felt so good—then turned and stormed toward the bedroom, needing to get away from him.

"Oh, no you don't," he said, chasing after her. "You're not going to run away again."

"I'm not running," she said. Well, she was, but she'd die before admitting as much.

He chuckled. Only the sound held little humor. "Go ahead and pretend. I know better. You *are* running. It's what you're good at."

She stopped dead in her tracks. "How dare you?" She blinked back tears and marched right back to him, not bothering to keep the hurt from her eyes. To hide emotions that seemed to suddenly spill out all the faster, she dropped her gaze to his chest. Her finger followed, stabbing him as if to make a point with her next heated words. "You know nothing of what I've been through."

"I dare because it's the truth." His lips twisted in a snarl. "I know enough to understand that we need to talk this out."

"What's left to say?"

"Plenty." Dillon grabbed her hand and held it. "Please," he added in a lower voice sounding grave and full of remorse. "Just talk to me." Even his eyes pleaded and tugged on her heartstrings, but she'd already been foolish once. Only a bigger fool would return for more.

"I can't." She pulled out of his grip. As much as she craved giving in, she didn't dare. "Talking at this point will only make things worse. I doubt I can handle any more honesty right now." Pride was all she had left at this point. She turned toward his guest room.

"I never thought you were a coward."

Again she halted and shook her head, expelling a long sigh. Finally she glanced back at him and smiled ruefully. "I think we both know who the real coward in this room is. You had your chance to make things right years ago and you didn't."

"Touché, Lauren." His voice held a cutting edge that was all Dillon. "I guess I deserved that." Unfortunately, she also caught an unexpected trace of pain that threw her.

She studied his face more thoroughly. He looked tired. And defeated. And just plain sad. So sad that she could no longer leave in an angry huff. Besides, his words about running galled her. She'd show him she was no coward.

"Let's call a truce, shall we?" she said, intent on proving him wrong while trying to assuage some of his pain. After all, he'd been stuck in the middle during her marriage to his brother.

"Fine," he said on a small sigh, adding a semblance of a smile that took years off the strain covering his face.

"Dinner is almost ready." She attempted a cheerful smile, one that lacked enthusiasm, so it probably came across as brittle instead. "While we eat you can tell me what Hutcheson had to say."

His grin widened and he inhaled deeply. "Smells good. What do you need me to do?"

Relieved that he was following her lead, she pointed to the silverware drawer. "You can set the table to start with." Reaching for the hot pad, she added, "The pasta is ready to drain. As soon as the steamed vegetables are done, we can eat."

"Great. I'm starved."

Acting as if they'd done it every night for the last ten years, they worked silently side by side. God, if only this easy companionship were real, she thought, furtively watching him open the cupboards and pull out two plates.

How she was able to finish preparing the food without an outward sign of the excruciating pain piercing her heart, she had no idea. Learning of Jimmy's betrayal really hurt, which meant she had to be strong. Stronger than she'd ever had to be, even stronger than those early days with DJ.

She dished everything out before handing the platter of chicken and the bowl of pasta to Dillon to take to the table. Then she picked up the vegetables and followed.

He held out her chair and helped her into it before sitting in the one across from her.

"Lauren, can't we talk about it?" Dillon asked as she draped her napkin over her lap. "Please?"

Something in his tone had her almost backing down. Only her deep-seated vulnerability wouldn't allow her to risk his rejection. She shook her head and stoically met his gaze, careful to keep her hurts hidden. "There's nothing to talk about."

"I disagree. There's a lot we have to talk about, the biggest being the fact that I've always loved you."

Her eyes began to burn and her throat constricted. Swallowing the small bite she'd taken seemed impossible. "Please don't," she whispered once she'd gotten it down. Of course he'd always loved her. As a friend or a sister-in-law. The same way she was supposed to love him. "I can't deal with platitudes tonight."

"No platitudes. Only the truth. I do love you. I've always loved you, even when I didn't have the right."

God, how she wanted to believe it! Was dying to believe it, but she couldn't. Not when her past appeared sordid and ugly. Full of lies. Without a handle on what was real and what wasn't, she couldn't risk another loss. "How's this for the truth? I don't want to hear any proclamations of love. Not tonight." Hell, she couldn't be sure he wasn't merely being the same old Dillon she'd always relied on to ease the pain his brother caused. How could she not have understood his motivations before now? "Let's just finish eating. Then we can clean up and I can retire to my room." She focused on cutting a piece of chicken covered with marinara sauce, pierced it with her fork, and brought the food to her mouth. "I'm really tired."

Still not looking his way, she concentrated on chewing with one driving need, to escape to the privacy of her room. Then she could mourn without an audience and plan a future—an insurmountable task when her life had turned out to be based on lies.

☙

Screaming silence pervaded the room for several long moments, during which Dillon kept surreptitiously glancing Lauren's way. Hell, even after she'd practically torn his head off, he'd still revealed his biggest secret. And her response? She didn't want to talk. Worse, she didn't seem to believe him.

He knew he wasn't the best communicator. He'd really botched things during that last argument fifteen years ago when she told him she never wanted to see him again. Obviously the past was repeating itself. He just didn't know how to get out what churned inside of him without making a bigger mess of the situation. His drunken raving hadn't helped back then, but now that he was lucid, he still couldn't seem to make himself understood.

Finally he pushed his plate away. His appetite had long since deserted him and he couldn't continue the charade of eating any longer. Judging by the way she just stirred food around on her plate, she wasn't hungry either. "I'm done."

"But you've barely touched your meal."

"I guess I wasn't as hungry as I thought."

"We can't just waste all this food." Her tone and expression said it all. The idea appalled her.

"Fine." He shrugged. "I'll put it away and eat it for leftovers."

"I'll help."

They stood and reached for the platter at the same time. His fingers brushed hers and she yanked her hand back so fast you'd have thought he'd burned her. Annoyance streaked up his spine.

"Damn it, you don't have to flinch like I'm some monster," Dillon blurted out. He'd felt the jolt too, but he wasn't the one who was running away again. She was. It made him mad. Damn mad. Mad enough to place his guilt over Hutcheson on the back burner. At least for the moment.

He bit his tongue to keep from calling her on her bullshit right then and there. Too many emotions still roiled around in his gut, a strong sign that now was not the best time to point out more truths. Damn, how he wanted to grab her by the shoulders and yell, hoping to shake some sense into her. He clenched his fists to still the urge to touch her. He didn't dare. If he did, he wouldn't be able to stop until she was in his arms and once there, he knew he'd have to kiss her. Then one thing might lead to another...

In the end he'd only muck things up worse and still be this needy bastard who'd always wanted his brother's wife. God, how had he sunk so low?

Together they stored the food, both lost in their thoughts, his becoming more and more agitated the longer the silence continued. As he worked, he struggled harder to see her position. How would he react if faced with the same betrayal? Maybe he didn't deserve to have her love him, considering his past sins, but damn it, life was too short not to at least try. When he stowed the last bowl in the fridge, he turned back to her.

"Lauren, why are we acting like nothing is wrong?" he asked abruptly, unable to stop the burst of anger. "Especially when you know full well we have to talk and clear the air," he said, almost shouting. Noting the way she jumped, he took a deep breath and rolled his shoulders back, fighting to relax and not yell louder. "You weren't at fault," he said a bit softer. "Jimmy was." And he was too, for falling in love with her in the first place. He had no idea how to make it better, even less how to make her see that his and Jimmy's failure at honesty hadn't been her failure. "You've done nothing wrong, so why keep running?"

"Then why do I feel so stupid?" Her sad voice twisted his gut into a tighter knot.

"Is that how you feel?"

She nodded, and silently continued washing.

Damn, why hadn't he stayed out of their relationship in the first place? He'd known she'd leaned on him when his brother had been distant. Hell, he'd relished the task. Deep down he wondered if he'd been waiting for Jimmy to admit the truth so he could swoop in and play Sir Galahad. Now, Jimmy was dead and she needed someone to lean on, a white knight. He was dying to be her hero. "You're not going to talk to me? I always thought we were friends who could talk to each other."

She took a moment to wipe her eyes then shook her head. Every bit of his anger died a quick death. It unmanned him to see her tears, knowing he was part of the reason why. Somehow, he not only had to make her see what was in his heart, he had to make her believe it. Deciding to honor her request for now, he picked up the dishtowel and began drying the pans she'd already washed.

"Okay," Dillon said, hanging up his towel after drying and putting away the last pot. He snatched the cloth she was using to wipe off the counters and draped it over the sink divider. "You've worked hard enough. Time to relax."

Lauren glanced at him.

"I'm not letting you escape without talking," he said, answering the question emanating from her eyes. "Resign yourself to it." He nodded to the black leather sofa in his living room. "I know you don't want anything to do with me, but I think it's important we clear the air. That way you'll understand why Jimmy did what he did and why I did what I did. Once you know, you won't feel so stupid."

"I gather I don't have a choice in the matter?" Her usual glib tone brought a smile to his face.

"None whatsoever." The fact that she was using humor was a good sign. "It may take some time, so you might as well make yourself comfortable."

"I have a feeling I'm going to need another drink, and something a lot stronger than beer."

"If I'm about to reveal everything, something stronger sounds like a good idea," he said in the same jovial tone. "I have bourbon. Is that okay?"

"Bourbon's fine."

"Plain or on the rocks?"

"Rocks," she said.

Dillon walked to the liquor cabinet at the far end of the kitchen, using the task to organize his thoughts. When done with pouring the bourbon, he picked up his drink and took a long sip. Unable to stall any longer, he snatched Lauren's glass and strode purposefully toward her.

She sat on his black leather couch, just staring at a distant point.

"Here you go."

"Thanks." She took the drink he held out.

He sat across from her, his gaze fixed on the condensation forming on the outside of the glass. He wiped away a few drops, still searching for the right words.

When he hadn't yet spoken after more long seconds, she folded her arms and said, "I'm listening."

"I'm getting to it." He swigged one mouthful and then another, letting the bourbon warm his insides as it slid into his belly. Dillon finally cleared his throat and admitted, "This isn't easy. I want you to know that."

"Then it's good that you're drinking bourbon. I'm sure after a few, it won't seem so hard."

He smiled. "Guess I should gulp the rest down faster."

"Knock yourself out. Just don't blame me for the headache in the morning. You're the one who needs to *talk*."

Great. She's still joking. "Here's to talking," he said, holding up his glass in an implied toast. He slammed back more than a mouthful and relished the burning as more liquid fire hit his gut. After a few seconds, a mellow, fuzzy feeling filled his brain. Amazing what a little alcohol did for taking the edge off and loosening the tongue, as suddenly talking didn't seem the same chore it had only minutes ago.

"I guess I should begin when I first realized Jimmy was different. Even as a kid, I'd recognized his sensitivity. As I got older, I just assumed everyone was like him. By my last year of high school, I noticed the dichotomy in his behavior. His sensitivity and caring just didn't coincide with his macho all-American, football-toting persona. I don't know why I instinctively knew he wasn't like the other guys on the team. Outwardly, he appeared the same. He was never without friends, both male and female." Even when Dillon hadn't understood what being "gay" really meant, he'd known Jimmy connected with the girls on a different level, and some of the guys he made friends with in college weren't the usual jocks he'd always associated with.

"In college, I guessed the truth. The female friends always seemed to be a cover. He still maintained his jock friends, but he started hanging out with guys more like him in personality. At first it seemed as if they were just brainier, but too many times I'd catch them noticing Jimmy in covert ways. I kept the information to myself. I loved Jimmy. His choice of friends wasn't any of my business.

"When Jimmy started hanging around Hutcheson more and more, I finally put two and two together, but he'd never admitted it outright. His being gay never really affected me one way or the other. It was part of who he was and I loved him. I mean, hell, he was still the same wonderful person inside." Dillon cleared his throat, remembering the way Jimmy had always consoled him when Sophie had hurled some snide comment meant to hurt. His big brother had always been there for him. "Sure, it seemed a little weird, but it didn't really matter. In my eyes, Jimmy was perfect, and God had to have a reason for making him that way, so who was I to mess with perfection? I was only too glad that he'd found someone he could connect with."

Ronald Hutcheson had seemed like an okay guy until Dillon found out he was married. But before he could confront Jimmy about him, the guy was suddenly out of the picture. He didn't start worrying until Jimmy met Lauren, married her only three months later, and within a few more had a baby on the way. Dillon had asked his brother outright what was going on. Jimmy had only brushed his concerns away, saying Ron had only been an experiment gone bad. It was time to grow up and face his responsibilities. The words had sounded too much like Kicker for Dillon not to grasp where they'd originated.

He looked at Lauren and more anguish filled his heart as he tried to explain his actions. "All those times you cried on my shoulder, asking why he seemed so distant, I wanted to tell you, but I couldn't. It wasn't my place." He scrubbed a hand over his face, unable to look her in the eyes any longer. "I can't tell you how many times Jimmy assured me he wasn't gay. Said he loved you and DJ. I knew deep down in my heart, he was just avoiding facing the truth."

"So, the affair with Hutcheson's wife was some kind of cover?"

He nodded and finally risked a glance in her direction. He swallowed a lump in his throat as she blinked back tears. "Yeah. That was Kicker's spin. My dad's never been able to accept the truth about Jimmy, and Jimmy could never disappoint him." He sighed. "Which I consider his biggest obstacle to being honest."

"Did Jimmy have an affair with Hutcheson while he was with me?" Her soft question, spoken barely above a whisper, held pain and her eyes flashed torment.

"No," he stated firmly, shaking his head and thanking God this truth didn't have to hurt her further. "I'm sure he didn't. In fact, that was the reason for the argument everyone saw. Hutcheson wanted Jimmy to do just that and Jimmy refused, saying he respected you more than he loved Hutcheson."

Whether the man used his wife as a cover or not, cheating was cheating, which is what Dillon had told Jimmy when Hutcheson showed up out of the blue again. His brother was worth more.

Dillon paused a moment to take another sip of bourbon.

"Around the time Hutcheson left the country, Kicker started making waves about us getting married and having grandkids. Jimmy had been out of college for two years and Kicker wasn't getting any younger. He wanted grandsons to carry on his name and fortune. No one was happier than my dad when Jimmy announced he'd married. Until he learned you were pregnant. He'd just assumed you were one of Jimmy's strays that he'd picked up."

Hell, that's what Dillon had thought too. In the beginning. "You were very pregnant when you first met Kicker and Sophie. What else could they think?" Dillon had been as shocked as Kicker, only for a different reason. He'd gotten to know Lauren and grasped early on that she wasn't in it for the money. She'd loved his brother. She'd been so young and vulnerable. "Jimmy kept insisting he wasn't gay. That he loved you. He said too many times how much you needed him, and that was all that mattered. I think he needed to be needed."

"You think he loved me?" Lauren asked, her expression hopeful. Tears streamed down the sides of her face.

Nodding, his heart swelled with love and compassion. "Yes," he whispered earnestly, allowing the truth to show in his eyes so she'd have no choice but to believe him.

"Shush," he whispered, wiping her tears away with the pads of his thumbs. She had the softest skin, now swollen and red due to too many tears. He now doubly regretted helplessly observing the emotional train wreck taking place. One that, in the end, left no one untouched. The worst was watching Lauren try to hang on to the Jimmy she'd thought he was when he'd withdrawn and hadn't wanted to admit the real reason. Dillon wrapped his arms around her, giving in to the urge to protect her from hurt, but realizing his silence had hurt her the most.

"All I'd ever wanted back then was for someone to love me and take care of me," she said into his shoulder. The soft words pierced his heart. Lord, he'd loved her and still did.

"Jeez, Lauren." He leaned away to view her face. "You're the most lovable person I know." He smiled and waited for her to look at him. When their gazes locked he hid nothing, wanting her to see the honesty in his eyes. "It was hard not to fall in love with you. I wanted you so damn bad, I got drunk and said things I didn't mean." His own eyes misted. "Can you ever forgive me?"

"I don't understand." Her brow furrowed in confusion.

"Admit it, Lauren. There's always been something between us. I know damn well you've felt it. I'd seen it too often not to mistake it."

"That was wrong." She tore her gaze away from his and shook her head. "I wasn't free to feel that way."

"No! Jimmy was wrong for trying to be something he wasn't and for holding on to something that wasn't his."

"But I was his," she insisted, recapturing his stare. "Don't you see? We had a wonderful marriage in the beginning."

"Did you ever have this with him?" he asked, lowering his mouth to hers. He never meant to kiss her, but jealousy reared its ugly head and spurred him on. Dillon couldn't believe after all these years he still harbored the sentiment toward his dead brother. Yet, hearing her words about being Jimmy's enraged him. God! Maybe he *had* misread his brother. Even as he kissed her, he couldn't expel that last conversation with him.

"You're just jealous because I have her and you can't," Jimmy had shouted.

"No. You're living a goddamned lie. To impress a man who doesn't deserve it," he'd yelled right back.

"You're wrong. Lauren loves me and we have a child together. I won't give that up."

"And what about Ronald?" He'd remembered hurling the words like a weapon, hoping to hurt his brother, but all Jimmy had done was shrug and ask, "What about him?"

Even as Dillon lost himself more in Lauren's mouth, jealousy and craving and unworthiness all warred with each other exactly as they had long ago. Need finally edged out on top.

Lauren might have thought it was true, but if Jimmy had owned her heart and soul, their attraction wouldn't have existed. And she'd never kiss him like she was doing right now. Nothing would change that truth in his mind.

He broke the kiss. Still breathing hard, he asked, "Then why is your heart beating so fast against mine." He nipped again, then kissed his way across her face, to her neck. Up to her ear, where he spent a moment nibbling. When she moaned, he whispered, "And why is your skin flushed and your breathing labored." He broke the connection, then caught her gaze and held fast, her chest still rising and falling in quick succession. "Tell me you don't feel it." He leaned closer.

Her heartbeat sped up and her "no" came out in a long sigh.

Smiling, he shook his head. "I don't buy it. This attraction is bigger than both of us. Always has been. From the moment we met. You and I were meant to be together, not Jimmy and you."

"No…" She averted her gaze, only his mouth lowered, caught her chin, and worked its way to her lips.

"Don't lie, Lauren," he said between kisses. "I won't believe you."

She moaned. "You're just doing this to be nice. To make me feel better. To make me feel desirable rather than stupid."

He laughed. "You are desirable. Can't you feel how much?" He then guided her fingers to his now full arousal.

She kept her hand in place for several long seconds. When she began stroking, he didn't think he could grow any bigger. *Wrong.* He closed his eyes, luxuriating in her touch. "Damn, I want to be inside you so much. It's all I've dreamed about for too long, even when I had no business dreaming it." His lips found hers again, becoming more urgent. "Love me, Lauren. I need you," he whispered between kisses.

 барб

Drowning in sensation, Lauren continued meeting Dillon's urgent demands. His kisses heated her insides and created a desire to give in and see what happened next. She'd never felt this rush of longing. She'd never felt so free, so alive, or so attuned to another's touch. She'd never felt another's need so readily. Knowing that she was the cause left her breathless and made her mind swim in a deeper sea of pleasure. Dillon's mouth left her lips and he slowly kissed his way to her neck and ears. Her head went back, opening herself to everything he offered and more.

"See what you do to me?" he said, taking little nibbles then spending an inordinate amount of time lavishing those hot lips on her ear.

Lord, it felt good. Too good.

Stifling a moan, she was able to get out a breathless, "But we're friends. You said so yourself." She inhaled. Then exhaled. Tingles of pure pleasure seeped from her core, through her limbs, all the way to her fingers and toes. Her lips parted and a moan slipped free. She had to stop him now. One second more and the strength to resist him would desert her. "You'll regret this." In reality, the regrets would be hers. "I can't live with your regrets." Or her own.

Leaning in, he positioned them so that they were both prone, then moved on top of her, his firm erection nestled too close to her center. "Can't you feel my need," he said, rubbing softly. Liquid fire consumed her and even two pairs of shorts separating them did nothing to slow the flames. Only increased her desire to shed the cloth barriers.

Jimmy never set her on fire this way. Of course not. He'd been gay.

The thought registered and she stiffened. She was about to push Dillon away when his mouth found hers again. At first his lips grazed hers with almost kisses, extracting another soft moan as well as more spine-tingling pleasure when the kiss deepened.

He broke the kiss. His breathing was ragged as he snared her gaze. "Do you really believe that I'd regret doing something I've wanted to since I met you?"

Too much honesty shone from his eyes, wringing more emotion from her heart. Why couldn't she have met him first? Then she wouldn't feel so guilty. Okay, so Jimmy had lied to her. But hadn't she been lying to him? Dillon hadn't lied when he said the attraction had always existed. She'd wanted him too, but she'd been too afraid to admit as much.

What would it hurt to find out? So what if she questioned his intent? So what if she'd regret her actions in the morning? For the first time in her life, she was willing to take a chance.

Her lips found his again. A surge of love filled her heart, and her mouth demanded more of him, one kiss at a time, as the emotion roiling inside her spurred her forth. She'd certainly never been this aggressive in the past.

Dillon groaned. The sound sent another burst of exhilaration through her. Made her feel powerful. Almost sexy. She increased the intensity of her kisses, using her mouth to entice him, even going so far as to add her tongue.

Another groan floated past her ears. She wasn't sure whether it was his groan or hers, but it didn't matter because she was too caught up in sensation to care or worry about embarrassment. Suddenly his hands were everywhere. Stroking. Caressing. Touching. Reaching places she never knew existed. Places kept hidden a lifetime.

Why him? Why did being in his arms, kissing him, having his hands possessing her, seem so right? Lord, but she wanted this. "Love me, Dillon," she whispered.

Right now, he owned her body and soul, she suddenly realized. He'd always been there for her when her husband hadn't.

"I already do." He rose up and helped her shed her shirt, along with her shorts. Then using his teeth, he drew her bra strap down an inch at a time, tugging until her breast was free. At that point, his mouth caught her nipple. As he suckled, pleasure shot straight to her core.

Dillon loves me…

She wanted it all and God help her, Jimmy didn't seem to matter any longer. Her husband had been dead and buried for too many years. Besides that, he'd lied to her. She'd be a fool to allow him to affect her happiness from the grave.

Now nearly naked and deciding he should join her, she tugged his shirt above his short's waistband. He flinched as her hands grazed his midriff to undo the snap. She gazed into his eyes and boldly unzipped his shorts an inch at a time. He caught on to her plan to tease him as she undressed him. He stood it for long seconds before the pad of his thumb lovingly traced the side of her face, continuing down her body, all the way to her hand. He squeezed her fingers and brought them to his mouth, sucking each one as he held her stare, watching her reaction.

Lauren inhaled a steadying breath and let it out as he quickly yanked off his shirt and tossed it behind him. He then slipped out of the shorts and stood above her, his erection poking out of his underwear. He was a magnificent man. Well-muscled arms attached to broad shoulders that narrowed to a firm waist. Her Adonis, she thought when he bent to take her in his arms. His muscles flexed, but he lifted her as if she weighed nothing, which almost made her laugh, since she knew better. Still, he carried her with the ease of a man who worked out regularly. His actions made her feel all the more feminine…all the more alluring. She'd damn well never felt this way with Jimmy. Only she didn't want to think of him. She wanted to think of Dillon. Of how well his body fit with hers after he'd carefully placed her on the bed, then shed his briefs, dispensed with her bra and panties and joined her. He rubbed his erection over that juncture between her thighs. In seconds, warmth flooded her system. Heavens, he was big. Even though he seemed to be allowing her to get used to its massive size. "Love me, Dillon. I've waited a lifetime for you. I don't want to wait one more second to have you."

"My sentiments exactly," he said, sliding inside her, much easier than she'd thought possible.

Dillon took his time slowly stroking in and out. As he continued, all she could think about, besides the building mind-numbing pleasure, was why she had run for so long when loving him seemed like coming home.

Chapter 18

José pushed aside the shabby blackout drape and peered out at the dark parking lot. One streetlight at the far end shone weakly, but didn't do much other than to create more shadows.

Swearing under his breath, he dropped the drape and began to pace. He was edgy and pissed off that he'd sunk low enough to be hiding out in the first place. He was José Sanchez, leader of the Warmongers. He shouldn't have to put up with this shit.

But the kid was still alive after the homies he'd called on earlier for help hadn't delivered. José didn't dare give the okay to try again. Even if he found someone else who'd risk it with two homeboys in jail, there were only so many times he could make it look like a gangland slaying gone wrong. Since every cop was probably on the lookout after every fucking effort on his part had failed, he was out of options.

As a precaution, he'd arranged for his son to head for Mexico.

His cell phone rang and he started. Glancing at the caller ID, he froze for a heartbeat, then angrily punched the CONNECT button and put the phone to his ear. "What now?"

The entire time the asshole on the other end railed him up and down about his ineptness, he subdued the impulse to throw the phone across the room.

"I ain't doing shit," he finally said when his caller demanded that he finish the job. By now, Carlos should be well across the border. He had no idea why he hadn't thought of it months ago when this monkey first climbed onto his back. If he had, he damn sure wouldn't be hiding out in this fleabag motel, running from the law like a scared little *chica.*

He'd already packed his bags back in Pemberton. Once he said his good-byes to his homies, he planned to be on his way to Mexico to join Carlos. A vacation seemed the best way out of this mess.

"If you want the bitch and her brat gone, then kill them yourself." As far as he was concerned those two had more lives than a cat, and killing them would only make his life more miserable. "You hear that, *mi amigo?* I'm done. "

"Have you forgotten about the evidence I possess against your son?" the caller asked. "It would be tragic for the DA to somehow obtain proof of his illegal activities."

He studied his fingernails and said, "Do what you gotta do."

The line went silent for long seconds, an obvious attempt to intimidate. Hell, he'd used similar tactics a thousand times himself not to recognize the ploy, but he was done with being intimidated.

"You realize he'll go back to jail."

José smiled. "That's a chance I'll just have to take."

More silence followed.

"How about money? Everyone can use extra money."

"I got your first hundred grand and I ain't giving it back, *comprende?*" That would pay for a lot of margaritas, not to mention a few senoritas. If the asshole wanted a refund, he'd have to find him first. "I figure we'll just call it even on your deposit, seeing's how I'm now a fugitive."

"If you'd done what I paid you to do a month ago, you'd be another hundred thousand richer and no one would know."

"Yeah, well, shit didn't go down the way you planned, now did it?" His main concern was staying out of jail. Once the heat died, he'd be back. Under an alias, of course. He had *amigos* who'd provide the papers. "Look, I gotta go." He'd ditch the phone on his way out of town. "It's been nice doing business with you," he lied. He was just about to disconnect when his caller hurriedly said, "Don't hang up. You haven't heard my proposition."

Against his better judgment, he brought the phone back to his ear. "Make it fast."

"An extra two hundred and fifty thousand ought to be worth one last try?"

"Yeah, right," he grunted, shaking his head. "You must think I'm *loco.* Keep your goddamned money."

"At least hear me out before you decide against it." The voice paused a moment then added, "You'll get that money up front, just like before, and I'll give you the number to an online account for another two fifty when the job's done."

"Keep talking. I'm listening." He couldn't believe he was actually interested, but that was a shitload of greenbacks. Added to his hundred grand, he'd have enough to last a lifetime south of the border in luxury. He and Carlos would never have to come back. "I suppose you have a plan?" Stupid frickin' question, since he knew the asshole had a plan and he was going to hear it, because he was too greedy a bastard to pass up so much easy money.

"Yes. How adept are you at breaking and entering, especially security gates?"

"I know my way around gates and locked houses," he boasted.

"Good. Then you'll have no trouble breaking into Kane's big house while everyone's sleeping. I can even provide his password."

He smiled knowingly. "You must be close to the owner to have his password." He'd always thought as much and it narrowed his search.

The caller just laughed. "Let's just say he's an arrogant son of a bitch who thinks he's smarter than everyone else." The caller snorted. "Any idiot who's known him a few years can figure it out." As the voice rattled on, Sanchez made a mental note to have Gonzales, his number two man, run his own investigation. "He uses the call signs of his first two planes. In his defense, I will say he switches them around every month or so."

José wrote down the numbers and his grin widened. The Internet made blackmail from Mexico real doable.

"And once inside, you kill everyone," the caller added, pulling his attention. "Then walk out five hundred thousand richer."

"Everyone?" That was new.

"*Everyone*. That won't be a problem."

"Hell no." In fact it made it easier, almost too easy for just spraying a few bullets. They'd be dead before they knew what hit 'em, and he'd make half a mil. All for doing something he was a pro at—sneaking into houses after picking locks or scaling walls designed to keep people like him out. He'd been doing that kind of shit since he was old enough to run.

His caller went on to explain the layout of the house and a few particulars, all of which he also wrote down.

The voice hesitated. "But it has to be tonight."

"Tonight?" He frowned, glancing first at his watch and then at the ceiling. A spider crawled into his line of vision and a foreboding chill ran up his spine. It was well after ten. "Shit, man I'm three, maybe four hours from Tampa."

"Not a problem. In fact, the later the better. That way the entire household will be sound asleep. They definitely won't be expecting an attack from within this soon."

As the caller went into great detail about where he could pick up the bag with half the money, José rolled the idea of another all-nighter around in his brain. He'd spent too long on the road last night and didn't relish doing it again. Still, how hard could it be? If no one would be expecting a prowler? Besides, stalking was his specialty, he reminded himself. So he had to drive a few hours. He'd use a silencer, get in, and get out.

Or maybe he'd just take off with the money. Yeah, that sounded easier.

"Once the job is done, I'll call you to fill you in on the online account information. Just don't get any ideas of stealing my money without earning it. Remember, I'll be watching. Screw me and you won't be able to run fast enough or far enough, because I'll eventually catch up with you," the voice said in a menacing tone that sent another chill down José's back and made him think twice about double-crossing his monkey. "And when I do, no one will care that a two-bit gang-banger who's wanted in three states got shot in the back. Do I make myself clear?"

"As glass," José said, smiling. He had to hand it to his caller. He understood human greed. "What about the lady?"

"I'll worry about that later. You just handle the others. Tonight!"

José hung up, suddenly in a hurry. He quickly gathered all his gear and headed for the stolen car with full intentions of making some easy money, then getting the hell out of town.

Killing everyone in the house might even ease some of his frustration over not being able to get his hands on the real person he wanted to kill. The frickin' monkey.

Chapter 19

Lauren inhaled a contented breath, luxuriating in the aftermath of their lovemaking. She never knew sex could be so wonderful, so satisfying, or so damned enjoyable.

"Did you ever get your degree?" Dillon asked, lifting her hand. The question registered amid tingles as his mouth lingered on the pulse spot at her wrist. Eventually he began kissing the length of her arm, stopping at her neck.

She smiled, remembering their long-ago conversation where she'd told him her one big regret. Dropping out of college to have DJ. Not that she'd ever regret having the joy of her life.

He gave her one last kiss, then situated her in the crook of his arm and shoulder and said, "Well, did you?"

"No," she said on the exhale of another deep sigh. She would have preferred to wait a couple of years, but Jimmy had wanted a child so badly. Then, once she'd gotten pregnant, he'd been over-the-top excited. "I always thought I would, but I never did." She shrugged. "Now a degree seems overrated and unnecessary. At least for me. I mean, it doesn't really matter in the scheme of things." She brought his hand to her mouth and kissed it. "I wasn't one of those who needed college as a stepping-stone to a career. I had everything I needed." She wasn't stupid, nor was she ignorant, and she certainly didn't need a degree to prove her worth.

"So, you were happy in North Carolina?"

The question brought her up short. Was she happy? "I always thought I was. But I realize now, those are the words of someone who was missing something." She kissed his shoulder and confided, "I had no idea of what I was missing." She leaned away from him to capture his gaze. "I was afraid. It seems everyone I've loved, I've lost. Can you forgive me for running?"

He gripped her neck and pulled her head closer, saying, "Shush." Then grazing her lips, he said, "There's nothing to forgive." He spent long seconds kissing her, then nestled her back between shoulder and arm. "We only need to concentrate on the future."

219

Warmth flooded her system when he kissed her forehead. Never had she felt so loved and protected, even with Jimmy.

"I've thought back on those months so many times over the last fifteen years and wondered if I had made a big mistake," he said, stroking her arm. His gentle touch soothed her more and added to her sensation of well-being. "After tonight, I know I screwed up by holing up and licking my wounded pride."

She put her hand on his mouth. "Let's not rehash regrets. We've found each other now. That's all that matters."

"We wasted so much time. I'm just as responsible. Hell, I should've tracked you down and forced the issue."

"It wouldn't have done any good. I was a new widow carrying a lot of guilt. I should've confronted Jimmy long before he died, but I was too afraid. I knew something was wrong between us. When you came in all drunk, challenging me to demand more because I was worth it, I just lost it. I didn't feel worthy, so I accepted. Looking back, I realize I accepted a man who couldn't give me what I needed, and rejected another who could."

"You are deserving, Lauren, and you're stronger than you seem. I wish my mother could've met you."

"I would've liked that. I could tell Jimmy really missed her."

He smiled. "He always said you reminded him of Mom. I'm sure that's why he was able to fall in love with you. You know…with him being gay and all."

"Really?" She glanced at him with the question in her eyes. "You really think he loved me?"

"I know so. I know if anyone wanted to make your marriage work, he did. Yet deep down, we both knew he could never be what you needed. I believe he hated knowing that I could. Sibling rivalry at its best." He shrugged. "My mother would not be proud."

"What was she like?"

"Outside of being the best mom in the world, she was fun to be around. I remember her always laughing and joking. She appeared docile enough, until riled. Once that happened, she'd put anyone in his place, including my dad." His smile died. "Then she got sick." He shook his head. "No one should die so early. Or suffer so much."

"I'm sorry you lost her. At least you have fond memories of your mom. I barely remember mine."

"Jimmy said your mom died when you were, what? Nine or ten?"

"Ten. My dad was in the Air Force and we moved around a lot. My Aunt Dory lived with us and took care of us."

"I don't recall ever meeting your aunt."

"You didn't miss much. She always said she stayed with me out of

220

duty to her sister, but I think deep down inside she wanted my dad to marry her. Then he died and she left too." Thinking about her dad's death and her aunt's rejection brought the pain she always kept buried to the surface. It was past time to expunge it from her mind.

"Losing my mom was hard, but losing my dad devastated me. I remember that day like it was yesterday. My best friend's dad was also a pilot in the Air Force. She and I were in the same class together at school. When we saw the man in a dress uniform at the door we looked at each other, knowing that something had most likely happened to one of our dads. Otherwise they wouldn't be there. It was the worst feeling, praying that my dad was okay while knowing that if God answered my prayer, it would mean something had happened to Katie's dad. When I learned the truth, my life stood still. I went into a deep depression. A few months later I met Jimmy. He was so wonderful and understanding, which brought me out of my shell. He became my family. All I ever wanted was a family and someone to love me." She closed her eyes, hurting for the girl she'd once been. "My husband was gay." No wonder she'd never confronted him. She hadn't wanted to lose him too. That thought saddened her even more.

"Shush," Dillon said, putting a finger to her lips. "I'm your family now, and I'm definitely heterosexual."

Lauren smiled and nodded as love surged in her heart. She now had his love and she had her son. Life couldn't get much better.

og

A knock on Rory's bedroom door drew DJ's attention from the video game.

"Yeah," Rory said, not looking up from the screen as Sophie opened the door and peeked inside.

Rory turned his head and smiled. "Hey, Mom."

"It's late." She stepped further into the room. "I didn't realize you were still up."

DJ glanced at his cell phone. Ten after two. His mother would shit bricks if she knew he'd stayed up this late.

Rory shrugged. "Got caught up in a game," he said and resumed playing. "I got nothing going on in the morning, so I plan to sleep in."

DJ totally agreed. Still, his mom's stern voice slid into his thoughts. No one but criminals and drug addicts were up all night without a reason. Like work. Of course, she'd been born before computers and cell phones and Facebook. Hell, all his friends stayed up well past two. He was the only geek who had a lights-out curfew at one a.m. Rory understood and was cool with pulling all-nighters just to play World Of Warcraft, which happened to be one of the reasons he loved hanging with him. His uncle was the coolest guy he knew.

"Are either of you hungry?"

Shaking his head to indicate no, Rory rolled his eyes as if to say, "See what I have to put up with?"

DJ smiled, but didn't bother to reply. Though Sophie had directed the question to both of them, he sensed she couldn't care less if he starved. It was no big secret Grandma Sophie didn't like him much. Her dislike had upset him at first, but not anymore. Mainly because he didn't much like her. Still, she was family. And an adult. Treating adults with respect was another one of his mom's edicts. He'd tried to be nice, but didn't get far. So, now he just respectfully ignored her like she respectfully ignored him—although she wasn't quite as nice in the way she went about it. Still, it worked for both of them.

"Why are you up so late?" Rory asked, drawing him out of his thoughts.

"I couldn't sleep." Sophie let out a loud sigh and added, in an obvious attempt to gain her son's sympathy, "I can't seem to relax, considering…" She cleared her throat. "You know."

DJ's focus darted from the wide-screen monitor to her and back to the screen, where it stayed. She was wringing her hands and her expression could only be called apprehensive. She hadn't taken the news of their earlier attack very well and DJ had a niggling feeling she blamed his presence for that too. She made no secret of her views. He'd brought mayhem and disruption into their lives.

"You're worrying over nothing." Rory continued playing. "The house is like a fortress. Dad has a guy watching it."

"Of course." Nodding, she rubbed her arms and glanced furtively around the room. "Your father wasn't feeling well, so he took a pain pill and is sleeping like a baby. I think I may stay up a little longer and read." She moved to leave, then paused. "Let me know if you want a midnight snack."

"I'm sure we can find food on our own if we're hungry." Rory laughed. "Good night."

As Sophie left, DJ turned to his uncle. "So, she'd really fix you something?"

"Yeah, it's her way of mothering me. But it's kind of stupid, considering Arletta's the one who cooks, then puts the leftovers in the fridge for us to heat up in the microwave."

"Oh." Having a housekeeper was so cool. He said as much out loud.

"Arletta's not just a housekeeper. She's part of the family and likes to mother me too, which Mom hates. She's a little territorial where

Dad and I are concerned and is always harping on Dad to get rid of her. I don't know. It never stopped Arletta from speaking her mind or doing what she's always done. It's a weird relationship. I doubt Mom could live without her help, considering all she does." He laughed. "And that probably pisses Mom off the most."

"So, it's like having two moms?"

"Kind of."

"That's pretty cool." If his mom had someone like Arletta, maybe she wouldn't be so sad all the time. Or so alone.

"I guess." Nodding, Rory went back to the game.

Some time later, Rory looked at his watch. "It *is* getting late. Let's continue in the morning."

"Man, time sure flies when you're having fun," DJ said, checking his phone. "I hardly ever play this late."

"So what?" Rory offered a half shrug, then shut his computer down. "We'll just sleep in tomorrow."

"Yeah, sounds good." He had nothing going on in the morning. DJ stood. Yawning, he stretched.

"Did you hear that?" Rory froze and his attention flew to the door.

DJ's followed. "What?" he asked, listening closely. "I don't hear anything."

"It sounded like a thump, then a bunch more thumps. You know? Like on the game." Rory stood. "I wonder if my mom is okay."

"Maybe it's something in your air-conditioning vent. We once got a mouse caught in ours." He bent to pick up his backpack, stuffing the book he was supposed to be studying inside, right as the door burst open.

He'd been playing World of Warcraft, and it seemed as if the action on the screen had come to life when a man carrying an automatic rifle started shooting. Everything happened in fast-forward as a million thumps filled the air.

Shit. That wasn't mice. Those were real bullets. Still in defense mode, he automatically dropped to the floor. Pieces of splintered wood and debris became shrapnel-sized missiles hitting him with force, some even drawing blood. He was too scared to notice any pain and rolled into the closet while Rory dove behind his desk.

DJ closed his eyes and scooted as far into the corner as he could get, praying Rory was out of the line of fire. DJ opened his eyes, peeking between the crack in the door to see the gunman shooting into the bed.

When he broadened his aim, shit flew all over the place. Bullets hit the window. Shattered glass spewed everywhere. More bullets sprayed, pinging against metal and splintering wood all around him. DJ just knew one would finally hit him, considering the guy seemed to be aiming lower.

A sharp blast filled the air.

The shooting stopped.

DJ inched closer to the edge of the door to see the shooter jerk around and aim his gun behind him, just as another blast sent him reeling to the ground.

Seconds later Sophie appeared, holding a wicked-looking gun in her hand.

DJ's heart was pumping so fast, he couldn't move. Could only stare at the man, lying on the ground bleeding. Hell, in video games it was pretend when someone died. Nothing like the real thing. Like seeing all that red against his pasty-white skin. And the smell? The cloying scent was enough to gag him.

He scrambled out of his hiding spot just as Rory went to the man who, judging from the blood seeping out of his mouth, was dead. Ignoring the urge to upchuck, he asked, "Is he dead?"

Rory bent over to reach for a pulse. "Yeah," he said before kicking the assault rifle out of the guy's hand. "Shit, man. He was trying to kill us. How in the hell did he get inside the house?"

"I don't know."

The soft voice drew their attention.

Sophie dropped her weapon and stared at the body at her feet. "Thank God I heard him and ran for Kicker's gun." Tears rushed down her face. "I had to kill him. Otherwise, he'd have killed you."

"What the hell is going on," Arletta said, appearing right behind her. "Oh my God! Call 911," she proclaimed after glancing first at the dead man and then at the mayhem in Rory's room. "I'll go wake Kicker and find out why that blasted man who's supposed to be guarding the house let this monster past him."

"I told Silas I was worried."

Rory looked at his mother, whose words were barely audible.

"He paid no attention to me," she said a little louder, then leaned back against the wall and slid to the floor as if her legs could no longer hold her. She buried her face in her arms and continued crying hysterically.

Chapter 20

Kicker listened a moment, trying to understand what had awakened him from a deep slumber. Seconds later, he drifted back to sleep.

"Kicker…Kicker… Wake up!" At Arletta's frantic voice, he opened his eyes to see his housekeeper leaning over him. "Something terrible has happened." Still not fully awake, he blinked, then closed his eyes. Only she shook his shoulder and said more forcefully, "You have to get up. There's been a shooting."

A shooting? Panic raced through his system and he staggered out of bed, grabbing the robe Arletta held out.

"Is anyone hurt?" He shoved past her and ran toward Rory's room, praying the entire time.

Not Rory. Not DJ. Please, God…

He didn't think he could deal with either loss. Better to have taken him than for either to die before him. Like Jimmy.

Sirens filled the air. The piercing noise sent his heart rate soaring.

"She's gone and done it this time," Arletta gasped out from behind him. "She done killed a man."

"What?" Still groggy, he shook his head. "Who?" he yelled, more than baffled. Not waiting for a response, he kept moving. He slowed at the open guest room DJ was using. His panic increased as he scanned the room. Bedding and pillow stuffing, along with bits of shattered glass from the lamp littered the floor. Splinters of wood were everywhere. When he realized the room was empty, he flat-out began running toward Rory's bedroom.

"Goddamn it all. What the hell happened?" he shouted, rounding the hallway to his son's room and spotting a body and an AK-47 at the same time. Then his gaze hit Sophie. Relief filled him as his focus quickly traveled to Rory and finally DJ. Safe! He sent up a silent thank-you to the man upstairs. He wasn't going to dwell over the fact that Sophie had been his last concern.

"Mom shot an intruder," Rory said, glancing up. He knelt beside his mother, obviously trying to console her. DJ stood back a few feet, his expression saying he didn't know what to think.

"I told you I was worried." Sophie glared at him, rage filling her tear-streaked face. "Where in the hell is your investigator? Fire him." She broke down as fresh tears erupted. "I had to do his job for him."

One of the guns from the display case in his study was on the floor a few feet away. Hell, he hadn't even known she knew where to find bullets or the key to the case, much less know how to fire a weapon to kill a man.

He bent down to check the dead guy's pockets, but all he found was a cell phone. Shouts and pounding from downstairs entered his consciousness along with Arletta's voice directing policemen and EMTs to the second floor. In a matter of seconds, uniformed men swarmed the hallway.

"We got a casualty out here," came a yell from the landing. "He's been stabbed."

Kicker's heart did a flip-flop. The casualty had to be McCall's investigator. As the two EMTs rushed downstairs, he said under his breath, "Please, Lord, let him be okay."

Minutes seemed to take days before one of the officers returned and said, "The man's hanging in. Ambulance just left."

For the second time that night, Kicker exhaled a sigh of relief.

Now, hours later, he wondered how he'd survived. What he didn't wonder about was the identity of the man Sophie killed. He recognized Sanchez from McCall's photos, but the police hadn't made a positive ID. Yet. Hopefully when they did, they could piece it all together, but if not, he damn sure would.

As he escorted the last police officer to the door, he was thankful that Sophie had been awake and astute enough to intervene. Sanchez had been too intent on killing. But everyone was safe. Rory and DJ. His wife. Arletta. If any one of them had been killed, he'd never be able to forgive himself.

"You're lucky we could establish what happened so quickly," the officer said, drawing his attention.

Funny, but he didn't feel very lucky.

"The intruder made quite a mess. There are a few companies that clean up crime scenes listed in the phone book."

"Thank you." Kicker's shoulders slumped in weariness as he led the officer to the front entrance. Their investigating had exhausted him. After taking thousands of pictures and everyone's statements, then removing the body and picking through everything thoroughly, they'd packed up and all but this one had left. Arletta, Rory, and DJ had already settled in at a nearby hotel. He and Sophie were joining them as soon as he showed this guy out and locked up.

226

The officer stopped at the door and glanced at him with a concerned frown. "Will you be okay?"

"Yes. I appreciate your help," he said, giving the man a handshake.

"We'll be in touch if we have any other questions."

Kicker nodded as the officer turned to leave.

Swallowing regret, he closed the door. He clenched a fist and vowed the person responsible would pay. He knew exactly who that person was, but he'd planned on verifying his suspicions before making any accusations to the law. Dillon's recriminations about leading the police to certain conclusions about Hutcheson still rankled, mostly because they held an edge of truth. He had no intention of giving his son any more ammunition to think badly of him.

At first, he hadn't wanted to believe anyone he knew was involved. Then after talking to his accounting department head earlier this evening and providing dates and a vague idea of what to search for, two eager employees hoping to earn brownie points had spent their Saturday night digging into the electronic files. The new generation of kids coming out of college had a much better handle on the techno stuff than either he or his finance officer. So much so, that it had only taken a few hours for them to find the transactions. Buried transactions negating each other so as not to show up on a month-end report. Yet traceable nonetheless, when the one doing the tracing knew how to find them.

The money had originated from an account bearing Frank Peters' name. He hadn't revealed that information to the police either. There was time enough for that.

He now had a sinking suspicion that Frank, rather than Hutcheson, had sabotaged the plane. That thought nearly brought him to his knees. Since his trusted friend had already proven himself crafty, he wasn't about to take any more chances where the safety of his family was concerned.

Kicker reached into his pocket for his cell phone to call McCall. He was about to hit the CONNECT button when out of the corner of his eye, he caught a dazed Sophie sitting up. He'd given her one of his pain pills to calm her down and thankfully, it had knocked her out for a bit. He cleared the phone and stuck it back into his pocket. Updating McCall could wait until he took care of his wife.

He made his way to the sofa where she sat. "Come on, Sophie."

She appeared so lost and frail, a huge contrast to the woman he knew her to be. He helped her stand, then wrapped a steadying arm around her waist. Hopefully this ordeal wouldn't diminish her spunk.

It was one of the few facets of her personality he admired. "Let's get you to the hotel so you can sleep more comfortably."

She stumbled at first, then found her footing, but as they walked toward the entrance hallway, she leaned into him for support.

The trip to the hotel took minutes. He parked, got out of the car, and hurried to the passenger side. "Wake up, Sophie. We're here. Once we get upstairs, you can go back to sleep."

Still out of it, she nodded. He helped her out and steadied her as they walked inside.

Once on the third floor, he found the right room number and knocked, saying softly, "Arletta, it's me, Kicker. Do you have our room key?" She'd taken care of checking in.

Arletta quickly responded, handing him the card. "Room 327. Rory and DJ are right next door in 325. I told them to try and get some sleep. But I doubt they will. They seemed too upset."

"Thank you, Arletta." He offered his best attempt at a smile. Thank God for his housekeeper. He mentally snorted at the term. She was no simple housekeeper. The woman was a well of strength to draw from, someone who'd always taken care of his family, and tonight was no different. "I don't know how I can repay you."

"You know I'd do anything for you and my boys."

He nodded and his smile deepened somewhat. If Sophie had been lucid enough, she'd take umbrage at Arletta calling Rory one of her boys. Hell, his housekeeper even considered his undeserving wife as part of her family.

"I promised Miz Catherine I'd look after you all and I always keep my promises."

The mention of his dead wife brought vivid memories of her to the forefront of his thoughts and sometimes, like now, he really missed her…missed the conversations they used to have. "Try to get some rest."

"I doubt I'll be able to sleep."

It did seem an impossible task. "Well, try," he said as she closed the door. He continued on past Rory and DJ's room to the door marked 327 and slid the key card into the slot.

Once inside, he hit the light switch as the door slammed behind him. He led Sophie toward the king-sized bed centered in the oversized room, tossed the decorator pillows on the floor, pulled back the fancy bedspread, and settled her under the blanket.

Soon her soft snoring filled the air. He peered down at her, suddenly feeling very alone and missing Catherine all the more. For all that he and Sophie had gone through, as a soul mate she paled in comparison with his dead wife.

Having no time for melancholy, he shoved the thoughts away and reached into his pocket for his cell phone to update McCall, who probably already knew that one of his men was in critical condition. The least he could do was make sure and offer condolences.

The PI answered after the second ring. "McCall here."

"Sanchez broke in and in the process, stabbed your investigator, who's at University Hospital in intensive care. Sanchez wasn't so lucky."

"Yeah, I heard," McCall said on a weary sigh. "I just got off the phone with his doctor." His voice sounded unusually gruff. Almost shaken, completely understandable since Kicker knew the PI thought of his men as family. "She says Williams is improving and is expected to fully recover."

"That's good news," Kicker said. "I'd hate to be responsible for anyone's death." He then recounted all that had taken place in the last few hours, as well as the information about the money transfers and what Hutcheson had told Dillon.

"I'm leaving for Tampa right now. I need to stop at the hospital first, but I'll be there as soon as I can," McCall replied after Kicker had repeated the name of his hotel and room number. "I damn sure plan on confronting Peters before TPD arrests him and the asshole gets lawyered up. He's in this up to his eyeballs."

McCall then recounted his own information. The investigator he'd assigned to visit the prison hit pay dirt. Records indicated a man who'd claimed to be doing a newspaper story on gang members in prison had visited Hutcheson's roommate, Sanchez, several years ago. "Supposedly he asked all kinds of questions and was nosy as hell, which is why the guards remembered him. And why we dug deeper, only to discover the reporter doesn't exist. Currently no one by that name works, nor has he ever worked, at any newspaper in Florida. My investigator went back twenty years and checked them all out. When showed pictures of our suspects, the guard picked out Peters as the guy. Quite a coincidence, wouldn't you say, considering the other?"

"Yeah." Kicker hung up knowing without a doubt that one of his best friends had betrayed him. Anger warred with disappointment, leaving him with unanswered questions, his biggest being why? He needed to call Dillon. His son's steadying presence was something he needed to keep from killing the bastard. Plus he had a sneaking suspicion Dillon would keep McCall in check if they all confronted Peters together.

"You brought this on yourself, you know."

"What?" At Sophie's caustic tone, he glanced over at the bed. "I thought you were sleeping," he said, not exactly sure he heard her correctly. "Are you feeling better?"

She ignored his question, saying instead, "I told you not to trust him." She'd obviously listened to his side of the conversation. "And now that Dillon is back, you've given him no choice but to retaliate."

His jawed dropped a foot. "How'd you know about my plans for Dillon?"

She snorted. "It doesn't take a genius to figure it out. Besides, Rory told me." She sat up, coming more awake. "He even told me about the changes to your will."

"Oh?" Kicker narrowed his eyes and leveled his gaze at her. "It seems the two of you have had quite a lot to talk about."

"Yes, we have," she said, folding her arms and glaring at him. "He's loyal. Unlike you. You could've told me, Silas. I've always been on your side. Screwing Peters by awarding a promised position to a family member I can understand and even applaud, but I can't abide you just handing it over to Dillon rather than Rory."

Clenching his jaw, he turned and headed for the door. "We'll discuss this later." After the night he'd had, he was in no mood to justify his actions. God only knew how she'd take including her nemesis, Arletta, in his will. Thankfully he'd be dead at that point and wouldn't have to listen to her haranguing.

"Where are you going?"

"To grab a cup of coffee from the lobby." Right now escape seemed the best option, otherwise, he might be tempted to do something violent. Once he calmed down, he'd call Dillon.

☙

The trill of his cell phone drew Dillon out of a dream about Lauren. He looked at the clock on the nightstand. Six a.m. He hadn't slept this soundly since Jimmy's death. It was as if his brother had sent his approval from heaven, which eased a ton of his survivor guilt.

Stretching, he rolled over. His arm landed on Lauren's thigh. She mumbled something in her sleep and snuggled closer. Wrapping his arm around her waist and spooning, he smiled as the memory of their lovemaking encompassed him.

The trilling began anew. Damn. No one would call this early on a Sunday unless it was important, and someone had obviously called twice.

Without disturbing Sleeping Beauty, he eased out of bed, not bothering to put something on, and started for the bathroom as his phone stopped ringing. The messages could wait until after he showered.

"What're you doing up?" Lauren's teasing voice penetrated into his semi-wakeful state. He looked back to see the sexy woman prop one eye open and flash one hell of a smile. Then she stretched and added a sultry, "We're wasting daylight." Her implication was clear as she lifted the sheet and patted the space next to her.

He closed the distance to the bed and bent to kiss her. "Someone's trying to reach me," he said, nuzzling his way to her ear. "But I need to feel human before I talk to anyone, so I'm putting on a pot of coffee and taking a quick shower." He'd never been able to think clearly without either and that was especially true this morning since Lauren kept him up half the night. "I'm having a hard enough time focusing on other stuff besides climbing back in bed."

"I should check for messages too, but first I need caffeine." She untangled herself from him and stood. "I'll make coffee while you shower."

Looking at her sexy backside as she walked naked as a jaybird toward the living room, he shook off the thought of dragging her back to bed. He headed for the bathroom, saying over his shoulder, "I love you!"

She laughed. "I love you, too."

Still smiling, he jumped in the shower. He was just rinsing off when Lauren shoved open the door and her frantic voice rang out. "Call Kicker. Something's happened. DJ texted me last night saying he's okay, but now he's not answering his phone."

"I'm sure he's fine. He's probably sleeping." He quickly dried off, threw on some underwear, and stepped into his shorts. Without bothering with a shirt, he reached for his phone. Sure enough, he had two messages from Kicker. "I'll talk to my dad and see what's up." Giving her a task might help calm her down. The scent of freshly brewed coffee wafted in the air. He nodded toward the door. "In the meantime, why don't you bring me a cup of coffee? And get one for yourself while you're at it."

"Coffee can wait. This can't."

"I need one." He headed for the kitchen. He poured two cups, and took a long sip of his before punching in Kicker's number.

His dad answered on the first ring. "Thank God you called me back."

"What's up? Is DJ okay?"

"Yes," he answered.

"Thank God," Dillon said, then covered the mouthpiece and whispered to Lauren, who'd followed him and stood a foot away watching his every move, "He's fine." His nod indicated the hot brew on the counter. "Drink up while I talk to my dad, then I'll fill you in."

"Everyone's okay," Kicker said. "But we're all shaken up. Sanchez broke into the house last night and shot the hell out of the place."

Lauren reached for the cup as he said, "What the hell happened?" His tone of voice drew her attention and she motioned with her hand for him to explain. He switched to speaker and placed the phone on the counter so they both could listen as Kicker spoke, telling what had transpired while they'd been making love, ending with, "I don't want to believe Frank Peters could be involved, but there's too much evidence against him." His dad sighed heavily into the phone. "McCall and I plan to have a talk with him before we hand the information over to the police."

"I'm leaving now." Dillon pulled out two travel mugs and filled them. "We'll be there in a couple of hours." His dad needed him. He knew it as sure as he knew the sky was blue.

"I appreciate that, son."

He disconnected and a sense of dread ran up his spine as he glanced at Lauren to gauge her reaction. She was a mother bear where DJ was concerned, and he figured she'd be livid over not being there to protect him.

"I'm sorry, Lauren." He only hoped the news wouldn't shatter the tentative bond they'd formed last night.

"Too late for regrets. I just want to get to Tampa as soon as possible. Give me five minutes and I'll be ready to go." Taking the coffee he held out, she pivoted and almost ran toward his bedroom.

He followed and prayed at the same time. Lord, don't let her blame me.

Chapter 21

"There, good buddy. It's fixed." Steve pushed the button for the hangar door to open and then went to connect the hand truck.

"Thanks." Dillon nodded as they pushed the plane outside so he and Lauren could finally take off. Luck had been on his side when he'd found Steve working in the shop, after arriving an hour ago. Otherwise, they'd be delayed longer and he'd never hear the end of it.

He glanced at the restroom where Lauren had disappeared, glad she had something to do besides pace and hover. He bent to open the cargo hatch, but suddenly remembered Hutcheson's claim and wondered how best to broach the subject.

"Oh, by the way." Unable to come up with a better way, he just blurted out, "I met with Ronald Hutcheson."

Steve's brow furrowed. "Ronald Hutcheson?" He thought for a moment. "Oh, that's right. Jimmy's killer."

He cringed. That's what the whole world thought of the guy, thanks to his and Kicker's actions. "After talking to him, I'm not so sure that he did it."

"He was convicted, wasn't he?" Steve's expression hardened.

"Yeah, but he says different."

"Don't they all?"

"I guess." Dillon cleared his throat. "Anyway, he wanted to talk to you. Clear up something about that day."

"Oh? What about it?"

"He said he saw you and Peters arguing about some problem with the twin." Dillon eyed him intently. "I was just wondering what the argument was about."

"You got me!" Steve shrugged and reached for a rag from his back pocket. He concentrated on wiping grease off his fingers before adding, "I don't remember an argument." Then he spun around and headed inside the hangar, aiming for the engine he'd disassembled earlier.

With an open jaw, Dillon stared after him as a streak of unease crawled up his spine. Why was his mechanic lying? He'd known Steve for too long not to recognize his tells, but he had no time to question him because Lauren chose that moment to storm out of the restroom and rush toward him.

"Are we ready to go?" she asked with an expression that said she wasn't about to wait any longer.

"Yeah." He opened the passenger door and helped her inside.

Just as he was about to climb into the plane, Hutcheson stepped into his line of vision and walked in his direction.

"He's lying and I want to know why," Hutcheson said, halting a few feet away.

Where had he come from? "This will have to wait. I'm on my way to Tampa. Sanchez went on a rampage last night."

"I heard." He'd obviously been lurking, Dillon surmised as the guy added, "News also said he was killed and I'm not taking the heat for anything this time."

"I thought we were ready?" Lauren asked, impatience bristling in every syllable.

"Look. I don't have time to sort this out right now. I gotta go." He grabbed the handle on the fuselage, ready to climb inside, but Hutcheson stopped him with an arm on his shoulder. He turned around and glanced at the man.

"You owe me," he said, losing some of his cool and pointing a finger into his chest. "Your old man owes me."

Just then Steve grabbed Hutcheson by the arm. "He just told you he had to leave."

If looks could kill, both he and Steve would be dead right now, considering Hutcheson's icy glare. "This isn't over." He yanked free and brushed himself off. "Not by a long shot," he said over his shoulder as he stalked away from the plane.

"It is for now." Steve nodded to Dillon. "You go on. I'll take care of him. Make sure he doesn't cause any problems."

"Thanks." Dillon climbed inside the aircraft, wondering what in the hell, if anything, was between the two men. More importantly, which man was lying.

 C3

Kicker paced, practically wearing a rut in the lobby's carpeted seating area. The entire time, his thoughts focused on what to do about Peters.

Dillon's flight had been delayed with a minor problem. McCall wouldn't land for at least another forty-five minutes. Then he planned to stop by the hospital, which would take longer.

He glanced up and noticed a room with a long desk and several computers beyond glass walls. A business center the hotel provided for guests.

If Peters had the kind of money to bribe a lawyer, he had to have more stashed away. He had to know the noose around his neck was tightening, especially since day-breaking news had pretty much centered on Sanchez's death. All Peters had to do was turn on his TV or open a newspaper.

Deciding not to take any chances, Kicker started for the business center, determined to check out countries with no extradition to the US. He wasn't a genius with the computer, but he knew his way around a search engine.

His task took a few minutes. Now to check on flights. After jotting down every morning flight with connections to airports that offered international flights to the countries on his list, Kicker grabbed his phone.

Concentrating on three flights, he punched in the number to the first airline.

"Hi, this is Frank Peters. I'd like to confirm my seat on flight 5760 from Tampa to Atlanta at ten thirty."

After giving the agent on the phone specifics, the man spent a moment checking before saying, "I'm sorry, sir. But I can't seem to find your reservation. Can you give me the confirmation number of your ticket?"

"Oops. I just realized I'm actually leaving tomorrow. My mistake. Sorry to have bothered you." He quickly hung up and called the next airline on his list, going through the same spiel.

This time he hit pay dirt. Peters had a confirmed seat leaving for Dallas at eleven thirty, connecting through LA on a flight bound for New Zealand. From there he'd take a puddle jumper to Samoa.

The guy's smart, Kicker thought, glancing at his watch. It was already after eight. If he waited for McCall or Dillon, the bastard might get away and there wouldn't be a damn thing he could do about it.

A surge of energy filled him with purpose as he pushed past the glass door and turned toward the elevators. He'd make damn sure Peters didn't get on that flight.

Once in the room, Sophie's soft snores drifted past his ears as he passed the bed on his way to the bathroom. Good, he thought. Hopefully she'd stay asleep until he was gone.

Less than ten minutes later, he slowly opened the bathroom door and peeked out. Sophie hadn't moved. Smiling, he started for the exit.

"You aren't leaving again?" Her drowsy voice stopped him in midstride.

He pivoted. "Yes. Someone needs to confront Frank."

"And why does that someone have to be you?" She climbed out of the bed and went up to him. "You're in no shape to get all worked up."

Annoyance coursed through him and he bit back a snide reply, saying instead, "I'm fine." She was always harping on his health. Lately he felt much better, so much so he no longer needed his cane to walk. Now that he thought about it, he realized events of the last few weeks had kept her from harping. There had to be a correlation.

"Remember what the doctor said. With your high blood pressure, you could easily have a stroke." Her tone changed to worry and his focus landed on her concerned expression.

He sighed. "Don't worry. I only want to talk to him." Delaying him was really his intent, but he didn't say so.

"Are we ever going to talk about the changes to your will?"

He threw out a half laugh. "You can't be serious?" If anything could get his blood pressure spiking, it was arguing with her over what he did with *his* money and *his* company.

"I'm very serious."

Of course she was. His shoulders slumped in weariness as she added, "You owe it to Rory."

He was damned tired of dealing with her demands. Oh, how he wished Catherine had never died. It should be the woman he'd always loved standing before him urging him to talk about his will, not the woman who'd always caused friction within his family. Which Sophie had done from the beginning, he realized, staring at her beautiful face. She'd never hidden the fact that Rory should take precedence in their lives. "Now is not the time to discuss this."

"When will be the time?" Her expression scrunched into a snarl. "After you're six feet under and I can't do anything about it? You need to change it back, Silas."

Catherine used to say that beauty on the outside sometimes masked ugliness on the inside. He had to admit that over the years, what Sophie held inside had often come out in ugly bursts, all aimed at his older two sons. Just like now.

Kicker snorted and shook his head, calling himself the worst kind of idiot for allowing her to get away with such behavior for so long. "My decision stands. Dillon will take over as soon as he wants to."

"What about Rory? You're completely disregarding him. He's not the son who left you in the lurch. He's the son who's poured his heart and soul into working for you."

"Rory understands." Kicker had made sure of that. It was Sophie who'd never understand, no matter how much he tried to explain.

God help them, she'd never relent on her bitching about it, either. She'd make everyone pay for his decision, Dillon and DJ in particular.

He finally recognized the full impact of his sin all those years ago. Catherine's death hadn't led to his family's demise. He had—by fucking Sophie and tearing his family apart with the consequences. He'd used Rory's birth to provide a new beginning, a place where he was still perfect to one of his sons. He tamped down guilt, ashamed to admit he'd been running from the other two.

But his sins were much worse than screwing and running. He'd also pushed—no, shoved was a better word—those he loved the most out of his life with lofty expectations that even he hadn't had the balls to meet.

As Sophie babbled on, trying to bend him to her will, he laughed, yet there was nothing jovial in the harsh sound. Even Jimmy had blamed him. Yet what had he done? He'd lashed out in anger. Another huge regret and one that ate at his soul, as his last conversation with his oldest son only hours before he'd died entered his thoughts.

Kicker had never told another living soul, especially Sophie, about the horrible things he'd said after Dillon had confronted him, implying that Jimmy was gay. No son of his could be gay. Unable to face up to the fact, he'd attacked his eldest with words, telling him to man up.

Like it had been yesterday instead of fifteen years ago, he could still hear Jimmy's disgusted response. Still see the sneer on his face, when he'd said, "Oh, like you did, Dad? By screwing your biggest client's daughter and getting her pregnant while mom was dying? At least I've done right by my wife and son."

"Your wife and son?" he'd yelled right back. "You're not man enough to have either. You're as bad as Dillon with your condemnation, only a bigger disappointment. You've hidden behind a slip of a girl who's afraid of her own shadow. You expect me to buy you had sex with her? I know exactly what you did. You up and married a pregnant nobody and you're not going to pawn off her bastard on this family as a Kane, goddamn it all. I'm disowning both of you. As far as I'm concerned, I have only one son left."

He'd allowed Sophie's suspicions to sever the bond with his son. Owning up to that fact shamed him further. He *had* led the investigators in Jimmy's murder to making an incorrect assumption and because of that Peters had gotten away with murder all these years. At the time, he'd thought he was protecting Jimmy's reputation, when in reality he'd only been protecting his own. What a goddamned hypocrite he'd been. But no more.

"Did you hear me?" Sophie's harsh voice yanked his attention to her face.

"Yes, I heard you," Kicker said, looking her square in the eye. "Now hear me. Get used to my changes because I'm not backing down, goddamn it all. Heed my warning. If you continue using the same nasty tactics toward those I love, I'll divorce your ass and split your share between Dillon and DJ."

Kicker ignored her stunned expression and stormed out of the room, wanting only peace. It no longer mattered that she was Rory's mother. Placating Sophie simply wasn't worth the price of the new relationships he was building with his son and grandson.

Chapter 22

Kicker drove straight to Frank's house and parked. Before exiting, he used his smart phone to check on McCall's flight. It had landed. He quickly gave him a call.

When transferred to voice mail, he left a detailed message about Peters, counting on the PI to check his messages before going to the hospital.

Once out of the car, he strode up the walkway uncertain he could stop the man, but he had to try. If anything, he could damn well slow him down.

Frank answered his knock within seconds. Astonishment lit his eyes for a brief moment before he smiled. He stepped back and opened the door wider. "What brings you here this early, Kicker? I don't work on Sundays you know," he said in a friendly tone.

"I'm sorry to bother you, but it's been a lousy night. I thought I could get a cup of coffee and pick your brain a little bit."

"Oh?" Frank's eyebrows rose. "What happened? And better yet, what can I do to help?"

"It's about Jimmy's death and Hutcheson's need for revenge," he said, sighing. "He's got an ex-roommate who's a member of the Warlords. His dad just happened to be their leader, who Sophie killed last night while he was shooting the place up."

"Oh my God! I hadn't heard. Are you okay? Come on in. You should've called me last night."

"It was late and I didn't want to bother you. Sophie's out of it this morning. The need to get away just took me by surprise and here I am." Kicker shrugged. "You were at the office the night Jimmy died, right?"

Frank shook his head. "I'd left at least an hour before that."

If Kicker went by Hutcheson's accounting to Dillon, he knew that was a lie.

"Come on in the kitchen and I'll fix you a cup of coffee."

Kicker smiled and followed him.

"Have a seat." His nod indicated a table and four chairs in an alcove. The bay window overlooked a small lake.

Frank grabbed the pot, filled it with water, and poured the liquid in the coffeemaker. Then he added first a filter, next a few scoops of ground coffee, and hit the switch. "Shouldn't take long." He started for the door. "I'll be right back. I need to check on my laundry. Don't want the shirts to get wrinkled, which is what happens if they sit too long."

Nodding, Kicker watched him leave. The second he was alone, he began opening drawers and cupboards, trying to find anything incriminating. In the third drawer, he spotted a cell phone. It was one of those throwaways bought at any discount store. After switching it on, he navigated through the device, and voilà. He noted only calls to one number, proof that connected Frank to Sanchez. Last night, before handing Sanchez's phone to the officer in charge, he'd memorized the number and had given it to McCall to check out.

"I see you found what you were looking for."

Kicker dropped the phone into the drawer and spun around, placing a smile on his face. "What? I was looking for a spoon." As Frank walked further into the room, he closed the drawer. Using the counter as cover, he reached into his pocket for his own phone and turned his camera on video.

"Nice try." Peters stopped a few feet away, pointing a gun at him. "Now why are you really here?"

He swallowed hard and locked gazes with his one-time friend. "To find out more information." He raised his voice, praying for enough power to record their entire conversation in case the worst happened. "And to stall you," he added honestly. "Are you going to kill me?"

"I'm not planning on it. Killing's a messy business that always comes back to haunt a person."

Kicker's chin edged a notch higher. "Did you sabotage Jimmy's plane?"

"According to the state of Florida, Ronald Hutcheson sabotaged the plane that caused your son's fatal accident."

His gaze narrowed on Frank and he offered a smile that could freeze an icicle. "So, are we playing semantics now? I found the electronic trail that led to the money you funneled to his lawyer to lose the case."

Peters laughed. "That's quite a tale. Why would I do that?"

"Are you saying you didn't?"

"I refuse to be baited." He waved the gun he carried. "Let's just say I played my cards wrong and bet on the wrong outcome."

"What outcome?"

"I thought I'd run Kane Aeronautics when you weren't around, but we both know that's not going to happen now that Dillon's back. I will say this. I do wish he'd been on that plane that night instead of Jimmy. It would've solved one of my problems."

"So, you did kill Jimmy?"

He shrugged his shoulders, not admitting to it, but not denying it either. "The accident served a purpose. I wanted it all. I wanted to be you. You were larger than life, with a gorgeous wife and an unending supply of money. But as I've learned, I don't have your balls." He snorted, shaking his head. "You Kanes got it all. Always have had. I've learned from the best how to protect myself and leave myself a way out. Damn good thing for me that I did, huh? I was smart not to trust either one of you." He went on, almost boasting. "I've been siphoning off money just in case Dillon came back, been preparing for years. I always suspected I could get screwed in the end, which I did. In more ways than one." He laughed. "No fool like an old fool, is there?"

"I was never planning on screwing you. You are a fool if you thought I'd leave you penniless. You may not have been my CEO, but you'd have been paid like one."

"Seems I've misjudged you. Unfortunately I set my course in motion. I can't go back now."

He waved the gun toward a door. "Get moving. Toward the closet." When Kicker didn't budge, he cocked the trigger. "Now!"

That got him moving. Near the door, Peters said, "I'm sorry about this, old man, but I already told you I have no intention of going to jail." Kicker didn't see the Taser coming at him until it was too late. He leaned away, but all too soon fifty thousand volts went through his system and he jerked. His body went limp as he lost control and dropped to the floor. Though he tried, resisting was useless as Peters tied his hands behind his back. Then he bound his legs. Seconds later, darkness surrounded him when the closet door slammed shut with a final click.

愉

"Kicker? Kicker? Where are you?"

"In here," he shouted, pounding on the door with his bound feet.

Seconds later the door opened. McCall reached in to untie his restraints and then helped him stand.

"Are you okay?" he asked, leading to him to the chair next to the bar. His forehead furrowed in worry.

"I'm fine," Kicker lied, in between deep breaths. "We need to go after Peters. He left about ten minutes ago."

"No need. He's already dead. Barely made it out of his driveway.

241

Someone sprayed him with bullets. The Warmongers obviously figured out who was blackmailing their leader and decided to get revenge. I called 911."

"Hutcheson didn't sabotage the plane. Frank Peters did. Our conversation's on my cell phone. Not the best quality, but hopefully it's enough to clear Hutcheson's name." He tried to stand, but his legs wobbled. His muscles still refused to work properly. He sat back down for a moment then tried again, this time more successfully. "I don't think I have the energy to answer a bunch of questions right now."

"No need for you to hang around. E-mail me the file and I'll wait for the police and handle everything."

"Thanks." Relief swamped Kicker and he gripped the PI's outstretched arm, using it for support to walk out of the house. "Guess I'm still a little unsteady on my feet."

By the time they reached the bottom step, he was feeling much stronger. As McCall helped him to his parked car, he spotted Peters' Town Car, not bothered in the least to see his lifeless form. The man got what he had coming to him for killing his son.

The PI opened his car door for him, and he quickly sat. His shoulders slumped. A brush with death certainly was exhausting, he thought, jamming the key into the ignition.

"Are you sure you're okay to drive?"

Kicker wondered if any of them would ever be okay after Peters' handiwork became common knowledge. "Yes. I just needed to gather my strength along with my wits." He offered a wan smile. "Having the shit stunned out of me isn't exactly what I expected from Peters, but I'm still alive and he isn't, which is what matters most." Now that he was sitting, he felt almost normal again. Almost. He still had to deal with apologizing to an innocent man. "If the police need my statement, I'll stop by the station after I meet Dillon's plane."

He'd draw the strength to do the right thing from his middle son. Hopefully full atonement would make things right between them. For all the shit he'd put him through, especially the sin of allowing Sophie to treat him and Jimmy so poorly for so many years. "It seems Lauren's in a dither to see DJ and make sure he's okay, so they need a ride." Kicker intended to make amends to everyone before anything else happened. His smile became genuine as he shifted into drive and mentally rubbed his hands together. With a little luck, he just might have a few good years left to enjoy his family.

A siren pierced the air as Kicker steered away from the curb and headed in the direction of the airfield. He drove straight to his company hangar in a matter of minutes. Entering the parking lot,

Kicker slowed and quickly pulled into an open spot, noting that Dillon's plane had just landed.

While the Beechcraft taxied toward the hangar, he hopped out and hurried inside. When Dillon shut down the engine, Kicker was ready for him. He hit the button and the massive hangar door began a slow ascent, rumbling and groaning the entire way.

☃

The propeller slowed its spinning. Dillon hopped out, then ran around to the other side to unlatch Lauren's door. Offering a hand, he helped her down. Out of the corner of his eye, he saw his dad walking toward them with a serious expression on his face.

Now what? He steeled himself and held out his hand. "Hey, Dad."

Kicker pushed his hand aside and pulled him into a bear hug. Dillon cleared his throat, suddenly uncomfortable. This warm welcome was a definite surprise.

"When did you start hugging?" he asked when Kicker released him and turned to Lauren.

"Get used to it. From now on, I plan to make sure everyone knows how much I care about them," Kicker said, wrapping his arms around her.

After returning his hug, Lauren looked over his shoulder. "Where's DJ? Is he okay?"

Kicker smiled and patted her hand. "He's fine, if a little shook up. He and Rory are back at the hotel. Hopefully they're sleeping. They had a pretty rough night. Hell, it was pretty rough on all of us." Kicker nodded to the plane and then pointed to the tow bar. "Here, I'll help you park her inside."

Once done, Dillon hit the switch to lower the door. The trio wound their way through several other parked planes before entering the lounge area.

Movement drew Dillon's attention. His gaze narrowed. "What the hell?" he said as Hutcheson stepped into view from a hallway with his hands up. Their eyes met.

"I told you I didn't do it," Hutcheson said as Steve suddenly appeared behind him. "We started talking and one thing led to another."

"What's going on?" Dillon's eyebrows shot up as his focus landed on Steve. "Why are you here?"

"Hutcheson isn't responsible for Jimmy's death. I am," Steve said, wearing a guilty expression.

Dillon's heart dropped. "What?" He shoved Lauren behind him.

243

"I knew something wasn't right, yet Frank Peters talked me out of speaking up. Then he told me the day after the accident if I said anything, I'd be blackballed.

"At the time, I thought he was protecting the company from liability, but now I think he switched the controls. Which means I'm responsible for letting him get away with murder. After talking it out with Hutcheson, we realized you might be in danger," Steve said, walking further into the room. "So, I flew us directly here to warn you."

"You don't need to worry about Peters any longer," Kicker said, stopping next to Dillon. "He's dead."

Steve nodded, but his expression was strained. Dillon's eyes narrowed in confusion when he saw that his hands, although closer to his side, were also raised.

"Seems we were right to be worried," Steve said, his nod indicating behind his shoulder. "Unfortunately, we were wrong about the who."

A second later, Sophie stepped into view. Taking note of the wicked-looking firepower she had pointed at Hutcheson and Steve, Dillon's chest tightened.

"Sophie," Kicker said, his face red with anger. "What the hell are you doing?" he roared.

"What does it look like," she asked, waving the automatic weapon around like a pro, indicating for the two men to join the others. "Sit."

Lauren gripped his hand and Dillon gave her a squeeze of reassurance, urging her to obey the order. They sat next to Kicker on the sofa as Hutcheson and Steve cautiously moved to sit on the love seat.

Ten eyes were aimed at Sophie as she added, "No sudden moves or I start shooting. I should warn you. This thing is pretty effective, compliments of Sanchez. I found it on him after I killed him and hid it without anyone being the wiser. The pig got what he deserved for daring to put my son in danger." She grinned, clearly gloating now. "Thought it might come in handy and I was right. All I had to do was wait for the opportunity to act. I took care of Frank and made sure they'll assume some scumbag Warmonger did it. And tragically, when they find your bodies it'll appear as if the same gangbangers took care of you too."

"So, you're just going to kill us?" Dillon asked, trying to keep her talking, to stall as the truth started to sink in. Of course, she'd been responsible. Hadn't she infiltrated their house and tried to erase their mother from the picture? Only Kicker stubbornly wouldn't let her destroy every memory. Dillon just assumed his dad held out because of a guilty conscience. What if Sophie had planned it all? From the very beginning?

"You're a very clever woman." He'd always thought his dad was the aggressor in their affair, but seeing her now, he was starting to doubt that scenario. "I'd bet my company you seduced my Dad all those years ago." He glared at her. "I've often wondered how you did it."

"It wasn't easy considering Silas wasn't interested. So, I gave him a little nudge."

"What do you mean by nudge?" Kicker asked, eyeing her with total disgust as if he could see his second wife clearly for the first time in his life.

"I mean, when you ignored all my attempts at flirting and kept going on and on about your dying wife, I had to slip something into your drink to get you in the mood."

Dillon shook his head, trying to wrap his mind around her admission. "So, you drugged him?" And they'd all had to live with the consequences because up until that time, his dad had been an honorable man.

Kicker looked dazed. "All this time I thought I'd drank too much and as a result, broken my vows. Now you're telling me it was all part of your plan? Was it part of your plan to get pregnant too?"

Nodding, Sophie practically cackled in glee. "Definitely clever. Not to mention well timed." Her gaze moved from Kicker to Dillon. "I saw what I wanted and went after it. Is that so bad?"

"No." Swallowing hard, Dillon placed a restraining hand on Kicker's shoulder as regret for his part in it registered. If he hadn't been so angry with his father, he might have realized the inconsistency in his father's behavior toward his family, especially toward his wife. Kicker could be a total bastard to outsiders, but until Sophie, he'd never shown Catherine Kane anything but the utmost respect and had made sure his boys did the same. He and Jimmy hadn't even been allowed to swear in her presence. "It takes a shrewd woman to plan so methodically," he said, his voice holding a note of admiration. Maybe acting impressed would get the conniving bitch to talk more. Anything to hold her off from spraying them with bullets.

"No one ever called you stupid." Sophie sighed, eyeing him wistfully. "If only you'd been in that plane that night."

"So, I was your target all along?"

"Yes. Frank and I had planned to point the finger at Steve, here." She tilted the weapon in the mechanic's direction. "Back then, I'd almost convinced Kicker to disinherit Jimmy because he was gay." Her stare hardened as she glanced at Dillon. "But everything went south when you got drunk and Jimmy died instead. So, my plan needed adjusting. I'd have figured out some way to get rid of you, but you broke ties with Silas and moved away. I'd already paid someone to kidnap DJ and sell him to an adoption ring. Only *she* left town with no forwarding address." Sophie indicated Lauren with the toss of her head. "Which worked to my advantage. Until almost a year ago, when Kicker started going soft and talking about reuniting his family. I knew I had to do something and fast."

"What about DJ?" Lauren asked, her entire body rigid as stone. Her hands curled into his so much that if she squeezed any harder, her fingernails might feel like they were cutting through the skin. "Do you plan on killing him too?"

"Not *now*." She shrugged. "Too risky. But I'll be there to console him." She hesitated. "And at some future date," her smile turned purely evil, "before his twenty-first birthday, he'll meet with some kind of accident."

"Are you crazy, woman?" Kicker interjected. "Why kill any one of us?"

She pointed the assault rifle at him and snarled, "Shut up. You had your chance this morning to make things right but, no…you just had to go and cut my son out of his legacy." She waved the weapon. "This should have been all his. Without me, it wouldn't exist. Without me, you'd be nothing."

Kicker started laughing. "You're full of shit."

"Wait, Dad," Dillon said, trying not to agitate Sophie any more than necessary. An agitated woman toting an AK-47 just might get trigger-happy. "Let's hear what she has to say."

Sophie whirled the gun around, aiming straight at him. "Stalling?"

"Sure. Wouldn't you?" Dillon offered a careless shrug. "Besides, you're going to kill us anyway, so why not satisfy our curiosity first?"

"Why not." Sophie's cold smile did nothing to ease his trepidation. "It's Sunday. No one's around to rescue you," she said.

He glanced at Kicker, conveying with his eyes *don't do something stupid.*

"Eyes forward." She lifted the gun an inch higher, the barrel pointing square at his face. "No communicating. Otherwise, I open fire. Trust me, I came prepared." Still aiming with one hand, she lifted her blouse with the other to show two clips of ammo attached to her belt. "That Sanchez was one armed son of a bitch. I'll be happy to tell you everything, but the minute anyone tries anything, I start shooting and won't stop 'til you're all dead. Understand?"

"Why'd you kill Frank Peters?" Kicker asked.

Her expression hardened once again. "He was a selfish man who thought himself deserving. He was only too eager to please because he wanted me. So, I used him." She glanced briefly at Kicker. "Imagine that toad taking your place, Silas?" She snorted. "But then you barely noticed me. I wanted us to be a family. Just the three of us." She again pointed the weapon at her husband. Her lips curled into a deeper grimace. "And you gave our child's legacy away. Rory deserves to be CEO, not Dillon."

"Goddamn it all, Sophie. Why couldn't you be content to let me handle my business? Rory didn't want to head up Kane Aeronautics so soon. It was Rory who wanted Dillon back. He knew it was best for the company." He wiped his face in frustration. Or disgust. Dillon wasn't sure which as his father added, "Why couldn't you see that? My boys would've loved you, had you given them the chance. Catherine taught them right."

"Don't you dare mention her name." Her face reddened in anger. "I'm so sick of living in Saint Catherine's shadow. My dad was right. I never should've picked you. He even told me to find someone else, but that only made me want you more. Now that the die is cast, my Rory is going to have it all."

She aimed. The wild look in her eye sent them scrambling for cover. She got off a few rounds, but the kick of the rifle sent those first shots into the air. Dillon dove off the sofa. Ignoring the sting in his arm, he pulled Lauren with him behind the flimsy barricade, and covered her with his body.

"We're all going to die," she whispered in his ear as bullets ricocheted around them.

Wood splintered. Lamps burst, spraying glass everywhere. He shook his head and kissed her forehead. "Not if I can help it."

Unfortunately, he had no clue how to go about meeting his promise as she mouthed the words, *I love you*. Bullets pierced the wall two inches from their heads. He flinched and covered her until the worst had passed.

"I love you, too!" he whispered, giving her another quick kiss, this one on the mouth. He then got on his hands and knees to scan the area for an escape. There was none, which meant Lauren was right. They were all going to die, just like Sophie wanted.

"Stop, Mom! What are you doing?" The shout came from the entryway.

Recognizing Rory's voice, he peeked around the sofa's edge to see his brother standing there looking baffled.

At the same time, a surprised Sophie whirled on him and stopped shooting, even though a few bullets went astray and hit the ceiling. "Rory?" she asked. "Why are you here?"

"Arletta told me you killed someone." His expression turned more solemn. "I didn't want to believe it, but it looks like it was the truth."

"I'm protecting your interests."

"By killing my father? My brother? People I love?" He threw her a grimace of disbelief. "How is that protecting my interests?"

Unable to continue holding the rifle under her son's scrutiny, she lowered it. "You weren't supposed to know."

During the distraction, Dillon crawled closer. Once near enough, he grabbed the weapon out of Sophie's grasp, and Steve and Hutcheson tackled her.

While Kicker called 911, he noticed his bleeding arm. He clutched the spot to staunch the flow as Lauren stood up and eyed him with horror etched onto her expression.

She rushed over to him. "Oh my God, you've been shot."

"It's okay." His heart swelled with love as he wrapped his good arm around her. She hugged him back and he added, "It could have been a lot worse." As far as he was concerned, a flesh wound was a small price to pay for not dying.

"Hold still," Steve ground out, holding Sophie's arms behind her back as she continued to struggle. When he had her hands securely tied, he helped her up.

Rory handed the gun to his father. "I'm sorry I didn't get here sooner." He ran a hand through his hair and glanced at Dillon, sighing. "I almost didn't come at all, but Arletta was beside herself with panic." He turned to his mother. "She followed you and claims you shot Frank Peters. She also knew of Dad's plan to pick up Dillon, and when you headed for the airport, Arletta feared the worst."

"I should've gotten rid of her long ago." The venom in Sophie's voice matched the fire in her eyes. "She was trouble from the very beginning."

"Yeah," Arletta said, stepping into view from behind the door, her hot gaze aimed straight at Sophie. "You could've tried, but no two-bit little missy was gonna do me or my boys harm." She snorted. "I suspected you were poisoning Kicker. Just couldn't prove it."

"He'd have been dead months ago if not for changing his will." Sophie's matter-of-fact manner sent chills down Dillon's spine but her statement damn near terrified him. What if they hadn't reconciled? His breath hitched in his throat as he looked at his father.

"You were poisoning me?" Kicker asked in a dazed voice.

After dealing with her cruel tactics for years, the news didn't surprise Dillon, but his father was clearly at a loss.

"She tried," Arletta said. "When you started getting sick, I felt something wasn't right. That's when I started feeding you on the side."

"I thought we were a team." Eyes wide, Kicker turned to stare at Sophie. "I've always done well by you. Given you everything you wanted. That's the thanks I get? You poison me?"

"You *gave* me everything I wanted? What a joke. All I wanted was your love and when I realized that was never going to happen, I waited for you to die, so I could find someone else. After a while, I got tired of waiting and decided to do something about it."

"Why couldn't you just divorce him if it was that bad?" Rory asked, appearing just as shocked.

"And have my father know he was right all along?" She shook her head. "No! I couldn't do that. Nor could I stand the thought of someone else taking my place. Better to die a widow and have people's sympathy rather than their pity."

"Look how that turned out," Kicker said. When Sophie displayed one of her spiteful looks, he just shook his head. "Now, *our* son knows you're a murderer."

Stunned into silence, she could only stare open-mouthed as the full impact of her actions finally set in.

Kicker's lips curled in disgust. "That's the legacy you've given Rory." He then turned and walked away.

As sirens blared in the background, her stricken look remained.

Out of the corner of Dillon's eye, he spotted DJ rush into the room.

"Is everything okay?" DJ asked.

"Yes, son. Everything's fine," Kicker said as Lauren rushed to give him a big hug.

"Are you okay?" she asked, leaning back and gently pushing a lock of hair out of his eyes. "I was so worried about you."

"I'm sorry for not waiting in the car," DJ said, glancing at Rory. "When I heard the sirens, I had to see what was going on."

Rory was about to answer, but EMTs and policemen suddenly swarmed the place.

Dillon watched his brother's expression sadden when an officer arrested Sophie. "I'm sorry," he said as she was taken away under guard. "I know what it's like to lose a mother."

"I almost think it'd be easier to accept my mother's death than to see her arrested for trying to kill my father." Rory shook his head and walked over to the opposite side of the room.

"It looks like the bullet just grazed you," a med tech said, starting to attend to his arm. "But you should still have a doctor look at it." He continued working, while Lauren, DJ, and Arletta stood nearby, fussing over the injury.

A few feet away, Kicker, Steve, and Hutcheson answered questions individually with three different officers.

"Thanks," Dillon said, the minute the guy finished dressing his wound. He reached for Lauren with his good arm, pulling her to him and giving her a quick hug. "See? I'm okay." His soul lightened as he stared into her shimmering gaze, seeing only love and acceptance. His heart mirrored the same sentiments. Then his focus turned to DJ. When the kid gave him one hell of a grin, he knew what he needed to do. He had to take care of them. They were too precious to let get away again. Besides, Jimmy would expect it of him. He had no idea why he hadn't figured that out before now, but now that he had, his heart swelled with love. He was one lucky man.

"I almost lost you. Twice," Lauren said. "I'm not letting you out of my sight."

Dillon laughed and kissed her forehead. "I can definitely get used to having you around. Both of you."

"That's good because I don't plan on running away. We'll stick around this time."

"I second that," DJ said. "I like the idea of us sticking around."

"Warms my heart to see you all together," Arletta chimed in, smiling. "At least something good came outta that witch's evil doin's."

Lauren nodded. "Can we go now?" A few tears trickled down the sides of her face. "I'm suddenly exhausted."

"Yes. I think we're all ready to go," Kicker said, coming up behind the group. "The officers just left." His shoulders slumped. "Seems I've done a grave injustice and I mean to fix it. I can't return the years the man spent in prison, but I can at least pay the attorney fees to have Hutcheson's name exonerated."

"I'm just glad we're all alive," Dillon said. He raised his voice. "Come on, Rory. I'll buy you a drink. I think we can all use one about now."

"I sure could," Kicker said, nodding. As Rory slowly neared them, his father reached out and embraced him for long seconds. "I'm so sorry, son." He stepped back, keeping a hand on his shoulder. "I never meant for this to happen."

Nodding, Rory cleared his throat. "I don't think anyone did. I just wish I wasn't the reason she went all loopy." He then turned and headed for the door.

Solemnly Dillon and the others followed.

Chapter 23

After arriving at the hotel, Kicker arranged for Lauren and Dillon to have adjoining rooms. Now in Kicker's room, she sat next to Dillon on the sofa and Arletta sat in an upholstered chair, while Kicker poured drinks.

Earlier, Lauren had gotten DJ alone long enough to apologize for her part in this tragedy. She'd been wrong to keep her son away from his family. Thankfully he seemed to be handling the ordeal without too much trauma, even opting to stay with Rory in his room, sensing his uncle needed his company.

When Kicker handed her a glass of bourbon, she took it, marveling over all that had gone on in such a short time. "I'm so sorry," she said to him, suddenly remembering her aunt's unhappy bitterness and deciding right then and there not to be like her. She would learn from her mistakes, work to rectify them, and then move on. As Kicker turned to Dillon, holding out his drink in the other hand, she added, "Can you ever forgive me? I should've stood up to you and said something about the kidnapping attempts." She deeply regretted running so far without contact, knowing that none of the affected men would ever recoup the time they'd been apart. If only she had confronted Jimmy all those years ago. It might have made a difference in all their outcomes. "I hate that I originally thought you might've been behind them."

"No need to apologize." Kicker's expression softened. "We've all got something to atone for. I'm just happy we're alive and able to actually do it." He exhaled a long sigh. "Sophie did a number on all of us and I was the person who let her get away with it. I should've known something wasn't right." He went back to the bar for the other two glasses. "I'd never cheated on Catherine before then, and truthfully never gave it a thought."

Arletta took the drink he held out. He sat across from the housekeeper and brought his own glass to his lips for a long swallow before wiping his mouth with the back of his hand. There was a faraway look in his eyes.

"She knows what really happened," Arletta said.

Kicker nodded. "She was my light, but all I saw was the darkness her passing would leave behind. Grief kept me from thinking coherently back then." He glanced at Dillon. Moisture glistened in his eyes. "And then when I told you boys what Sophie claimed had happened, both of you believed it so readily, I guess I believed it too."

"I'm sorry, Dad," Dillon said. "I should've known better."

Sighing, Kicker shook his head. "I hated that you looked at me differently afterward and didn't see how I could change things. I saw the chance to start over with another son and do things right, so I took it." A sad expression crept into his face. "Little did I know the only thing right about it was Rory."

"Do you think he'll get over this?" Lauren asked. DJ always seemed to appear okay, but inside he was probably tied in knots.

"Lord, I hope so. I'll make sure of it. As well as making sure his mother gets the best defense possible. Not for her, but for Rory." Kicker hesitated. "He's upset enough that his mother would try and kill us, using him as an excuse. I don't want him to ever find out what Sophie did back then to conceive him. The knowledge won't do him a damn bit of good and will only hurt him." He cleared his throat. "I told him she's unbalanced. I just didn't see through her illness. I made sure he knows how much I love him. None of this is his fault. It's mine. It's a legacy I'm responsible for."

"How is it your fault?" Dillon asked.

"I didn't love her like she wanted, which drove her to extremes. It wasn't enough that I honored her or took care of her because she was my son's mother. She couldn't handle the fact that I loved my sons equally." His look turned pensive. "How could I love one above another? I've always loved my boys and I always will. Even my grandson. I thank God he and his mother are part of our family." Kicker offered Lauren a wan smile. "It's too late for Jimmy." He then glanced at Dillon. "But not you, son. Can you ever forgive me?"

"I told you, I already have." Dillon was silent for a moment. When he next spoke, his voice cracked with emotion. "Mom told me she forgave you. I didn't see how because I couldn't forgive you for hurting her. But she also told me when you love someone, you forgive even the most grievous errors." His revelation brought another round of tears to Lauren's eyes as he gripped her knee. He squeezed gently and met her gaze. "I've since learned that's what loving is all about."

She inhaled deeply, knowing without a doubt that life was good. "I'm glad it's all come out. Anger and fear can be horrible things."

She and DJ would get through this and come out stronger and happier because they now had a family to depend on, she quickly realized as Dillon added, "Even though Mom didn't know the full story, she said it didn't matter and that you were hurting, too afraid to live without her. She asked me to take care of you." He wiped at his eyes and swallowed hard. "She said you weren't as strong as you liked everyone to believe. That your inside was soft, which was why you had such a hard outside." He smiled. "I didn't know what she meant at the time, but now I do. I hope you can forgive me for judging you and hating you. I hope Mom can forgive me for not watching out for you."

"It's all in the past, son. We've got a few more years to work on loving each other. A good start would be to marry Lauren. It should've been you all those years ago. Never Jimmy. I knew he was different. I just couldn't accept him that way. I pray he'll forgive me. I hope you and Lauren will find in your heart to forgive me."

"Well, all this forgiveness is making me cry." Arletta stood, then set her glass on the table. "Since you've obviously worked things out, I think I'll go and see to my other boys."

"I don't know about you, but I like my dad's idea," Dillon said, with love shining in his eyes. "So, what do you think?"

Grinning, Lauren nodded. "You and your dad are definitely on to something."

Dillon laughed. "I was hoping you'd see things that way. I say we get married sooner rather than later. We've wasted too much time already." He took her into his arms. Glancing over his shoulder, she spotted his dad's approving smile just before Dillon's lips touched hers.

Yep, she thought. Life was full of hardships and surprises, but at the moment, it couldn't get much better.

~~The End ~~

Thank you for reading *Kicker's Legacy*. If you enjoyed this story, please help others find it by posting a review wherever you bought it—share a link, tweet about it, Facebook it… Everything helps in this new internet world.

Email her at sandyloyd@twc.com to sign up to receive notice of her new releases.

Like her on Facebook at www.facebook.com/sloydwrites.

Follow her on Twitter at **www.twitter.com/sloydwrites**

About the Author

Sandy Loyd is a Western girl through and through. Born and raised in Salt Lake City, she's worked and lived in some fabulous places in the US, including South Florida. She now resides in Kentucky and writes full time. As much as she loves her current hometown, she misses the mountains and has to go back to her roots to get her mountain and skiing fix at least once a year, otherwise her muse suffers.

As a sales rep for a major manufacturer, she's traveled extensively throughout the US, so she has a million stored memories to draw from for her stories. She spent her single years in San Francisco and considers that city one of America's treasures, comparable to no other city in the world. Her California Series, starting out with Winter Interlude, are all set in the Bay Area.

Sandy is now an empty nester who has published twelve full length novels—five contemporary romances, four romantic mystery/suspense/thrillers, and a series that starts out with a time travel and follows up with two historical romances in the past. She strives to come up with fun characters—people you would love to call friends. And we all know friends have their baggage and when we discover what makes them tick, we come to love them even more. She doesn't skimp on the romance. And because she loves puzzles, she doesn't skimp on intrigue, either. Yet whether romantic suspense, contemporary romance, or historical romance, she always tries to weave a warm love story into her work, while providing enough twists and turns to entertain any reader.

Other books by Sandy Loyd

Contemporary Romances
The California Series
Winter Interlude – Book One
Promises, Promises – Book Two
James – Book Three
Dancing With An Angel – Book Four

Second Chances Series
Tropical Spice – Book One

Contemporary/Time Travel/Historical
Timeless Series
Time Will Tell – Book One
Games – Book Two
Temptation – Book Three

Romantic Suspense
D.C. Bad Boys Series
The Sin Factor – Book One

Running Series
Running From Love

Deadly Series
Deadly Misconceptions

A Matter Of Trust
Kicker's Legacy